THE WOOD'S END SERIES IS DEDICATED TO ALL THOSE
THAT HAVE COURAGEOUSLY UNDERTAKEN TO HEAL
FROM ABUSIVE AND CONTROLING CULT-SYSTEMS IN
WHATEVER FORM THEY TAKE.

I0692093

THE YEAR BETWEEN THE WOOD

A Psychodrama of Murder, Intrigue, and Mistaken Identity

DIAMOND HEDGE PRODUCTIONS, LLC

This book is fiction. Any resemblance to real people or actual
events is unintentional and entirely coincidental.

Cover Design by Churchill Studios, Memphis, TN
E-Book conversion for download by, Paul Mayer:
paulmayer@live.com

Thank you to Martha Burnham for her wise council,
valuable feedback and editing skill.

Thank you to Ray and Marj Pierce for providing an inspiring
environment from which to write. The views at Deerwood will
always be cherished in memory; even more
so your friendship and support.

Thank you to my friend Paul Mayer for his technical
expertise and feedback.
Although he is no longer with us I am indebted to Brian
Churchill for that snowy Tennessee day that we climbed a fence
so he could capture the images from which this cover design
comes. Brian - I look forward to seeing you again in that
glorious place called Heaven.

*"...and He will wipe away every tear from their eyes;
and there will no longer be any death; there will no
longer be any mourning, or crying or pain; the first
things have passed away." Revelation 21:4*

Note: Pedophiles are drawn to wherever children are vulnerable.
Ambitious parents that abdicate control, at risk families, foster
children, and professions that involve children attract
pedophiles. While one sport is a theme in this book the setting
could be any sport, any number of areas where children are
involved.

THE YEAR BETWEEN THE WOOD
PROLOGUE

JARED

Life had stopped. A strangled hiatus gripped him in a useless regime. It wasn't that he couldn't stay busy. Fact is, every hour was pretty much occupied with some aspect of physical therapy, scans and x-rays, blood work, doctors and waiting for doctors. When he wasn't so engaged, he was bone weary and slept far more than he ever had in his adult life.

Yes, Jared reminded himself. He no longer needed the despised wheel chair, but when a new treatment plan was proposed, he put on his implacable, out-of-practice detective's expression; failed to acknowledge what was said, which was taken for agreement; and knew that he was done. What was left of his body would stay as it was.

More and more, Jared's mind raced. He thought of all those delicate, changeable details of happenstance. If any aspect of that day had been altered even slightly, he would have been saved this debt of suffering. Why had God allowed it? Jared recalled the crimes he helped solve, the cases built brick by brick, and the many criminals brought to justice. In the bargaining stage of grief, he reminded God that he'd be more useful engaged in his past life as a homicide detective.

All this remonstrating took his mind as far back as that first crime that had launched his career path and left him so curious he couldn't think of anything else. For weeks he had so badgered his famous uncle, Burns Padgett Shiel, until the usually indulgent and patient man, with an artist's capacity for expanse and pathological aversion to media attention, had finally put his foot down.

"Enough already! It was a horrible tragedy for that family, and if that little girl is ever found she'll probably be dead."

"She's somewhere, so why the hell not? Seems to me someone

3

needs to be asking questions."

"You're nine. What do you expect to do that the state police and finally the FBI couldn't? And when did you start swearing?"

His uncle tossed him a dog eared copy of Webster's Dictionary. "Only lazy people suffering from intellectual poverty rely on profanity. Find a new word! One I haven't heard before, and give it to me over dinner tonight."

"I want to go there."

"Where?" Burns asked, having already moved on.

"Please. I want to see the place she disappeared from."

"Has it occurred to you that there was no crime? She might have gone back to the beach. Maybe no one saw her enter the water and she was swept out to sea. Some do ascribe to that theory, you know."

"It wasn't an accident! Someone took her and I think she's still alive."

Jared could never say how he knew that a crime was a crime, how he managed to sense the unseen confluence of evil that hovered at the rim of such awareness. It was a gift he took for granted, even when those he worked with pointed out his uncanny success in fixing on the truth while others were still formulating a theory.

"Oh," his uncle grimaced. "I see where this is going. You'll join the police force. Now, go. Find something to do. This is a working farm; there's always work to do on a farm. And if Pastor isn't falling over his feet in a rush to do something about this miscarriage of justice why should you?"

Jared gave up on Burns. At the mention of Pastor he realized he might elicit better results from that quarter. Thor and Pastor were at least related to the family and Rockport was what? Four hours away? That was nothing, he reasoned.

Jared exited the old milking floor. One side backed flush to the east meadow where a well worn depression, trodden by generations of dairy cows, had returned to the timber-framed barn twice a day for milking. Now the space was an art studio and the cows were long gone. At the opposite end of the studio, Jared grabbed hold of the rope swing and hurled his agile body out the hay window, dropping thirty feet to the barnyard. Off in the distance he saw that Thor was working alongside his father whom everyone addressed respectfully as Pastor, since from the time he could talk, he'd been a Bible prodigy, reciting whole passages of scripture from memory.

If Pastor would let him off, Jared would wrest Thor away to have lunch at the drug store soda fountain in the village. Here they could plot a trip to see firsthand the scene of the crime: the apparent kidnapping of Lydia Dillihunt. They wouldn't have any money, but that was never a problem in Wood's End. Everyone knew his uncle, and if Burns didn't have an account somewhere, Jared could open one with a word. In winter he went away to boarding school, and for at least a month of summer and for the mid-year holiday, he was at the farm.

Jared smiled at the memory of those sunlit days of fly-fishing in the running streams, hiking and camping off the mountain trails with his best friend, Thorson Dillihunt III -- Thor to everyone who knew him.

Here in the present, Jared was in danger of being swallowed by depression. He had to find a way to banish the blues from his heart, for heart-sick is how he felt. Depression was his enemy, tightening its vice grip, grinding him to powerlessness. Something had to change.

Following that thread the thought dropped into his mind. Jared latched on to it like the drowning, desperate, utterly bored and rudderless man he was. *What happened to Lydia Dillihunt? Was she still alive? And if so, who took her?*

Here was the diversion he needed, a chance to test his metal, because there wasn't a chance that he would let the Wodsende case slide. At the right time he would be back, looking for his attacker.

After seeing Andrea and attempting to interview her, Jared and his partner, Ed, were looking to shatter the alibi of ex-husband, Dr. Dudley Wodsende. But then he had been shot and out of commission; the entire first year focused on reclaiming his health. Others took over the case and didn't interpret the evidence as he did. If the attack on his life hadn't happened on hospital grounds, Jared knew he would have died and ironically, a few hours after emergency surgery, he landed in the same trauma unit as Andrea.

Until they were done searching for his attacker, Jared was prevented from interfering. So, here was a chance to challenge his limitations. To push the envelope beyond the safe confines of physical therapy and see how ready he was to take up the threads of his past life.

Jared thought about little Lydia Dillihunt, six years old when she vanished. Her case had been reopened and investigated anew several times. There were no answers, but Jared knew the truth was out there. Her parents were no longer living, but the elder sister, as the inheritor of one of the less well known paintings of his uncle, would be known to the foundation. They tracked the provenance of all Burns' work and would have Nora Dillihunt's contact information. Burns had known their mother and painted the two little girls the year before Lydia disappeared. Later he had given the portrait to the grieving family.

Jared's mind jumped ahead. The crime had gone cold, but the files would be somewhere, collecting dust on a numbered warehouse shelf, each year pushed higher and further out of reach. He could still pull a few strings since he had not yet been officially let go. He needed a project, something to sink his teeth into.

"Someone to see you."

Jared wondered if he had time to stand and balance. His legs were strong, but the head injury still left him reeling in dizziness if he rose too fast. It was a year ago that Stephanie Wodsende had been murdered, and he had laid in a coma for thirteen of those weeks. It was now necessary to face some hard truths. For one thing, the old days were gone. It was only a question of time before Boston PD cut him loose. The union rep had said as much, echoing what Jared already knew, but testing to see if the head injury had left him addled and slow. Jared hated that -- the insult of lowered expectations.

"What's going on here? What's the deal?"

Jared recognized the booming voice before Thor put his head in the door.

"How'd you find me?"

"Stopped at the house. That snooty housekeeper of yours finally checked your schedule, like any one really had to look. A deep muscle something or other and then an hour in the pool before dinner. What is this! A spa?"

"They call it aqua therapy," Jared acknowledged. "Come on

in. Sit down."

"I don't have time to sit and neither do you. Stuck in neutral is no way to live and you've vegetated in that state a bit too long. Grab your gear and let's go."

Joy rose up in Jared. He loved the confidence.

"I know what you need and it's not coddling and pronouncements on what you can and can't do for the rest of your life. *'Life and death is in the power of the tongue'*," Thor quoted from proverbs. He had emerged as a slightly less knowledgeable version of his father.

"If you can lift weights you can lift a few bales of hay. If you can walk to the sissy pool and back you can drag yourself up the lane to collect the dang mail. Still remember how to shoot that Glock of yours?"

Jared nodded and wondered if Thor had been cleaning his collection of guns. Over the years Thor had sent him reports about the status of the land and buildings, but Jared had been too busy with his law enforcement career to pay much attention to the farm, coming out only on the occasional weekend for a little rest and relaxation. Thor had functioned mainly as a caretaker, which included keeping curious tourists off the property, now that Burns was no longer living, and tending to the few animals that remained.

"What brought all this on?"

"Brace yourself. This will be hard to take."

"Okay," Jared played along.

"There are a few weasels up to no good. We lost four hens and one turkey this week alone. I had plans for that turkey. Hey, they belong to you; I would think you would care."

As always Thor was transparent, one of his more redeeming characteristics as far as Jared was concerned. The timing was spot-on.

Jared couldn't quite swing his legs up to the floor boards. He backed into the seat, grabbed the bar above the open door and pulled himself up with his arms. Then he swung his legs around, pushing the bad leg with the good. When finally settled he was sweating with exertion and the world was a circling carousel. Jared closed his eyes and waited for the nausea to subside. Thor hadn't offered to help. They'd get along just fine.

"We need to stop and pick up some of my things at the town house."

"Already done," Thor fired back. "Over the objections of your housekeeper, I might add."

"Swing by anyway. Then I have a couple of stops to make. State Police headquarters, science park exit."

"Then where?"

"Wherever they keep the cold case files now-a-days -- hopefully with a requisition in hand."

"Not the Wodsende case. I mean, I can understand why you'd want to, but maybe you need a little more time. And ... your partner, Ed. I talked to him a week ago, and he told me they're still working the case."

"No," Jared said. "This would be the Lydia Dillihunt disappearance. I know that rings a bell."

"What brought this on?"

Jared could tell Thor was interested. Lydia Dillihunt had been a cousin and, however remotely impacted, one never forgot such a tragic connection.

Thor turned the white pickup into traffic. They hung a right onto Marlborough. Jared lived on Louisburg Square. His mother's family had kept a townhouse there, and like the farm in Wood's End Township, it now belonged to him. He might have inherited his wealth, but he'd cut ties with that life and always worked.

It was five thirty and pushing dawn as Thor walked toward the house from the barn. He'd left his daughter, Victoria still in bed asleep and his wife, Brenda with a cup of hot tea by her bedside. An early arctic storm had swept down from Canada and claimed the landscape where drifts were chest high along the drive to where the mail box needed to be swept of new or blowing snow. This was the season to clean and upgrade the machinery with new parts. Early morning and late evening there were the animals to tend. Thor liked this time of year which freed him to concentrate on the small congregation and country church nestled at the intersection of Ridge Road and old postal route three.

As Thor approached the house he thought about Jared. The limp had nearly disappeared, but he still paused upon occasion to steady himself from random spells of dizziness. While the seizures were no longer a problem, Thor knew that Jared lived in fear of being vulnerable.

For the most part Jared was just plain restless. The injustice of his attack and the Stephanie Wodsende murder was never far from his thoughts. Unable to interfere with an ongoing investigation, Jared absorbed himself with the Dillihunt case. Thor had never met that branch of the family, and the summer they arrived to have Nora and Lydia's portrait painted, Pastor had kept his distance, expecting Thor to do the same. A family break had occurred and no one had ever offered an explanation. Given a choice and being an only child like Jared, Thor would have welcomed a few cousins in his life.

Thor removed his boots in the mudroom and hung the canvas barn coat on a hook. He unzipped the navy sweatshirt and then removed the overalls layered over a white Henley and jeans. Led by the rich coffee smell, he entered the kitchen. A bagel stood upright in the toaster, and he set to work layering it with cream cheese and paper thin slices of lox and red onion.

"That you?"

"It's me. For certain that dappled mare is with foal. My guess, early May."

Thor entered the dining room. He sat across from Jared pushing aside a pile of papers.

"Careful with that."

"So... anything interesting?"

"The two cases are connected, albeit remotely."

Thor was immediately attentive, though he kept his body language in check. "How can that be?"

"I don't know, but I'm going to find out."

They exchanged a look and in unison recited one of Pastor's many sayings. "Coincidence is divine timing laying claim to proof."

"You'll appreciate this." Jared picked up the stack that Thor had moved and placed it crosswise on another stack. He had a system and he didn't like it messed with. His eyes were red rimmed and Thor could see he'd been at it all night.

After a generous donation to the police widows and orphans fund, the cold case files were picked up on their way to the farm. They languished in a corner of the kitchen until two weeks ago.

Jared figured they had until the anniversary of Lydia's disappearance spurred some footloose journalist to ask the requisite questions. He prepared by making two complete sets of copies, freeing the originals for return the next time they had a reason to be in the city.

"You gonna tell me about it."

Jared stood, stretched and then massaged the length of his bad leg. "Well, now. A Marstead connection means a Dr. Dudley Wodsende connection, wouldn't you say?"

"Might be a stretch, but yes, maybe."

Jared guided his body slowly back into the chair. "I'm sure he murdered his wife and he nearly killed me."

"There was a conviction," Thor reminded his friend.

"The best system in the world can mess up, and Ed and I were pretty sure Andrea Wodsende was set up to take the fall for Dr. Wodsende."

Jared no longer took pain pills, though Thor knew he could make a case for needing them. Instead, when the sleepless nights piled up, he settled for too much Irish whiskey. It was a long road back and no one could deny the fight in the man or the progress he'd made so, for now, Thor was holding his tongue.

"So, what progress have you made?" Thor asked.

"I got Nora Dillihunt on the phone once. After that she didn't return any of my calls. I wanted to sound her out; tell her I was unofficially reopening the investigation."

"And?" Thor prompted.

"Surprised me that she didn't seem at all pleased. Was even defensive; not quite hostile, but close. Not the reaction I've come to expect from families desperate for answers."

Thor was just relieved not to be dissecting the Wodsende murder.

"I did a background check on Nora Dillihunt after we talked. Then I moved on to key relationships among family friends and neighbors," Jared continued. "Nora's best friend is now, and was at the time, Paul *Marstead*. Paul Marstead was with Nora when Lydia disappeared."

"And I'm guessing that's not a coincidence."

"Samuel Marstead's father had a house in Rockport and I'm pretty sure..."

"Dudley Wodsende's attorney? Are we talking about *that*

Samuel Marstead?" Thor interrupted as he covered his disquiet by repositioning the sliding lox on the overburdened bagel before taking another bite.

"Where is your napkin?" Jared asked.

"I'm not touching anything. God forbid one of these papers gets stained with cream cheese. Now that would be a crime."

"Samuel Marstead has two siblings, Howard and Paige. Samuel, Dudley Wodsende's attorney, was the baby of the family."

"And to think that old snake was ever young," Thor commented.

"Paige was the middle sibling and guess who her son is?" Jared answered his own question. "Paul Marstead, Nora's childhood friend and neighbor."

"Paul Marstead and Nora... Are they an item? Thor asked.

"He's gay, has a long time partner. I haven't had time to get to him yet; Herb something or other," Jared continued. "It appears Paul took his mother's maiden name. Has to be a story there, don't you think?"

"There could be a number of innocent reasons for him to make that decision. Maybe he just didn't like his father," Thor offered.

"Might get confusing here so listen" Jared continued. "The eldest Marstead sibling, Howard, had one son, Hank. Hank is also an attorney, and like Paul he was raised by his mother... father out of the picture. Samuel, the Wodsende family attorney had no children."

"Thank God for that."

"Yeah, well, as far as I can tell these three Marstead siblings are not close. Samuel took over his father's law firm, but never extended a hand to assist his nephew, Hank, in launching his law career. Howard and Paige, for the most part, live on family money of which there seems to be an inexhaustible supply."

"So what does this have to do with the disappearance of Lydia Dillihunt?" Thor asked.

"Surrounded by Marsteads."

"Can't be good," Thor affirmed, not liking where this was going. Next they would be talking about Andrea Wodsende; a subject he was determined to keep Jared away from.

Thor sat back in his chair, crossed his arms, and surveyed the dining room table covered with stacks of paper, some with various color labels marking the pages. Only Jared knew what the colors meant. Isn't this what he wanted for Jared; to reenter life and wake in the morning with a restored sense of purpose?

"I'll be looking into it," Jared asserted.

"Looks like you already are," Thor said, keeping his tone neutral. "My guess, there is a trip to the office supply store in our future. There will be a chart or two on that wall tomorrow showing all the familial relationships networked with the Dillihunt, Wodsende, and Marstead families with pertinent photos networked to these case files, just so we don't get confused. You'll want a recent photo of me, right?"

"I'm sorry, Thor if all this bothers you. Brings up old ghosts or something."

"I don't know," Thor mused. "Maybe it's time."

"But, I'm thinking," Jared spoke over Thor. "Burns and Pastor are gone. Who is there left to care why your father severed ties with this branch of the Dillihunt family? Why the Wodsende family has such a hold over this part of the county."

"It's forbidden," Thor ventured. "That's the script that runs through my head. Worse still, it's the feeling that comes with the script." Thor literally shook himself as though tossing off the physicality of unseen chains. "Where will you start?"

"With Lydia's last living relative, besides you that is; her sister, Nora. The foundation borrowed the portrait for the last museum tour. Nora was invited to the launch, but didn't show. And," Jared hesitated. Something Thor would not approve of. "A few weeks back I visited her studio in Rockport. She's an artist. Pretty fair."

'Pretty fair' as an assessment coming from Jared was a compliment.

"I bought one of her paintings," Jared added still concealing something.

"And ... "

"Wanted to see the town; get a fix on the geography I'd be reading about in these files. So, I've been trying to reach Nora. I told you that. After our first uninspired conversation when she tried to get rid of me as quickly as possible, she hasn't returned any of my calls."

"Nothing you can do about that," Thor was relieved.

"Yes, maybe that's a good thing. Better to get a bead on all this first," he said gesturing to the files. "I don't want to be influenced by anything she would say until I'm familiar with the record."

Jared held up a photo. "The technology has continued to improve. This looks pretty life-like."

Thor reached for the photo-sheet, which showed Lydia Dillihunt with different hair styles, weight, and various processes of aging in real time. If this woman could reach across time to enter the room, it almost seemed she would do so.

"I see a family resemblance; Pastor's chin and eyes."

"In other words she looks like you. Looking into those eyes, it's disconcerting," Jared offered. "I think she's still alive. I feel it."

Thor nodded. "The cases might possibly be connected; I'll give you that, but how connected? Having a Marstead for a neighbor isn't nearly enough. And if you start digging will this paint another target on your back?"

"You've been pushing me to get out of the house. Build a life. Mingle. Well, I'm about to do just that."

"Not exactly what I had in mind, and you know it. You're not ready. It's too dangerous, and if Samuel Marstead thinks you're poking around in another crime, one remotely connected to Dr. Dudley Wodsende, you can consider yourself dead meat."

"They are connected. I've always been drawn to this case and the Wodsende-Marstead connection. If it turns out I'm right, is just a bonus."

Jared grinned. As far as he was concerned it was Christmas. Like a kid about to attack a pile of packages under the tree, he was straining at the bit. What worried Thor was the snake coiled about the wrappings, colorless poison bleeding into the ribbons under the shadow of fir and glitzy tinsel. Where Wood's End Township was concerned, nothing was ever quite what it seemed.

Thor studied Jared. There was a nearly ten year difference in their ages. Ever since they were boys, Thor had been charged with protecting Jared. He'd promised, and in that promise Thor had accepted certain terms and conditions more binding than any legal document. Burns, Jared's uncle, and Pastor, his father, were still pulling strings from beyond the grave.

Thor let his gaze take in the neat stacks of file folders, the legal pads upon which much was already written, the open laptop, a law book. Jared had a hazardous momentum going. One he couldn't control.

Thor folded his arms and leaned back in the chair as Jared got busy with a computer search. Yes, it was true. Burns and Pastor hoped he might forget; encouraged him to think about the events of that day in an entirely different light. But that is not how Thor was wired. His was not a personality that lent itself to suggestion or molding. Thor remembered quite well the Indian summer of that autumn day, with the crimson and gold tree-line bordering the pastures, and the two heifers that failed to return home for milking the evening before. Burns had set out at dawn, calling their names.

Thor shut his eyes, and now, as clear as any scene on a television screen, the images sprang to life. Burns, shirtless, running fast across the dew laden pasture, down the fenced run that brought the cows to the barn; a screaming something cradled in the jostling crook of his arm, wrapped in the paint-stained denim shirt.

Responding to the uncharacteristic panic, not able to fathom what the crying could be ... a rabbit, a puppy. Pastor lit out with, as always, Thor not far behind.

He remembered asking about the markings on the baby's naked body as they submerged it into the kitchen sink's warm water, wiping away grass and dried blood, not, as it turned out, that of the child. Burns then wrapped the still screaming infant tight in a clean flannel shirt, tying the arms together as they would a package.

Then... out of desperation, Pastor did what worked for newborn calves and dipped his finger in molasses and cream. The baby turned its head and sucked and Thor could tell that the sudden quiet unsettled the two grown men far more than the outraged protest.

"Now, what," Burns had asked?

This was the first time Thor ever heard desperation in a grown man's voice. He knew enough not to offer his opinion. They might remember the witness he was and send him away as oft had happened. Thor had been thinking like this for many years, discerning as children do, the weight of conversations cut short, inference and body language that told one or the other men that he was within hearing distance -- and then the complicated mesh of code and double entendre. Thor absorbed this, just as Jared later did, acquiring acuity for reading what wasn't said; but eventually, as they entered their teen years, contemptuous of what was never adequately explained; and even later, put down to eccentricity. Only Thor knew the label didn't quite fit. He'd been there the day that Jared entered their family as a baby, no more than three or four weeks old.

All three of them had gazed at the now sleeping infant until, Pastor, ever the pragmatist stated, "We can't turn him over; they'll just get him back. You know this."

"I don't. Not at all! He belongs in a hospital."

"They must think he's dead," Pastor stated with a tone of resignation that lit Thor's curiosity.

"He's a strong little thing. Look at him."

They gathered around the emptied biscuit tray layered with hastily gathered towels sitting on the kitchen table. The baby was on his side, placed that way by Pastor with another rolled shirt at his back to keep him in place.

"Babies are a lot of trouble. They need things," Burns remarked.

The two men regarded one another and silent words flew between them. They looked at Thor.

"You can't tell anyone Thor. You understand?"

"He won't," Pastor said.

Thor was glad for his father's vote of confidence. He basked in the center of that inclusion, savoring the hope that in future he'd be privy to everything they knew; no longer shut out. Now, when Thor looked back, he wished he had been anywhere else than in the path of Jared's arrival on that day.

"For the bye and bye ... until we know more," his father said, as though just making up his mind. "Thorson, you run to the barn and bring the truck. You and Burns here have some shopping to do?"

Always thinking ahead. One step removed from a kind of world weary paranoia. "You'll be going to Springfield where they won't know you," his father elaborated. "I'll make a list."

"Why don't you go and I'll stay here," Burns suggested.

Thor gestured toward the sleeping infant. "What are you going to do when he wakes up, sketch him? You wouldn't have the faintest."

"We can call someone. Maybe locate Emily Capra. When was the last time you heard from her? She'd take him off our hands."

"Have you forgotten they're no longer in this country? We're not in the loop. We asked not to know."

"You can't be serious," Burns erupted. "We're not talking about a puppy. It's not staying here."

"Skedaddle, Son. Bring that truck," Pastor spoke, over Burns' continued protest. It was rare that his father and Burns would disagree about anything within his hearing.

Thor left without a backward glance and soon arrived at the mudroom door with the truck. By this time Burns wore a sullen mask of resignation. Silent and visibly shaken, a fist full of cash taken from one of the many tins stashed under the floorboards, he climbed into the driver's seat. In this same hiding place were gold bars and three passports, among many curious items difficult to conceal from a curious boy. As far as Thor knew they were still there. Thor imagined one day sliding back the floor boards to reveal this contraband. Perhaps the only way to jumpstart what was perhaps a long overdue conversation with Jared.

Thor lacked patience for Burns' periodic mood swings. This intruder, little though he was, would challenge Burns' stability. Despite appearances, it was his father who called the shots and Burns was somehow emotionally damaged and even limited by what his father intermittently referred to as "her" or some event or incident related to "her." Then there was the "it", of whatever tragedy "it" was, that he never quite recovered from. All this was confusing and at the time, beyond Thor's maturity level to understand, though today he had a few theories.

Burns drove to Springfield without speaking. A hundred questions swirled in Thor's brain. The silence continued as they sat in the mall parking lot, until Thor grew restive.

"What happened out there?" he demanded, not expecting an answer.

Roused by the question, Burns counted the cash. "How much

do you think baby things cost?"

"Better give me more than I need so I'm not coming and going from the truck."

"Good thinking. Don't forget diapers and baby formula. As far as I'm concerned we can do without the rest, since the kid is not staying."

Jared knew this was unlikely since, judging from the list which seemed extensive, his father had decided otherwise.

"You're not coming with me?"

"I'll be recognized. Here is five grand. Spend wisely and keep what's left over."

Burns was bribing him and they both knew it, telling him not to let Pastor know the assignment had been handed off to a boy. Thor thought about the shift in power this represented. If he wanted to know more, now was the time to push.

"So, what happened?"

"Your father and I agreed a long time ago that we'd keep you out of it."

"I'm already *in*, or weren't you listening? And, maybe I already know more than you think."

Burns looked at him then, taken aback. "It's a kind of private war."

"Kind of like war of the worlds?"

"Not at all. Anyway ... they are fixated on that stretch of land narrowed now to Wood's End farm which the Wodsende family owns. It borders your grandfather Brown's place. We rent it for pastureland."

"You graze a small herd, having to bring in straw and pump in water since not much edible grows there. The herd is there so you have an excuse to keep watch. I'm not entirely blind."

"For our purposes, it's one family. Kind of an assignment to keep an eye and report on what's going on over there."

At this Thor sat up and paid careful attention. It was the proximity and access to Woods End farm. This is where the crying infant was left to die of exposure.

Thor was still speaking. "The farm draws them at regular times during the year. Only for a while they had to lay low and nearly abandoned the place, and we hoped we would never see them again. Until now, that is. They suddenly, willy-nilly show up. So, bottom line. What you need to know. We are not keeping this kid. We can count on the fact that he was dedicated to demons, and they expected him to die, and that was feeding some power they wanted. But... who knows. Maybe they were interrupted."

"By what?"

"Because, they were sacrificing that baby with a badly mutilated cow, *my* cow, out on the edge of Brown property and Wood's End Farm. Now your father says we're keeping the kid for a bit. Not for long you understand, just for a bit."

"Are they looking for him?"

"We'll pray they think he's dead, dragged off by animals. Tomorrow morning I'll have breakfast at the diner and tell the sheriff that a bobcat's come down and got one of our dogs and a goat. A little gossip will spread this idea to whatever plants they have living among us. Everyone that's lost a pet will take it up, and fish and game will be investigating."

At the threat of conflict, Burns had a habit of fading into an unreachable place of withdrawal, but that isn't where he was at the moment. He was white-hot enraged and barely keeping the boiling anger in check. '*My cow.*" The torture of this animal was a personal affront he would not forget. The war had come to his doorstep. Although he had enjoyed and painted his cows grazing with Crum Hill rising in the distance, he let the small herd go the following week.

There was a word for how Thor interpreted what was revealed as he added Burn's disclosures to the weight of a thousand other incidental clues. Burns was big on vocabulary. The word Thor tried to remember conveyed one view of truth and then another reality that wasn't obvious, but was the part of the actual truth that was the whole unseen of a strategy that was surreptitiously unfolding. The word was *"dystopian."* Sitting in the parking lot on a beautiful fall afternoon, Thor suspected that the little that Burns had just shared with him represented a dystopian cesspool of secrets.

"Thanks," Thor said.

"For what?"

"For telling me the truth instead of some story no sane person would believe."

"You're too smart for us. One day soon we'll tell you more. Now get on with you."

Only they didn't, because Burns never told Pastor about their conversation. In vain Thor waited, finally accepting that there was no plan to sit him down and tell him what was really going on.

Baby stuff -- he needed baby stuff. Thor had grown up without a mother, accustomed to premature responsibility from a father who had little understanding, neither of youth's foibles nor of a growing child's life-stages. In his element, he savored this reversal of roles.

"My sister," Thor lied to the sales lady, "just had a baby and we need some things"

"Came earlier than expected," the sales lady smiled. "For a girl or a boy."

"A boy."

"I always suggest buying a size up. They aren't in the newborn born stage very long. So what do you need?"

He showed the list and flashed the cash. She seemed to buy the story. Apparently it was common for babies to come early.

That was the start of Jared as a Shiel, accepted as though he really had been born into that family and completely unaware of his real history. Not until they forged a birth certificate and brought Burns' brother, Bradford and wife, Nancy into the scheme did the baby ever see a pediatrician.

Thor remembered the quite fierce debate about adoption. "He can't be adopted," Pastor stood firm. "If he's adopted, then one day he'll look for his birth parents. Then what?"

"Do you know how hard it is these days to fake a birth?"

"*They* do it all the time," Pastor knowingly said. "If *they* can do it so can we, and clearly this one is no hybrid."

"He was a failure of some kind or they wouldn't have considered him expendable."

Thor pretended he wasn't paying attention. They had always seen him as the weak link and, as soon as Jared was old enough, sent him off to boarding school in Canada, effectively separating the two until sure that in a weak moment Thor wouldn't impulsively disclose the truth.

Thor considered the past as Jared shuffled papers, still worried a glob of cream cheese might land where it shouldn't. By this time Thor had fried three eggs and was eating a second bagel.

"Can't you eat that at the kitchen table?"

"No."

"I hope you're planning on cleaning up after yourself."

"Maybe. Maybe not."

"Are you soaking the pan?"

Thor grinned. "Maybe. Maybe not."

They were the closest facsimile each would ever have to a brother. They could talk like that. Thor hoped it would always be so. But still, secrets kept and then revealed could shatter relationships. Now, the question: to tell or not to tell? Thor decided he'd wait for a sign. Pastor was big on signs, and as it turned out, he was too.

THE YEAR BETWEEN THE WOOD

PART ONE
CHAPTER ONE

MATEO

Dressed for the occasion,
I'll lean over the casket,
Thinking of those who've known you as I have,
I'll slip this poem into the breast pocket of your
human disguise,
Then I'll go back to where I am today,
In the clearing,
Free of you - It's warm.

The young priest, young to be so far advanced, glanced at the large envelope, newly delivered into his charge. Though he had tried to ignore it, his eye was continually drawn back. Written in a light pencil script in the top corner was the name Mateo Araujo and attached by clip was a plane ticket to LAX from Shannon. Though Mateo couldn't know it, he was running out of time.

Father Guido Woods had enjoyed a rare and safe respite. Three months to make his decision. The envelope represented more of the same, while refusing the assignment would send the message that he was retreating to a solitary life in a Swiss monastery where the Abbot, part of a clandestine Vatican underground, was told to accept him anytime he showed up. After the last two years of constant travel, it had been a luxury to be in one place with nothing to do but watch wild sprays of surf crash against the west Irish rock face.

He was alone, but not lonely. There was something about the ascetics of breakfast on the scarred plank table, the hand turned pottery, round plates looking like sunset and the austerity of an open hearth reminding him of a bygone era.

Guido stood in the closeness of the room, feeling grateful and refreshed, when just as suddenly the atmosphere changed. An alien presence of the pre-Flood watcher variety had oozed through the crevices of the slate floor, off-loading the scent of death and decay and trailing lesser demons under strict control not to make their harassing and oppressive purpose known.

Guido thought about what it meant. He had prayerfully closed all portals when he arrived, but a new one had been ripped open, probably by a human spirit sending the advance guard on ahead and not understanding that by doing so, their hand was tipped. Most people would not have marked such a preternatural arrival. If felt at all, it would have been just as quickly dismissed. But Guido was different from most people. Barriers which existed for others were porous for him.

The demonic visitation was the harbinger of those human vehicles of destruction that would follow. Guido closed the cover of his Bible, slipping it into the ready knapsack. He held the envelope that had arrived by courier that morning -- perhaps the means by which he was found.

In a pretense of ignoring what was afoot, probing for understanding beneath the surface of the watcher company he now had, Guido made a last pot of strong black tea. He poured in milk and two teaspoons of sugar before adding the steeping brew to a travel cup. Then he walked outside, making the rounds and seeing nothing untoward.

It had rained the night before. The sky was brilliant at his back, sun just lightening the rural lane down from the Byone Mountains. Soon a warm blanket would lay over the green landscape, and he would not be here to appreciate the splendor of one more day. To sit in the rush chair, meditate on scripture, and leisurely read. He felt the abrupt ending, to what had been for him an idyllic time of refreshment, as a physical loss -- time to go.

Time is up!

Now!

Guido sprinted up the foot path and back to the cottage. Before he arrived the path was nearly covered by the encroaching vegetation and, all too soon, would be again. He would hike overland five miles and pick up the car well hidden in an abandoned farm building. But first ...

Just one thing. *Was there time?* Father Guido Woods

hesitated at the fire. He held in his hand the large envelope destined for Mateo Araujo. Photographs -- stills taken from old video that would shock the sensibilities of a good and decent man. The decision was his to make. Burn them or accept the assignment, implement the plan, guiding the process to the desired outcome.

He thought of the recent project. A pedophile British rocker who, cloaked in fame and ready cash, was also a warlock and a baby rapist. He was born in Wales and had adopted a stage name, but Guido and his cohort referred to him simply as Smith #62. Always last name Smith and sequentially numbered. Too often common and blending in; not recognized for the monsters they were.

The man had been charged five years earlier, but the case went nowhere. Evil protected its own, and in this case there was a pedophile crown prosecutor who influenced the higher ups, arbitrarily deciding there wasn't enough evidence; then planting that mantra until it was generally assumed to be correct. Charges were bought off and the irate family member discredited with the threat of also being charged. But now, Smith #62 would be locked up, and if they let him out early, or some manipulative legal technicality obstructed justice, he'd be otherwise taken care of.

There was something about the symmetry of such swift and righteous outcomes that appealed to Guido's sense of justice.

Guido drew the envelope back from the flame and tucked it into the backpack just as a first beep was heard, followed by others in ever-increasing frequency. Taking his gear, not forgetting the travel mug of tea, Guido headed for the guerilla style blind skillfully crafted into the hillside. He approached in such a way as to confirm that his unwanted visitors hadn't already done reconnaissance and found it.

Guido lay prone upon a rocky shelf, his view toward the cottage unobstructed, his body cloaked by vegetation. There wasn't long to wait. A beat up red car, engine cut, rolled down the hill, stopping short of the cottage. From overhead two men and a woman passed inches from the blind. He watched their descent through binoculars as they skirted the hillside and joined the others below. Only when the first man slid through the front door did Guido set off the devise. In swirling hunger, oxygen was sucked from the surrounding area. Half a second later the cottage imploded in flame.

Almost immediately Guido crawled from the blind and disappeared over the hillside. He was jogging above the road when he heard the sirens and at his back... he felt it, the watcher-demon keeping pace. Turning in a rush of anger, his will, the presence of Jesus Christ within Guido, met the hatred full throttle.

"In the name of the Lord Jesus Christ of Nazareth, who came in the flesh, and by the covering of the blood, I send you to the throne of grace for immediate judgment, to be cast into the abyss never to be heard from again! Father God, with the fire of the Holy Spirit, destroy all backups and replacements and send them to the burning pit ...

His course was set. He was going home to America. He'd have to contact his brother, Mario to meet him. Guido preferred to work alone, and his handler, Cardinal Brandon McMurry, who only worked with clergy, allowed him more freedom than he did the others. Even though Guido was the youngest, he was in many ways more prepared for what they dealt with.

Guido uncovered the car and drove south passing another fire truck and An Garda Síochána as he went. First step a pub in Galway, then the airport at Kerry, and next a direct flight into Kennedy before heading for Los Angeles.

For the first time Guido would meet his mentor and handler in person, Cardinal Brandon McMurry. Advisor to three Popes and past member of the Vatican Intelligence Service, he was a man who understood the dual worlds to which Guido was called. He would also meet McMurry's protestant liaison, Thorson Dillihunt. Both men were important to Guido. It was Thorson's father who had saved his life on more than one occasion. The first was when Pastor and the Cardinal orchestrated his family's escape. Guido's vocation and calling as a Christian was cemented in the realization that he must never have children, must never further the cult's bloodline by doing so. Pure bloodline represented a rare and valuable commodity in cult circles for the vast accumulation of demonic power that accumulated through succeeding generations.

Once in New York Guido planned a side trip to Boston. There

he could look up the father they had left behind. His mother, Emily, related to Guido and his brother how Henry had assisted in their escape and then stayed behind in a sacrificial attempt to cover their trail, pretending ignorance and posturing outrage. Although it was dangerous, and could put at risk this latest assignment, Guido privately hoped he might actually set up a meeting between himself and the father he barely remembered, now a Boston circuit court judge, Judge Henry Capra.

Alexandra Clair

CHAPTER TWO

As he sat in the screened section of the veranda in the first light of dawn, Mateo Araujo studied the trellis lines perfectly spaced against the rolling prospect of the valley. For the first time in memory this familiar sight, which had occupied his family for four generations, failed to offer solace.

He thought of the images now lodged at the back of his mind and felt that he did not deserve Daria. If photos could give off an odor of putrid offense, these did. He had systematically lied to himself, and now that ostrich-retreat from reality could no longer keep at bay the mountain of inconsistencies that should have been obvious long ago.

He had not a shred of doubt that other photographs would follow, along with the demand for money in exchange for silence. *Isn't that how blackmail worked? Isn't that how the plot unfolded in countless books and movies?*

Before following Daria to bed, Mat had switched on a reading light and settled into his favorite rattan lounger. He saw it now in defining relief against his racing mind. This was the second that complacency had been stripped away as his hand closed over the envelope and, irritated that for overkill the flap had been additionally closed with packing tape, he slit the contents free with a pen knife.

Here was the depraved, amoral side of life that only occurred in the lives of fictional characters and strangers. Mat was about to reject what was before him, but then he made out her features. How could he not? The quelled suspicion, countless ignored incidentals, broke the bondage of denial in a mocking sneering flood. Nothing of life would ever be the same again.

With envelope in hand, Mat walked into the bedroom just as the sun cast slanted tentacles of light across the width of the veranda. Daria lay sleeping, her red hair a ribbon-stain against the stark white sheets. With her features reposed in sleep, she looked very unlike the aloof young woman the press had dubbed 'the ice princess.'

For Mat the recriminations were just beginning. Why hadn't he noticed that when invited to speak of her childhood she sounded like a walking press release? Why didn't he pursue more details when she claimed not to remember her past as a Russian orphan? Then, in a fairytale that aggrandized the Russian system, but defied common sense, she was placed in a state-sponsored skating program? He bought it all hook, line, and sinker.

Mat wished he could jump back in time, and erase forever the frozen look of utter revulsion on Daria's face and then the forced smile cued for the camera which, in grotesque parody, could not conceal her shock or pain. Nothing! Nothing, would ever wipe from his memory that look of stark terror as she was brutally raped.

He thought of his young female students and guessed she would have been six or seven. Faced with such evidence, the temptation to do nothing and let events take their course, beckoned. This was not his Daria, not his wife. But there was no mistaking the lock of hair that would not be tamed as it fell over her brow and in the last photos, all numbered for his viewing in grotesque sequence, that same absent stare which still today unsettled him. This was the signal that, though Daria walked and breathed in his sphere of reality, she was in point of fact, mentally elsewhere, some place unreachable.

It could be any vehicle that promised fame and wealth, where access to children existed. With that thought Mat focused on the perpetrators. He recognized two, Daria's former coach and the other a broadcast executive. The third man, poised over Daria, kept his back to the camera, even when awkward. It was evident to Mat that this pedophile rapist had made a conscious decision not to assume the risk that the other two believed would never be compromised.

Mat examined the camera angles and realized they were too deliberate for a tripod. A fourth unseen presence was there operating the camera, and in one earlier photo from the sequence, it seemed that Daria was looking in that direction with pleading eyes.

Mat forced himself to think. He had to protect Daria, but he also had to go on the offensive. Whoever it was that handed these selected stills to Hillary in the overcrowded rink of an out-of-town competition had taken quite a risk. Was this an innocent courier pressed into service or the blackmailer? There was no getting around the task ahead. Mat needed information.

"Tell her it's important," he told the mother who picked up.

Hillary would be on the ice for the first lessons of the morning and would not have her cell phone with her. When she finally came on the line her abruptness jarred his nerves.

"Couldn't this wait?"

Mat's relationship with his assistant coach had begun as an affair that ended after Daria came into his life. Hillary had never overcome her jealousy of Daria. Several times, Mat made up his mind to fire her, but she always seemed to anticipate what was coming and managed to modify her behavior.

"That large envelope you gave me yesterday? Remember?"

"I'm not brain dead."

"There isn't a postmark. Where did it come from?"

"Boston -- the competition last week."

"Who gave it to you?"

"How would I know?"

"Well, how did it come to get into your hands?"

"Honestly I don't have time for this."

"Hillary, just answer the question."

"Someone passed it to me while I was checking scores. I put it in my bag and later in my suitcase, and then I forgot about it until I unpacked, but was careful to keep it flat. Photos, right?"

"Yes, that's right."

"The only reason I didn't open it myself is because it was labeled confidential. Was it important?" A note of curiosity had crept into her voice.

"Think about this, Hillary. Did a man or a woman give it to you?"

"Someone may have slipped it into my bag; whatever, I wasn't paying attention enough to remember."

"How can you not remember something like this?" As soon as the accusation escaped he regretted it.

"Well, Mat, that would be because you haven't had to handle more than two students at competition at any time in your life, while I am left with all the rest, some of them on new ice for the first time in their lives."

Mat swallowed the retort that sprang to mind and, yet again, regretted their past intimacy. If Hillary thought she was still in love with him, that love had turned to hatred. There was no getting around it. He would have to fire her, but with the demands of Daria's career and the attention she would need, that also meant closing the program.

"If you remember anything at all Hillary, no matter how trivial, I'd like you to call immediately. Will you do that?"

Hillary hung up without saying goodbye.

With exaggerated care, Mat gathered the photographs and slipped all but three into the envelope. Daria was usually up for morning practice by six, but the night before had flown in from a charity exhibition in Palm Springs and would indulge the rare luxury of waking slowly. As the sky lightened, Mat knew he had little time to compose himself. Daria was an astute observer and would suspect immediately that something was wrong.

Mat walked across the wide hall into what had once been his parents' bedroom. Built into the floor was a safe. He lifted the rug, spun the dial, and opened the heavy door. The three photos' that most clearly revealed the identity of the two perpetrators were slipped into a leather binder. On automation now, he knelt by the hearth and struck a match against the adobe fireplace.

"What is that, Mat?" Daria asked.

When she wanted to, Daria had a disconcerting habit of moving without making a sound. She actually seemed to enjoy startling him. If he complained, she would laugh in ironic detachment and remind him, "But I am an angel. Angels can do such things."

"You are an angel," he would agree. "You are my angel."

The term had become for Daria an endearment that she could never quite accept as a compliment, and now he understood why. Now he understood so much more, and he dreaded the prospect of having to reevaluate all those ill-conceived notions that had held his marriage together.

Daria had loosely belted a green satin robe with ivory trim. As his eyes locked on hers, he felt a fierce protective emotion, completely new and almost foreign for its zealous intensity. This, he thought, was how men felt with home and hearth, farm and country, in great peril.

Mistaking his look Daria smiled, but he turned back to the

task at hand. He placed a log over the burning photographs and caught a last glimpse of a child's face frozen in shock from the curling edge of the paper. Quickly he reached for kindling and fed the narrow pieces of wood into the glowing embers until the log flared.

"It's almost too hot for a fire."

"I know, but it makes me think of our time together at the fishing cabin."

"When we first met?"

"When we met later," he corrected her. "As adults. For me it was love at first sight. Not for you, but for me."

Daria had an unsettling habit of shifting temperament with a speed that was difficult to keep up with. The night before, she had skated flawlessly. Her show program, skated to a fifties rhythm and blues tune, had brought the crowd to their feet. She had turned professional only after pressure from him, but now he was transitioning her into an acting career, insuring longevity as a marketable commodity. With very little training, Daria proved a natural and, as it turned out, the camera loved her. Her amateur skating career had been cut short when she left her native Russia, but not before she won a bronze Olympic medal. Mat had managed to gain his wife a theatrical agent. As a result she'd been cast in a plum role that had nothing to do with skating. Soon she would make the rounds of talk and morning shows to promote the film's release.

It didn't hurt her celebrity that Daria was married to one of the most celebrated male figure skaters in history. Her dramatic story of rescue from an abusive coach had once made dramatic copy. Next month they, as husband and wife, would appear on the cover of a popular magazine with broad national circulation.

During the interview Mat had deliberately promoted Daria over himself, and hoped the story would read that way. When he had doubts about Daria's happiness, he told himself that she thrived on her success, but now he wondered if he were the only one thriving in their personal and professional relationship. At times Daria seemed blatantly contemptuous of all the attention, which made him feel she didn't appreciate how hard he was working on her behalf. She was slow to make friends among the other professional skaters, even though life on tour usually forged quick and lasting friendships among former competitors.

Daria's surprise at her notoriety and the humble way that she received public attention was an endearing trait that only he saw. When the cameras were aimed in her direction, a metamorphosis took place and she was transformed. It was clear that she possessed that indefinable star quality that spoke through lens and image in a provocative and compelling language that drew or repelled, but always captured attention. He had guessed correctly at that wide gulf between Daria's public persona and deep insecurity. He had guessed at, but chosen not to probe for understanding. He had committed blindly to his own selfish agenda for Daria, and now they would both pay a price.

Mat turned from the fire and watched as Daria raised her hand to smooth back her long lustrous hair. He noticed how the green satin of her robe fell over narrow hips. The slightness of her body, an impression of fragile beauty, were as deceptive as her public persona. She was physically strong, and though she was now older, could still launch her body into high, beautiful jumps with an athletic grace that was stunning to watch.

"Why don't we have breakfast before the fire?" he suggested.

"A good idea, Mat. I'll run down and tell Rosa," she called over her shoulder, already halfway across the room.

Mat sat on the veranda as the late afternoon sun drifted over the rim of the oak-covered ridge. Daria bent to kiss his forehead. She was dressed in purple tights and an oversized white shirt tied in a knot at the waist, and she had yet to drop her skating bag. It came around and hit his shoulder as she leaned in to kiss his lips, her long burnished hair enclosing his face like a tent. She tasted of juicy fruit gum, a favorite American product.

"What is wrong?" she asked. "Rosa tells me you haven't moved from this spot all day. Are you sick?" She reached out to lightly place the back of her hand on his cheek in a way that reminded Mat of his mother.

"You didn't even come to watch me practice, and my triple Lutz is over-rotated," she scolded. "I needed you, and Hillary is useless. That woman will not help me. And beads are falling off my new dress. Imagine Mat, three thousand American dollars for almost no fabric."

She looked at him, waiting. She had dropped the heavy bag and stood with hands on hips inviting him to share her exasperation, knowing that he would only be amused, but today she could not raise even that response.

"Three thousand American dollars. You pay too much, Mat. We pay too much."

Daria was decidedly frugal and could not grow accustomed to the high cost of skating after having all such expenses met by her former country. She had grown up poor. The only clothes she had were gifts from her former coach, Sasha Eymrnov, who kept a tight reign over her in every possible way.

Mat looked at her face. A lifetime spent in cold ice arenas had slowed the aging process, and her skin was virtually unlined. Her cheekbones and wide green eyes gave the impression of endearing youth. She wore makeup only when competing and otherwise seemed not to care for artifice of any kind, traits totally out of sync with her public image.

"Come here," he said and held out an arm. She nestled beside him in the wide chair and he pulled her close. They sat like that, comfortable and still for a few minutes.

"You will come to practice tonight?" Daria asked.

She knew he was thinking about something that worried him, something he had yet to confide, but he was not a secretive man, her Mat. He was not complicated in the bad way she had grown accustomed to shielding herself from. He was open and honest, with an endearing vulnerability, and soon he would tell what was on his mind. In the threatening scheme of possibilities that life could potentially cough up, she could depend on it being easily rectified -- nothing to worry about.

Perhaps another fight with Hillary or a script for another movie that he knew she wouldn't be interested in. His life was firmly rooted in routine, his way of thinking and behaving entirely predictable, which was precisely what made her presence in his house and in his life possible. How long that would last she could not say.

"I'll come to your practice and I'll even sew those beads back on your dress," he announced. Like most skaters, in a pinch, Mat could repair a costume.

"Crystals," she corrected him. "They are Austrian crystals at four dollars each and two of them are lost forever."

They sipped from the same glass of wine. "This is certainly a great tragedy," he teased and put up an arm to block her punch.

"You are making fun of me again," she laughed, but he did not laugh back in his usual way. Daria looked at him intently. She felt safe when Mat was near, and she had learned to let the feeling stand rather than send her off in a roaring panic of displacement as it once had. But now, a silent alarm rattled the checking mechanisms of her mind, and a shift took place. Nothing was forever. In the beginning, he had meant nothing to her, only a means of escape, but time had brought the unexpected. When she looked into his face and saw happiness there, she actually found a little for herself.

Mat finished the wine while Daria pulled a bottle of water from the top of her equipment bag. Without looking at him, she probed for what the change might be. She did so as an animal sniffs the air for alien scents that have infiltrated the territorial enclosure, running various scenarios through her mind.

Despite the fact that she had far more notoriety than was safe, Daria was sleeping and sometimes even straight through the night. And she was eating and tolerating the physicality of her body and even his. More important, that feeling of not being real, of being absent from consciousness had ceased to plague her as often. She didn't need her husband for a place to live and for food to eat. So, why did she stay when their marriage had already provided the legal status needed for residence?

Daria watched the shadows climb like fingers from the depth of the valley. Lulled by the barrier of security that Mat offered, she had neglected her primary responsibility. Names written in a childish Russian scrawl tacked to the inside of the collective consciousness by an immature personality, now stunted and long since having receded into oblivion. That list and those names, a central task and reason for living.

Daria looked into her husband's eyes. "What are you thinking?" she inquired and held her breath, fearful of the answer.

Mat paused, "I'm thinking about my mother. I'm thinking she did a good job of protecting me when I was young, and I'm wondering about you. Who," he asked, "protected you?"

Most questions presented as slippery slopes of entrapment and this seemed no different. Daria didn't recognize the expression on his face. Was it pity? She stood abruptly and hoisted her equipment bag as though it weighed nothing.

"That's your job, and I'm starving. Shall we see if dinner is ready?"

For the first time since Mat had known her, although he had heard it many times before, he only truly heard it now. Her tone was evasive, faintly defiant, but decidedly foreign.

She was at the door to their bedroom when she stopped. "Don't think too much about your mother, Mat."

"Why not?"

"Because... perhaps she would not have liked me." *Perhaps*, Daria added to herself, *she would have hated me.*

"She would have loved you," he called after her, knowing it wasn't true, and besides, it was already too late. He had spent the afternoon thinking about his mother and those early years when he had hated skating and looked for his father to take the initiative to rescue him from long, sometimes painful, practices.

Mat laid the palm of his hand on the place beside him that Daria had newly vacated. He thought of his father's guns. There were two gun cabinets in the house and a display of antique pistols, but much to his father's disappointment Mat had disliked hunting and refused to learn how to shoot.

"Every civilization is a hair breath from chaos. A man needs to learn how to defend himself and his family," Thierry had said.

Mat never expected to agree with his father and especially not on this topic. However, in the space of sixteen hours his world had profoundly shifted, and a new reality hit. He would learn to shoot and he would learn to shoot well.

Alexandra Clair

CHAPTER THREE

Irene entered the office of her son's coach and settled her large frame into one of two newly upholstered club chairs. Glen Winston looked up from his desk inquiringly. He glanced at his itinerary for the day and saw that her name did not appear.

"What can I do for you?" he asked, failing to disguise his annoyance. Irene was seriously overweight and Glen Winston had a penchant for perfection. He found lots of reasons not to like Mateo's mother and primary among them was that he could not neatly slot her into a skating mother category.

"I've told Mat that he can pack his things. We'll be leaving this afternoon," Irene said, offering no other explanation.

Glen had noticed that most communication between mother and son came from her vast repertoire of looks and shrugs, which Mat seemed to interpret without difficulty.

"Leaving?" Glen laid aside a heavy folder. Even before learning that Mat's former coach was ready to retire, Glen had campaigned to acquire him as a student. The boy was far too valuable a prize to give up without a fight, and yet Glen was not worried. The boundless ambition of most figure skating parents was easily manipulated, and he was a master at serving up just the right confluence of censure and validation calculated to keep the most astute parents off balance.

"What's the problem? May I offer you some coffee?"

"Mat is not happy," she said ignoring the offer of coffee. She had no plans to stay long enough for such niceties.

"Happy!" Glen's smile was a smirk of condescension. He could summon no enthusiasm for another whining exchange with one more parent seeking assurance that they were valued. But smoothing the feathers of a disgruntled parent was as much a part of his job as introducing a new jump, so he forced himself to appear attentive.

"If you're worried about Mat's program you should know that I hired the best choreographer money could buy, and at no expense to you," he added.

Even as he spoke Glen considered the circumstances that had brought Irene to his office unannounced and threatening to remove her son. Obviously the brat had complained about the altercation they'd had over Mat's wish to alter certain elements of his program. Inwardly Glen bristled. He still had a thing or two to teach that boy about how things were done under his tutelage.

Just yesterday he had looked out one of the two windows at each end of his office that afforded him a full view of both Olympic-size ice surfaces. A smooth, pristine surface had been left in the wake of the Zamboni, until Mat had burst into view, an explosion of energy, remarkable after a full day of training. Glen felt pleased that one of his two prized students should be working long after the others had disappeared into the locker rooms. This was not unusual for Mat. He was nearly always the first on the ice in the morning and the last to leave in the afternoon.

Glen was about to turn away when he noticed that Mat was doubling his triple jumps. This allowed him to concentrate on the changes to his program that Glen had clearly stated could not be made. Judging by the fluid ease with which Mat skated, it was apparent that he had been practicing these changes behind his back. More important, so close to the first qualifying competition that would lead to nationals, he was confusing the muscle memory that most skaters relied on.

Glen was infuriated. Mat had been at the prestigious Winston Skating Center only a few months, but he could not allow his authority to be challenged in such a way. Only Ryan Kollyn could get away with that sort of rebellion.

In a fit of rage Glen had bounded down the stairs and out a private door that led directly onto the ice. Student and coach met at the music booth where Mat was about to key up his music for another trial run.

"What do you think you're doing?" Glen erupted.

"I have a couple of ideas about changing my program," Mat began, but Glen cut him off.

"When I need your help, I'll ask for it. And let's get something straight right now, Araujo. You have a reputation as a mama's boy, but she's out of the picture because we're sending her packing."

Warming to this tongue-lashing, Glen realized he did not have Mat's full attention. A few of the younger students were drawn to watch.

"When you step foot on my ice, I'm your mother and your father. Are you listening to me?"

Glen punctuated his words, by stabbing a finger repeatedly into Mat's chest, until Mat caught his arm and held it in a tight grip. Infuriated Glen noticed a look of mutual pity exchanged with Ryan Kollyn who had joined the younger students observing from the boards.

The implied criticism fueled his rage, but Glen had gathered what self control he could. What worried him most of all was that Ryan and Mat were not enemies. A possible growing friendship could not be tolerated. Skating was not a team sport and Glen believed it better to fuel the jealousy of rival competitors, keeping them apart. He'd have to find a way to deal with this and deal with it fast.

Glen appeared oblivious to the undercurrent of fear that impacted his dealings with his students. Whether love or hate, he counted on that energy to drive a fierce competitive edge to win at all costs.

Out of the corner of his eye he had seen Ryan scoop up his skating bag and walk from the rinks parameter. Ryan's angry exit contained an element of hushed drama, not missed by the younger students as they made room for him to pass; but then Glen had the kind of captive audience he liked best and escalated his tongue lashing of Mat.

Now he narrowed his focus and looked at Irene, speaking with what he hoped was the right tone of sincerity. "What can I do to restore your confidence in me?"

There was nothing. Irene had listened long enough to other mothers' gossip about Glen's former students. Two were dangerously anorexic. One had committed suicide and others had substance abuse problems, being in and out of rehab more often than Mat had celebrated Christmas. Irene didn't like those odds. She especially decried the policy that prevented her from watching lessons and practices. The invitation to abdicate parental responsibility was built into Glen's program. Of late, his staff had stepped up their attempts to have her return home, leaving Mat to untested authority. But a nagging sense of caution restrained her. Irene had prayed for clarity and yesterday's altercation between her son and Glen had sealed her decision.

Glen tried a new tactic. "Perhaps what we have here is a spoiled young man and an overindulgent parent."

Ignoring the attempt to draw her into fruitless debate, Irene got right to the point. "If you'd had the opportunity to meet my husband, Mr. Winston, you would realize that you should never threaten Mat. Never raise a fist, or in this case a finger, that in any way connects with my child's physical person. Am I making myself clear?"

In all the years that he had jealously watched Mat compete and wished he could be the coach guiding that talent, he had never seen Mr. Araujo at any event. If he could keep the parents at odds, they had less time to interfere with his own plans.

"Does your husband agree with your decision to remove Mat? Perhaps I should call him," Glen said, making a move to reach for the phone as though he and Mat's father talked often.

Irene continued as though his words and manner had not insulted her intelligence. "The Winston Skating Center is not a good fit for my son. I'm sorry for you, I know you're disappointed, but I'm sorry for us as well. Valuable training time was lost."

"I did you a favor." Glen summoned his best facsimile of martyrdom. "I've gone out of my way for Mat, and there were some, Elliott included, who said I shouldn't take him on because of Ryan."

Irene had never been impressed by Elliott Smythe, as others were. Sports commentator and journalist for a major network, Elliott and Glen seemed to have a solid friendship. Elliott often flew in from New York to spend his free time with Glen, and the younger children appeared to adore him as he generously passed out sporting equipment and footwear autographed by football and basketball greats."

"You must be pleased at how Mat is progressing," Glen continued. "I imagine you watched him skate last Friday."

"I've seen nothing that tells me Mat has gained anything by coming here."

As competition season loomed, the students ran through their programs each Friday in full costume for interested observers and other skaters. This provided a dress rehearsal without the option to re-skate a program because of falls or missed timing. Glen made a mental note to ask his staff to pay Irene more attention and launched into a recital of the number of his students that had competed at nationals over the years, including those who had finished high enough to make a world team. The statistics were impressive.

Glen accepted only the best students and had a long list of families anxious to defer to his every wish in the belief that he could win their child acclaim, prestige, and riches. Glen was confident, warming to the subject of his many accomplishments, when Irene stood abruptly, interrupting him in mid-sentence. She had heard all this before.

"My judgment was clouded by your reputation. I was unduly flattered by your interest in my son. That was my mistake."

It had been Glen's record as a champion builder, combined with what she suspected of Ryan Kollyn that had convinced Irene that Glen would be the right coach for her son. Now she bitterly regretted that decision and especially the very valuable training time that was lost and could not be recovered.

"Is it Ryan Kollyn? Are you actually pulling Mat because of Ryan?" Glen blurted out. Damn Ryan, he thought to himself. He would fix that brat if he had sabotaged his plans for Mat.

"Because if you want us to step up the skill level, even though Mat will probably not medal at nationals this year, we can do that and ... "

"Any other coach would have already done that," Irene stated. "By reining Mat in and not presenting him in the best possible light, you hoped that next year you could have both the junior and senior national champions. This would be carried out at Mat's expense. You don't care about Mat or Ryan. You care about your reputation."

Ryan was rumored to have a substance abuse problem, and Irene believed that he could self-destruct at any time, leaving the field open to her son. Although immensely talented, Ryan would not have the longevity in skating that would place him in direct competition with Mat in the important years to come for those precious few spots on the world team.

Alexandra Clair

Despite the gloss of professionalism, Irene had felt uneasy from the first day that she entered The Winston Skating Center. As she headed in the direction of their small apartment, where Mat was even now packing the car, Irene looked about her with fresh insight. For the first time in his career Mat had been offered nearly full financial sponsorship when he entered The Winston Skating Center. Wealthy patrons had gravitated toward Glen, and his students enjoyed the best of everything. When sponsors visited, Glen made a point of parading them through the lobby and introducing them to parents as a subtle reminder of the control that was lost because of the financial help they'd accepted.

Irene had briefly met Howard Marstead and the well known broadcaster Elliott Smythe, and like the other parents, she could not help noticing that they paid particular attention to Ryan Kollyn. He was often taken off the premises for dinner, and they gave him gifts, which tended to make the younger students jealous.

The best coaches were well known and worked out of select skating centers across the country. There could be no delay in replacing Glen. Without consulting her son, Irene had already decided on Susan Eberly. All that remained was a conversation with Mat and the confirming telephone call.

Irene had carefully weighed her decision. It was well within Glen's power to poison the minds of judges and officials against her son and, in fact, he had just threatened to do so. All too often the exchange of favors determined the outcome of a close competition. At times the problem was so pervasive and so well known that it was openly talked about. Susan Eberly could claim only one national champion, but she had a stable personal life and a solid reputation for honesty that Irene felt would counter a bit of the slander she expected from Glen's camp. Irene felt comforted that Mat would be back in California, and yet far enough from home, that she could conceal her illness long enough to see him settled with what she hoped would be the last best coach of his career. Irene had determined that no one would use her illness to undermine her son's career for their own selfish purposes. Especially not Thierry, for in Irene's mind her husband was as much the enemy as Glen Winston ever was.

CHAPTER FOUR

Despite Glen Winston's predictions of disaster, Mat Araujo came in first, winning the coveted gold medal as a junior competitor at American Nationals. This accomplishment was often cited among the many accolades of his career, but even before this first place win could be recorded in official record books, Mat knew something different about this event that would trouble him for the remainder of his life.

Those few months of training with Ryan had shown Mat how wrong his impressions had been of his chief rival. There was no boasting or posturing, no sabotaging of equipment or secret measuring of tracings to see whose jump was higher.

Both boys had heard the glib analysis many times. Ryan was the more artistic, purer athlete, while Mat worked harder and longer and had better stamina. If Mat came in first, it was luck. If Ryan won, it was skill. Going into American Nationals, it was the consensus of skating insiders that Ryan Kollyn, coached by Glen Winston, would come in first. Given a clean program and Ryan's riveting presence, few expected any other scenario.

Those who knew skating, when they finally sat down to watch, were almost bored. Too many people owed Glen favors and disapproved of the way that Mat's mother had recklessly switched coaches. Glen's reputation and his contacts would carry the day and only a freak infusion of blind luck could win Mat anything more than third or fourth place.

Glen had been Ryan's only coach, while Mat had four during his long career. The first was discarded after only a few months when his mother caught the skating virus of obsession and began to view figure skating as something more than mere recreation. The second coach retired and the third was Glen Winston. Susan Eberly was to be Mat's last coach, taking him on as a junior competitor just before the same American Nationals that would forever shatter Mat's insular view of himself and others. He had just turned sixteen, had never attended a school dance, never been on a date or had the dubious distinction of being challenged to a fight on a school playground. Rites of passage experienced by most young men of his time never happened.

Glen's threat of ostracism had not materialized, but Mat's satisfaction in winning the gold medal quickly soured. Only a fraction of a point had separated the first and second place ordinals when Ryan fell on what should have been a simple jump. If he had recovered quickly and moved on, he might still have come in first because the judges could easily have cited his superior artistic delivery. But he had hesitated, prolonging the agony of that fall into an eternity of suspense, all the more painful because this was so rare an occurrence in such a predictable athlete.

With the last event completed and his gold medal firmly in hand, Mat was too elated to be tired. When he finally got around to showering and changing out of his costume the locker room was deserted.

Mat pulled on jeans and felt the slap of the gold medal against his chest. He anticipated the satisfaction he would experience each time he looked at it, feeling a certain vindication for both his mother and his new coach. As he reached for his shirt the locker room door swung open and a loud metallic crash reverberated through the room.

"What was wrong out there? Are you on drugs?"

"What of it? You going to send me to rehab again? Hey, anything to get away from you."

"Pull a stunt like that again and I'll kill you myself." Another loud crash. "Are we clear on that?"

Mat had witnessed Glen lose his temper many times, but never with such fury in his tone. Believing that he and Ryan were alone, Glen had let slip the public face of unruffled ease and polish, entirely different from the private face he showed his students.

"You can't cut it, can you?" Glen ridiculed. "We both know you can land that jump sleepwalking, so why not today? That medal was in the bag, and all you had to do was skate clean!"

"Maybe I fell on purpose," Ryan taunted. "Maybe I did it to make you look like a fool after all your smug boasting about Araujo ruining his career because he fired the great almighty coach. You can't stand it that Mat skated well in spite of you.

That's right, isn't it? You're jealous! I can see it in your face. And you know what? I'm sick and tired of your face."

Mat heard the unmistakable sound of a fist connecting with flesh and then a loud noise that could only be a body thrown against one of the lockers.

"You touch me again and I'll kill you," Ryan hissed back at Glen. "Do you hear me, you pervert. I'll kill you. Because unlike everyone else, I know who and what you are. I know all about you and your pervert friends!"

"Are you threatening me? Because if you are...."

"I'm not afraid of you. Hatred and utter disgust supersedes the fear you've used to control me. Get it. I hate you! Only God knows how much I hate–" Ryan's words were abruptly cut short as Mat heard the sound of another blow and then a scuffle. He knew he had to intervene. Leaving his things behind, he exited the cubicle to find Glen gone and Ryan on his knees, bent over and holding his stomach as he gagged involuntarily in violent heaves.

Ryan seemed unaware that he was not alone, and feeling awkward, as though trespassing, Mat brought him a moistened towel. In response Ryan tore the towel from his grasp with unexpected fury and tried to stand. Mat reached out a hand to help, which Ryan pointedly ignored as he gingerly lowered himself to a bench.

"Are you all right?"

"What do you think?" Ryan rasped.

"Should I call someone? My mother and Susan are just outside," Mat offered, already starting for the door.

"No! Not unless you really want him to kill me?"

"You might need to see a doctor."

"Not tonight."

"You have to get another coach! Tell your parents!"

Even as he said the words Mat realized he had never seen Ryan's parents at any of the countless skating events they had competed in through the years. He wondered what it would be like to have two disinterested parents instead of one, and if that was truly the case, what kept Ryan skating?

"In your world that would be the thing to do, wouldn't it? You could actually tell Mommy and she would do something about it," Ryan said with biting sarcasm. "You're lucky, you know.

Glen's a master manipulator. I've seen it over and over again. Another few weeks and your mother would have been silly putty in his hands no matter how you complained."

"I know something about how bullies operate."

"Sure you do," Ryan was disbelieving.

"If you'd seen how my mother has stood up to my father over the years, you'd know she could handle Glen."

"Yeah, well. Count yourself lucky."

Mat detected a note of jealousy at his escape from Glen. He took a close look at Ryan's eyelid. It was quickly swelling and would soon close without some attention. He went to his equipment bag and retrieved an ice pack.

"You don't have to stay with him. Everyone says that someday you'll win a medal at the Olympics."

"Yeah, well they say that about you too; and they've said that about lots of athletes no one ever hears of again."

"I have to work a lot harder than you. Even I can see that," Mat said over his shoulder as he filled the bag with ice and tossed it to Ryan. Now it was his turn to feel a tinge of jealousy.

"So why not leave?" Mat asked. "Coaches would line up to have you."

"Pretty naive aren't you, Araujo? Glen has a long reach, but I will get away!" Ryan vowed. "I have a plan."

A heavy stillness settled over Mat's chest. He had to ask, but already had a sneaking suspicion of the truth he didn't want to hear.

"Did you really throw the competition?"

"You won by a slim margin, but a fair one. I like winning too much. I'm addicted to the spotlight, I live for the applause, and much to everyone's distress, I'm destined to be the next media darling. Isn't that what they say about me?"

Ryan could be as flamboyant and spontaneous, as he was composed and predictable. While he personified the ideal for a male figure skater, Ryan pushed constantly at the parameters, but always with an air of nonchalance that others, who didn't have to spend much time with him, found charming.

Ryan's trademark costumes tended to be severe, almost stark, and it was known that he and Glen fought long and hard over what he would wear. He refused music reminiscent of any of the old skating standbys, as well as movie sound tracks which required him to reenact a dramatic role on the ice. When Ryan took the ice, he skated as himself, which never seemed to disappoint his audience.

Glen was reduced to bribing Ryan to gain his cooperation and was openly criticized for failing to control him as he did his other students. Appearing to make the best of a difficult situation, Glen coolly capitalized on Ryan's bad boy image, leaving many to conclude that he possessed immense patience to suffer repeated rebellion with such élan.

The older, more conservative judges and officials found themselves wishing that Ryan Kollyn would fade from the scene fearing he would tarnish the image of skating. Glen had noted the tide of opinion turning against Ryan and thought that with Mat in his pocket he could work the images of both boys to his advantage. But his plans had failed, and he was still reeling from the disappointment, an unfamiliar emotion.

Ryan's superior athletic ability and engaging style could not be ignored. On the ice he was a riveting presence and had a mystifying following of loyal fans, particularly among young girls. Mat would never generate that same raw, almost palatable excitement.

After what he had just overheard, Mat was now fairly convinced that for one parting shot of sweet revenge Ryan had made a calculated slip, giving up his first place standing to the skater his coach least wanted to win. There would be plenty of time to study the tape of Ryan's performance, but instinct told Mat it would only confirm his worst fear.

"I saw you go into that double at the end of your combination. It looked good," Mat probed.

"Yeah, it's a muscle thing. Your brain confirms perfect and your body rebels. Or is it a mind thing? Your mind says, 'yes' and your body says, 'screw you man.' Which comes first?" Ryan asked in a perfect imitation of Mr. Rogers that made Mat smile. "The chicken or the egg?"

"It's happened to me a lot," Mat offered.

"Yeah, but it didn't happen to you tonight, did it champ?"

Mat picked up Ryan's large silver medal, which had fallen to the floor during his altercation with Glen and lifted his own from around his neck. He compared the two, weighing each in one hand.

"Which one belongs to you?" he asked, searching Ryan's expression for an answer.

Ryan's all black costume was ripped at the sleeve, and vomit splattered the elegant velvet vest. His longish bangs fell over his swelling eye, and blood trickled from his nose. Still, there was an air of dignity and even pride in Ryan's manner, which Mat could only admire.

"Well?" Mat prompted.

A hapless expression, something like despair washed over Ryan's face. Mat was sure Ryan would cry, but as quickly as this fissure opened, it closed and he looked away. Mat had his answer. With Ryan's face averted he slipped the gold medal into Ryan's skating bag and placed the silver back onto the bench.

"There's nothing wrong with second," Ryan offered, pulling the blood stained costume over his head with a grimace of pain. Rolling it into a ball he lobbed it into a nearby trash container.

"Why don't you join us for dinner? My mother and Susan wouldn't mind."

"I should. It would send that paranoid sleaze-bag screaming, but ... I've got a date," Ryan brightened. "Come with us. You don't really want to celebrate with two old women do you?"

"Sorry, can't."

"You'll always do what's right. I can see that, Araujo."

Despite the bravado Ryan didn't sound all that keen. He was a sad figure sitting alone under the harsh lights of the locker room and was isolated in a way that Mat felt he couldn't understand.

"Yeah, thanks. By the way, if you see a blonde in a white jag outside tell her I'm running late. And don't say anything about tonight. It will only make things worse."

"I have to tell someone. Glen should not get away with this. Susan can file a complaint and they'll interview you. I'm a witness. Maybe we can get Glen sanctioned."

"No, you don't understand! They'll just assume we both had an ax to grind. And ... you can't tell anyone," Ryan was alarmed.

"It will only happen again."

"I don't plan on being with him much longer. If you say something now, before I have everything set, I'll never get away," he added, almost pleading.

The two boys regarded one another until Mat nodded in agreement.

"What will you do?"

"If I want to keep skating, it has to be in another area. I'm thinking pairs."

Mat was stunned. He couldn't imagine not having Ryan to compete against, and to have him switch to pairs at this late date seemed a terrible waste.

"So we're agreed, "Ryan said stopping Mat at the door. "You won't say anything?"

Mat nodded, knowing that Glen would not give up Ryan without a fight and especially not after he'd already lost his replacement.

Mat no longer looked forward to the celebration dinner ahead. When he got home there would be no explaining the absence of the medal. Before he walked away he could see that Ryan's facade of haughty amusement was firmly back in place. The switch of persona, given the violent altercation just witnessed, unsettled Mat.

"Good luck," he said.

"Yeah, good luck, Araujo."

CHAPTER FIVE

Mat leaned against the frame of the bathroom door and watched his mother apply moisturizer. He thought she looked tired. Perhaps this was why she had not asked for the gold medal she would add to the display case when they arrived home. Mat had long since given up seeing the location of this shrine, in the center of his father's library and office, as anything less than strategic.

"If someone we knew needed a safe place to live for a while, could they stay with us?"

She gave him a look of inquiry and Mat knew she had focused on his use of the word 'safe'.

"I can't tell you the details. I promised not to," Mat said, fending off her wordless inquiry.

"You might offer that person our help but," she cast him an icy stare. "If this is Ryan Kollyn we're discussing, we might have to find him help elsewhere. Assuming only half the gossip about that boy is true, then he has more problems than you and I am equipped to handle. I also think a close association would tarnish your image, and you know what people say?"

"Maybe you're wrong about Ryan. Maybe everyone is."

Irene didn't care if she was right or wrong. She knew that she had just attended her last competition and felt a deep, pervasive weariness far more debilitating than the pain. Just getting ready for bed required a supreme effort, and she wanted nothing more than to sleep.

"I know you're disappointed in my answer, but I can't help that right now. If we opened our home to Ryan, it would look like we had some agenda. Maybe this just isn't the time. For more reasons than you know."

"You're thinking about my career. You can't think about anything else. Well, people are more important than winning all the time."

Irene bit back her reply. She simply could not afford a friendship to develop between her son and Ryan, convinced that his freedom would prove overwhelmingly attractive to a boy as protected as, Mat. Whatever Ryan had learned about life had come too fast and too early, and now he was growing up at the expense of ambitious adults who had failed him from the start. But Irene would not share her thoughts with Mat. She could not risk a conflict there would be no time to resolve.

Irene turned to speak, knowing that she had not said enough, but Mat had already left, and it struck her that he had forgotten to kiss her good night. She could not recall a time when he had failed to kiss her goodnight.

The next day, as Irene checked out of the hotel and Mat organized their luggage, Ryan breezed into the lobby, laughing raucously and flanked by two female skaters. Ryan lifted his chin in greeting, the black eye and the angry swelling of one cheek a reminder to Mat that Glen's abuse was not a onetime occurrence. Only now Ryan was big enough to fight back.

"I have something that belongs to you," Ryan whispered as he pulled Mat aside to speak privately.

"Keep it. There'll be other nationals, and maybe next time I'll get the medal I deserve."

"You don't understand," Ryan whispered. "I don't want it."

"Then throw it away because I don't want it either." Mat had found it increasingly more difficult to conceal the flood of guilt he felt each time he was congratulated for winning.

Ryan nodded and once more Mat glimpsed that haunted, almost desperate expression, which swept Ryan's features.

"I don't know how you plan on getting away from Glen, but I spoke to my mother and … No," he rushed to assure Ryan when he saw the panic. "I didn't tell her. But she did say you could come to stay with us for a while," Mat lied.

Ryan grinned, and Mat understood how that smile could disarm the worst of suspicions. It was radiant and wide, showing perfect teeth, and would sell anything from condoms to sugary cereal. No wonder he had already been approached to do several television commercials.

"Does it hurt?" Mat asked.

Ryan touched his cheek, as though just reminded. "I guess people are talking?"

At breakfast Mat had overheard those at the next table assert that Ryan had been in a drunken brawl the night before over his disappointment at finishing second instead of the much lauded and expected first. There was no one to defend Ryan, and Mat had felt a frustrated inadequacy over the promised silence.

"I haven't heard anything," he lied again.

"Well, you can be sure the gossip mongers, or should I say the gossip mothers, are at work." He looked about in a parody of furtive paranoia. "I guess the legend grows whether I want it to or not," he said as the two girls, impatient to be off, interrupted them. "See," Ryan said in parting. "All you need to attract girls is a bad rep and a black eye."

The two boys smiled at one another, sharing what for Mat was a rare moment of alliance with another boy his age.

Mat Araujo could well remember when he had hated skating. Caught between two equally strong personalities, with wildly divergent ambitions for their only child, his participation in this expensive sport became the single most damaging source of friction between his parents.

He was seven when his mother got him started, after his father demanded Mat be involved in some sort of organized activity as a means of toughening up their undersized child. Irene announced that Mat would skate, and Thierry approved. Skating for a boy could only mean ice hockey, and although Thierry didn't actually make the time to follow sports, he approved. Ice hockey was clearly a masculine endeavor bound to reinforce manly attributes.

Thierry was an expansive man who did nothing with restraint, but he was far too busy with the vineyard and other farming duties to attend practice. He failed to notice the absence of hockey equipment and did not scrutinize the bills his wife presented for payment. Not until eight months later, when Mat was measured for his first costume, did Thierry discover there was another altogether different dimension to skating.

The last thing Mat wanted was for his father to see that first costume, for unlike his mother, he suspected the scope of his father's ignorance. But Irene had insisted, and so like a lamb before the slaughter, he was paraded out in the mock military uniform, a light blue polyester blend with sequined epaulets at the shoulder and gold fringe that swayed with the slightest movement. As if that were not enough, Irene had insisted on matching sequins at each cuff and down the outside seams of his trousers. Thierry's reaction of stunned disbelief, followed by booming protest, in no way fell short of the expected tirade.

Thierry attended that first competition with the express purpose of telling his wife, "I told you so!" After that he never came to another. Battle lines were drawn and he the pawn between.

Before she died Irene had seen her son win two national titles, while Thierry had remained intentionally oblivious to these accomplishments. When Mat qualified for the world team and was to compete at the Olympics, it dawned on Thierry that his son had accomplished something beyond his reach, and his first urgent thoughts were for the winery. People he barely knew from town began to stop him on the street to ask about Mat, and even more disconcerting, complete strangers began to offer advice. *As though,* Thierry inwardly raged, *ice skating could actually be a career.*

For the first time Thierry realized that his plans for Mat were seriously undermined. When Mat returned from Europe, Thierry was primed for confrontation. Mat parted from his coach at the airport and joined Joey Santos in the red Jeep with the farm's name and logo emblazoned on the door for the ride home.

Jose Santos, called Joey by Mat's father, was a good friend. The two had known one another since they were boys. Unlike his parents Joey was an American citizen. His mother had gone into labor during picking season, and she had been rushed by Thierry to give birth at the charity clinic near the mission. Although very different in background and temperament, they loved to fish; and it was a rare luxury for Mat to pack a lunch and, with squirming bait in the bottom of the tackle box, to disappear with Joey for a leisurely day at the river.

Joey's parents had been migrant workers who came to the vineyard each harvest. One year after the grape was safely fermenting in their huge vats, Joey's father had mysteriously moved on, leaving his wife and son behind, and Joey had taken to trailing after Thierry, who didn't seem to mind. Accustomed to taking charge and compulsively shaping objects and people alike to fit his own private vision, Thierry soon had Joey attending school and joining them at meals, becoming a new fixture that Irene tolerated but never quite accepted.

"I hear the old man gave you a promotion," Mat said to Joey once his luggage was stowed and they were settled in the Jeep.

"He did," came the measured reply. "He gave me the promotion he wanted to give you. He told me it was only temporary." Joey shrugged and gave Mat a sidelong glance under thick eyelashes.

He was almost as tall as Thierry with glossy straight hair that he wore in a ponytail, tied with various pieces of tooled leather. Tourists often stopped to talk with him, and soon he was offering advice on the best wines for them to purchase and send home in cases. Noticing his natural sales ability, Thierry moved Joey into the store where sales soon tripled. Then he began sending Joey to various wholesale markets, expanding the gift shop and increasing their drop-in trade. At Joey's suggestion, a string quartet from the local college came in each week, and they sponsored an afternoon of wine tasting. Joey even opened the old mission chapel, which predated the house, for weddings. Try as he did, Thierry could not convince Joey to cut his hair, and, although he disapproved, Mat knew that his father would accept such behavior from a man he sweated and worked beside, but that he would openly berate in his own son. It was obvious to Mat that the two shared an easy regard and tolerance that would never be extended to him in any comparable measure.

"As far as I'm concerned the job is yours," Mat said, surprised at the note of bitterness that had crept into his tone.

"You okay?" Joey asked.

"It's not your fault, and I hate to sound jealous, but I know he likes you more than me."

"Likes, not loves. That's the operative word, Mat, because there is a world of difference. He just doesn't understand what you're about. He can't relate."

"Doesn't understand or doesn't choose to understand?" Mat countered. "Because there's a world of difference there too, and I think we both know the answer."

"Yeah, well, don't get into it with him this trip. I've been a little worried about the old man," Joey said with obvious affection. "He can't do everything himself anymore, and he hates it. You know his energy level. He can go forever, but lately he tires quickly. Had to bring my mother in to run the house, and even she has noticed it."

Before she died Irene had always had help with the large sprawling house, but never live-in help. Mat knew the two were probably lovers and perhaps had been for many years. There was talk that Joey was his half-sibling. Although it did his mother no good, and she was now beyond caring, Mat experienced a sudden stab of jealousy on her behalf.

Even before Mat walked across the worn and scarred threshold of the large Spanish-style mansion of stone and adobe with the red tile roof and the weathered companario of burned brick, he experienced his usual sense of foreboding. Joey's mother took his suitcase and reached up on tiptoe to kiss his cheek.

"Your father is in the library," she said ominously. "Don't fight with him tonight, Mat. Just agree with him if you can. He needs peace and quiet, and you must not provoke him."

Mat felt a flash of defensiveness. It was none of her business what he did. Separating him from skating was Thierry's last obstacle to the son emerging from the father's mold. Mat felt ganged up on. Even at the risk of losing his inheritance, no relationship with Thierry was preferable to continuing under the immense weight of that limitless disapproval. Mat wished he could be any place in the world but home. In his mind he reviewed the upcoming itinerary. There was an exhibition to do at Lake Tahoe. After that he was off to St. Moritz. He would use that trip as an excuse to cut the planned two-week stay at home to a few days.

The library was a combination study and office with floor-to-ceiling bookcases. It had always been his father's retreat, the place he did his planning for the farm.

Thierry stood as Mat entered the room. He had a full head of white hair, complimenting the rough-hewn features of a distinguished face. Perhaps because of Joey's warning, Mat thought he could detect pallor beneath the tan, and despite the athletic build and overall impression of health, a disturbing hint of frailty.

"How'd you do?" Thierry asked in a gruff approximation of a greeting.

"Fine," Mat said, understanding that Thierry did not want to know the details of his second place finish. Mat felt a grip of anxiety. He could see in the set of Thierry's face that chomping –at-the-bit gleam of avarice that was always a precursor to a tirade of opinion.

"I'm not going to beat around the bush, Mat."

"No, I don't imagine that's possible."

"Don't be flip with me. We've reached an impasse and this is important to your future and that of our family."

"It's always important. Whatever you have to say that the world must agree with. Okay, I'm listening -- a skill you haven't learned, I might add."

"If you're picking a fight with me you won't win."

"I've given up fighting with you. Go ahead. I'm listening."

Mat understood that his father had already rehearsed what he would say, and it was his one job to listen and agree. Joey and his mother had both advised him to tread lightly. Well, this time he might not accommodate.

"You know this skating business cannot be a career. If you continue, the best you can hope for is touring in some fairy skating show, and you know what people will say about you then."

"I know what you would say."

"Well then. I've had Joey doing your job until you got back, but now you can call that coach of yours, what's her name?"

"Susan Eberly. You know her name, Dad."

"Okay, that's right. Call Susan and tell her to cancel anything she has you down for."

There was a haunting ring to his father's words. Almost against his will, Mat remembered a recurring childhood fantasy in which his father rescued him from the grueling monotony of long, sometimes painful practices. "Enough, Irene," he would thunder to the unfailing hope of a boy's imagination. "Mat is my child too, and I say no more skating." In this fanciful revelry, his suddenly docile mother would look at her husband in loving submission and agree, and the skating would end. He had been disappointed in his father then, and now oddly, he was even more disappointed. Thierry had never rescued him, and yet, that perpetual disapproval had pervaded their lives and sapped the joy from each accomplishment.

The pressure to stop skating had been building almost since the day of his mother's funeral. Mat had rarely been openly defiant of his father, but as he looked into that stubborn face, an overwhelming rush of resentment washed over him. Even now, after all the trophies and accolades, Thierry would not appreciate the accomplishments, the past ambivalence, the discipline, or finally the determination to rise above it all. As he glanced about the room Mat realized that the trophy case his mother had been so proud of was missing. Its absence exposed the truth of his father's disdain, which Mat could no longer excuse.

As Thierry spoke of his responsibility to the Araujo legacy and his new role as the heir apparent, as though the vineyard were a small country, Mat wondered how he had evolved from hating his craft to loving it. There was not one particular incident that he could recall and hold up as the crisis point of change, and yet a love of skating had seeped into his blood and burrowed a place in his heart, quietly tilting a subtle balance from one extreme to the other. Now he was symbiotically tied to the sport and there was no going back. Mat looked into his father's determined face and saw his features relax in smug victory. He had taken his son's silence for agreement.

"Now whatever it is you have coming up next. What is it? Switzerland? An exhibition? Cancel it!"

Mat placed two shaking hands on the desk, which filled the space between them. "Dad," he began tentatively.

"You need to get that so called coach of yours, what's her name? Susan, is it? Get her on the horn and tell her to cancel everything else too. There'll be no more trips to Europe for you for a while."

"Dad," Mat spoke a little louder.

"And while she's at it, tell her to call that damn skating association and tell them you're out. You hear? You're out," he shouted with undisguised glee.

"DAD," Mat nearly screamed. "Will you PLEASE listen to me? I'm not going to stop skating. I'm training for the next Olympics. That's eighteen months away and I could come home with a gold medal. Don't you understand what that means?"

"Your life is here. Now I've got Joey doing your job, but thanks to innovations he's made with my backing, there is room enough for both of you. Plenty of work, and he won't mind having you over him."

"Won't he? If what you say is true, I would."

Thierry picked up the phone and held it out to Mat. "You are no longer a child. It's time to grow up and take on your responsibilities as my son. Here," he jabbed the phone toward Mat's face. "Call that damn coach of yours and cancel."

"Cancel what? Cancel my life? The only life I have? If you force me to make a choice between you and skating or the vineyard and skating, you'll be making a huge mistake. It's not that I don't appreciate all you're trying to do. And maybe later ..."

"I don't understand you," Thierry interrupted. "Your grandfather nearly lost this place during the great depression, and my father and I built it back up for you. This farm is your heritage. You'll have a son and it will be his. If you can't feel it now you soon will. You are the only son I have."

Mat looked into his father's face. "That's not what I hear," he said, warming to the subject, realizing how much he wanted to know the truth. Was Joey Santos his half brother? Is that why Irene had so resented mother and son?

"What did you say?"

"I hear that Joey is your son. And he loves this place. Why not adopt him since you already love him more than me."

"Gossip! Tell me who has said such a thing and I'll kill them."

"I need you to see how hard you are to talk with. I point out something that you don't choose to admit, and rage is your only response. I have news for you. You are not God. There is no argument left with my mother that you can win by controlling me. Chew on that for awhile."

"Your mother would roll over in her grave."

"My mother is dead, and you were an abusive prick. If she's going to roll over in her grave about anything, it would be about your mistress sleeping in your bed, living under her roof, every night."

"Get out!" Thierry's face was contorted in an ugly parody of rage.

"Just for once let's have a rational conversation. One where I speak and you actually listen."

"You get out of here, until you're ready to accept

responsibility. See how you get along without a monthly allowance and someone to subsidize this very expensive hobby of yours. Your life is here."

Thierry pounded the desk and sent a vase of sunflowers flying with the sweep of his hand. "Do you think you're better than your ancestors who struggled to make a living picking someone else's grapes in Spain? You dishonor their memory."

To argue with his father was to lose. Mat turned his back and walked slowly toward the door, unable to deny a liberating sense of release. He wouldn't give Thierry the satisfaction of seeing him cry because his father hated such weakness, and yet, there was something profoundly sad, and even wrenching, about leaving the only home he had ever known.

Thierry was nearing the end when Joey finally called. Mat sat in that whitewashed hospital room and held the large beefy hand, scarred and wrinkled from years of hard physical labor and recalled how, as a young child, he had loved the feel of that hand cuffing his cheek, ruffling his hair.

They had never said, "I love you," to one another, and yet even as he watched, Mat could not quite grasp that this seemingly invincible man could leave the world forever. In the sterile arena of the hospital Joey was fearful and awkward, already grieving. Joey lingered in the room and refused to leave the corridor, while Mat was content to hold a grieving son's vigil by the bedside, even helping the nurses change the linens and make his father as comfortable as was possible. Secretly he hoped his actions would somehow alleviate any residue of guilt in the years ahead for that last argument and ensuing estrangement.

At the end, Mat leaned his elbows on the narrow bed and held his father's hand to his cheek. Silence seemed to encase the small huddle of their bodies as, choked by expectation, a final opportunity slipped beyond reach without the healing balm of what each knew should be said. That call to apologize, those words of reconciliation, overtures well within their power to make and often on their minds, never materialized. In stunned disbelief Mat felt his father's hand relax in his. He watched the stillness of Thierry's chest as life emptied from his face, and for some time he sat paralyzed in the grip of that mysterious absence.

He knew that he should wake Joey, who was sleeping in a recliner in the corner of the room. He should ring for the nurse and think about arrangements, but his only thought was for the last goodbye, hollow in its finality, a goodbye that was no goodbye at all.

Mat expected to feel a similar loss that could ambush him even now when he thought of his mother. Like a visitor intruding where he least belonged, Mat organized the funeral and played the role of grieving son. In those weeks he often thought to pray, but pushed from his mind that subtle call to talk with a loving God. He felt guilty for the love he could not feel and for the humiliating surge of relief over his father's absence in his life.

In a daze of self-hatred Mat moved through the formality of what was expected of him. He placed Joey beside him in the receiving line, a move not missed by employees and neighbors. Friends and family thought him brave and generous. Mat knew that he was neither.

Alexandra Clair

CHAPTER SIX

With no hint of her future importance to him, Mat first saw Daria at the competition in St. Moritz. Like everyone else, he was impressed by the flawless jumps combined with graceful artistry which she evidenced in practice. She looked younger than her years, and for the first time the western press took notice and predicted a promising career. In spite of this Daria did not skate well. The flawless jumps displayed in practice did not translate to the spotlight, and her standings plummeted to the last tier of competitors.

With the ladies' event over, Mat had pulled the last practice of the evening, which was sparsely attended. Most of the judges, who attended practice in order to become familiar with the skaters and promote their country's hopes for a medal, had wisely stayed in their hotel rooms. A large storm was predicted, and already snow blanketed the boulevard where the complex was situated. Mat had arranged to meet friends in the hotel bar, and to save time he came prepared to shower and change at the rink. Over his clothing he wore a black leather bikers' jacket, a gift from Ryan the night before. It was Ryan who occupied his thoughts as he made a wrong turn exiting the American locker area.

Although the truth was carefully guarded, the rumors of Ryan fighting a drug habit were true. American hopes for a medal had been pinned on Ryan and his partner to unseat the eastern Europeans, and especially the Russians, at the upcoming Olympics. The fast and secret cure in a private clinic proved difficult to hide.

Following an argument with his partner and her parents, Ryan had disappeared without explanation. Now the team doctor stood by ready to conduct a discreet and unofficial drug screen. If America's most celebrated pair team needed to withdraw from competition, then whatever illness was currently making the rounds would be cited as the reason and all rumors to the contrary glibly denied.

"Hey Mat, this is all I had time for," Ryan called with his usual polished élan as he flipped on the lights tossing two leather jackets on the bed. "Take the one you want. As you can see we have company."

It was after three. Blurry-eyed Mat fought his way awake to see the association president, Elizabeth Cannon, enter their hotel room, followed by Ryan's coach, his partner's father, and the team physician in tow. No one looked happy.

"I know we can count on you not to say anything about this," Elizabeth said to Mat. She looked grim-faced, convinced that Ryan had relapsed, already writing the press release in her head.

"Damn partner," Ryan drawled in a mock Texas accent. "These marshals work too fast for me."

Mat smiled as he recalled Ryan rolling up his sleeve for blood to be drawn and then being dispatched to the bathroom for a urine sample, nonchalant, as though he did this as often as he brushed his teeth.

"And no privacy either," he lamented flashing the huddle in the doorway.

Little was known of Ryan's absent parents. When they returned to the US from this trip Mat was concerned about Ryan being on his own. In Los Angeles the temptation to party with old acquaintance and forgo training was a self- destructive certainty. Mat had just decided to invite Ryan to the vineyard for Christmas where they could practice together at his home rink.

Mat stopped abruptly. He'd been so lost in thought that he'd made a wrong turn. Industrial grillwork loomed overhead and nothing looked familiar. Mat was about to turn back when he heard the unmistakable sound of a cry, which seemed to emanate from above. He wondered if it was merely an echo from a far off location carried by the duct work until the plaintive sound of a sob choking back tears and very close was unmistakable.

"Hey," he called, just as the lights snapped off, replaced by a dim glow from the auxiliary system. "Can I do something to help?"

Silence.

"What are you doing up there?" He tried again. Mat had hoped to get away without complication. Tonight would be his last chance to relax with friends until all was over.

"I'm hiding."

In spite of himself Mat smiled. "And how, may I ask, did you manage to get up there?"

"Like this," came the reply. Suddenly Daria dangled before him. He recognized her instantly as he guided her descent to the floor.

"I'm sure there's a pretty interesting explanation for why you've been hiding, but I don't have time to hear it. They're closing the place down, so if we don't hurry we may find ourselves locked in."

"I'm not going anywhere!"

Mat studied her small upturned face.

"Well you can't stay here," Mat asserted, noting the stubborn set of her jaw. "People have to be worried about you. I'm surprised they're not tearing this place apart as we speak."

"They don't care about me. I'm nothing and I failed to skate well. They'll be looking to punish me and that's about all," she stamped her foot in childish defiance.

"Now you know that's not true," Mat cajoled. Up close he could see that her hair was over-bleached from harsh chemicals, the choice of color all wrong for her. Her pale skin had a washed-out, almost wizened quality that made her seem unwell. She wore black tights with matching practice skirt and a sweatshirt emblazoned with her country's flag. On her feet were cheap slippers, comprising the incongruous detail that typified her country's teams, whose equipment and dress could range from the very best to the most decrepit he had ever seen in serious competition.

A story had circulated of a silver medalist at European Nationals who, despite blades over-sharpened until there was almost no edge to skate on, finished second when he might otherwise have managed first. Because his upset had not been anticipated and because he was not the political choice, his equipment had been virtually ignored by an inflexible and unimaginative regime.

"There's a storm brewing out there so we need to get moving."

She stubbornly refused to budge.

"I'm not leaving you behind."

Her face was tear-stained and her restless eyes red and

swollen. Mat knew very well what it was to have one's confidence shaken after a disastrous performance, but to be so young and to have it happen in front of an international audience with so many expectations was brutal.

"I know who you are," she changed the subject. "You are the American skater, Mr. Mateo Araujo. You might take me home. And why shouldn't you?"

"Because you're a minor and much too young to make such decisions. I don't have time for this, let's go."

Mat was puzzled by her accent, which lacked the British inflection of most East European language programs.

"I want to go back to America."

This last was a plea which Mat ignored. "I don't know about 'back to America,'" he said, "but I do know this... I'll take you back to your hotel. And that's about as far as this nights' trip will extend."

Mat held out his hand which she ignored.

Torn, Mat looked at his watch. Without him to run interference and ignored by the other skaters who would have been warned by coaches and parents that it wasn't wise to be seen socially in his company, Ryan would most certainly strike out on his own. After the violent locker room altercation with Glen and that disturbing glimpse into Ryan's life, Mat felt responsible for the former competitor, now friend.

Bringing his thoughts back to the present he tried sympathy. "I had a coach like yours once, but if possible Sasha could actually be worse. So I understand..."

She emitted a cynical, mirthless laugh. "You understand nothing at all."

"Enough! I don't have time for this. I'm going with or without you." Mat headed down the corridor listening for her footsteps.

It was not unusual for Sasha to confront a judge if he disagreed with a score, and he seemed to have inexhaustible contacts and influence in the international skating community, where he was looked upon with a disturbing mixture of fear and respect. Little of importance happened in the skating world without his being among the first to know, and although no one took it seriously, it was rumored that he sometimes acted as unofficial courier for his government, or some said, for the Russian crime syndicate.

Concluding his bluff had failed, rehearsing stern words to gain her cooperation, Mat was surprised to feel a small hand slip into his. This was a gesture of defeat, and he felt her sadness. For an instant, only an instant, Mat wondered if there was something more to know, something beyond the superficial that deserved his attention.

As they opened the door hard pellets of snow, whipped by the wind stung their faces. Mat noted how inadequately dressed Daria was which quelled his concern for this waif of a charge. He concluded that her plan to run away had to be an impulsive act by a distraught child too disappointed in her performance to face her coach.

Mat removed the leather jacket and settled it about her thin shoulders. As she pushed her arms into the sleeves, he placed a knit Bruins cap he had picked up at Logan Airport on her head, grateful to note that the car he'd ordered was still waiting. Once settled in the back seat he told Daria how talented he thought she was.

"Who are the Bruins?" she asked, ignoring the compliments and removing the Bruins cap to study the name.

"They're a Boston hockey team," Mat said, calculating how long Ryan would wait.

"I know Massachusetts," Daria offered in the clipped, almost breathless way she had of speaking.

"Good," Mat replied absently, now concerned with the level of security Sasha routinely maintained about his competing skaters. With the Berlin Wall down and the shift in fortunes his paranoia had become a running joke.

"It doesn't appear anyone's been looking for you."

Quietly Daria began to cry. Feeling awkward Mat fished a handkerchief from his pocket.

"Listen," he said, thinking this was about the three falls and the rest just a bit of drama. "I'm an excellent judge of skating talent. You do believe that, don't you?"

"Yes," she said solemnly.

"Sasha might be angry because you didn't skate well, but no other girl your age has the jumps that you have. Your country is well aware of this. Talent in our world is currency. Capitalize on it while you can."

Even as he said this, Mat knew that many skaters could

deliver the goods in practice but not when it counted in competition. He hoped this was not the start of one of those heart-breaking patterns for Daria.

"But I want to go home," she said.

"You will," he soothed.

"No," she whispered in hushed exasperation. "I want to go home with you, to America."

"They wouldn't have you. You're a minor without parents." Everyone knew her story of being orphaned and then sponsored by Sasha into the state-sponsored skating program. "You do understand this, don't you?"

"I know. I must wait. I must always wait," she said almost in a wail. "And I may never have another chance. You do understand that, don't you?" In this last there was a sudden shift to anger.

Mat looked nervously at the driver's profile. A broken window separated the front and back seats, but the driver appeared to ignore them as he skillfully maneuvered the car through the snow, which was accumulating at an alarming rate on the roads and embankments.

"Look," he said, opening the inside flap of the jacket he'd lent her and that Ryan had given him only the evening before. "See this patch? Only the American team has these, and each has a name on it."

Under the light from the passing street lamps, Daria traced the letters of his last name with her finger. Carefully Mat ripped out the stitching that he had sewn around the rim only hours before and placed the patch, symbolically in her hand.

"Someday we'll be at another event together. You'll be older, and if you want help to get clear of Sasha, or whatever else they think you owe them, I'll help. Send this patch as a signal and I'll know. I'll know, and I'll find a way to help you have a different life."

"You don't mean this," she challenged.

"No. I mean what I say. I'll help you."

Instantly she smiled, and the transformation was so complete and unexpected that impulsively he grinned back.

"You are most sincere Mr. Mateo Araujo?" she demanded.

Thinking her pretty for the first time, Mat nodded. She was dwarfed by the size of the jacket, which extended below her knees. Snow had settled in her hair and made him think of fireflies as they glistened under the shifting glow of street lamps and shop windows. They were almost at her hotel.

Like all athletes he had been briefed on how to behave in certain situations, and he had already broken several rules, but the late hour and the storm dictated his decision to handle this himself. Mat believed that he would never hear from Daria again. She would evolve from skating to coaching, produce several children who didn't skate and would forget entirely his promise of future help once puberty set in.

Mat did not reveal these thoughts. This was no more than a transient meeting, and she, just a little girl who needed his encouragement.

Mat opened the door. She stepped from the car clutching tightly his patch in her hand.

"This is a solemn promise you have made," Daria reminded him in the overly-dramatic stance that childhood can sometimes assume.

Appearing both vulnerable and cute in the cap and oversized jacket, she turned all the force of her intense stare on him, and Mat fought hard to stifle a smile. He had let her out a block from her hotel, and now he attempted an expression of equal seriousness as he nodded in answer.

Daria turned and walked away. Suddenly concerned for whatever repercussions might follow on the heels of her runaway attempt, Mat directed his driver slowly forward. As Daria approached the door of her hotel a man stepped from the shadows, grabbing her slender arm and nearly lifting her from the ground. With a force that was excessive for such a little girl, he roughly directed her toward the lighted canopy of the hotel entrance. Mat opened the cab door to object.

"I wouldn't do that if I were you," the cab driver offered.

"Who are you to tell me what to do," Mat responded with misplaced anger.

"You don't know who these people are."

"And you do?" Mat said as he slammed the car door. For a moment he stood in the snow, forgetting Ryan. Forgetting everything except the fear of a young girl and the inappropriate, rough way she had just been handled.

When he peered into the lobby there was nothing to see. No sign of Daria at all. Mat's concerns for Ryan were forgotten as the cab drove the short distance to his own hotel. Getting out on the cold sidewalk he turned to pay, planning a generous tip for waiting outside the rink. The words came to him again ... *You don't know who these people are.* But the cab was gone, the question of payment obviously an insignificant detail leaving Mat with more questions than he started with.

Ten days later, after a strong technical program, Mat was first in the standings and ready to skate the final freestyle event. He had picked by lot what most skaters consider the worst possible placement, slated to skate first in his elite group. No matter how well he skated, the judges would be conservative, leaving room for any better performance after his.

With Susan nearby, Mat listened to his music and visually imagined skating through the best possible performance. All conversation and background noises were shut out, but nothing could diminish the excitement and sense of expectation that clenched the backstage atmosphere in a tight grip of organized anxiety. As he tied his skates and stretched out his long legs, Mat reminded himself to allow that energy to work for him and not against him.

Mat noticed that Susan had wandered off to speak to an official. Beyond her he was startled to see Sasha Eymrnov striding toward him, with a murderous scowl on his face. On Sasha's head was the same Bruins cap that Mat had given Daria only days before. Instantly he knew that he was about to be confronted and that Sasha, who had a student slotted to compete behind him, had strategically chosen this very moment. With unexpected force Sasha bent down and snatched the ear piece, causing a sharp edge to scratch his face, leaving behind a thin welt of blood.

"We know what you did with that child," Sasha whispered venomously into Mat's ear, sounding more like a jealous lover than a protective coach.

Sasha could not have chosen a more inappropriate moment. All of Mat's carefully constructed focus was instantly shattered. Even the great Sasha Eymrnov would have difficulty explaining his actions should either Mat or Susan decide to file a formal complaint. With concentration lost, Mat could slip significantly in the standings and Sasha's own student could end up with a medal.

A lifetime of watching his mother be bullied by Thierry had left Mat scornful of such manipulation. With skates on, he towered over Sasha, as he stood with menacing slowness and retrieved the ear piece. He glared into Sasha's face and was gratified to see that this was not the expected reaction.

"I don't know what you're talking about." Mat allowed his voice to rise in anger, deliberately calling attention to the exchange.

Sasha glared at him and muttered something in Russian that Mat couldn't follow.

"I simply escorted Daria back to her hotel. She was scared and from what I observed she had reason to be. Maybe you should thank me for getting her safely back in that storm."

A swift change came over Sasha's face. Mat was not intimidated nor was he matching Sasha's whispered tone, which invited a curious expectation of secrecy. Something was not quite right, but Mat had no time to explore the possibilities. Still, there was an unsettled aspect to their exchange, which nagged at his sensibilities. He couldn't help wondering why Sasha would risk confirming his reputation as a bully if there was nothing to hide."

Susan looked their way. Sasha's back was to her, but there was no mistaking the expression on Mat's face. It was the epitome of poor sportsmanship for a rival coach to speak with another student minutes before competition, but to do so at such an important event was tantamount to being criminal. Already several officials looked curiously at Sasha, wondering what the two could possibly have to discuss at such a time.

"I do believe this belongs to me," Mat said and snatched the cap off Sasha's head.

"But of course, and I am simply returning it." Sasha's pleasant tone was in sharp contrast to the look of abject hatred on his face.

Susan Eberly was a small woman with gray hair and a penchant for dressing always in black. She had an unassuming manner, but when it came to protecting her students, she was like a mother bear with new cubs. Taking a handkerchief she dabbed at the trail of blood that marred Mat's cheek.

"What's happened here?" she asked, staring incredulously at

Sasha's back as he sauntered away. "I'm going to file a complaint as soon as your program is over. That man has finally gone too far."

"No. I'll handle this," Mat said, brushing her hand aside.

"Right, you're right. We'll talk about this later. Think about your program; get him out of your head."

Mat's name was called and a monitor frantically waved him forward. Mat stepped up to the rim of the ice and removed the skate guards as the signal was given to announce his name over the arena. With difficulty he attempted to empty his mind in an effort to regain the concentration that was lost, but he could not shed the uneasiness he felt at his encounter with Sasha.

An image lingered in his mind of Sasha's cold gray eyes and skin stretched tightly over careful, deliberate features. As he glided to the far corner of the arena to await the start of his music, Mat brushed the place on the side of his face where Sasha had snatched off the earphones.

Suddenly Daria's desire to run from her coach no longer seemed melodramatic, and he felt truly sorry for her. As the first notes of his music filled the stadium, Mat vowed that if the patch ever made its way back to him, he would keep his promise to help her.

CHAPTER SEVEN

Nearly ten years later Mat watched Daria take the ice at the Montreal Olympics and could not quite reconcile the image he had carried in his mind of this waifish girl to this stunning beauty that bore her same name and credits.

Head bowed, hands on hips, she paced like a caged animal before the gate, as her coach, Sasha Eymrnov, looked on. Mat knew just what she was feeling, and when her name was announced and she erupted onto the ice in an infusion of energy, he could almost feel himself skating with her. The restlessness that had marked her pacing just seconds before was gone, and she lit up the arena with a spontaneous smile that drew people in as she glided to her starting spot. A metamorphosis had taken place, and Mat found his eyes riveted on her face as she lifted her arms and seamlessly glided into the first notes of her music, eager to embrace whatever fate delivered.

Few recalled the thirteen-year-old wonder that had stunned the skating world at practice years earlier in St. Moritz with her flawless triple jumps. With a less than spectacular showing at the European Nationals, Daria arrived in Montreal by default when another skater suffered a serious stress fracture.

Ryan Kollyn was covering the event and was slated to join the better known Elliott Smythe as commentator on the dance and pair events. He had sent Mat tickets and back stage passes, followed by a phone call from his New York Office.

"Come on, Mat. It'll be fun. Just like old times."

"I guess a week in Montreal could qualify as a vacation. I could use a break."

"And you've got Hillary to take over your students," Ryan finished for him.

"Yeah, but you'll be pretty tied up."

"I only look like I work," Ryan said. "Making Elliott, that relic from the dinosaur age, look foolish in front of millions of spectators has become my sole purpose for living."

"If that's all you have to look forward to, then you're in trouble," Mat laughed.

The generation of skaters that suffered most under Elliott's biting commentary had now grown up and remembered well his ungenerous, often caustic remarks. Mat himself had suffered as a result, although no skater more than Ryan. To all appearances Ryan had turned his life around, but Elliott never missed an opportunity to remind others of the past and seemed to find sadistic joy in fostering Ryan's bad boy image. Teaming up the younger, more dynamic Ryan with the polished and sophisticated Elliott was considered a mistake among controlling insiders. But the camera loved Ryan and the network that brought him on board saw only ratings.

Shortly after the altercation with Glen, Ryan hired a lawyer and emancipated himself. Packing his belongings he moved to an obscure town and rink in rural New Hampshire, in order to skate with a partner four years younger than himself, under a pair coach who had never produced a medal holder beyond the regional level. Ryan's abrupt departure raised eyebrows. Rumors of drugs, promiscuity, and outbursts of temper became subjects of speculation, and Elliott made certain that, at least in print, Glen was portrayed as the surrogate father, overly generous and patient, his trust betrayed by an ungrateful student.

With more people wishing him ill than good, Ryan and his partner had gone on to win silver at the same Olympics that saw Mat take the gold in men's figure skating. Ryan had an unbeatable combination of looks and charm, wit and intelligence, which he projected on and off the air. Younger generations of skaters believed that Elliott, who was thirty years older and had always been vain, could only be jealous.

"You win," Mat said, accepting Ryan's invitation. "How could I possibly turn down the opportunity to witness you and Elliott politely decimate one another in front of a national audience."

Ryan and Mat sat in reserved seating with easy access to the back staging area. Mat had not been present for the ladies' technical program and was surprised to learn that Daria was being touted as the stunning upset, now in third place. If she finished the evening with a medal, any medal, she would be the dark horse winner at a time when there were very few upsets in skating.

Along with the other spectators he was mesmerized by her unique presence. Her simple red dress with the handkerchief skirt and square neckline lacked the intricate bead and sequined look of the other costumes and reinforced the image of a skater not expected to be competitive. In the opening minute of her program Daria two-footed a triple and then doubled the second jump in what was intended to be a triple-Lutz, triple-toe combination. Knowing that she was short a triple jump, Daria seamlessly added another toward the end, insuring that her presence was strong enough to move her into second place with four other competitors still to skate.

Almost immediately those spectators seated around Mat and Ryan complained that her scores were higher than they should have been, as they shuffled through programs for the bio section. Daria had soundly captured the spotlight from her teammate who was the actual favorite to win a medal. Some close by murmured that the judges had been distracted by her beauty, complaining that she did not deserve the bronze medal that she ended the night with.

While it took the western press a heartbeat to adjust to the unexpected, it would take others a bit longer. For the first time in her career Daria could be viewed as a useful commodity.

As Daria finished skating, Ryan got up to leave. He had a few prearranged minutes to interview the Canadian expected to come in first, just after she stepped off the ice to hear her scores. It was an interview he had wrested from Elliott, who was furious.

"If you see Daria back there, tell her I said hello."

"You know her?" Ryan was clearly surprised.

"From a long time ago. She may not remember."

Mat watched Ryan's live interview on one of the big screens set up around the arena. Just as the last skater took the ice, he returned.

"Here," he said, feigning an indifference that Mat knew was not genuine.

Mat looked down at his hand. The patch was so faded it was difficult to make out the insignia of the former world team.

"Where did you get this?" Mat asked, amazed.

"The question is where did she get it? Slipped it into my hand like it was stolen diamonds or heroin or something. For getting too close, I was nearly roughed up by her bodyguard, who happened to be twice my size and not at all charmed by my press credentials."

"She has a body guard?"

"Listen carefully, Mat. Don't cross Sasha and especially not over this particular skater. He has connections you don't want anywhere near you, nor near anyone you care about. And let me tell you right now," Ryan uncharacteristically lectured. "If you're thinking of making her an offer and bringing her to the states my advice is, don't."

Mat shrugged his shoulders unconvinced.

"Why do you think anyone bothers with security for someone like her?" Ryan pushed. "In the history of skating she ranks among the most unreliable, though talented athletes. In a month no one will remember she medaled at this Olympics. Trust me on that."

"They may not remember her skill level, but the artistry was unforgettable."

"Thanks. I'll use that line. But seriously, Mat; I know more about Sasha than you do, and I wouldn't cross him if I could help it."

"Did anyone see her give this to you?" Mat asked, changing the subject.

"Maybe. I don't think so."

Mat considered. If Daria was ready to leave her coach Ryan had just provided the perfect rationale. He actually could agree to coach Daria as a way for her to escape Sasha's draconian control.

Mat walked into the lobby area, cell phone to his ear. To make an offer he first needed to see Daria. At the prospect he felt a rush of excitement. The skinny little waif had turned into a beautiful young woman, and there was no doubt that he felt an instant attraction. Feeling somewhat guilty, he made an obligatory phone call.

"Did you watch the Russian girl compete?" he asked Hillary.

"Of course, we're all glued to the screen. Popcorn and fried chicken, the whole bit."

"What would you think if I made Daria an offer?"

"I think that's an atrocious, horrible idea. And you can't approach her unless she contacts you first."

"What if I said she did contact me first?"

"As your partner, I say, no; not in this lifetime. Not only can she not deliver, but she's mentally unstable. They covered it up, but last time she was in New York I hear she disappeared and no one knew where she was or what she was up to for something like a month. They found her wondering the streets in Philly with no identification."

"That can't be true."

"My source is rock solid. You don't listen to gossip or you would have heard this story. They admitted her to a locked psychiatric unit where Sasha finally located her and against the doctor's advice he bundled her up, chartered a private plane and immediately left the country. You call that stable?"

"If it's true," Mat parried.

"Okay, just for the sake of argument forget that she is mentally ill, which she is. This event is the first she's competed in since that happened three years ago. And you want to bring her here and disrupt what we've built. Don't do it, Mat."

They said the obligatory 'I love you,' the words dry like sand paper sticking to the roof of his mouth. Just before leaving on this trip, Mat tried to articulate his doubts, introducing the idea that they should break up. Hillary wasn't having it, stating that she loved him enough for both of them.

"When are you going to produce the ring?" was a common taunt from mutual friends, which not only surprised Mat the first time he heard it, but also made him feel he was being manipulated. The idea of marrying was never his intention.

Although he once planned to remain celibate until the right girl came along, Mat failed to live up to that standard of moral purity. He didn't feel good about Hillary. In the entanglement of their relationship, he was sleeping with a woman he didn't love. When he got back to California he would sit Hillary down and tell her the truth.

Mat cancelled his plans for dinner in order to attend the final party held for all the skaters, families, and coaches. Security was tight at this function in order to keep away press and fans alike, and as a non-participant Mat had not been invited. Still, he knew that as soon as he was recognized he'd be welcomed. After months of intense training, skaters could let loose. With a coveted medal in hand, Daria was sure to be among those celebrating.

Mat was no longer as readily recognized by the general public as he had been, but here in the skating community he would always be famous. As he walked through the crowd some of the younger athletes and their parents asked for his autograph, which he signed and quickly moved on, scanning the room. Other skaters from Daria's team were in attendance, but he saw no sign of her.

Deciding to give up and call it an early night, he saw Sasha with a small group of men clustered around him. Curious Mat realized they were not coaches or parents. Among them Sasha appeared even smaller than he was. At 5'6" he would be lost in the huddled intensity if not for the force of his personality that dominated this huddle of tension so at odds with the celebration around them.

Mat had no reason to connect this group with Daria, but he did. Some instinct, the bodyguard that threatened Ryan, the strange meeting in St. Moritz and other accumulated details gave him pause. *There was some 'thing' to know and he should know it.*

"Would you like to dance?"

The question startled Mat. He looked at the young woman before him and recognized her. Sophie was Daria's teammate and was the favorite to win a medal, but had actually finished behind the first ten. Through the years he and Sophie had been at various competitions together and had a nodding acquaintance. An accomplished athlete, Sophie lacked the grace and presence that Daria so naturally exuded, but she was a seasoned competitor with an impressive record of wins. More importantly, Sasha was her coach.

"I've admired your career," she told him as they danced.

Mat was aware of the group around Sasha fanning out, allowing him an unobstructed avenue of censure as he caught sight of Mat and Sophie. One of the other men put a hand of restraint on Sasha's shoulder. Mat caught Sasha's eye and felt a threat more substantial than if words had been exchanged.

Responding to the bully in Sasha, he pulled Sophie toward him in a burst of defiance. Sasha's predictable reaction gave him pleasure, and he didn't care if Ryan's warning about Sasha being dangerously connected were true.

"And I've admired yours," he returned the compliment, keeping Sophie's back to her coach, knowing that Sasha recognized this ploy. If he wanted to make a scene, he could march over to break them apart. But no, it wasn't happening, and suddenly Mat's curiosity jelled. These men meeting together at this unlikely event had such significance that Sasha would not make a scene. Would not be allowed to make a scene. Why?

I know you expected to do better," Mat focused on Sophie, needing information.

"Thank you," she nearly spat out the words. "I would have if not for Daria. There was no intention for her to be here. She did not deserve alternate, but Sasha wanted her with him. No one imagined she would actually compete."

Mat was surprised at the rancor of Sophie's tone. The music stopped, but he kept her on the dance floor. The next song was fast, which prevented them from speaking. Afterwards he offered to get her something to drink.

"I can't," she said, clearly discomforted. "You're persona non grata, and Sasha has noticed us together. He hates you, and here I am dancing with you."

"So you are courting Sasha's legendary rancor. Very courageous," Mat teased.

"Why does he hate you, anyway? Why should he care?" She asked and at the same time acknowledged Sasha's stare with a nod. Time together was at an end.

"I think it stems from an argument over a certain hat."

"I heard it was more than that, but okay," she smiled. "Be careful. He never, and I mean never forgets a slight."

"You're the second person today to tell me I should be careful. So, why isn't Daria here?" Mat asked, leading Sophie into the crowd, out from under Sash's watchful gaze.

"She is unpredictable. Crazy, as you Americans like to say. They can't let her go anywhere alone."

A photographer walked by and snapped a picture. Mat's arm touched Sophie's as he leaned close to catch her words over the blaring music. Tomorrow people would speculate that they had managed an affair. He could expect a thinly disguised call from Hillary, who seemed to have a limitless supply of girlfriends that plied her with news of his every move whenever they were apart.

They danced once more. As he held Sophie and moved in time to the music, he imagined that it was Daria he held and wondered at the strong attraction he felt for a woman he didn't know. He had not thought of Daria much in the intervening years. Perhaps, Mat cautioned himself, what he really wanted was an excuse that would force a break up with Hillary. Her attempts at control had made him feel claustrophobic. He hadn't been firm enough and she hadn't wanted to listen.

"Under the circumstances it would be difficult for you to share a room with Daria," Mat probed.

"She stays in Sasha's suite. He can keep a close watch on her that way."

She gave him her room number.

"It's unlikely you can get up there," she added, "since I'm on the same floor as Daria. This has been my last year to compete, and I'd hoped to finish better." She lifted her head and looked into his eyes. "I didn't know you liked me."

The invitation was there, but Mat was adept at deflecting.

The music started up again. He just had time to say goodbye, wishing her well, before another asked her to dance. Mat saw she was disappointed he let her go so easily, but she was not the woman he had come to rescue. If, in fact, rescue is what Daria had in mind. Whatever happened, Mat felt obligated to follow up on his promise to help her start a new life away from her coach. As an added bonus, getting past Sasha's legendary security would be a slap in the face. A reminder that bullies didn't always win.

Delaying as he improvised a plan, Mat danced with an old friend, a former competitor turned coach. Over her blond head he kept an eye on Sasha Eymrnov. At the door to the bar the groups' *secret conclave*, for that is how he had begun to think about whatever it was they were so engrossed in discussing, were joined by Elliott and Glen Winston. A lift of spirits was observed as greetings were exchanged.

Now the gangs all here, was the thought that sprang to Mat's mind. And then, *what are they up to?*

"I can see you're just as suspicious of them as I am," Ashton

Bennett said.

"What?" Mat stopped dancing and looked into her face. Was he that obvious?

"Do you recognize who those two men are with Sasha, Glen, and Elliott?" she asked following his line of vision.

"Not, a clue."

"Howard Marstead and younger brother, Samuel Marstead. Samuel is a lawyer with offices in Boston, San Francisco, New York and London."

"Really?" Mat's fascination jumped a few decimals. "How do you know this, Ashton?"

"The Marstead firm defended that pedophile gymnastics coach from Minneapolis and got him off on a technicality. You read about that, right?"

"I don't recall."

"My point exactly. Well, I'm mercy coaching one of the casualties, if you can call it that. She's had a rough time; she so wanted to testify. A few child actors where victims as well."

"I didn't know he got off."

"With a slap on the wrist, while the others, one a well known Hollywood agent, were never charged. Then along came the Penn State-Sandusky debacle. That had a higher profile, but as always the investigation stopped short."

"I don't think I've ever met Howard Marstead, but I do know that at one time he offered my mother money for my training with Glen Winston. She turned him down."

Engrossed in conversation they moved to the sidelines.

"Afraid strings would be attached, no doubt; smart mother. Howard is hardly ever seen anymore. He's a kind of recluse. Something important must have happened to get that vampire out of his coffin."

"You don't think too highly of him I see. Many would say Howard was a skating icon."

"Let's just say that because I gave that girl a safe place to land and stood by her as this case moved forward, I've learned more than I ever wanted to, more than is safe to know."

"Could just be a social occasion. A chance for old friends to get together," Mat offered weakly.

"Not a chance."

"Any connection to that group and Daria?"

"Just that Daria is a loose cannon and Sasha her svengali. She can't function without him. I have no firsthand knowledge of that you understand. Just what has made the rounds."

"If I can do anything to help, you'll let me know?" Mat said by way of goodbye.

"Serious?" she said, hopeful.

"Yes," Mat turned back to face Ashton."Whatever you need."

"Well," she hesitated, her eyes following Samuel Marstead's every move. At present he was deep in conversation with Elliott Smythe. "I might need a job."

"No problem. Just give me a call. The door is open, and you can bring whatever students you want, or should I say, need to come along with you."

"Would there be room for another coach if I came with no students?"

Mat hesitated. "It's confidential, but Hillary may be leaving. I'd like to keep the program going before I make any firm decisions. With or without students we'll make room for you, salary and benefits."

"Thank you," she said. "You wouldn't be afraid how that might impact your own career?"

Mat saw real fear in her expression. What he knew of Ashton Bennett told him she wasn't one prone to exaggeration.

"What can they do? Erase my record and take the gold medals away? No, the offer is genuine. I skated under Glen Winston for about half a second. Felt like a lifetime. I don't trust any of that lot."

"Elliott Smythe... watch your back with him. He's so phony," she added. "I could tell you a thing or two." They exchanged cell phone numbers.

A year would pass before Mat regretted not asking more questions about Elliott and his many secrets from a colleague who didn't normally speak so freely and never took him up on his offer of a job. Instead, she traded coaching for law school.

In light of what had just been shared, Mat surveyed the group that had gathered about Sasha with fresh insight. Mat's growing reputation as a coach made it unwise for Elliott to snub him, despite the hated friendship with Ryan. Elliott went out of his way to be cordial, often feigning a closeness that did not exist. Mat didn't need Aston's confirmation to recognize Elliott's fawning congeniality for what it was. Whenever possible, Mat made an effort to avoid contact.

Catching Mat's eye, Elliott waved as the group moved toward the bar, seeming to invite Mat to join them. Only those who watched from the sidelines endlessly regurgitating the skating gossip were deceived that this was any kind of a genuine invitation. Mat ignored the gesture and exited the ballroom.

He had already called the front desk and asked for Sasha's room number which was not being provided except to a select few. He located the service elevator. It was close to midnight and time was running out for Cinderella. Placing empty cups on a tray, Mat covered all with a napkin, and reaching for a wall phone was instantly connected to the hotel operator. He asked for Sasha's room number, knowing that the in-house kitchen call would have registered on the call screen.

"I can't give out that number. You know that. Look it up yourself; you haven't lost the room roster, have you?" she accused without pausing between sentences. "You'll lose your job for that."

"I'm temporary," Mat said, knowing the hotel would have hired extra help to accommodate the influx of activity.

"Okay, but don't bother to ask again. I'm not going to break the rules, just so you can screw up twice." She recited the room number. "You better have your ID or you won't get off the elevator. You do remember that much from orientation?"

Mat disguised himself as best he could with glasses, a waiter jacket, and stolen identity badge. He gathered up the largest gift basket he could find which contained a collection of chesses, biscuits, fruit, and a bottle of champagne. The service elevator opened on the eighteenth floor where a single guard greeted him while others stood idly about the row of passenger elevators down the hall. Mat handed over the basket before anything could be said.

"Compliments of Sasha Eymrnov," Mat announced and pressed three one hundred dollar bills held in readiness into the man's pocket. Hoping he wouldn't be stopped he walked brazenly to Daria's door. Helping him out, the man followed, swiping the key card before joining his friends down the hall, balancing the basket and holding aloft the bottle of champagne.

Even as his eyes adjusted to the dimness, he saw her. She sat alone, motionless on an art deco sofa. Wet hair had deposited shadowed patches over the shoulders of an oversized denim blouse, and with a hairbrush suspended in mid-air, her eyes locked on his. Mat felt mildly ridiculous and had just placed his tray on a nearby table when Daria threw herself into his arms with such force they nearly toppled to the floor.

"You came," she said. "I prayed that you would remember. I dreamed you would help me, and now, here you are," she marveled, clearly amazed as she kissed his face in tiny, fevered pecks, her impulsive tears smearing both their faces.

Her reaction brought him abruptly to his senses. Clearly he should not have come, and yet he had made a promise to a distraught child years before. That she remembered and even counted on the seriousness of that promise, and he had not, suddenly struck Mat with potent alarm.

"We do not have any time," she said breathlessly and rushed into the adjacent room for a sweater, socks and boots. She pulled the sweater over her wet hair. "What is our plan?" she demanded.

He shrugged his shoulders and felt foolish. "I thought we might dance and then saunter out the front door like normal people. However, it seems you've missed the party."

Daria stopped her frantic activity and regarded him with astonishment. "You did all this for foolish sentiment. But you got here. How did you manage?" she asked.

"If I'd actually planned to help you I would not have gotten this far. That's the plan, right? You're leaving Sasha?"

"Planned or not, you are late. Sasha will be back any moment."

"What do you suggest?"

"This is fate," Daria pronounced decisively, shoving her feet into fur lined boots. "We must do something to distract them. We must get to the elevator right away."

He had known all along that her purpose in sending the patch was a cry for help. He felt a new rush of adrenaline pump through his body. If she chose to escape one of the most ruthless coaches in skating, why shouldn't he help? For once in his life he would not overanalyze or even think about the consequences. This was just the sort of impulsive action Ryan was famous for.

The kind of mad spontaneous exploit that no one would ever connect with him, and this alone might buy the time they needed.

Mat could not help notice that Sasha's belongings were everywhere in evidence. He saw that the second bedroom was unoccupied. Somewhere along the way, coach and student had become lovers and now Daria, who was clearly more a prisoner than a volunteer, if in fact she had ever been anything else, was desperate to leave Sasha.

"I have an idea," he told Daria and quickly removed the loose waiter jacket. He explained as he helped her pile her hair under the ball cap and settled glasses over the bridge of her nose. He then picked up a bottle of vodka and spilled some over his shirt.

"This is too dangerous," Daria asserted when he finished explaining. "How can they not catch you, and then what will happen to me?"

"That's the idea. And what can they do anyway? I'm drunk and in love and for what we hope will be at least an hour Sophie will be shrouded in romantic mystery."

Mat stood back to look at Daria. The loose chef's trousers hid her figure and the back of the white jacket would be all anyone would see as she walked to the elevator. "Not very convincing," he mused. "If they see you at all, let's hope it's only a short glimpse."

"Wait," she said and returned seconds later with the same jacket he had given her in Switzerland.

"Looks like you've hardly worn this," he said as he slipped his arms into the sleeves, mildly surprised that it still fit.

"Sasha hates that jacket. I take it to every competition, but I've only worn it once," she said softly and looked him fully in the face for the first time. Something was there when their eyes met. Even if mere gratitude, Mat could no longer regret the risk he'd taken.

"Here," he said and handed over the key to the suite he shared with Ryan and a cameraman friend. Their hands touched and his involuntarily lingered seconds longer than necessary. Sliding bills from a money clip he instructed Daria to have the cab drop her off at the Hilton before walking the four blocks back to his hotel.

"Give me forty seconds. Forty seconds, then walk, don't run

to the elevator. I'll meet you at the hotel within the hour. Once you're in that room, whatever you do, don't leave, don't answer the door or pick up the telephone. If I don't come back, you can count on Ryan Kollyn to help you."

At the mention of Ryan's name an expression of fear crossed Daria's face.

"You do remember Ryan? He's a friend," Mat assured.

She nodded her head and turned away. "And this is your good friend?" She clarified, her tone halting, full of tension.

"I know there's been a lot of gossip about Ryan, but he's a different person today. Don't worry."

There was an inscrutable expression on her face that made Mat uneasy. He had to ask; "Daria, is this really what you want? Because, you can change your mind, find another way. But once out that door there will be no going back."

"No, no!" she asserted. "I must get away from here."

Far too much time has already been wasted. Flashing a last smile of encouragement, he walked to the door and opened it. Her whisper came to him like a kiss.

"Thank you," she said, so low and soft that he almost did not hear.

What passed for Sasha's security, were congregated near the public elevator. They passed the bottle among themselves and Mat hoped this would work to his advantage. Wishing he had the power to make himself invisible, he ducked around the corner toward Sophie's room, now in full view of the guards but still unnoticed. Without hesitation, he began knocking loudly at the door until the sound of running converged on him and he was pinned roughly to the ground.

"You can't be up here," one guard shouted in his ear. "How did you get up here?" With his arms pinned behind him Mat nodded toward the stairwell, keeping his face averted. The four guards regarded one another.

"What did you want?" they demanded in such broken English that only because he anticipated what was asked did he understand.

"I'm meeting Sophie."

"Mat counted the minutes as the muscle-bound guards argued amongst themselves. They had no authority to detain him, or so he hoped. Mat imagined that by now Daria would be exiting the elevator and just entering the service room off the kitchen where she would rid herself of the disguise. Visualizing her progress, as though his thoughts could carry her forward, he imagined her walk to the side entrance and around the building to the line of waiting cabs.

With his face still pushed into the carpet Mat heard more conversation back and forth. "You are Mateo Araujo, is that not right?" one of the guards demanded, pleased at his powers of observation, as the two others jerked him to a standing position. They were all larger than he and although it wouldn't have been legal, Mat guessed they were armed. He did his best to appear both drunk and compliant.

"You are a stupid man," one guard finally pronounced after more words were exchanged. "Now you may go and do not please, come back."

Mat realized they wanted to be rid of him as quickly as possible. If deciding to report the incident to Sasha, he would have been detained longer. Sasha would certainly have recalled his connection to Daria and would have discarded the notion of a drunken Mateo Araujo pursuing Sophie. As he was shoved none too gently into the public elevator, he glanced at his watch, wondering if Daria had changed her mind. Or was she even now following his instructions.

 The door opened on the lobby and there was no mistaking the group moving toward the open door. "Mat, how are you doing? Join us for a drink."

Resisting the impulse to turn and run, Mat acknowledged Elliott's invitation. A tall reed of a man, who could only be Howard Marstead, looked briefly at Mat before moving on.

"You've met Sasha, haven't you," Elliott deflected.

Unable to do otherwise, Mat extended his hand, but Sasha pushed ahead of Howard ignoring the gesture.

"Nice to see you again, Mat. I'll shake your hand even if my friend won't. I hear you've got some promising students. I'll stop by sometime."

Mat nodded trying to move away.

"Great," Elliott slurred his words. "I'll be seeing you then."

The others were holding the elevator for Elliott, the sound of the doors trying to close finally penetrating Elliott's drunken haze. Still holding Mat's arm, this time for balance, the two turned about and Mat almost pushed Elliott through the door.

"We'll have lunch when all this is over," Elliott called with his usual polished buoyancy, holding the door open a bit longer.

The others glared at Elliott's back. It was clear a cardinal rule had been broken by calling attention to their little group.

"Call me when you're in New York," Elliott slurred and leaned heavily into Howard who shoved him aside forcing his hand off the door.

Not in this life time, Mat thought, his gaze locking with Sasha, and in that moment the distinctive bikers' jacket registered and rattled Sasha's composure as comprehension dawned. Mat had a last satisfied glimpse of Sasha as he frantically pushed forward, too late to catch the closing door. Strangely elated in a surge of adrenalin Mat sprinted across the lobby. Now he was responsible for Daria. The thought lodged in his mind, giving him new purpose and direction. Daria had called this fate, and Mat now saw their meeting in the same terms.

Wasting no time, Daria had pulled a valise from the closet, tossing in a random mixture of his and Ryan's clothing. As she indiscriminately emptied the contents of the bathroom into a leather duffel, Mat scribbled a note, trusting that Ryan would understand the meaning. *Gone fishing* was the telling signature.

"You can stay here, you know," he hesitated at the door, giving her one more opportunity to change her mind. "You're an adult, not a minor. No one can tell you what to do."

"You don't understand. Sasha will kill me before he lets me go."

Was that an exaggeration? True or not he could almost feel the fear lift off Daria like a living thing, filling the space between them. He would save for later, the news that Sasha had recognized the jacket, there being no mystery whose company she was now in. Nor would he relate until later Sasha's frantic attempt to push his way out of the elevator before it closed. Mat was frankly surprised that a few of his goon-contingent were not already breaking down the door.

"We'll buy ourselves some time," he assured her, gathering up what Daria had packed. "We won't give Sasha a chance to interfere without significant distance between us. I know a good immigration attorney, and we'll make a case for persecution due to domestic violence," Mat soothed, unsure if that was a valid precedent. In former days she could claim political asylum.

Mat located the keys to Ryan's rental car and tossed Daria a warm parka. Once again he was loaning her a jacket, but this time the fit was considerably better.

The first challenge was to dump the rental and its GPS tracking. What he needed was an older model 4-wheel drive of anonymous color. Mat had noticed a used car lot near the freeway. He made arrangements for Ryan to pick up the car and paid for the new wheels with a credit card, the last time he would use it until a week later when an immigration attorney was hired. He had no idea if Sasha was really connected to the Russian mob, but he was now more concerned with the Marstead firm's international presence. Every discerning cell in his body told him not to underestimate the danger his actions had placed him in. And there was Daria to consider.

They stopped only for gas and for the few groceries limited by the convenience store selection. Once into Maine, Mat pulled into a residential neighborhood and locating a similar truck parked on a side street, he changed out the plates.

Not until they hit a stretch of dark, deserted road did Daria refrain from looking over her shoulder every few minutes. Mat had a destination firmly in mind, but Daria had asked no questions. She was quiet, almost withdrawn as she rested her weight against the passenger door appearing to sit as far from him as possible. *She doesn't trust me,* he thought, not taking offense. The degree of security around Daria, controlling access to outside persons and keeping her a virtual prisoner in her hotel room, spoke to problems he could only guess at. With the advantage of knowing who she was with, Mat felt the search would be concentrated west, toward the border crossings closer to California. No one but Ryan, he hoped, would remember the fishing cabin in Maine.

As first sunlight slanted through the canopy of firs onto the forest road, Mat was struck with the beauty of his surroundings. The color reflected off the snow was a wash of pink, and the tops of black pine boughs laden with heavy drifts of snow an abstract touch of divine artistry. He looked toward Daria, ready to comment but she had dropped off to sleep, her long hair, pulled into a pony tail, draped over one shoulder. She needed him, and he realized suddenly how drawn he was to that helplessness.

Mat scrutinized the roadside. The old logging road would be obvious for the wide drift of white snaking long into the deep wood, unmarred by tire tracks or footprints. Finding it Mat turned the truck and hoped the snow would not impede their progress. Only when the chimney and frozen lake came into view did he wake Daria, relieved to note that, except for the blanket of winter, this fishing camp, owned by Ryan's pair coach, was unchanged. The key was still tucked in the false bottom of an old milk can that in summer had hosted a pot of red geraniums. They would get some rest and decide what to do next, but Mat was already making plans to engage the immigration attorney at the first opportunity.

Mat located oil for the lamps and built a fire. They piled pillows on the floor and wrapped themselves in woolen blankets as he told her of the restless teenagers who felt like men as they grilled their catch each evening. She seemed to be put at ease by his aimless conversation, and so he related how they had gone at night to the local bar at the back of a small grocery store. No one had asked their ages, as beer was served up on demand, and they found themselves giving up their cash in game after game of darts to the local clientele.

Daria listened to his story as though she could read something more in his words. She had avoided answering anything but the most routine questions concerning her own life. Other than that one frantic embrace at the hotel, they had barely brushed hands, and so he was surprised when she leaned forward to kiss him. Without intending to do so, his lips parted hers.

It occurred to Mat that he should question this sudden change of demeanor. They had all the time in the world to get to know one another, or so he reminded himself as he stifled his first inclinations, and prepared to withdraw. He expected her to follow, grateful for his restraint, but instead, as he put distance between them she moved aggressively into the breach. Almost immediately her kisses shifted with devouring fervency as all thoughts of retreat fled.

Instinct warned that this was too sudden to be at all meaningful. She couldn't and didn't care for him. But if they had time to get to know one another, then there was hope for a future relationship. He had to stop this flood-tide of desire before their emotions overwhelmed them.

Later Mat would admit that Daria had ambushed him with a skill he was too stunned to analyze, and now she was firmly in control. It was as if a channel had been flipped, a page turned by a wayward gust of wind. She was not what he expected, and this state of being slightly off balance, perpetually surprised was a strangely familiar stimulus; a danger welcomed by the dysfunctional part of him that concealed the proof of what she provided. Mat told himself that he did not want a repeat of the premature intimacy that had trapped him in a relationship with Hillary. But here he was sliding down that same slippery slope.

Once more Mat pushed Daria back and looked into her eyes. He saw there an odd mingling of emotions he could not discern. Enveloped by a new wave of passion, the time to question was gone.

Alexandra Clair

CHAPTER EIGHT

As the sun slanted through the trees, invading daggers of light slid across the barren plank floor. Mat studied Daria as she slept. Twice during the night she had struggled awake and seemed disorientated as she wildly surveyed her surroundings. Each time he'd gently reminded her of where they were, speaking quietly until realization relaxed her features, and he could see that she believed him.

Now that daylight had more fully infiltrated the room, she slept soundly. Mat watched the shadows flee from the surface of the old quilt tucked tightly about her and grew increasingly uneasy. He was disappointed with himself. He had wanted to begin with Daria on firmer footing, but he had given in to temptation.

"Wake up," he whispered in her ear and kissed her lightly on the forehead. He already felt that he loved her. As she stirred and shook the tight quilt off her legs, he lay down and drew her against him. But her body, unresisting and pliable in his arms the night before, now stiffened as she pushed a space between them.

Mat looked at her confused. Didn't she remember the intimacy of the night before? "Time to wake up," he spoke and buried his face in her hair.

Daria sat up abruptly. "Don't touch me again. Never touch me under any circumstances unless I say you can," she announced with chilling aloofness.

"But I thought last night that … "

Their eyes met and he saw in hers a sudden influx of confusion. The search for recollection wrinkled her brow and she put a hand to her temple as though struck by a sudden, blinding headache. Her shoulders slumped and she looked away, the shift in persona so subtle and fleeting that when she engaged him again, he forgot to question.

"What did you say?" she asked politely, the tone one of girlish compliance.

"I'm sorry. I really need to apologize. I don't know why I can't learn this lesson. It's so wrong to be intimate this soon. Undermines any hope for a solid relationship. And I really want to get to know you better, Daria. I know this isn't logical because we've just met and we don't know one another, but I really feel that I could love you and...."

He looked at her. The blank expression on her face almost frightened him. "Not to worry," she said innocuously.

"It's just that last night I thought maybe we had something."

"Of course I remember. I'm just tired. You are right. I didn't sleep well."

Had he said that? He knew he didn't. What's more, it was he that hadn't slept, waking often to look out into the darkness of the wood, listening for the sound of a motor or the muffled tread of footsteps on the porch, but he let her statement pass.

"Do we have a plan for today?" she asked in a sing-song, well-bred tone, deftly changing the subject in a way that would become all too familiar.

It took three weeks for them to reach California as certain measures were set in place by the immigration attorney. Along the way they stopped in Philadelphia for a curious meeting with two FBI agents. Daria was pale and shaken when she exited the office.

They want to know about Sasha," she confided. "And they want to know who I am." Mat was alarmed at the near hysteria in her voice. "How can I know everything when I am an orphan," she cried, her voice breaking.

"Just explain," Mat told her.

"I explain and explain, and they ask me again. Over and over the same questions and something they do not believe. And I cannot tell them. I cannot answer their questions," her voice trailed.

The vineyard had always been a haven for Mat. It did not occur to him that Daria would not view its lush manicured setting in the same way, but almost immediately upon her arrival she had fallen into a deep hole of depression, which he, Joey and Rosa, had worked hard to bring her out of. Then, without explanation she had disappeared. With her absence Mat felt as though he had lost a necessary appendage, and although he waited and prayed for news of her, there was none.

Mat recalled her second interrogation by the FBI. The meeting had been set up through her attorney and, although he accompanied Daria to the appointment, very little of what transpired was shared with him. Mat was reluctant to petition emigration for Daria's current address, not wanting to raise any kind of alarm. Instead he threw himself into the work of the vineyard with a zeal never before witnessed by Joey. He turned over more and more students to Hillary until she too talked of hiring an assistant, and he came less and less to the rink, helping instead to prepare the huge vats for the next harvest.

Mat had never known true loneliness. After his parents died he had Susan, who remained devoted to him, and he had the friendship of Joey and Rosa, as well as a community of good friends in skating. But nothing could fill the hole left by Daria's departure, and until he found her again, there was no escaping the gnawing void of loss left by her absence.

There were clues about her life with Sasha. Indications of what she might have suffered, but Mat would not allow his thoughts to take him down a path of no return.

One incident remained fresh in Mat's memory. The brittle blonde of Daria's hair color, chased by the rich burnished shade she was born with, was obvious. Daria seemed particularly fascinated and Mat wondered how anyone could have preferred that false color to the natural beauty of what was emerging.

He found her sitting before the dressing table with her hair parted as she studied the emerging shade of red. In her hand was a sharp pair of scissors. Something about the way she gripped the handle and the blank stare as she studied her image, almost as if she did not recognize the face that stared back, gave him pause. Frightened, Mat walked up behind her. When he reached for the scissors he found that her grip was so tight that he had to peel white fingers off the hilt one by one.

Perplexed, he spoke to her gently. "Daria, did you want to cut your hair?"

Stiffly she nodded her head in assent, never shifting her gaze from that of the stranger in the mirror. Fearful that she would harm herself, Mat trimmed off a narrow row of over-treated hair, speaking in soothing innocuous words that later he could not recall.

"Rosa can take you into town and you can have your natural color matched if you like. You don't have to wait. Would you like that?"

With coaxing, Daria sipped the healthy soups that were Rosa's specialty, but otherwise wanted nothing more than solitude and sleep. Rosa had already suggested that a professional evaluation was needed. Something was seriously wrong, but Mat resisted.

"She's in a depression, Mat. I doubt we can help her. She needs a psychiatrist or at least a good evaluation by a medical doctor. Maybe medication," Rosa stated.

"She won't go. You know I've tried."

"You didn't try hard enough. You wouldn't ask a sick child if they'd like a little something to bring down a raging fever. You give it to them, even if they resist."

"I'm not buying that psychobabble. There's nothing wrong with her time won't fix."

"One week, no more. If there is no change, I'll make the appointment myself. We have an excellent psychiatrist at St. Patrick's and I've already talked with him about Daria. From what I described, he agrees that she needs help."

"I didn't ask you to do that," Mat challenged.

"Too late. From what I described ... "

"I don't want to know what that quack, someone who has never even met Daria, has to say."

"Well you're going to listen, Mat. He thinks she might be suffering from post traumatic stress syndrome. She is finally safe enough to feel her feelings, and she is overwhelmed by this. You want her to have help, don't you?"

Rosa insisted Daria sit on the veranda part of each day and supplied her with a catholic missal and devotional from her church. Joey informed her that he was short handed and soon had her exercising their most predictable mare up and down the long drive. One day Mat came home from the rink and found Daria in the kitchen chopping vegetables as she laughed with Rosa. A sound was never more welcome, but so sudden a change seemed almost unnatural until he forced the disquieting thought from his mind.

She was apparently better, and yet their relationship was firmly altered. Her sudden disinterest in the physical side of their relationship seemed abrupt and final. Although they continued to occupy the same bed, she no longer turned to him for whatever solaces their coming together had previously satisfied. Mat almost felt that Daria was another person entirely, and yet, apparently oblivious to his confusion, she neither explained nor apologized.

Sometimes at night Daria would turn into his arms and he would hold her. He felt the thin, highly-muscled frame against him, almost grateful to avoid that combat-like passion that had sometimes typified their coming together.

Under pressure from him, she resumed a training schedule and continued to improve. He was surprised at how little she had lost in her months away from training, and when she was invited to perform several exhibitions, he accepted on her behalf. After a television special, in which she was a last minute replacement, Mat laid out plans for a professional career.

This resulted in their first major argument. In no uncertain terms she told him that she would never skate to her former level again. Mat had heard that old lament too often and did not believe her. He knew many skaters who, with every good intention, left the sport only to find that they could not easily redirect the discipline and intensity of those formative years into a new, seemingly bland, direction. As he watched her perform, he was struck at the instant rapport she established with her audience. From the moment she took the ice, the excitement and energy she inspired was electric, and that genuine smile which lit up her face as the audience erupted in applause made him think that this could provide the much needed healing that would give their life stability.

His plans were shattered when, with no premonition of impending loss, Mat returned from the rink one fine October day to find her gone. Leaving nearly every new possession he had bought her behind, Daria had borrowed a suitcase from Rosa and called a cab. Bewilderment was followed by hurt and finally anger.

"Where did she go?" he demanded accusingly of Rosa.

"How should I know?" Rosa was defensive. "She packed a few things and called a cab."

"And you let her do that," Mat demanded. "Without calling me!"

Rosa was a graduate of Penn State and a third generation Mexican American. She had married Joey, who had struggled to obtain a high school education and had spent his entire life working at the Vineyard. Only in the last year had her family begun to forgive her. Now she leveled a stare at Mat and took a deep breath as though weary of having to explain a basic and obvious truth.

"You cannot keep her prisoner just because you feel compelled to indulge a rescue obsession."

"Is that what I've been doing?"

"Maybe not entirely, but any fool can see that she's unstable. Maybe you've told her what to do too often and not listened enough"

"I only want to give her a safe haven," Mat said, hurt. "Time to recoup and get strong."

"But you didn't give her time, did you? You got her right back out on the ice and then put her in the spotlight when she told you very clearly that this is not what she wanted for herself. Daria is a woman who has been controlled all her life. She went from Sasha to you. Why wouldn't she decide it was too much?"

"I'm not Sasha. I don't abuse her."

"A father figure is not husband material, Mat. Never has been, never will be. You spent most of your life tightly controlled by a sport you started out hating. It gave you stuff, but it took stuff away. Ask yourself if control is not your idea of love."

"She has a very slim window of opportunity to rebuild her career. She doesn't know what she wants."

"Will you listen to yourself? No woman will tolerate being treated like a child forever. God didn't design us to be cattle."

The words stung. Mat turned away, but Rosa came up to touch his arm.

"Sleeping with someone is not a bridge to intimacy. I just think she's complicated, and maybe none of us really know her as well as we'd like to think."

"What do you mean? I know her very well. I was going to propose marriage. After everything we've been through, how can you believe that it's right for her to go without even saying goodbye?"

"If she loves you, Mat, she'll come back on her own terms. And despite what you say, she is not well. I didn't major in psychology, but I suspect there may even be something clinically wrong with her. You're pretty practiced at denial; seeing what you want to see. It might be time to know Daria, not as you want to make her over and imagine her to be, but for the woman she really is."

Mat was silent and Rosa took advantage of the opportunity. There was more she wanted to say.

"Think about it, Mat. If Daria had told you she was going you would have done everything in your power to stop her. Maybe she wasn't strong enough to withstand that pressure; felt she didn't have any choice. I don't doubt that she loves you Mat, but ..."

"You seem to know quite a lot," Mat's words were an accusation.

Ever since the blackmail photo's arrived Mat had spent the day going over the past, looking for clues, trying not to reject out of hand what common sense said was a thread he should follow. The world was no longer the orchestrated, safe and secure bubble of the past and denial no longer a viable choice.

If he loved Daria, truly loved her, he would fight to protect her. That meant learning, all that she had, in such an intensely guarded manner withheld. It meant being willing to know, without condemnation, what she had done during that time that she had left him and before they finally married. This time he must not allow her to change the subject, to raise the usual smokescreen or derail a line of questioning by assaults of passion.

In the wake of tonight's practice, on the way home he would broach the topic. The following day they would both be flying east; Daria, to resume her PR schedule before hooking up with Glen Winston's ice tour in Kansas City and he to confront Elliott Smythe. Informed by the blackmail photos, Elliott was the place to start and, in Mat's mind, the weak link in any conspiracy.

Mat stood before the gun cabinet in his father's study and wondered where he might find the key. The gentle sound of the dinner chime rang through the rooms, calling them to the table.

Mat heard, but remained as he was, every muscle straining against what self control he could muster.

"All men," Thierry liked to claim, "need to know how to protect their land and their family."

The masculine bravado of the statement had once offended Mat's sensibilities. Only now, he saw the world through a different lens entirely. The poison assault of what he'd taken in by way of those photographs, images he would never be free of, had shattered all pretense of complacency.

CHAPTER NINE

Daria came up behind him. She wrapped her arms about his chest laying her head between his shoulder blades.

"What are you doing here all alone and staring at these horrid guns?"

She took his hand and Mat allowed himself to be led away. There was a lot to do. He had a plane to charter, a decision to make about how to approach Elliott, and a few pointed questions to ask his wife. This time he would not allow her to avoid being honest. He needed answers that only she could provide.

At the table Mat forced himself to smile and look attentive, but made no real attempt to follow the conversation. Joey joined them late and seeing that Mat was preoccupied, engaged Rosa and Daria in conversation.

Joey and Mat worked well together and yet there remained an underlying competitiveness. Under the terms of the will, the Vineyard was to stay intact for future generations, but Mat had never seriously considered children, and now he wondered if that too was a kind of passive rebellion against his father's perpetual disappointment in him. And what about Daria, he wondered? Daria had never mentioned children, and suddenly Mat thought it significant that they, a married couple, had never once broached the subject.

Daria looked at him and furrowed her brow even as she continued her conversation with Rosa. She slid her foot over to touch his, and he returned the pressure as he checked off in his mind all that needed to be accomplished before he could leave for New York the following morning. He would have to revise the rink schedule and then phone Hillary and arrange for her to take his students. He recalled Hillary's reaction when she learned from Rosa that Daria had left him. She wasted no time in letting him know that she was willing to take him back on any terms, but there was no going back for Mat and, not for the first time, he wondered how her persistence and refusal to accept the truth continually brought them back to the same old stalemate; each confrontation producing an animosity that took longer to dissipate.

"I thought we meant something to each other," Hillary demanded in tears. The next day when he saw her at the rink, Hillary took him aside to apologize, but by now Mat knew to doubt the sincerity of her words.

"I'm sorry, Mat. I want you to be happy, and if that means another woman, I can accept that."

"Are you sure?" Mat asked. "You wouldn't rather stop working together? I know you've had offers and maybe you'd be happier with more distance between us."

"No. I've helped you build this skating program from the ground up, and I'm proud of what we've accomplished. I can keep my personal feelings separate. But Mat, do you realize that Daria may never return?"

"It doesn't matter, Hillary. Whatever happens I want you to understand that our relationship is over." Mat made a point to hold her gaze. He was wary. Always before she had failed to take him seriously, and when Daria returned and began to train at the rink, Hillary could barely be civil. Shades of that same jealousy remained even today in how the two women related to one another.

As the initial shock of the photographs receded, Mat decided that knowing where Daria had been and what she had been doing during that absence was the key to containing the blackmail threat that loomed over their futures. If he had not been so busy trying to reconstruct Daria's life, she might have confided in him, and then perhaps she would never have left. The abruptness of that ten-week separation, as he agonized over her safety, was a torture he never wanted to experience again. He considered hiring a private detective, but Rosa and Joey had dissuaded him. Only Ryan understood his feelings and promised to make inquiries, letting him know if he learned anything at all about her whereabouts.

The Holidays had come and gone with no word of her welfare. Mat filled his days with any mindless activity until at last fate played a hand in bringing them together. An unexpected call from his agent was most welcome. Several board members of a company intending to launch a new electrolyte drink had extended an invitation, and suddenly the prospect of flying to New York and mixing business with pleasure appealed to Mat.

He was accomplished at socializing with people he hardly knew and exuded a polished charm that drew others to him. The party had spilled over into several rooms and every so often Mat looked for Ryan, who had also been invited, but had not yet shown up. Feeling stranded, Mat knew he could persuade Ryan to make a quick exit as soon as he arrived. The prospect of having a drink with Ryan, quizzing him about Daria and catching up on what had been happening in their lives was preferable to this vivid party atmosphere, so contrary to the self-pity which held him in an unaccustomed grip of introspection. He could confide in Ryan who would not feel sorry for him, but would bring him up sharply with a mixture of truth and caustic humor. Mat suddenly felt the need of such emotional surgery for with Daria gone he felt oddly incomplete.

As he glanced surreptitiously at his watch, Mat bristled with well concealed impatience. He had been cornered by a woman who held him captive with a string of comments on the emerging American gymnasts as if she were commenting on racehorses rather than human beings.

Mat glanced beyond her in search of Ryan, and caught sight of Daria. Disbelieving, he blinked and looked again. She was changed. There was a sophisticated polish to her appearance that he had never seen before. This near stranger gave no hint of ever having suffered from a paralyzing depression and was difficult to reconcile with the needy and lost young woman who had fled his home without so much as the courtesy of a goodbye. Her hair had fully grown out and she wore a simple sheath of hunter green with sequined straps and the flash of diamond and emerald earrings that could only be real.

This was not the reunion he had envisioned as he watched her intently, uncertain of his reception. He had imagined her walking into his office at the rink or looking out from the veranda that surrounded three sides of the house and seeing her drive up in a taxi through the iron gates of Araujo Winery. He had envisioned every scenario except a party such as this. A party he would never have thought to attend, except to escape some measure of his own pain.

When he first arrived, Mat was impressed to note the eclectic group assembled. He recognized several actors and public officials, including his own senator. There were presidents of corporations and philanthropic boards, like the woman who still held him captive as she prattled on, apparently oblivious to the fact that his attention was intently riveted elsewhere. The host of the party, whom Mat had not yet met, was Howard Marstead's son, Hank and given the Marstead connection to Sasha, Mat was astonished to see Daria here and seeming to enjoy herself as though she had not a care in the world.

Current gossip said that Howard had suffered a debilitating stroke. No one in the history of figure skating had raised more money for the sport or prepared so well for what would eventually become a marketing and licensing bonanza. The speculation concerning Howard Marstead's health, and especially his state of mind, had been intense, and many were avid to confirm the rumors.

As Daria's eyes locked with his, Mat recognized the same fleeting shock and uncertainty that must have been evident on his own face seconds before. Once again he felt that familiar, blind infusion of lust rush through his body. It was a torrid, primitive energy that Daria rarely failed to recognize, and now she smiled in return; an unguarded and open smile that promised everything but assured nothing. Daria turned from her companion and unceremoniously walked to meet him.

"Where did you go, why did you leave?" He hated himself for asking. He hated the agony that drove the question from his lips without so much as a greeting of hello.

"I had to go, Mat. You must try to understand," she said in that breathless way she had of speaking when confronting the unexpected.

"Of course," he said, touching her cheek. "I do understand. I was smothering you. Making too many decisions without taking your feelings into account. Can you forgive me?"

Even as he apologized Mat knew that he understood nothing, but would not risk an argument that would take her away again. The shifts of persona and mood, never knowing what to expect, was the impetus that set his pulses racing, even now.

"Mat, I have a favor to ask of you. An important favor," she ventured, getting right to the point, not caring if they were overheard.

Mat had a thousand questions.

"I would have called but I was afraid to ask. Afraid that you would say no. But now my situation is desperate and I must ask you my question."

"You can ask me anything. Don't you know that? I love you."

"I may not be able to stay in this country. They think I know something about Sasha and money missing from my country." This was the first real information concerning her ongoing immigration problems that she had ever confided.

"What I need, Mat, is a husband. If I marry you, no one will send me back."

Mat looked at her stunned. Marriage had never been discussed, and only he had ever said the words, "I love you." But he had thought of marriage many times and assumed that she too had anticipated this as a normal progression of their relationship. They were standing in the middle of a crowded room, and the moment was awkward. Mat longed for privacy as someone called Daria's name and she turned to wave and smile in return. Out of the press of bodies a woman asked for Mat's autograph.

"It's for my daughter," the woman said. "She won't believe I met you here tonight."

Mat scribbled his name on a monogrammed cocktail napkin. "Now if you'll excuse us," he said abruptly and took Daria's hand, leading her out into the hallway. When the next person stopped him, Mat could no longer control his impatience.

"Can't you see we're trying to have a private conversation?" he snapped, forgetting that his purpose for being there was to be charming and accommodating, while his agent lobbied to keep his name on the narrowing list of candidates considered as spokesperson for the new sport drink. On impulse he opened a closet door and pulled Daria in behind him. They could smell damp wool and fur tickled their faces. Mat found the overhead light so that he could study her expression.

"I love you," he said. "But I won't marry you unless we agree to have a real marriage." He hesitated. He was afraid to suggest that she love him in return. Love could never be demanded, so he said instead, "I won't marry you unless you have feelings for me."

She leaned against him, encircling his body tightly with her arms.

But Mat stopped her. He would not be distracted.

"And you must confide in me, Daria. There is no real love without trust. It can't be the way it was. You must tell me everything so that I can help you."

Mat held his breath and waited. He could not quite believe he had found the courage to give her an ultimatum, when they both knew he would gladly have her back in his life under any circumstances.

Daria looked at him, a serious expression on her face. "I won't lie to you. I love you very much, but I don't know if I am capable of the kind of love you deserve. There are particulars you cannot know, Mat. It is because you are good and generous that you do not see. It is I who will never deserve you. Not at all!"

"Nothing you can say will alter how I feel about you. Don't you believe that I love you and that I can never stop loving you?" he pleaded.

"Then I will marry you," Daria asserted and smiled in that radiant way that never failed to bring a surge of infectious joy to his heart. It struck Mat that she had forgotten that the proposal had originated with her, and for a moment he felt confused and inclined to question that odd shift of interaction. Looking into her face in that moment of questioning was like peering into a fun house mirror only to emerge into the reality of the circus arcade, blinded by light.

But he wouldn't question. The old Daria was back. She stepped closer and like an addict hungry for a fix he buried his face in her hair. She turned her lips up to his, and they fell together. It was a deep, hungering kiss that blotted out the memory that she had ever left him. Once again he was whole and complete simply because he held her in his arms, and the truth of that greedy need was as blatant and palatable as the physical space they stood in. Mat could no more control his obsession with all that she had awakened in him than he could stop breathing.

"Let's get out of here," he said. "I came with my agent, so I'll call a cab."

"I have a car and driver," she said and kissed him again. "There is just one little thing I need to do. You go on and I'll meet you outside in fifteen minutes," she urged.

Mat sat in the darkened limousine and watched the snow drift under the lamplight. Daria's driver offered him a drink, but he declined. Instead he sank into the comfortable leather and watched white flakes, thick and heavy, accumulate on the drive and settle in a white line over the ink-black branches of the trees. The night reminded him of their first meeting.

Fifteen minutes turned to thirty. With growing anxiety Mat watched the front door. He had just decided to go in search of Daria when from the opposite direction a cold blast of air permeated the car, and she slid onto the seat beside him.

"Where did you come from?" he asked.

Thinking back later he recalled that he had not seen her emerge from the house, but noted a flash of color as she slipped something into the pocket of her coat. They fell together and kissed. Her hands on his face felt cold and her face hot. The scent of her perfume came to him from the open neck of her coat, and he failed to wait for an answer. Eventually a deluge of questions would flood his mind, but for now every doubt could wait.

"Are you sick?" Daria's question brought Mat sharply back to the present.

They were still seated around the old monastery table gleaming from layers of polish. Daria reached across to touch his hand.

"Are you not feeling well?" she repeated, "You've hardly touched your dinner."

To cover his discomfort Mat took a sip of Rosa's specially blended herb tea. The pattern of the cup was 'Chinese Tigers' which Daria had glimpsed during the opening scene of a movie they had watched together. It was the first and only time she had asked him for anything, and so he had been happy to track down a full service, although the pattern itself was discontinued. They used the china each night that Daria was home, and Mat could see that she derived a certain pleasure from looking at and handling the pieces. He was certain the pattern reminded her of happier times in her life, but when he asked she only thanked him again for the gift.

Leaving his own skates untouched, Mat sat in the bleachers

and watched Daria land her jumps, absent the usual calls of encouragement. He had to think, but as usual, when Daria skated, he could not take his eyes off her.

He thought of what a skilled lover she was. At the Maine cottage she had stunned him with the abruptness of that first passionate encounter and despite the flawless execution of that skilled and heightened dance, he could not entirely shed a lingering impression that she, as a real woman, was profoundly and mysteriously absent.

In a painful flash of insight he recalled how Daria would tense at the moment of penetration and even seemed to prolong the inevitable for as long as possible. He saw himself seeking unconsciously to ease that moment and always failing. Mat knew that he would never again make love to Daria with the same blind and careless excess. Those black and white images had shattered an illusion, and at the same time revealed his insensitivity. Was she only giving him what she thought he wanted? In the midst of pleasure was there remembered pain? Was their lovemaking truly reciprocal, and why had he not seen and known and sought the truth?

Mat remained on the top row of the darkened stadium. He watched Daria glide around the parameter of the rink as she lined up her jumps with graceful ease, and he thought of their wedding in January, hastily put together after their return home.

The ceremony was held in the chapel on the grounds of the winery. Once an outpost to the network of missions that spotted the California coast, the building had been restored by Thierry and often brought tourists to the farm. Only Ryan, Hillary, Rosa, and Joey were in attendance as a local justice of the peace officiated. Joey and Rosa were pressed into quick service as attendants, and Daria wore an off the shoulder dress trimmed with Mexican lace and tonal embroidery which Rosa had helped her select. Afterwards they had a barbecue on the lawn and Mat thought it the happiest day of his life, even paling in comparison to the day he won gold at the Olympics.

Now, as he thought of that day, Mat felt a stab of pain. He had loved Daria and believed his love was returned. He had ignored the truth and replaced his doubts with a fantasy marriage in order to stave off what evidence presented. He should have found the courage to coax the truth from her long ago, for nothing else could have armed them better for what lay ahead. It struck Mat that the survival of their marriage, and perhaps Daria's life, depended on his willingness to fight this battle for their protection.

Mat watched Daria turn her body for the backward approach into the double Lutz. She shifted her weight onto her left foot, and using the toe pick of her right skate as a spring, she propelled her body into the first revolution. After two rotations she exited the jump on her right foot. Now she would try a triple. It was the jump she was having difficulty with, but there was no hint of that now as he watched her come around for a second try. Her speed was good and as she pushed off with her toe pick, her leg came up and she flew into the final spiral, gliding out in perfect form. She looked up at the stands for his reaction, seeking his praise. Mat accommodated, gesturing a thumbs up and forcing a return smile.

Mat watched Daria leave the ice. Although skating required great physical exertion and skill, she seemed more relaxed on the ice than any other place. In many ways she reminded him of Ryan. Locked within the perimeters of the boards and isolated on that frigid surface, they were both focused inward and aware of little else. It was enough to 'be out there', on that private island. He suspected that if Daria had never turned professional, she would still skate as Ryan did for a sort of unconscious release.

As Daria reached for her guards, he joined her below. "Here, let me do that," he said and bent to unlace her skates. Daria extended one leg and leaned back against the row of bleachers. He could feel her eyes studying him, and as he slid off her second skate she leaned forward to plant a kiss on his forehead.

Mat avoided Daria's gaze as he wiped down her blades and slid the terry cloth protectors into place. How many times had he performed this mindless ritual for himself, for his younger students, and now for Daria? There was comfort in the familiarity until a swift dart of icy presence, a premonition of what lay ahead, intruded. In a fierce protective surge Mat wanted nothing more than to freeze the utter normalcy of such routine forever.

"Soon you must tell what is wrong, Mat?" Daria spoke softly.

He studied her face and knew that he could not protect her. Rosa would even say it was wrong to conceal vital information she had every right to know. Just not now!

"I'm going away for a week," he told her once they were in the land rover and heading north. He didn't look at her but studied the road ahead.

"Where are you going?" she asked, curious.

"Our agent wants me to meet with a potential sponsor. They're sending a plane for me." The ease of this lie as it slipped off his tongue surprised him.

"So it is an endorsement you've been worried about," Daria said, relieved that this was all that was bothering her pensive husband. "We don't need the money. This is what you always tell me, so why should you worry?"

"I know, but still it would be nice. Good exposure for you and especially combined with the upcoming article. You'll be out of town anyway, so I thought as long as I was in New York, Ryan and I might head into New Hampshire or Maine for a little fishing. No more than a week, maybe a few days," he lied.

"I love you," she said. "You deserve a break." She leaned across to kiss the hollow of his neck.

This would be their last night together, but Mat knew he could not risk making love to Daria as would normally happen before a separation. The blackmail photographs represented only the tip of the iceberg and Daria, who had withheld so much, would fight him at every turn as he sought to uncover her history. The thought of this, that she couldn't or would not trust him, was more than he could bear to think of.

Mat pushed the self-pity away and fought for control of his emotions. Rage burned behind his eyes mitigated only by the knowledge that what he felt was nothing to the torture endured by her. It was fortunate that he did not need Daria to tell him where to start. Mat knew enough of Elliott to know that he would be the weak link in any conspiracy. He only hoped Elliott could be persuaded to talk before he sank a fist into that pompous face, for Elliott was the man who watched as the child Daria, was raped. His Daria!

Mat rammed a fist into the seat. Beside him Daria jumped, startled by the force. She looked at him in astonishment.

In a squeal of brakes, Mat cut across two lanes of traffic. Behind him a horn blasted and dust rose as tires spun onto the shoulder. He turned in his seat.

"Daria, something has happened. I need you to tell me where you were before Christmas. I want to know what you did after you left California!"

Daria looked at him wide-eyed, and as often happened when there was a sudden shift of mood or topic, there was a pause -- a certain interlude of blankness as she prepared to answer.

"I'm sorry," she said finally, speaking in a childlike tone calculated to undermine his anger.

"I need concrete answers, not vague phrases about being alone in order to think. I want to know where and what you did during those weeks that you disappeared from my life."

When Daria spoke again, her accent was more pronounced, and she pressed one hand to her forehead as though in pain.

"This is important to you, Mat?" The little girl voice was gone, but she was stalling and they both knew it.

"We agreed to have a real marriage, and now it seems you still can't trust me. Not even enough to share minor details and answer simple questions with a straight reply."

"You are being very tiresome and melodramatic," she accused. "I went away. We were reunited and got married just as you wanted, and aren't we happy together, Mat? Isn't this enough for you?"

This was his cue to reassure her, but this time he could not accommodate.

"I asked you a simple question that you seem unwilling or unable to answer."

"What question?" she asked and looked around as though suddenly unsure of her surroundings.

"I want to know what you did during that time that you left me without so much as a thought for how I would worry. It was a mere fluke that we met at Hank Marstead's party after the Holidays. You asked me to marry you, and we agreed there would be no more secrets, that you would tell me everything. But the fact is, Daria, I know nothing more about you today."

Daria reached over and shut off the air conditioner.

"Why is this important? Why now when you never cared before."

"Not true Daria. And it's important because we are a married couple, and maybe someday we'll have children. There can't be secrets between us."

Daria rolled down the window and looked out at the Pacific. A pale sickle moon hung overhead. Curious, Mat followed her gaze. Above, on the hillside of a jutting peninsula, houses clustered on the sloped landscape, giving the appearance that they might slip into the sea. Daria held herself erect, as though in readiness for flight, even as her face remained an impenetrable mask of neutrality. Mat waited. As always, he waited in vain.

PART TWO

CHAPTER TEN

DARIA

Imprisoned in the claustrophobic closeness of the car as traffic flew by and that sickle moon hung overhead like a distracting slice of lemon rind, Mat demanded answers. Daria formed her thoughts and opened her mouth to speak, but nothing came out. Talk, as an exercise of will, was not, at that juncture, possible.

How could she explain that she had not lived alone for a very long time? At times her only clue that autonomy had been given over to *others* was lost time. If she could not explain in the beginning, why did Mat imagine she could do so now?

Mat was never satisfied, always striving and planning. The very qualities that drew her toward him in the beginning had become the threat she must now escape. Daria regarded her husband. He was handsome. His glossy hair was neatly trimmed, and even when he woke in the morning it was almost never out of place. His warm brown eyes reminded her of the velvet depth of flowers. But his ambition for her career brought with it a level of notoriety that put at risk certain plans the *others* were committed to and, by proxy, she as well; that singleness of purpose that motivated survival, allowing no dissent.

Daria had no illusions that some were immune to Mat's charm; *okay... that was all well and good,* but some viewed him with suspicion, even hated him. Daria had stayed present, growing stronger, flexing internal acuity and stamina to protect him; something he failed to appreciate.

If Mat knew, really knew what he had welcomed into his home and bed he would be horrified and think her insane and a waste of that love he so eloquently claimed to feel. And she was jealous. Yes, Daria acknowledged, startled at the accuracy of that term for the emotion felt. She was truly jealous and could barely tolerate sharing her beloved Mat any longer with those *other* alter personalities.

Daria had seen the bruises on his hard strong body and knew that she would not have inflicted them and that he, loving her, would never raise a fist in self-defense. What set some off was the wet, filthy coupling so reminiscent of the abuse she had once been helpless to oppose. Daria had become more successful at fighting the imperative to switch, refusing to let *others* take her place, but in consequence she could feel a frenzy mount under a canopy of rage at her presumptuous usurpation of what, until Mat, had rarely been her territory.

Daria reached across the seat to touch Mat's cheek, but he tilted his head away and gave her a steely look of determination. Something had shifted the delicate axis in the rules of their relationship. Mat was not falling into line, playing the part the demands of her dysfunction had so carefully cued him to act out.

"By the time I've finished in New York you'll be picking up Glen's tour in Kansas City," he reminded. "I'll meet you there, but I must warn you, Daria. This time I expect the full story. I will not settle for anything less."

As so often happened, Mat took her silence for agreement and maneuvered the car back into traffic. It was unlike Mat to brood, but he remained troubled and failed to pick up the threads of their argument. He hated to have her angry with him, but this time he didn't seem to care. He wasn't falling over himself to make a truce.

Once home Mat stayed late at his desk. As the pearl gray of dawn lifted the mantle of darkness, he lay down beside her. She rolled into his embrace and he held her and stroked her hair, but his touch was not the same. Even as she dozed she felt his eyes on her face and marked his sleeplessness like a dog worrying a sore, relentlessly licking, licking.

Daria tried not to think, but despite those efforts she fell into a state of twilight awareness where unwanted flashbacks could take on nightmarish proportions. She recalled in great detail that moment that she realized the dangerous, precarious state of her survival. A boy of ten, Rhyming, expressed it best, his voice echoing to the forefront

"He doesn't want breasts; he doesn't want hair, not down

there."

Daria hated to think another child would suffer what she had, but she knew they had and did. She'd once witnessed the murder of a girl. Naked and drugged, she sat huddled in a metal dog pen as she peered through the candlelit obscurity of the bars. The murmurs of ritual required the screams and then the blood which Sasha told her gave him satanic power and protection.

Daria remembered little of these rituals, except when triggers orchestrated flashbacks, or violent dreams tickled at memory receptacles. When she felt herself tantalizingly close to grasping at the outside rim of such a picture, those other alter personalities stepped forward to whisk them away like a putrid dish of diseased garbage.

"Starving and training is no longer working, what will we do, what will we do?" became the chorus of alarm that woke others, long dead in the somnolence of thoughtless exchange and rising paralysis.

"It is our murder he'll require."

"No, no," Daria argued, denial a powerful program.

"Look in the mirror. You're not a girl."

"He needs us dead."

"Or worse, sold to the highest bidder."

They were right, Daria finally had to acknowledge. While she practiced her skating, a possible ticket to escape, *others* became indispensable. *Lie* and *Mocking* mothered Sasha, stoking his acid humor, always sadistically offensive rather than amusing even as they breathed secret poisonous ridicule. *Kill* conspired with earliest memory to compile an assassins' hit list. But, Daria, who was practiced at giving over the field of sensory assault, did her best to fine tune those dual skills of avoidance and flight. This allowed her the safety to put in play her greatest talent. That of capitalizing on Sasha's primary weakness; the egocentric conviction that he was beyond the ordinary flow of consequence which he believed he had effectively inoculated himself against by preternatural wiles, spells, hexes, and blood-alliances.

Daria delved into his business affairs until Sasha wondered how he had ever survived without her. This chameleon-like response to trauma was something Daria had fine-tuned to a craft of superior sophistication. She was, in essence, a survivor. The strength to be so derived from the earliest wellspring of stability among the loving family that, until they lost her, had prayed for her, protected, and loved her.

Mat checked Daria's bags and escorted her to the security check point. His kiss goodbye was all too brief and his words perfunctory. Daria watched him walk away, and almost it seemed he would turn back. When he did not, she wanted to run after him, throw her arms around him, confiding everything. He was her knight in shining armor, her protector, and defender. It was in his nature to help and to love, and yet the prospect of trusting Mat bred confusion. Far better not to exercise that failed muscle. It would, she felt, be a relief to get it over with. To have him finally reject her so that she could simply walk away as she had done once before... that time he wanted to know about.

Daria found her first-class seat and hoped that no one would sit beside her. As the airplane aligned its nose on the runway she made up her mind. The decision came seemingly from nowhere, and she was grateful. She would tell him. Inviting rejection and maybe even death, she would tell him everything.

Like any good actress who learns her lines as well as those of her fellow actors, she ran those weeks in question through her mind like the dailies from a disjointed day of shooting. She had to practice. What she could not say by rote might not be said at all. She could never entirely know everything, but regarding those larger gaps of memory, she knew to ask *KEEPER*. The one who believed in truth even at the threat of death.

Daria grabbed a pillow and feigned sleep. For the first time she went to *KEEPER*, before he came to her. Greedily she sank into the internal place of a multiple existence to share from the pool of a collective consciousness, making every effort to be small and unobtrusive. Doing so rendered her an observer and not a participant, the role she preferred. But thanks to Mat that passive role was no longer the luxury afforded. Loving Mat had changed so much.

Daria would start, not at the beginning, but at that place he asked -- the day she left him.

By Boston standards it was a mild winter day. The sun shone and the streets were dry with banks of snow indented by snow plows. The contrast from sunny California was stark, but she felt almost happy. First thing she bought herself a winter coat, boots, gloves, and hat. She strolled up to Court Street and smiled at the huge teakettle, which hung off a grappling hook and sent a flow of steam up the overhang of the building. Nothing at all was concrete or specifically remembered. But everything was familiar and came to her like bouquets wrapped with ribbon about green trailing stems that elongated behind her as she walked. Like a safety rope, like bread crumbs, like buoys on the surface of the water.

From Court Street, Daria turned down Tremont toward the old State House. Sights and smells and thoughts were stirred out of the vast numbness of her being until an avalanche of memory assailed her, and it almost became too much. And it was too much. Tripping over the tender green stems, Daria and a few of the *others* lost hold of the safety rope, lost sight of the sign posts and sank.

Significant time had been lost, and so she did what she always did on those occasions. She couldn't rush the procedure. It happened of its own accord and in its own way. She came to herself slowly, still feeling heavy and cumbersome and weighed down, the absence of herself fixed far from that space that her physical body occupied and yet reaching and yearning for that return to place.

Vision was a rainy windshield obstructing the eyes that looked out from a body that was not yet hers. Daria squinted into a winter sun and waited to see more clearly.

"Where am I?"

The answer was always unexpected and sometimes cruel. So she stood small. She stood quiet, in no hurry to learn her circumstances, and especially because she didn't seem to be in any imminent danger. She concentrated on her breathing. She was breathing. She concentrated on her heartbeat until she felt herself filling the internal spaces more fully. As always, she must consider physical pain, and it was better to explore this before feeling rendered her incapable of control. This is how she'd once ended up on the locked ward of a psychiatric hospital before Sasha found her and whisked her away.

Daria had a routine that smothered anxiety. She felt a certain pride in taking over for those who couldn't cope and knew how to handle these dense situations fraught with risk. She continued the inventory, looking down at her hands and whispering off the checklist. No blood. Good. The nails. No manicure. Not good, but not too bad. They weren't broken, and she could see the remnants of the last one, which provided an approximation of how long it had been that the Daria personality had been displaced.

What was she wearing? A coat. A winter coat. Yes, it was cold and she needed warmth. She was no longer anywhere near her home in sunny California, but now she recalled leaving and the plane landing at Logan and the coat she'd bought at Filenes. Daria decided to test her legs and found them in good working order. The overriding physical sensation of hunger now registered. She pushed it off for later. Fingers trembling, stiff from cold, she reached for a purse that wasn't there. Instead there was a smart leather briefcase stuffed with papers and blue plastic file folders all neatly arranged.

This provided a clue as to who had been preeminent during that missed time away. It could only be the banker, the money manager who had made them very rich, knowing everything there was to know about business and finance so that they could finally deliver a fatal wound to Sasha where it most counted -- his pocketbook.

Daria had left the park bench and heavy briefcase in hand, much too heavy to contain just papers, she moved to the window of a store filled with bric-a-brac and an antique mirror low in the center. She bent to see her reflection. Her dark red hair was caught back in a tight low ponytail, but at least her hair was clean and neat. It wasn't cut and her scalp hadn't been shaved and there were no bruises on her makeup-less face. Makeup-less. That was good. No makeup translated to, no abusive sex with strangers. Daria breathed a sigh of relief.

Suddenly another face appeared in the mirror beside hers. Daria tried to take in the features, but her eyesight was still somewhat clouded.

"Do you live around here?" Daria asked, more to see if the face were a memory or a flashback than for any answer.

"Yes, Deary, all my life, and look what I've come to. Stand up now, I'm an old woman, I can't bend over like this for long. You going to buy that mirror?"

Daria straightened her body and shook her head. "No, I don't think so."

"You look like you could spare a twenty. Twenty dollars for an old lady who's come to nothing."

Long pause and then, "Ten if you don't have it. Five will do."

Long pause through which Daria decided the company was real and not a figment of her imagination.

"Cat got your tongue, Deary? Can't talk, is that it?"

Daria struggled to bring the woman's expression into focus. Dirt was caked in the lines of her wrinkled face, and her steel-gray hair peaked out from a low cap, which fell almost to her eyebrows.

"I may have lived there, in a big house," Daria pointed, the weight of the outstretched arm heavy and unfamiliar. But, as soon as the words were off her tongue she knew they were true; the reason she was here, standing on this particular street.

Daria blinked and blinked again. *Of course!* The assassins list had brought her to this place.

"They tore it down, Deary, and the rest on this block too. Urban Improvement, don't you know? It's the latest thing," she commiserated. "And displaces the likes of me and you. I used to live in an apartment over there," the woman offered and pointed also. "And a snug place too. Had a fire escape with plants and a place for my cat to sun."

Daria let her gaze follow. She could see it -- a brick apartment building with ivy on the walls and an intricate wrought iron canopy that sheltered the door.

"I don't have the cat anymore."

The woman's gray coat was threadbare, and her gloves were missing fingers. She seemed to like having someone to speak with. The odor that emanated from her person was atrocious, but Daria was just glad that it wasn't rotting corpses or her own stale urine from days of isolated confinement. She thought of walking away, but had not yet fully filled the space of her person. It couldn't hurt to stand here on the sidewalk and listen to this harmless stranger. It was like listening to someone else's background music while she skated a scripted program. The woman provided ballast. Daria was satisfied to keep company until she was strong enough to plan her next move.

"Would you join me for lunch?"

"You must be daft, Deary. Blind or retarded. They wouldn't let the likes of me in any restaurant, and besides that they all know me. They know I can eat at the church. But they do have a cafeteria in that building. It's only for employees, but dressed like you are they won't know the difference. They have high turn-over. I hear things sitting at that bus stop there. Why don't you just march over there and get us something to eat. I like tuna on rye with dill pickles." Daria saw that her mouth was watering.

"Where can we eat?"

"There." The woman pointed to a transit shelter where a young mother and her child waited for a bus. The image of the little boy leaning against his mother as she sat with a toy on her lap slipped past her defenses, tearing at the internal flesh of unwelcome recollection.

"The very minute we sit down, they'll leave. They always do."

Daria decided. "Wait here. Watch my briefcase." With knowing fingers, fingers that knew what her conscious thoughts didn't, she reached for a small slim wallet of red alligator, and she caught site of the matching red gloves and looked down at her feet. Yes, matching shoes, and the colors of her coat softly blending with the artfully coordinated silk scarf.

"And don't forget cake."

Daria crossed the street, entered the building, and returned a short time later with two Styrofoam containers and her pockets stuffed with extras. She could see that the woman had fully expected her to return. She sat alone in a corner of the transit shelter hugging Daria's briefcase to her chest with a fiercely protective expression on her face.

"Lordy, what you got in here?" she asked as she put the briefcase at her feet. "A gun or something?"

Daria handed over one of the two Styrofoam containers into avid, outstretched hands. Immediately her companion was absorbed in her food, while Daria forgot that she had ever been hungry.

"Did you get us something to drink, Deary?" Daria passed over two cartons of milk. "Chocolate! How did you know?"

"I used to live over there," Daria recited softly. "It was a big house. White stone, I think, with a tall stained glass window on the second floor landing. Do you recall this house?"

"I remember. The family lived there a long time."

"That's right," Daria agreed, a small thrill of excitement racing from her stomach to her throat, causing her heart to constrict. The feeling scared her. She didn't want to feel. Not yet. She only wanted to know.

"What happened to them? Where did they go?"

"I used to make better tuna than this. I had a kitchen once. Why you interested, Deary?" The woman looked at her fully for the first time. Her wizened eyes squinted into the sun beyond Daria's shoulder. Her tone was sympathetic.

Daria didn't answer. She knew the value of silence. She knew how stillness unsettled curiosity and guarded secrets worth keeping. She picked up the briefcase and hoped she could know the contents without looking. She thought about the gun. *Kill* would never own a gun that wasn't cleaned, primed, and loaded. Did her companion guess right? Was there a gun?

"I'll tell you if you want to know. There was a tragedy. They lost a child, I think." A stab of electricity shot through Daria at the old woman's words.

"Something happened to that child. I forget. But the mother went to live elsewhere, and the father stayed and worked during the week in Boston. He was a handsome man. Movie star handsome. I liked him."

"Why?"

"Oh, you know. You just like some people you might not know well. He'd ask about my Judith, my cat. He was nice to everyone and he loved his two little girls. He played with them in the park on winter evenings, pulling their sleds and they'd watch out that window for him to come home."

Daria's new friend paused and pointed across the street to the precise place where the window would have been. Daria saw it clearly.

"He was older than his wife and he walked with a cane. After he died they tore down the house to build that ugly monstrosity, and I lost my home too. I haven't been on my feet since."

Daria glanced at the woman's feet. She wore men's tennis shoes with several layers of socks to make them fit.

"What would it take to get you on your feet?" she asked.

"More money than you have, Deary. Food is expensive and

the landlords want references and first and last month deposits. I haven't collected a social security check in two years because I don't have an address. The priest said he'd help me, but I won't go in any shelter. As dangerous as the streets. A woman I know was raped there, and she was older than I am and uglier too. You wouldn't know this, Deary, but I was pretty once. I held down a job and I had a life. I miss my Judith."

Daria lifted the briefcase. She slipped knowing fingers into the zippered side compartment that was stuffed full, as wide as it could be, with a bit of Sasha's money. It pleased her to occasionally direct some of those resources to what he would decry as self serving, ego-boosting righteousness. She counted out the bills without removing them. "Do you have a place to hide this until you can get to a bank?"

"I got lots of places to hide things, Deary. I've been on the street a long time." She opened the flap of her coat to reveal multiple pockets, pockets within pockets sewn securely with bits of thread and even string. Daria identified with what bred the need for such ingenuity.

"Take that priest with you to the bank; open an account. Let him help you. Will you do that?"

The woman nodded. She looked at the money and hoped there was as much as two hundred dollars there; enough to get her off the street for Christmas. She watched as Daria walked from under the transit shelter.

As one bus approached and another pulled away, Daria breathed in the scent of diesel exhaust. That too was familiar. She had ridden this bus. *Not this precise bus, but a similar one... with her mother and... older sister.* Its route went to Copley Square and the Boston Public Library. They went there for children's hour each Tuesday, rain or shine. They stopped for afternoon tea and then took a taxi to North Station and rode the train home with father for a light supper before bed. The memory came in a cruel wave of grief that stung her eyes with salty tears.

"Goodbye, Deary" the woman waved at the departing bus. Then she counted the zeros on the first bill. Was it real? Yes, the paper, the ink. It all felt real. She'd get another Judith. She'd have a kitchen and a little room with a comfortable bed. She was too happy to smile. After she'd had a good cry, she went looking

The Year Between the Wood
for the priest at the church up the block.

Daria found him at the Boston Public Library. His face looked back at them from the glossy cover of *Legal Jargon*. There was something about his expression. She recognized the overdone polish of one committed to function and capacity rather than substance. He believed in the role that he played more than he believed in himself. Some of the *others* were adept at spotting this sort of putrid ooze, that very ooze that seeped from this man's pores and would flow from his mouth with dangerous disdain.

Lie and *Mocking* began to argue and almost made them walk away, but Daria thought that perhaps she had seen that face before, and there was something compelling about his name. She repeated it to herself over and over again. Marstead, Hank. Hank Marstead. Marstead....

In a professional register in the third floor gallery Daria found it again. Marstead, Henry otherwise known as Hank. His reputation seesawed between notorious and respectable, and he had recently been up before the bar to combat charges brought by a disgruntled client, but somehow had managed to walk away unscathed. In his world money was the eternal lubricant, and denial, when cloaked repeatedly in the timely phraseology of seamless accommodation, the great salve.

The next morning Daria boarded the shuttle to New York. Christmas decorations lent a festive air to the hazy winter light. The sight tugged at Daria, but the *others* had no memory of Christmas in the midst of family, and it struck Daria as sad, and then she thought of Mat. Like her he would be alone for Christmas. She knew he would miss her and wondered if he would come here, to the very city she looked out at from the window of her cab, to spend the holiday with Ryan.

It occurred to Daria that she might phone Ryan, but a chorus of *others* warned against it so she left that for later. There were things that he could tell her that it seemed no one else would.

Daria took the cab directly to Hank Marstead's building and then the elevator to the top floor office where she walked the length of the Persian runner to the reception area, unannounced and without an appointment. Hank looked at her with an inward tug of curiosity that prevented him from sending her away.

Hank often acted on what he liked to term his 'lucky hunches', and after he learned how rich she was, and especially how unencumbered by family, he congratulated himself for having the good sense to have heeded those instincts. But he also felt that he knew her, and there was something more. An odd confluence of disquiet merged with a strong feeling of déjà vu, which needled him.

Now, some weeks later he was not so sure. In moments of complete honesty he could almost admit an underlying tug of fear, although he felt completely foolish for indulging such a sentiment; and by then the serpent's head of greed had reared its ugly head, and he was determined to acquire something more than his usual fee from Daria.

There was very little to do really, although he did his best to make his work look as complicated as possible, amassing billable hours. He transferred money and made a few investments that he explained to her in overburdened detail. She was maddeningly conservative and agreed to almost nothing he suggested, as though completely uninterested in making a profit. He was suspicious of her strategy, for he suspected she had one; but he couldn't figure it out.

A few things became clear. She, or someone else, for he didn't think she could have done this on her own, had been deliberately obscuring a money trail. Some of the off-shore accounts had not seen activity other than interest accruing for ten years or more, which would have made her ten or twelve years old at the time that they were opened.

"What happened to this fund?" he asked, as he tried to access an account.

"It was closed," she said simply.

"Closed? Why closed?" he asked, alarmed, for he felt proprietary where money was concerned -- all potentially his.

All his usual tactics to gain the upper hand failed. In the beginning, still grossly underestimating Daria, he tried to make the process complicated, until she phrased the legalese back to him with perfect ease. Hank even flirted with her though, as pretty as she was, she left him cold; and when that fell flat he treated her like a daughter; and finally, at the end of his rope, like an equal. Finance was not Hank's area of expertise. New

York was the financial hub of the world, so why, when there was real cutting edge advice to be had a block away in any direction, had she sought him out?

It drove him crazy how she roamed his office, walking the perimeter like a caged animal and exhibiting an appalling lack of reverence for all the decorative investments he was so proud of. They had been chosen with great care to send just the right message, proof of his worth. Above a mantle was an original Turner borrowed from his father's condo. At the opposite end of the room the equally talented, John Stobart. Daria peered at the faces in the silver-rimmed photographs, which offended him when, if she'd been any other person, he would not have cared one bit.

Hank would invite her to sit, and she would drop into the nearest chair, often located across the large room so that he was forced to walk from behind his desk to sit opposite her. Then, just as he was again feeling comfortable, she would rise unexpectedly, often in mid-sentence, and resume her same circular stroll. With eye contact lost and focus disrupted, Hank seethed in barely suppressed exasperation. He could see that she was distrustful, and that absence of trust, although completely justified, affronted his senses like fingernails across the surface of a chalkboard.

It was an office worker who finally recognized her. He was both astonished and relieved now that he could set aside the nagging suspicion that they had once personally known one another. And with figure skating in common, he could build a little trust and perhaps end up managing her celebrity as well as her fortune. He had, in fact, never made so much for doing so little.

There was only one photograph of his father present and that was a black and white still taken during Howard's studio days of brief movie star fame.

Of course she had noticed that photograph in her forays about the office, but not until Hank mentioned his father's name did she really see it. Did the color of her skin plummet to a paler shade of ivory? Were those beads of sweat on her brow, and did he imagine that she slid her hands in her pockets because they trembled? His curiosity was piqued. Perhaps his father's fame and reputation would be the leverage he needed to forge a new bond with her. She had to be a fan. Anyone who knew anything at all about the history of figure skating held his father in high esteem.

"I know of Howard Marstead," she admitted when he questioned her. "And this is him? Your father?" She scrutinized the photo.

"We didn't know one another well."

"Your parents were divorced?"

Hank nodded his head. "Howard had a serious stroke a few months back. My wife wouldn't hear of him going into a home. He lives with us now."

"Very admirable."

"Yes," Hank said, liking the compliment. During their brief exchange he had even thought of extending an invitation to lunch, but Daria changed the subject, and once again there was only the mechanics of their business dealings to cover.

As usual, she was dressed in what seemed to Hank a painfully nondescript manner. Her hair was up off her neck and pulled away from her face. She was dressed in gray flannel trousers and a white sweater with a men's oversized raincoat which hid her figure.

"Don't you ever wear your hair loose?' Hank asked without thinking.

The question caught Daria by surprise and became a trigger. Rough hands and burning chemicals poured over her scalp. She thought about Mat and his kindness as she had watched the stark platinum chased off by the rich strawberry red; how Mat had liked the change and told her she was beautiful.

Daria turned from the mirror of her memory and wordlessly regarded Hank. She could tell that her scrutiny and especially her silence made him uneasy. But now, suddenly, she no longer enjoyed playing him. Instead she felt sorry for him. He too had once been a child, and to have a father like that …

As Hank led Daria to a conference room, he knew she would prefer he not speak until they were alone, but he could not resist disguising his nervousness with talk as they walked past his secretary and down a long hallway. Daria's refusal to reply to superficial banter with anything more than a nod or shake of the head seemed to him rude. Under the ballooning raincoat she wore a straight gray skirt and matching sweater with her hair caught in a tight bun. The absence of jewelry in view of her vast wealth was a glaring particular that irritated him, and he wondered. *Why not red? Why not a limousine rather than a cab that smelled of stale cigarettes and last night's drunk?*

Hank had searched through his father's collection of skating magazines and programs until he came upon a single photograph of Daria standing on a podium in a glittering blue dress with silver sequins. Her hair was blonde, and because she was young, the overdone makeup made her look far less attractive than she actually was. He admired her legs and the outline of budding breasts, which she now seemed, bent on concealing beneath loose, colorless clothing. Daria, he realized, did not want to be admired or even noticed, and this grated against every conception he had of women in general.

By three in the afternoon they were finished. There was no repeat of the previous meeting in which they had all too briefly discussed his father. Daria seemed committed to a polite and distant protocol. As usual she had her gloves on before she would shake his hand. He wondered if that wasn't because she disliked the clammy wetness of his palm, a symptom of anxiety that surprised him, and that he hadn't had to concern himself with since adolescence.

Hank did not know Daria well enough to dislike her and yet it was more than that. He sometimes felt repelled by her strangeness. His feelings had progressed toward loathing, and yet conversely, he felt compelled to show her more courtesy and attention than any of his other clients. As though she might be dangerous, and it wasn't entirely safe to turn his back on her.

As the elevator door closed off her face, he calculated how soon they would meet again. Why must they meet so often? Hank felt an inexplicable surge of repugnance that was nearly physical, and decided, as he had decided several times in the past, to end their association. Let her find another attorney.

Daria sat or reclined against the low stone wall. Before her was the house, at her back the cemetery, and then the sea. As the sun came up from behind to reflect off the tall narrow windows of the second floor, she maintained her vigil. The wide shutters could be fastened and secured in the event of a hurricane and were still painted the same shade of bright green. The burgundy window boxes, which overflowed in summer with impatiens and wayward springs of ivy, were now packed with snow.

At Daria's back the pull and thrust of the waves rolled over the yellow sand of Front Beach, obscured now by a sculptured wall of layered, frozen spray. Overhead, flocks of gulls took wing on currents of frigid morning air, their clear, penetrating screech a haunting reminder of summer. From June through Labor Day, during the first years of her life, Daria had fallen asleep in a bed under the eaves of this house.

She'd caught the train from North Station and arrived in Rockport in late afternoon. It was the same train her father caught each Friday night in summer so that he could spend his weekends with the family. Daria had a vague memory of going to meet that train and being caught up in her father's arms, lifted high above his shoulders. She closed her eyes and almost heard anew the infectious thrill of that innocent laughter.

From the station Daria had walked up King Street and then down the hill toward the beach. Many of the summer businesses and restaurants were closed. She studied the wood sculpture of the pirate perched above the sign before the shuttered windows of Peg Legs. What surprised her most was how little all this had changed. The trees looked no larger and the houses no different, and as night fell she walked off the mounting anxiety through narrow, twisting streets until finally she came to the place she'd always intended.

The house before her was confirmation of memory matching reality. She was still there at dawn when the hall light snapped on and she counted the steps until the kitchen light filtered through from the back of the downstairs rooms. Daria could almost smell the coffee brewing and the tea steeping, and her mouth watered at the thought of her grandmother's raisin scones.

The thought came. Why couldn't she just go on up and ring the bell, or walk in. The door was never locked. She walked a few steps forward and stopped. A bicycle came up Mill Lane from the direction of the pond that the winter children skated on. She had been a summer child, staying only in season, but if the old woman's memory could be trusted, her parents had moved here.

Where else would they have gone?

The pond was covered now under a pristine blanket of new snow, but today was Saturday, and soon the boys would arrive to shovel off a hockey surface; and then the girls to compete for their own space. Sleds would line up just beyond her view at the edge of the hill that ran down to the pond and over the bridge to the foot of the old mill. There had been a painting of that scene at the house in Belmont. Seeing the town draped in winter jogged that memory which slashed at her heart with biting cruelty.

The layer of new snow over the cobblestones gave the bicycle traction as the boy tossed his newspaper in a wild arch in the general vicinity of the few houses that faced the cemetery wall. The paperboy of her childhood had been the son of a fisherman. His wife hauled the lobsters up a barnacle encrusted wall, to huge boiling pots in her kitchen and sold them out the front, wrapped in waxed paper with Dixie cups of butter.

For a moment the boy's eyes locked with hers. She wondered how she must appear to him in the first light of a pale dawn. Obviously startled, his bicycle swerved and he averted his head and moved as far as possible toward the curb. With a last look over his shoulder, he peddled faster until soon out of sight.

Daria looked at the second house. Compared to her grandmother's, it was small and low, painted a deep red that looked almost black in the emerging light. She stepped up to the curb and let herself in the gate and walked around to the back. It was difficult to tell beneath the layer of new snow, but the garden seemed larger and there was a greenhouse, which had never been there before. These changes nagged at her and for a long moment she hesitated, but soon she had regained that even, emotionless veneer.

A short time later Daria emerged through the front door. She was in no hurry. There was no need to run and hide, for she knew that as long as she remained in that moment she was invisible and immune to any harm. By now the newspaper was gone. Invigorated she looked at the indentation in the snow bank where it had been recovered, proof that she was truly present to the circumstances.

Daria breathed in the crisp morning air and stepped through the frame of a painting. She followed in the tracks of the bicycle down the hill, over the stone bridge, by the old mill toward the railway station, wrapped in the impenetrable bubble of invincibility.

It was okay. She had failed to murder an enemy who was already dying. Let him suffer. She sent the information back to the far reaches of her skull where a scribe would cross his name off the assassins list.

Five names more, two accounted for; three dead, that's the best, Rhyming sang as Daria sank back to grateful oblivion.

CHAPTER ELEVEN

Nora placed the coffee cup down in its saucer with a clatter and reached for the indestructible coast guard jacket of indeterminate years. For as long as she could remember, the jacket had hung by the door and was present even in photographs of times before she was born. Letting her pink flannel nightgown trail over the tops of black Wellingtons, Nora Dillihunt walked out to retrieve her newspaper. Once again the boy had missed the landing.

Although it had snowed quite a bit this winter, Nora had never once shoveled. With skill she picked her way over the little that could be seen of her front steps. Trying not to get caught up in her trailing nightgown, she found the newspaper in a mound of snow, which when melted, would blur the print and stain her fingers.

"Hello, Paul," she called to her neighbor as in unison they bent to retrieve their newspapers. Her short red hair fell over her eyes, and she pushed it up over her forehead in the unconscious gesture that had been hers since girlhood.

"How's Herb this morning?"

"The same," Paul answered, which meant he was worse. As though his optimism could stave off death, Paul tended to exaggerate Herb's real or imagined improvement. For sixteen years they had been together, and now Herb's body was attacked by a far more aggressive and new strain of the AIDS virus.

"Come on over for breakfast," Paul called.

"Can't. I have a shipment due at the Gallery. Why don't I cook for you tonight? I'll bring it over," Nora quickly added, knowing that Paul rarely left the house since Herb had returned from the hospital and was now bedridden.

"Hey. There was someone out here last night. Did you notice her?"

Nora was alert to the tension in Paul's voice and his emphasis on the word 'her'. Later she would recall the icy feel of the doorknob in her hand and the prickly wool of the jacket lapel

131

that brushed her cheek as she turned her head in his direction. She had been thinking of spring and the sight of redbuds lighting the rim of the wet forest and anticipating the first whiff of thawing soil still some distance off.

No more than a few yards separated the houses. Each sat perched at the curb and belied the fact that behind was a sweeping yard that meandered toward the edge of a wood.

Paul stood at the foot of his carefully swept steps, dressed in jeans and a Red Sox sweatshirt. His house was smaller and simpler than Nora's but much better kept; and he had gone to the trouble of hanging a Christmas wreath with garland about the windows. The house was painted a dark shade of red, and in summer the back was filled with flowers and shrubs that were the envy of all the county garden clubs.

"Did you get a look at her face? Was she young or old?" Nora couldn't help asking.

"Don't know. If she comes back, we'll call the police."

Paul and Nora were comfortable with one another in the way of long time neighbors and friends. Nora's house had been her grandmother's before her parents moved to Rockport from Belmont. Paul's home had belonged to his mother. They attended Rockport High School together until Paul went on to Harvard and Nora across the Charles to Emerson. The last year of college they shared an apartment. His mother, Paige Marstead, had expressed disapproval, but was secretly relieved, assuming they were lovers, and took her last breath comforted by that fallacy. At fourteen Paul confided to Nora that he was gay.

"Probably just another tourist watching for ghosts in our famous graveyard," she soothed.

"I don't think so. She looked to be watching the house. If I'd learnt sooner I would have chased her away."

"Herb off on another obsessive rant?"

"Off the charts. He hates it when people loiter about. His nurse has evidently told him, although she denies it, and now he's all worked up about this stranger."

An unsettled disquiet slipped past her defenses. Nora walked into the living room and gazed up at the oil above the fireplace, just as a gust of wind off the ocean rattled the windows in their frames.

The Year Between the Wood

Burns Padgett Shiel had painted the portrait at his farm at Wood's End, Massachusetts when Lydia was five. Nora was taller, and older than Lydia. The two sat with their arms touching and their long, windblown hair, two different and distinct shades of red, intertwined as the bright, fractured sun gleamed off the barn behind. Nora was in a cotton sea-foam sun dress with tiny daisies so small they looked like dots, and Lydia wore the same dress in pink.

The portrait was not staged. Lydia's ribbon was half out of her hair and Nora's trailed from her lap. Their socks were soiled from an afternoon of play and the white Buster Brown sandals hopelessly scuffed. The portrait had just been returned to Nora from a tour of the artist's work. As she looked at it now, she knew she would not part with it again for the house seemed particularly lonely with it gone.

As far as Nora knew, except for a cousin and any children he might have, she was the last Dillihunt. There were times when she thought of contacting him, but all she knew of Thorson Dillihunt was that he was the son of a minister who lived in the far western reaches of the state. The trauma of loosing Lydia had brought premature death to her parents and grandmother. There were no scones, no Formosa oolong steeping, and the breakfast china of Chinese Tigers had not been removed from the breakfront since her grandmother had lain in her casket in the living room for a traditional town wake.

Impulsively Nora walked to the kitchen. His phone number was still there, tacked behind a lobster magnet on the refrigerator door. Jared Shiel. Since his first call there had been several messages, none returned.

Nora kicked off her boots and slid up onto the antique butcher block in the center of the kitchen. Although it was hopeless, she lifted the lid of a cookie jar in search of a half packet of cigarettes. She'd stashed them somewhere... and then forgotten and been looking for almost a week now, fairly convinced that Paul had thrown them out.

Nora thought about where she might look next and counted the rings as the coast guard jacket slid to the floor. In their one conversation Jared had identified himself as the nephew of Burns Padgett Shiel, giving them an immediate connection.

"I'm not surprised you don't remember me," he said in that

first unexpected phone call. "If memory serves, I hated girls and resented your visits."

They spoke of the friendship between Nora's mother and his grandfather. One of Burns' biographers had speculated in a recent New Yorker article that the two had become lovers that summer, but both agreed that this was not true. The painting, which, until recently, had never been on tour and appeared in few catalogs, had raised a certain level of interest, not least of all because of the notoriety of the kidnapping. After a while Burns had made a gift of the portrait to their family.

"What are you doing now?" Nora asked, feeling awkward. She wasn't good at aimless conversation.

"I'm a homicide detective."

Nora's guard came up. "Forgive me for being blunt, Jared, but I'm guessing you did not call to reminisce about my mother and your uncle and a summer in which we hardly talked to one another. Exactly why have you phoned?"

"As it turns out I have some time on my hands. Thought I'd take a look at the case and see how I might help."

"What does this have to do with me?" Nora demanded, already resigned to the answer. "My parents are no longer with us. They kept up with the case."

"But not you?" Jared was surprised.

"Look, it's in the past. I'm resigned to the fact that Lydia will never be found."

"I thought I might go through the files. Review evidence in light of all the new technology. Even the age progression photos they are doing now are remarkably accurate."

"And you'll want photos of Lydia. No need; that's already been done?"

"This is different, Nora. By seven a child has seventy percent of their facial growth, and Lydia was six when she disappeared. What the police did was a series of sketches by a composite artist. Potential witnesses do not study or remember a drawing in the same way they do a photograph, and that is precisely what this computer program can produce. A series of actual photographs."

"Do you really think, even in your wildest dreams, that after all this time my sister could possibly be alive?"

There was a pause on the other end of the receiver. Jared was taken aback by her resistance.

"I must tell you that I am profoundly weary of well-intentioned people with useless suggestions which inevitably come to nothing," Nora stated bluntly.

"I am sorry if this opens old wounds for you. Lydia's disappearance inspired me to go into police work. I've never forgotten her."

"And you think I have."

"I didn't say that."

Nora was only half sorry for how she had come across. It was true that she would like answers. After he started therapy Paul had adopted a new vocabulary. He would call this "closure", but Nora doubted if such a thing was possible. The authorities concluded that Lydia had been a victim of a stranger abduction and held out little hope.

Only Nora had doubted, as she witnessed firsthand the burden and ensuing cost of all those unanswered questions. The uncertainty and worse still, imagining Lydia's fate, had tortured each waking thought. The attic was full of gifts from missed birthdays and holidays in the hope that Lydia would be recovered. Just the thought of all those unopened presents, which sat under the Christmas tree each year, made it impossible for Nora to enjoy the festivities.

In their anguish over Lydia, it often seemed her parents had forgotten they had another daughter, and Nora felt a responsibility to be strong and endlessly solicitous of their sorrow. Grief had become a shrine to hope, and in defense, Nora had ceased to feel obsessed with the need for answers. Her sister was dead.

Nevertheless, here she was, dialing the phone number of another crime-obsessed outsider. Why must she put herself through this? Nora's ear began to throb, and she realized how tightly she pressed the receiver to her face.

"Shiel farm, Wood's End, talk fast I'm busy," a male voice said.

"This is Nora Dillihunt calling for Jared Shiel."

"Not here," Thor was taken aback.

"When you see him, tell him I called."

"Should I track him down? Is this important?"

"Not at all. Something happened, but probably wasn't at all to do with the case. Just say ... Say I called. I got his messages and he can ring back or not."

Nora checked inside and behind the breadbox for the cigarettes. Calling Jared Shiel was a mistake. If she let him in it would start all over again. The weirdo free lance journalists obsessed with crime would crawl out of the woodwork expecting her to fall at their feet just because they offered to peel away the scabs.

Paul was thinking of Lydia when he told her about the girl in the lane, but Nora was prepared to forget it. And Jared Shiel too. Someone like him could not even imagine how Lydia's disappearance had altered her family forever. Nothing was ever the same again.

Where were those cigarettes?

None too gently Nora pushed aside the contents of a drawer and ... bingo.

Matches? Her father's lighter? It appeared Paul had even removed the wooden matches to light the gas stove with. His gay lover was dying and his life in general a chaotic mess of dysfunction and he was worried about her getting lung cancer.

Nora caught her reflection in the mirror. Short hair askew, cigarette dangling from chapped lips, no makeup, pointy chin and... oh my. Faded flannel night gown so old it was fraying at the collar. The image wasn't pretty, but examined by her artists eye, Nora thought would make a pretty interesting self portrait. At least it would be accurate.

"You look like hell," she said aloud and shoved the cigarette back into the crumpled pack, breaking it in the process.

Okay, she would consign the nightgown to the rag bag which, from earliest memory, hung on a nail at the cellar door, but she would demand Paul return her father's army lighter and henceforth stop the search for lost cigarette packages.

Nora then leaned very close to her reflection in the mirror.

"You're hanging by a nail. You know it. Paul knows it, and if you let Jared Shiel within five feet of this house, he will too."

Better keep your distance.

CHAPTER TWELVE

By the time New Years had passed, Hank had almost forgotten his dislike of Daria. She had cancelled her last appointment and cancelled again the first week of January and what business there was, was conducted succinctly over the phone. Convinced that Daria had begun to trust him, Hank could not resist once more to scheme. Putting his investigator to work he learned that she lived in a single room in a rundown building on Marlboro Street and had flown into that city directly from Los Angeles. It was further reported that she had been living with Mateo Araujo and that he was acting as her agent, but there was some kind of conflict, and she had left.

When his investigator persuaded the landlord to let him see Daria's room, it was discovered that she lived austerely, with no more than a bed and a table and little clothing. For this reason Hank was fairly astonished when Daria announced that she was buying a condominium that overlooked the Charles and a small cottage on Sanibel Island in Florida. Clearly help was needed if she was to furnish both places. From habit and to be polite, he recommended his wife's decorator and was flabbergasted when, a week later, the decorator called to thank him for the referral.

"Darling," his wife Cynthia oozed, during one of her late morning calls to the office, in which they discussed the logistics of two equally busy schedules and weighing the merits of one invitation over another. "Why didn't you tell me that Daria was a client?"

"Who told you?" he asked, having adopted Daria's wariness, at least where she was concerned.

"Well, you must know, Darling. You recommended Helen, who claims she has exquisite taste. Not mine or yours, you understand. Far too simple a penchant for negative space and less is better and all that rot. But she may authorize Helen to bid for her at the Richmond auction, with no ceiling, if you can imagine."

Hank's thoughts spun ahead. He had not seen a withdrawal

from any of the funds he monitored. Did that mean Daria had even more money? Money that he knew nothing about? The thought of her seemingly endless resources set his pulses racing. With effort he brought his thoughts back to the present.

"We ought to get to know this girl, and I've just had a thought," his wife was saying. "Let's have her to dinner, especially in light of your father's skating connections."

Hank groaned inwardly. He didn't want to hear any more, but Cynthia continued as though she'd just come up with a completely novel idea. "We do already have that party planned, Darling. We could include more skating people and wheel your father down for a brief introduction if he is alert enough. Mateo Araujo's agent has already replied, and we'll include that young sports commentator who visits father so faithfully."

"Believe me when I tell you, Cynthia, Daria is not a client to entertain. She is a recluse of sorts and most decidedly not at all inclined to be social. Do not invite her anywhere."

"But she doesn't sound like a recluse, Darling. If she's buying a house and decorating it, she plans to see and be seen."

"You must tell Helen that she is wasting her time. I can safely assure you that Daria will never buy a thing from her. Why, she doesn't even wear jewelry or makeup."

"But how can you know that? I–"

"Enough, Cynthia!" Hank cut her off and the subject was mutually shifted to more benign topics.

Cynthia had not disputed his judgment, and so Hank was surprised when he opened the door that snowy January evening to see Daria standing under the foyer lights. The house was overflowing with guests. He called them his wife's charity crowd, for they mostly sat on boards of educational institutions, museums, and various other non-profit organizations. Hank had gleaned many clients for his firm from Cynthia's social involvements and had learned it was wise to be on hand whenever his company was required.

The moment Hank looked into Daria's face, he regretted not leaving the door to the help, but he had been passing when the bell sounded, and now he was required to play the reluctant host. One look at her impassive face and all joy evaporated from the evening. To make matters worse, Hank was convinced that

Daria was acutely aware of his discomfort.

For a heartbeat he failed to recognize her. Her luxurious hair glowed with highlights, pulled up with tiny curls let loose at the hairline. She wore a green evening shift and quite fabulous diamond and emerald earrings. He couldn't help notice that her arms were visibly muscled and as though oblivious to the plunging temperature, a mink coat was draped carelessly over one shoulder. The unexpected shift from calculated neglect to stunning elegance made for a dramatic transformation. Hank looked over her shoulder to see a limousine parked at the end of the curving drive and blocking the walk.

"Your man can move the car around back," Hank said when he noticed more guests gingerly picking their way around the vehicle in the snow. He waved in the general direction of the back drive as he took her coat, but she looked beyond him and said nothing. Hank suppressed an urge to slam the door in her face.

"I won't be staying long," Daria retorted as though reading his thoughts.

Despite that assertion she did stay. When later he checked, her car remained inconveniently blocking the front walkway. Hank could not help noticing that Daria visited with uncharacteristic animation, feigned interest in various charities, and smiled as though she might actually be happy. He found that smile disturbing. She even accepted an unlikely invitation to lunch with Joyce Meadows, the elderly wife of Brian Meadows, financier. As much as he disliked Daria, the thought of all that money being handled by someone more capable set Hank's heart racing at a fast clip, and he rushed Cynthia over to charm her way into the conversation, wrestling Daria in another direction.

Hank remained silent as Cynthia greeted Daria like a newly garnered prize, introducing her to others with a smug satisfaction that only, because he knew her so well, did he recognize. Soon his duty as host required his presence elsewhere, and for a time he lost track of Daria, but that absence proved more disconcerting than the task of keeping tabs on her. She was like a different person tonight as she moved from one group to another, laughing and talking with that odd edge of an accent that came and went, the one subtle reminder that she was not American.

This new Daria seemed the antithesis of the severe and composed young woman who was his client. The abruptness of her transformation did not seem to him quite normal. Hank felt anxious. He walked into the dining room and checked the buffet area. He waded through the crowd in the drawing room, and then the living room, and breathed a sigh of relief as he concluded that she had left. Now he could return to enjoying his guests.

It was a successful party, and Hank experienced a burst of pride in Cynthia. No one knew better than she how to combine the right mix of personalities, the right professions, with the current and popular proclivities and trends. Cynthia always claimed that she counted a party productive when people overstayed and became informal, as they did tonight. Guests had spilled into the cavernous foyer, draped themselves over the wide staircase, conversing with enthusiasm, occasional raucous laughter drowning out the music.

Hank caught sight of Lawrence, his English trained butler. The man spoke with a Bronx accent but performed his duties with élan. "Did you see Daria to the door?"

"Who, sir?"

"The redhead in the green dress."

"Oh, her, sir." Lawrence nodded in the direction of the guest coat closet. "But I wouldn't go in there if I were you," Lawrence suggested politely when he saw Hank step forward.

"Why not?"

"The lady is not alone, sir, if you get my drift."

Hank was astounded. The implication was clear, but he could not imagine Daria experiencing passion with any man. His own attraction had been so fleeting that he no longer remembered it and had actually come to think of her as asexual.

"Get them out of there. People will be leaving soon. They'll need their coats!"

"The door is locked, sir."

"As you well know there's a master key around the place somewhere; I don't care how you do it. Just get her out of there and out of the house entirely, if you can do it without insulting her." He thought of telling Cynthia, but he knew she would only be amused at his reaction. "By the way. Who is she with?"

"Miss Daria is with Mateo Araujo."

"The gold medal, the coke commercials, and the winery!" Hank was astonished. Why had he not recognized Mat?

During the evening he and Cynthia had fielded questions about Howard. Some asked to see him, but that would not be allowed.

Occasionally, people called Cynthia to have her ask Howard's opinion on a subject. Always an elitist Cynthia enjoyed getting to know these people. She used the opportunity to learn about the skating world, which she found fascinating and fraught with unusual stories and endless gossip concerning details of people's lives not normally available. It almost made her wish she had a child who skated so she could stay in the loop after Howard died. It was only a question of time, although she hated to think of that happening, since Howard had certainly enriched their lives. He had not only brought her husband business, but had also given her a new area of interest for what she freely admitted was a fairly useless life. If only she'd had a child of her own, she might have been a different person. Maybe, she thought, she and Hank would find a young child to sponsor in skating or some other sport. Maybe she would even invest in a horse and hire an up and coming child prodigy to ride for her. One whose parents would allow her to pull the strings.

Taking these requests for Howard's opinion seriously, Cynthia took detailed notes and promised to call back as soon as she had an answer. When she did, it was her own opinion she rendered, although she did certainly discuss the matter with her father-in-law, who could not even grunt in response. But often, when she talked of skating, an intelligent gleam stirred the cloudy surface of Howard's eyes, and she almost felt him straining toward her, actually seeming to listen intently and taking in each word.

While Cynthia knew it was only her imagination, Hank seemed to believe his father understood far more than his doctors admitted possible. Outside of staff and family members, Howard had only two regular visitors. Both men had known him well through the years, and although she was doubtful in the beginning, she now knew she could trust them to maintain the image of Howard as disabled, but in no way mentally-incapacitated.

Hank stomped off to look for Cynthia, and Lawrence, following instructions, raised his hand to knock on the door just as it opened. Daria looked at him as though it were entirely normal for her to lock herself in a closet with the guest everyone else had been looking to meet. Trained not to react, Lawrence returned the courtesy.

Three hours later Cynthia and Hank Marstead closed the door on the last of their guests. Cynthia looked at Hank with an expression of deep satisfaction. From her perspective the evening was a great success.

"It's charming, really. I do believe we are responsible for rekindling a love affair. Did you recall that Mat Araujo helped Daria escape the clutches of that abusive coach? Lawrence tells me they left together," Cynthia congratulated herself.

Hank did not answer.

"Darling, do say that you are not angry with me for including her. She was a great success. Everyone loved her."

But Hank was reluctant to forgive.

"I don't understand how you could dislike such a delectable creature." Cynthia kicked off her heels and sighed. Automatically Hank bent to pick them up and their hands touched. They never stayed angry with one another for long, and although Cynthia often appeared to defer to Hank, she was actually the stronger personality.

"Come," she said and led him down the hall. It was their habit to retire to the library filled with books they rarely read and sip brandy as they gossiped over a successful evening.

"First let me check on father."

"Let me," Cynthia soothed. "You've been upset, and you need to relax or you'll never sleep tonight."

Howard had lived with them since released from the Hospital after suffering a severe stroke which required round the clock nursing care and ongoing physical therapy.

Hank walked to the row of decanters and selected one. Slowly he poured just the right amount of rich amber liquid into each glass. He placed Cynthia's on the federal walnut table and settled himself in one of the twin chairs that faced the fire. He wrapped his hands around the glass and thought of his father.

The Year Between the Wood

They had spent more time together in the last few years than all of his life. Hank's parents had been divorced when he was a child, and he had spent his school days at Choate and then Harvard and summers near Gloucester, Mass. The Marstead family had a mansion that overlooked Rockport Harbor, and after it was lost by fire, his mother continued to return for an annual vacation, staying with her former sister-in-law, who was also divorced.

Rockport had never been a fashionable place to summer. The coastline was rocky and the beach, by comparison, was postage stamp modest. Hank hated the visits. Most of his friends were at the Cape or traveling, and he had nothing in common with his younger cousin Paul.

Despite his objections his mother, Pearl, was committed to a stay each summer at the rambling cottage on Mill Lane. Pearl spent hours in whispered conversation with his Aunt Paige, and he and his cousin, Paul were left entirely to their own devices. Not until Paul was old enough to sail did Hank resign himself and stop complaining. The two shared a passion for sailing, and this alone redeemed the visits.

Hank would never follow in his father's footsteps to take up skating, either as an athlete, judge, or benefactor. He had to wonder if his mother had not deliberately set out to insure that father and son have nothing in common. Howard Marstead had been a true intellectual. *Committed* and *passionate* were words often used to describe him. He had played tournament chess and collected stamps as a boy and had only begun to skate at the doctor's chance suggestion, after contracting a mysterious illness that left him bedridden for nearly a year.

Hank, on the other hand, collected nothing. Pearl kept her son busy during the summer with camps that emphasized outdoor activities, and his interests rotated randomly with the seasons. Fall was football, winter was basketball, and summer was golf and sailing. From the time he was young he had a personal trainer who taught him the fine points of various sports, and if he had any physical ailments, his mother refused to respond unless he was vomiting or had a raging fever.

She never spoke of her former husband, and Howard never attempted to visit his son. Only as an adult, after his mother had died and Hank unexpectedly became responsible for his father's affairs, was he confronted with a first objective view.

While sorting through the New York apartment that had been his father's principal residence for thirty years, it was immediately evident to Hank that, even with no foreknowledge of the stroke that had so suddenly incapacitated him, Howard's affairs were meticulously organized. Through the years Howard had kept everything, including tax records from the first year he made an income, to every shred of documentation pertaining to his divorce.

Feeling like an intruder, Hank read the terms of his parents' divorce and realized for the first time the lengths at which his mother had gone to gain complete and total custody. Interpreting the legalese that he had grown so good at weaving himself, he concluded that his mother was privy to some sort of unsavory information and may even have resorted to blackmail.

As he pored over the initial documents between his parents' respective attorneys, he was surprised to learn that Howard had begun by insisting on equal custody, a novel idea at that time, when mothers were considered by the courts and society to be the only caregivers for children. Howard modified his demands, asking for alternate holidays and summer vacations, which seemed only reasonable; but his mother's attorney responded with a flat refusal. Then, after more ambiguous correspondence, and just before they were about to go to court to fight a bitter custody battle, everything was settled.

Howard now gave up all claims to his only son. Inexplicably, he doubled his child support payments and agreed to lifelong alimony and maintenance, which would not terminate even if the former Mrs. Pearl Marstead decided to remarry. Hank was curious, but an inward tug of fear prevented him from investigating further, and he was unable to ask his father, who, as a result of the stroke, had lost the ability to speak.

It was a pleasant surprise to learn that Howard was in possession of a sizable estate, including his choice apartment that overlooked Central Park. In contrast, his mother had spent every cent she got her hands on. After her death it was a bitter disappointment for Hank to learn that he was broke. The two homes his mother maintained were heavily mortgaged, and by the time creditors were paid and almost everything sold, nothing remained. All was compounded by the fact that Hank was about to enter law school, and for the first time he took out a school loan and was required to work just to purchase essentials. Hank had no time for his former social life, and only because of Cynthia and her support was he able to keep up appearances.

During that autumn that his mother passed away and as he wrestled with the reality of his new circumstances, it occurred to Hank that he should contact his father and ask for help. He started several awkward letters, which he quickly abandoned; and then impulsively he boarded a train for New York. Train fare back and forth was all he had. He had already walked and hitched several rides down Massachusetts Avenue, over the Charles River toward South Station. Now arriving at Grand Central, he began the long walk to his father's apartment; but the closer he came to his destination, the more reluctant he was to continue. It was a fine fall day. The sun was shining, the air was crisp, and only the thought of his total lack of resources propelled him forward.

When he came to his father's building, several leather suitcases were lined up on the sidewalk. A boy about his own age grumbled about how difficult it was to obtain a taxi in New York, as he ineffectually waved from the curb whenever he saw a flash of yellow amidst the oncoming traffic.

Hank was taken aback by his appearance. His hair was colored a most unnatural shade of mustard and his dark eyes smudged with traces of what could only be liner.

"Where's the doorman when you need him?" the young man complained and lifted a finger haplessly into the air as though checking wind direction.

"You'll never get a cab with that gesture," Hank offered and walked to the door.

"Can't get in without a key or 'less the doorman is standing there. This is an exclusive building," the young man offered.

Hank felt contemptuous of the explanation, acutely aware that he was being looked over in a way that made him feel decidedly uncomfortable. They were about the same height, but vastly different in appearance. Hank wore chinos and an Oxford shirt with his monogram on the cuff. On his feet were loafers, no socks, and he had slung over his shoulder a cordovan leather jacket.

"Just wait and he'll be back. Went up to get more bags. We're off't Europe. Paris and Rome," he offered proudly and then scrutinized Hank's face for a reaction. Disappointed that there was none he turned away and once more gestured for a cab, this time already a block beyond the curb.

Disgusted, Hank walked between two parked cars. Putting two fingers between his lips, he whistled and lifted his arm as a cab stopped at the curb. Behind them the door opened, and the doorman, dressed in mock military uniform followed a tall man with graying hair and finely defined features. There was a feline grace to his bearing, and his manner of walking was both elegant and regal.

"He got us the cab," the young man said, motioning in Hank's direction. Howard placed a hand on the young man's shoulder, and some aspect of this possessive gesture both alarmed and repelled Hank. He watched intently as Howard smiled as though indulging an underling. The Marstead family resemblance was evident. Howard was taller than he, but the cut of the jaw and the eyes were the same. There was little doubt in Hank's mind that he was looking at his father.

"Thank you," Howard's tone was dismissive as he pressed a twenty into Hank's hand. Hank was so stunned that he did not protest, as Howard slid into the back seat of the cab. He stood at the curb and watched the car disappear into traffic and wondered why he had not introduced himself. This first sight of his father had come and gone so quickly that it hardly seemed real. He thought of his mother's years of silence on the subject. Shrugging his shoulders as though he could just as easily shake off his bitter disillusionment, he turned and walked away.

Hank spent the money on two chili dogs and a large coke, purchased from a street vender, and with the food he choked down a profound sense of disappointment. For the first time in his life he felt like an orphan. His mother was dead, and the father he hoped would claim him not only did not recognize him but was also homosexual.

When Hank got the call years later that his father was in the hospital after suffering a severe stroke, he could only wonder why they were calling him. Would his father have put his name down as next of kin? The thought was astonishing. He wondered what to do. It was Cynthia who took over, dutifully conferring with the doctors and Howard's attorney and making daily trips to the hospital to monitor his care.

Both were stunned at the number of letters and cards and hundreds of gifts of flowers that began to arrive at the hospital. The wealth of contacts made that first year as a result of Cynthia's management of her father-in-law's care began to send Hank additional business. Unaware of any previous estrangement, some quickly embraced Hank and his wife as one of their own, all too glad to endear themselves to Howard through this handy conduit of a son.

Hank was amazed to learn from Howard's attorney that under the terms of the will, he was named nearly sole beneficiary of a sizable fortune. The one exception was a plot of land in Rockport that had contained the family home before it burned, which was curiously left to his cousin Paul. When it became obvious that therapy would never restore his father's mental faculties, Hank was appointed legal guardian and given power of attorney.

Hank and Cynthia decided to sell Howard's isolated summer home at Martin Point in Maine. They sold his Austin Sloop, the log cabin in Aspen, and donated his extensive collection of skating memorabilia to the Skating History Museum in Colorado Springs. He and Cynthia kept the Manhattan apartment, which Cynthia determined was outdated and wanted immediately to overhaul and redecorate. Hank felt such a project was premature, so they put the furnishings in storage, making only superficial changes. But slowly the twelve-room apartment filled back up with Cynthia's antique and auction finds. Now they used the premises for entertaining, and Hank stayed over on weekdays when he could not get home to Southampton. It was a convenience he had come to rely on, and only last week he had given Cynthia the go-ahead to begin the renovation project that would put their personal stamp on the place.

The introduction of a father into his life evolved into more than an opportunity to own a valuable piece of New York real estate. Hank actually liked having Howard under his roof. On Sundays they took breakfast together, and Hank read the Times aloud, imagining shared interest; and he rarely went to bed, no matter how late, without looking in and planting a kiss on that sandpaper brow.

Hank convinced himself that Howard liked his company and looked forward to that private time together. He enjoyed having others ask after Howard. "My father," he would say, liking the sound of those words and with a vague sense of how not having that parent had left a hole in his heart, now partially filled by the possessive utterance of a child's desperately coveted phrase.

He and Cynthia hired round-the-clock nursing companions and refitted one of the guestrooms for physical therapy. They hung a lift over the pool so that his flaccid body could be lowered into the heated water for his daily constitutional. Hank even installed an elevator that went directly to Howard's third floor quarters. In some way that he could not explain, the old man with the impaired faculties and faulty, aimless attempts at speech became the child he and Cynthia never had, and his dependence and presence added a new dimension and even depth to their marriage.

It seemed to Hank that Cynthia was taking a long time. His own brandy was nearly gone when she walked into the room. He did not allow himself to think much of the past, and his thoughts had evoked a discomforting state of mind. Hank was relieved when he saw that Cynthia had changed into a dressing gown before going in to see father. This, he decided, was what kept her so long, but as she stepped into the light there was an odd, unfamiliar expression on her face. Time seemed to slow for Hank, and he wanted to stand but could not. Cynthia came to him immediately and knelt at the edge of his chair. Hank felt the first infringement of fear curl an icy grip over his thoughts. He almost knew what she would say.

"I'm sorry, Darling. I am so sorry for you, but father has left us. He is now in heaven and no longer suffering. You must think of him in this manner, Darling. Do you understand what I am saying, Hank?"

"But he was fine," Hank choked. "The doctor was just here and said his heart was strong, and he could live another twenty years, and where was his nurse? Why didn't he call us?"

"Father was put to bed and thought to be sleeping. This is how painlessly and simply he left us. I myself believed he was sleeping until I kissed his cheek," she lied leaving out a salient detail until later, after Hank had absorbed this first shock.

"But why? How could this have happened?"

"He was not well, Hank. You know that." She spoke to him as if he were a child. Her love and grief reached out to him, and Hank responded. He pulled her up until she sat on his lap and he buried his head in the softness of her breasts, and she wrapped her arms about his back and smoothed his thinning hair.

It was then that Hank felt an almost electric stab of alarm. Invited though she was, she had almost been an intruder. He saw her that way. The hairs on the back of his neck rose, and despite the warmth from the fire he shivered and thought of Daria. Why, at this precise moment should he think of Daria?

Alexandra Clair

PART THREE

CHAPTER THIRTEEN

PAUL

Paul's delivery was dispassionate as he informed his psychiatrist about the abuse, explaining that it had nothing at all to do with his current problems. Although it was completely unnecessary, he was willing to subject himself to a little psycho-babble for the sake of Herb, his long time partner. He was fine. There was nothing wrong with him, only with the relationship, since Herb tended to be critical and wanted him to change a few of his habits.

"Like what?"

"Like, he cannot do the laundry because he's too careless. I could do the laundry, but I hire it done and they know what I like. He thinks I'm a snob. So if he does launder, I have it sent out again. He claims he can't find what he needs which is a gross exaggeration. He says I drive him crazy."

"What else?"

Paul sighed, knowing how he sounded to people who didn't understand. "I buy our underwear at the new year. Three hundred and sixty five pieces and I throw them out after one use."

"Yes?"

"He thinks it a waste. You probably do too."

It mattered not at all to Herb that the clothes in his closet be arranged by color and style, or that the cups on the shelf have their handles pointing out for easy access, or a thousand other details of organization. Paul believed that Herb's unwillingness to be tolerant was unreasonable. A symptom of the neglected state of the relationship which could easily be repaired.

"You mean," the doctor asked, "you could change any of these habits?"

They got around to the subject of his childhood. With some

151

reluctance but amused by his own rendition of the story, and inviting his doctor to be equally entertained, Paul admitted that his need for a controlled, predictable environment might be remotely associated with his experience of being molested as a child. He then apologized for presenting such a transparent and unchallenging case and promptly changed the subject. Child molestation was too much of late in the public lexicon, and Paul confessed to feeling like a cliché when he discussed the subject which, except with Nora, he never had. After some months, the doctor suggested hypnosis, which Paul adamantly rejected, convinced that he recalled most of the experience anyway, which was in no way impacting his current problems. The relationship with Herb, he reminded his doctor on numerous occasions, was why he was there. Still it was proving difficult to keep his doctor on track and away from subjects Paul had long since stopped dwelling on, if in fact he ever had. Why think about the past anyway? To what purpose and to what end?

Therapy was no longer a diversion to appease Herb. Nevertheless, Paul continued to return for nearly a year. Herb was worth the effort. He seemed impressed by Paul's supposed sacrifice on his behalf and had threatened to leave if he stopped. Now Herb would never leave, and, for a while at least, Paul felt safe canceling more appointments with his doctor than he kept.

Still, he thought about it. Even as he denied that he did, he couldn't help himself. It was as if therapy and his doctor's gentle, incessant prodding had opened a fissure that would not be closed. At odd moments, when he least expected it, he was besieged by memories, which threatened more memories, and it became exhausting work to monitor that floodgate. Of late he felt his emotions were captive prisoners of that intellectual record keeping of the mind that paraded images of what he most wanted to forget. Paul knew he should have the power to shut that visual slide-show down, but increasingly found that he could not.

As a child Paul had loved the boathouse. It was a large musty building with the ocean lapping under half the floor when the tide was up. The place was filled with long forgotten treasures. There were spools of twine, torn nets, a half disassembled Johnson outboard and even an old lobster cage, and above all, suspended from large grappling hooks, a row of dinghies. Paul was able to climb the ladder at the inside of the building, which went up into the rafters. From there he crawled on hands and knees across a support beam until he could drop into the highest boat. It was a perfect place to be. In heightened excitement, Paul lifted away a corner of the tarp. The outside of the boat was a weathered blue, his favorite color, but the inside was painted a fresh, pristine white.

Paul stocked the interior with supplies. A jar of peanut butter, match box cars and baseball cards; a flashlight, sticks of whale bone from an old corset resurrected from the attic, a rabbit foot, a pocket knife and a few of his favorite books, the current being, "Treasure Island." His mother thought he read too much. She called him a solitary boy and often chased him outside.

After Paul discovered the dinghy, he didn't mind at all. He knotted a rope and secured it over the rafters. When it was time to descend, he could swing down and around and land on a pile of nets in the corner of the boathouse.

He got the idea from watching Tarzan, the Jungle Boy. On television this neat trick appeared easy, but on that first day the jarring realization of just how far from the floor he actually was struck Paul with the force of a paralyzing weight. In panic, he struggled to regain his place in the hull of the boat, but it swung out from under him, and he was forced over the edge. Breath fled from his chest in a rush of air, and with what seemed like great speed, he found himself standing miraculously below on two legs barely able to support his weight.

It was a frightfully thrilling experience making him feel invincible, intensely alive, and immensely capable. After that first day Paul perfected his technique until he had mastered the fine points of a smooth drop. Sometime later, Uncle Howard found him in the boathouse.

"I'll have to tell your mother," he said. "She wouldn't approve. It's far too dangerous."

"Oh, please don't," Paul had pleaded.

It started that summer, although Paul could not say precisely which summer or how old he was, but he was certain it hadn't lasted very long. It started with inappropriate holding and then touching. When Paul threatened to tell his mother, he was threatened in return. Uncle Howard would harm his mother, and in order to demonstrate how simple the matter and how this could be accomplished, he began to leave tortured chipmunks for Paul to find in strategic places like the cab of his Tonka dump truck and even his shoe, which he then had to chase down the rotting smell of and make up a story that explained the loss of new loafers.

Howard informed Paul that when his mother learned the truth, she wouldn't want him anymore and would get another child. A boy that she could love better. But Paul knew that his mother could not have any more children. She had already confided this. If Uncle Howard could be wrong about such an important detail, he could be wrong about everything else.

When the abuse games escalated, Paul decided he would go to live with his father in order to both escape the torment and put his mother out of harm's way. All the gifts of toys went largely unappreciated because he had plenty, but his mother monitored his diet with a vengeance so the candy was at first a distraction. Soon he hated to wake in the morning, and nothing could dislodge the stone of immense reluctance that constricted his child's heart and robbed his life of peace.

Paul understood something important. Howard wore a mask, and when his mother swept into the room and kissed her brother's cheek, she had no idea of the danger she was in. Paul alone, in the entire world, knew that beneath the outward friendliness of that handsome countenance lived the monster of nightmares come to life.

If only his mother could see, then she too would recoil in disgust and horror. But Howard's face remained perfectly disguised. Each morning that fixed mask smiled at mother and son from across the fruitwood French breakfast table, a cunning and constant reminder of the snare that had trapped his spirit and threatened to destroy his mother by mere association.

To have his tormenter under the same roof and all around him, rooted in the routine of any summer, seemed a cruel parody. Paul began to suffer nightmares, unexplained bouts of anger, and a penchant for having all in his room arranged in a particular order. This work kept him in the house and out of Howard's reach for precious long hours, and it was this proclivity which dogged him, even into adulthood.

Paige Marstead lacked the patience to extract confidences.

She abhorred being alone, preferred to be the center of any gathering and liked the sound of her own voice. After weeks of vigilant surveillance, Paul finally found her at the far end of the dock during a time when Howard had taken the train up to Boston.

For the wealth of details, Paul recalled the incident more clearly than any other of his young life and described it for his psychiatrist. The tide was out and Paige had removed her stockings, which sat rolled in a ball in her lap. She leaned back on her arms, her head tilted toward the sun, eyes closed.

As he walked toward her, ever so slowly, putting one deliberate foot in front of the other, Paul had never been so scared. His neck felt hot and his palms wet, and his breath came uneven with a loud roar to the internal place of his hearing. The sun was behind them, and when he stood beside her she smiled, her blue eyes bright amidst the tan, freckled skin of summer. Paul sat beside her and concentrated on details rather than on what he would say or how he would say it.

Paige Marstead was careless with her clothing, and yet it was nothing for her to spend exorbitant sums on her wardrobe. Today she seemed unaware of how the wood of the dock could tear tiny holes in the gossamer overskirt of her dress, but Paul was acutely aware, and he worried and thought of this as he attempted to summon the courage to speak.

She wore the white strapless dress from Worth. Paul had been with her, sipping apple juice from a highball glass, when the model emerged from the dressing room. Paige often asked her son's opinion, and when he said he loved the dress, a word he reserved for the very best, she bought it on the spot, right off the model's back. The white skirt had an iridescent overlay of blue with silver flecks that sparkled when she moved, and her silver sling-back pumps, with the three-inch heels, sat between them like diamonds on the weathered gray planks of the dock.

Paige would be attending the ritual Saturday dance at the yacht club, and already a recently delivered corsage of pink tea roses had preceded her escort's arrival. Paul would be ushered in to shake hands with her date, one of several she had known in college or from one club or another; and like a 'little man', he would stand back and watch as the corsage was affixed to his mother's wrist or bodice.

155

In the quiet hush of a gathering twilight, mother and son looked out at the flats and the gleaming sea beyond, and until she spoke, Paul felt certain she had forgotten he sat beside her.

"Pretty, isn't it?" his mother asked. "When the tide is out of the inlet, you can almost forget the sea and think we have a river."

"I've decided to go live with father," Paul announced.

"You'll be visiting next month, dear."

"No, I mean forever. Go to school there and live there."

"But why, Darling? I wouldn't give you up. You are my own precious boy. You are all that I have." These were the words Paul longed to hear, and yet the monster had made him doubt they would ever be spoken.

Paul kept his voice neutral. He tried to imitate the unconscious tone of authority his mother used when conferring with the help.

"I'll ask Marta to pack for me," Paul said and began to stand. "I can be gone by tomorrow if you'll just call and make the arrangements."

An expression of alarm came over Paige's face. Paul's father was a concert violinist who was rarely home. He and Paige had already decided to separate when Paul was conceived in one last futile burst of intimacy. They divorced before he was actually born, and each summer Paul spent three weeks with his father and new wife. Immediately the new marriage produced two children who absorbed his father's attention with a devotion that excluded Paul. Eventually, when he was older, Paul would refuse the visits and adopt his mother's maiden name of Marstead. She did not see why she should object, and his father did not protest too long or too hard. Nevertheless, at this juncture of her child's life, Paul's request seemed very odd indeed.

Paige coaxed the truth from Paul and was duly horrified, but on some level not surprised. A few months before, Howard's wife had divorced him; and for reasons which Paige could not understand, Howard had given up all parental rights while paying a fortune in child support and maintenance. Howard had insisted the family have no contact with his former wife whom he accused of driving him to a nervous breakdown. The charges against Pearl were many but on the whole insignificant, and the entire affair was baffling to Paige who, by virtue of her sex, was left out of family business which favored the men over the women. Still Paige was curious and knew that there had been something about the divorce that had to be covered up, raising more questions than could easily be answered.

It was true that Howard was harried that summer. He seemed unusually preoccupied, easily angered, and prone to solitary drinking spells that he tried to conceal. Only the sight of little Paul seemed to cheer him. Not in the know, Paige believed Howard was mourning the loss of his own son, Hank, and felt only compassion for her eldest brother. By the time they left the dock that summer day, the tide was in and the lights from the house came up and fell across the manicured lawn and down to the dock where mother and son sat talking. Paige's escort had come to the door and been sent away. Now the sea hit his mother's ankles, but Paul, who was small for his age, had to scoot to the edge of the dock and lift himself down while his mother held his arms, just to have it brush the soles of his feet.

She would not allow him out of her sight until her brother left the house late that night. Any fledgling doubt and tendency to denial had been squelched by a candid conversation with her former sister-in-law, Pearl Marstead. With Paul in tow Paige had sequestered herself in the library. Paul would never forget the look of utter horror that came over her face as she listened to what was related from the other end of the line.

Perhaps, Paul had speculated to his psychiatrist, it was because Paige had handled his experience with such swift and certain intervention that it was easy to forget. She had gathered him into the tight embrace of her arms and informed him that evil people did exist, often appearing deceptively normal, and a child could not be expected to know the difference. When he tried to speak and tell of his experience, she hushed his words in a flood of her own. Over and over again in those first hours, with the library door locked, she encouraged him to think of all that had transpired as a bad dream; a nightmare of no importance that must be put immediately out of mind and never thought of again. To illustrate her point she picked up a book and placed it out of sight, under the cushion of a nearby sofa.

Paige Marstead took responsibility entirely upon herself. "A mother should know," he heard her lament. "Why didn't I know?"

The pathetic plea of her voice was a long whine of despair that confirmed for Paul that he was permanently scalded. When she pulled him against her, he stiffened in her arms. Her manner and the convoluted rhetoric of her ranting had consigned his pain to ash and hers to fire. He never trusted her again.

Finally Paige picked up the phone and called her father, Samuel Marstead the elder, not to be confused with his namesake and youngest son who was also an attorney. This was a call that Paul knew his mother hoped to avoid, for they all lived in reasonable intimidation of his seemingly limitless power and resources. Paul sat under the desk and fiddled with the silver strap of her shoe and counted the lines in the wood grain and the red sword shapes in the Persian carpet.

Of everything that happened, the bleed-through of this memory had begun to haunt Paul and especially of late.

The old man's cultured tone was so uncharacteristically loud and demanding that it shattered Paul's impression of his grandfather as almost god-like; a man above the fray of ordinary humanity.

"You will not report this!" he demanded.

"I'm his mother. It's my job to protect my son and I failed. I'm calling the police and having him arrested."

"Do that and you'll find yourself seriously discredited, cut off from every penny. Can you seriously see yourself supporting Paul as a single parent making minimum wage in some dead end job."

"Something has to be done," Paige yelled and sobbed simultaneously. "You could have told me. Howard was under this roof and you said nothing."

"We'll take care of this internally as we always do. Your brother Samuel will talk with Howard. He'll handle this, and you will let him."

"My Paul will need to see someone."

"I'll select the counselor and you just mother him and make him forget. You have no other choice, my dear. Be careful. Be very, very careful."

"Is that a threat?"

"If you want to protect your son, you'll cooperate with how things are done. Am I making myself clear?"

When finally Paul fell asleep, Paige was still on the phone, the emotionally charged tone of her conversation deflected by the web of his withdrawal.

"We have a situation here," the elder Samuel Marstead said to his youngest son, also Samuel.

"What now."

"Howard ... he went after Paul and Paige is livid. We all agreed to keep both Hank and Paul out of it; we'd groom them for another track."

"Has Paul been programmed to keep our secrets?"

"Yes, but he's never been tried and tested as you children were," the elder Marstead answered.

"Okay then. Reinforce that. Send him to that school buddy from Harvard days. He's one of us, I believe, though different family group. Still in Cambridge and a practicing psychiatrist, the right sort all-round."

"I'll call him tomorrow. But I want Paige on a tight leash. She's my daughter, but she's also a fool and a mother. I don't want her drinking too much and spilling secrets all over the place. And I don't want her in Italy especially. No more trips to Europe for her; take her passport away. Tell her we'll know if she gets another, in which case she'll find herself with no monetary support, and I'll take Paul away. Make it very clear."

"What about Howard?" Samuel the younger asked. He sat up in bed, and the man beside him stirred and turned on the light. "Talking to my father," he whispered with his hand over the receiver.

"You sit him down and scare the living day lights out of him. Call old man Woods and have him picked up. A few weeks at the farm in Wood's End, and he's successfully hobbled. I hate to do that to one of my own ... "

"I understand, father. He is what he is. We can't fix him. But he has to learn not to defecate in his own backyard."

"And I want Howard to lower his profile. Check out who his proclivities have him associating with these days. I want no one in his life that isn't tied in some way to us."

"Consider it done, Father. Now go back to sleep. I'll drive out to Rockport and meet with Paige myself tomorrow."

"Thank you."

"Good night."

Paul saw the psychiatrist in Cambridge, a former classmate of grandfather Marstead. All that Paul ever remembered of those sessions was walking in the door and walking out. From Paul's perspective the appointments were bearable only because his mother allowed a stop at Brigham's on the way home. Here he was indulged with the rare luxury of a huge chocolate sundae with coffee ice cream and a mountain of whipped cream. As he devoured his sundae, his mother sipped her raspberry Ricky, and they talked of the Red Sox player she was currently dating and the boat she would buy him when he was old enough. They talked of school and books and a trip to Disneyland. Paige wanted her 'old happy boy' back, and Paul did his best to oblige.

Almost immediately, mother and son had come to a tactical agreement, the complicated details of which never really had to be discussed. After that first evening on the dock where he had finally confided in his mother, they would never speak of the events of that summer again. He learned to act the resilient child his mother told him he was. It was the Marstead way after all, to bounce back quickly from adversity, or so the Latin phrase on their family crest proclaimed. Dutifully, Paul expunged from his mind as much as possible, as quickly as possible, never reckoning a later price for that premature gloss of peace.

Fall was well advanced when mother and son said goodbye to the fieldstone mansion on the hill. Leaves lay a patchwork quilt over the ground, and shiny wet trails of red and gold snaked into the wood, leveling each depression. They left the boathouse, the private cove, and most difficult of all for his mother, the luxury of a car and driver. True to his promise, grandfather Marstead settled a trust fund on Paul and purchased the house on Mill Lane. The house was not Paige's choice for she considered it far too modest, while her allowance, controlled by her brother, Samuel, in how funds could be spent, proved more than sufficient.

Although Howard was the sinner, Paige felt that she was unjustly punished as was the way among men and women in their family group. Women bore the children and male ancestors were reincarnated into the bodies of subsequent generations. Or so they believed. Most galling of all, Howard, after a period away, was thereafter welcomed back home as she was not.

Paul welcomed the move and almost immediately met his next-door neighbor as she was outside pruning her roses. Grandmother Dillihunt took one look at Paul and decided that he wasn't entirely normal, and it was her job to help. She told him he was always welcome, and with the literal mind of a child, Paul began to spend more time in her kitchen than his own. The next summer Paul met Nora and Lydia.

"I have two little granddaughters who come each summer. You'll like them," Grandmother Dillihunt informed Paul over hot gingersnaps and milk.

"Where are they now?" Paul had asked. It had been a long silent winter and hard, in that small house, to escape his mother's scrutiny. The baseball player had left, and she was dating a banker from Boston, a business associate of Grandfather Marstead, and for some reason she had taken to confiding in her son details of her relationships that he would have preferred not to know and did not always understand.

Despite school, Paul felt lonely and disconnected from the world in general, although he often crossed the narrow yard to visit with Grandmother Dillihunt. She was a no-nonsense sort of woman who preferred listening to talking. The silences between them were often prolonged, although entirely welcome so that neither seemed to mind.

"They live outside Boston and come for the summer," she answered his question. "They'll be here at the end of June. Those two wouldn't miss the parade and the bonfire and the fireworks on July fourth. Not for the world." Grandmother Dillihunt laughed at the thought of her two granddaughters, and intrigued, Paul laughed in return.

With great expectation Paul awaited their arrival. In some ways, he already felt he knew the girls since Grandmother Dillihunt had let him play with their toys, and he had read many of Nora's books. He and his mother had been invited to join the Dillihunt's for their traditional Fourth of July dinner of salmon, creamed onions with peas, and strawberry shortcake.

Paul was sitting on the steps when they first turned down the lane. The family came on foot and the luggage followed later in the town's only cab -- a flat bed truck that existed solely for the purpose of ferrying the luggage of the summer folks from the train station. Mr. Dillihunt wore a suit, and the girls were formally dressed in hats with white gloves. Within the hour the formal clothes had disappeared, not to be worn again until church on Sunday and then the trip home two months later. Paul wondered why they couldn't live all year in Rockport, never dreaming he would someday get his wish with tragic consequences.

What Paul remembered most from that first meeting was that Nora punched his arm so hard it left a bruise, and he tripped her going up the steps, resulting in a scraped knee. Instead of crying she scrunched her face in a fleeting demonstration of pain before bestowing on him a dramatic look of withering disdain. The battle of stares that ensued resulted in a tie, and for the remainder of the summer the two were inseparable.

What Paul remembered about Lydia was that she was beautiful. Her skin was a porcelain shade of ivory, absent the freckles that scattered across the bridge of Nora's nose. Her red hair shone in the sun and was a prettier shade than her sister's, and her green eyes were vibrant and alive.

Immediately she complained of being left out, and Paul recalled Grandmother Dillihunt patiently explaining that before long she would find some friends her own age. Although this was true, Lydia was never satisfied. Red rover, pirate ship off the raft, and stick ball and tag, in which the smaller, younger Lydia was often 'it', was not her idea of fun. She whined when she was not included and cried and complained even more when she was. In all their dealings with Lydia, Paul and Nora unfailingly emerged in the wrong and often found themselves standing side by side as they explained their side of the story. The inevitable result was an enduring lifelong bond of friendship.

One incident concerning Lydia stood out in Paul's mind with certain clarity, and when he thought of her he often recalled it. On a rainy day, Nora had taken the train with her mother to see the family dentist. Paul spent the afternoon doing Lydia the very great favor of indulging her with his company. No one but his own mother had ever been so thrilled to have him all to herself. They played with Lydia's Barbie dolls and rearranged the furniture in her dollhouse. They dressed the neighborhood cats in party dresses, tied makeshift leashes to miniature chairs, and served them a special concoction of tuna and milk out of Grandmother Dillihunt's green and white breakfast china. Paul was impressed with the scope of his generosity and her admiration.

Later, as though to confirm this impression of himself, Mr. Dillihunt had thanked him for entertaining Lydia, as though the whole experience of dressing up the neighborhood cats and playing with dolls must have been entirely abhorrent. Mr. Dillihunt had shaken his hand and treated him with a respect that was foreign to Paul.

Paul came to love the Dillihunt family. He liked the wonderful cooking smells that emanated from Grandmother Dillihunt's kitchen. He liked the structure of bedtime and meals at specific hours. "You better watch out," Nora would mouth behind her mother's back in anticipation of the inevitable warning should one fail to cooperate with clearly defined expectations.

When Nora's mother announced bedtime, Paul got in the habit of returning home and climbing into his own bed. His mother had stopped imposing these sorts of restrictions and the first night thought him lost and never thought to check his room as she rallied the neighbors for an inconvenient midnight search. Nora's mother suggested that he might actually be asleep as all normal children were at this hour. The neighbors crowded the small doorway of his bedroom, as his mother scolded and informed him that only boring people with not an ounce of creativity retired so early.

Paul especially liked Mr. Dillihunt, who was a man of few words, always with a book under one arm. He used his cane with the skill of another appendage, which had become a necessity after returning from the war as a young man. At Nora and Lydia's request he would roll up one pant leg, and to squeals of exaggerated horror, exhibit the ugly scars that encircled his shattered kneecap and puckered the skin down to his foot in an ugly, trailing burn scar. Sometimes the girls would not pretend horror at all but would ask for an explanation, and he would use that occasion to tell them a story about trusting God. Because of

Mr. Dillihunt's resolute faith, Paul never doubted the existence of God.

He had his own corner in the front room with a large leather chair and a pipe stand with gleaming pipes of various woods and each with a different smell. He always had time for his daughters and since Paul and Nora were inseparable, for Paul as well. They sat on his lap, and he read them books and he graciously limped around the backyard croquet wickets with the three of them. He liked nothing better than to sleep in the sun at the beach and, more agile in the water than anywhere else, he often swam with them out to the raft.

When weekends came and he was expected back from the city, the entire house was hushed and focused on his arrival. Special foods were cooked, and Mrs. Dillihunt turned herself out in bright Lilly sun dresses with white lace trim contrasted against her tan, and the delicate scent of citrus trailing in her wake. She was as thrilled as the girls to welcome him but would stand back as they rushed into his arms.

In those first moments, over the heads of Lydia and Nora, Paul noticed that Mr. Dillihunt never took his eyes off his wife. That they loved one another was a silent certainty, the glue of their security. It was something to aspire to, but deep inside Paul suspected he could never be clean enough or good enough to deserve a similar prize. This family that he had come to love and wished desperately were his entirely and permanently, could make him forget for a little while the gnawing sense of worthlessness, but not for long. No confluence of carefully spun logic could convince his child's mind that he was not damaged. Planted in the dark recesses of unresolved trauma, the evil rhetoric of his tormenter, restive in sleep, was a perpetual hibernating threat.

Sometimes Mr. Dillihunt would look at him in mock exasperation and say, "In a house full of women we men must stick together, right Paul?"

He pushed Paige to allow Paul sailing lessons and golf lessons, often saying, "I'll have a little talk with your mother." And they had career talks. "Some children, you know what they'll grow up to be," he would confide. "Now, Lydia will have a career until she settles down and has children. Nora loves art and will never give that up. But you, Paul. We have to give this some real thought, because you'll see so many choices that it will be hard for you to decide. That's how smart you are. The world's your oyster, my boy."

And Paul, listening attentively, wished he could confide in Mr. Dillihunt, but that was not possible. He didn't have the words. He didn't understand enough to begin, and this feeling only increased his isolation.

One year for his birthday, he was given a dark blue Bible with his name engraved in gold letters. Paul saw right away that it was a grownups book and this pleased him. Inside Nora's father had written: *For by grace you have been saved through faith, not of yourselves, it is a gift of God, not as a result of works least anyone should boast (Ephesians 2: 8, 9).*

What did those words mean? He asked his mother.

"We can't have that book in this house. I'll return it for you."

But she never did since Paul kept it well hidden. Paul had never regained any measure of respect for his mother, so he tended to believe Mr. Dillihunt, who had encouraged the three children to memorize passages of Scripture. Long into adulthood, the words of various verses and passages would flash to mind, and when they did, he was transported back in time, a small boy taller than Lydia and the same height as Nora standing before a proud Mr. Dillihunt, reciting in the sing-song way that children have, their voices joined in unison, confident of praise. *For God so loved the world that he gave his only begotten son that whoever believes in him should not perish, but have everlasting life (John 3:16).*

Scripted by the deep recesses of a scarred identity, Paul was convinced his life course had been permanently hijacked. Compulsions merged with lifelong habits, separating him forever from the boy Mr. Dillihunt had loved. Out of reach were the attributes and character Paul had most wanted to emulate and he often wondered what Nora's father would say or do; or worse still, make of him today. Knowing that he would somehow still be loved made the contradictions all the harder to accept.

With Mr. Dillihunt Paul had been admitted to some exclusive club that Nora and Lydia were exempted from simply because they were female. He felt safe with Nora's family, and especially her father, in a way that made him forget; allowing the stronghold of misplaced shame to relax its grip. Paul never doubted that if Mr. Dillihunt had really been his father, Howard Marstead would have suffered the consequence of exposure and all that went with that.

Mr. Dillihunt had loved him easily and truly, and when he roughed his hair or slapped his back, or reprimanded him for not being patient enough with Lydia, Paul was happy just to be basking in the center of that masculine attention.

When Mr. Dillihunt died of a heart attack four years after Lydia's disappearance, Paul grieved as though for a real father; the only father that ever counted. He was inconsolable all of that long winter and even now visited the gravesite, while Nora hardly at all. The loss was one that faded in freshness but never in sincerity; the past anchor of love securing a goodness which sustained Paul when depression might otherwise overwhelm him.

CHAPTER FOURTEEN

When Herb became sick this last time, Paul stopped making time for his psychiatrist. Regardless of how often he was assured otherwise, he felt certain that when he was gone, Herb tended to do worse, and so he made his forays away brief and infrequent. Herb lay with his emaciated frame propped up on a snowy white pillow. He'd lost all of his wonderful glossy black hair and his expressive brown eyes appeared unusually large.

"Have you tested?" he asked Paul.

"You know that I have."

"And you're fine?"

"I AM fine."

"You're certain, are you?"

"Very certain."

"Maybe you should get tested again."

Paul suppressed his irritation. Lately Herb's mind had begun to wander. He often focused on an idea or thought, only to need constant reassurance of the same answer. The idea that plagued him today was testing. Yesterday it had been a weather report of flooding in California, but Herb seemed unable to make the distinction that Massachusetts was on the opposite coast.

The very worst occurred just before the holidays. A substitute nurse, unaware of Herb's tendency to obsess, had looked out the window and seen the girl who had stood out in the lane for much of the night. She'd waited until shift change to tell Paul, but Herb was already upset, demanding they call the police. For two days he insisted she was dangerous and made the outrageous claim that she had entered the house and stood over his bed.

Paul had crushed an extra sedative and put it in Herb's tube feeding. Connor, his good friend and the only doctor in town, had warned of personality changes as the virus invaded Herb's brain. Paul could not accept this, telling Nora that these symptoms of confusion were only a temporary result of new medications and terrible side effects that sometimes wreaked havoc on Herb's ability to cope.

Paul took Herb's hand. The skin was paper thin and black and blue from endless probes with IV needles. Connor, Herb's doctor, was due to stop by in the afternoon. The plan was to insert a permanent shunt so that Herb would no longer be tortured by the painful search for a vein strong enough to infiltrate without soon collapsing.

Paul saw the frown form over Herb's face. He saw Herb struggle to put the words in sequence. Just as he opened his mouth to ask yet again if he had been tested, Paul changed the subject.

"Nora's going to make you that bread pudding you like so much."

"With caramelized brandy?" Herb whispered the deep masculine tones of his voice now painfully frail. Paul missed that rich, firm voice which had been such an important part of his life for so long. He nodded and tried to smile.

"Nora never liked me."

"Of course she likes you. She loves you."

"Nora loves you, not me." Herb sounded resigned. "She thinks you're too good for me. Just like everyone else in this god-awful town."

"I thought you liked this town."

"Well, it's not New York, is it?"

Paul refrained from answering. He walked around the foot of the bed to look at the IV bag. He drew into a syringe the correct dosage of an anticoagulant that would prevent blood clots from forming and inserted it into the catheter. Since Herb's illness, he and Nora both had acquired a host of skills they never imagined they would need.

Paul did not try to reassure Herb that he was wrong about Nora. It was impossible these days to reason with Herb, and in any case, he was certain that despite a tenuous, sometimes rocky beginning, she had grown genuinely fond of him. Paul had done all he could to prepare Nora for that first meeting, but still she had looked at Herb in incredulous disbelief, almost as though she were regarding a bizarre science exhibit. Herb was so unlike any of Paul's former partners, and her instant perplexity, if not shock, was obvious. Paul smiled to think of it now.

"I need to remind you," Paul had said. "Appearances can be

deceptive, and I'm planning to do a complete overhaul."

"What is he, a used part for one of your boats?" Nora had asked as they cut through the cemetery to Peg Legs, where they would meet Herb for lunch.

"Stop being cruel. I love him. Don't spoil this for me by being too practical."

"You just met him. How can you love him?"

"Three months can be a very long time, and besides, you're jealous because you've never been in love!"

Nora punched his arm, and he ducked away.

"True. You fall in love too quickly, and I not at all. Which, I ask, is worse? While you cry and agonize, I can at least sleep nights. Just do me one favor, Paul. This time proceed cautiously. Don't commit yourself too quickly. It seems that only yesterday I was sweeping up the pieces of your last broken heart."

"I'm going to ask him to move in. I'm tired of traveling to New York every weekend just to be with him. I hate that city."

"Do you mind if I get quietly drunk at lunch? So I don't have to watch you make a complete fool of yourself without a little liquid reinforcement."

"You worry too much, and you've never been drunk in your life, Nora."

"I have to worry. You worry about the wrong things and when it comes to men, you have a blind spot where your common sense ought to be."

"Don't be so dramatic," Paul chided.

Nora did not think she was overreacting. Unlike her, Paul could barely tolerate being alone and seemed to need the drama of a new romantic interest on a regular basis. He was able to keep his friends forever, but not so his partners; seeming to reject the more stable relationships, craving instead those fraught with drama and tension. If she was reading between the lines of Paul's glowing description correctly, this great love of his life, the one destined to last forever, sounded like a street punk. Too much like what Paul himself had sometimes characterized as rough trade. A type he claimed he could never be attracted to but had slowly been gravitating towards for a very long time.

Nora had given up trying to stem the self-destructive slide inherent in a lifestyle she neither understood nor approved. But her love and dashed hopes for Paul and herself, the conflicted trauma of their shared past, and her respect for the integrity that colored all other aspects of his life, was a fierce bond that would not be broken.

When Nora was truly tormented by the consequences of Paul's choices and her total helplessness to protect him, she would pray, *God you must have a plan. Whatever it is please tell me, because only you can heal Paul from whatever it is that requires he be hurt to feel alive.*

When Nora turned to God at these moments of trial and uncertainty, she felt guilty. She had spent her early life attending church and yet now rarely went. Even as she prayed, she knew something more. Her parents and grandmother had shared an intimacy with Jesus Christ that she could not claim, and yet tenuously she held on to the conviction that God was personal and real; and if she could just shed the bitterness of the past, and if God could truly forgive her for abandoning Lydia, then He might actually love her the way he apparently loved others.

Herb was already seated at a reserved table when Nora and Paul walked into the restaurant. Herb shook Nora's hand and sensed Paul's scrutiny as he made the introduction. Right off Herb realized the outcome of this meeting was vitally important to Paul. Why Nora's approval should mean so much was baffling. Herb could feel the first talon of jealousy invade his good spirits and was immediately attentive.

From the way that Paul described Nora, Herb had expected a judgmental, surrogate mother type. As he took her measure, Herb knew that Nora was in turn assessing him. Her manner was polite and coolly distant, but when she turned to Paul she changed. The rapport between them was close, almost like siblings. This in no way quelled the jealousy he would continually struggle with.

Herb wore white jeans with the pant legs tucked into black calf-length boots and a black tee shirt that showed every bulge of his muscled arms and chest. Traces of mascara clung to the top and bottom lashes of his eyes, and Nora was almost certain that he had applied a natural shade of lipstick with gloss. He wore his hair long. It was freshly washed and hung in a straight line to his shoulders.

Despite the makeup, there was nothing feminine or even

tentative about Herb. He had a raw physical presence that made Nora think of trapped steam searching for any crack from which to escape. She guessed he could be a tough opponent, but now that she had met him she was relieved. He would never last. A few months were all she would give the relationship, for she was certain he would be unfaithful, and Paul expected his partners to be exclusive while they lasted.

Nora doubted that Herb would do Paul the favor of giving up his life in New York for the quiet predictability of a town like Rockport. The more he talked of his friends and round of social commitments, name-dropping an occasional celebrity, Nora felt relieved. *Yes,* she assured herself. *This relationship is doomed.*

Paul and Nora were dressed almost alike in summer shirts and cargo shorts. Nora's shirt was peach, embroidered with her initials in a tone-on-tone color that made the script barely discernible. Herb noticed that she had the sort of warm, effortless glow to her skin that came from slow, natural exposure to the sun, and her chin-length hair was pulled to one side with a flat, tortoise shell barrette. Paul wore deck shoes with no socks and a faded green polo which had the look of having been professionally laundered.

Herb looked at them and wondered how they could look so carelessly thrown together and yet so perfect. Nora wore half-carat diamond studs in her ears and no other jewelry. Herb tended to wear every possible piece he could manage, but now, as he studied Nora, he suddenly regretted the heavy gold chain that hung over his tee shirt. A recent gift, he had actually worn it to make Paul jealous. As he looked at Nora he realized that manipulations which worked with others might backfire with Paul.

Nora had difficulty tearing her eyes off Herb's hair, which was streaked a peroxide shade of orange. She picked at her shrimp and mango almond salad and with fixated fascination, studied Herb as he scraped up a layer of runny eggs from the top of a charred T-bone. This particular dish had never been on the restaurant menu, but Paul had prevailed upon his friendship with the owner and had it cooked regardless. Anything for a new love. Nora sighed and kept her thoughts to herself.

After lunch they skirted the cemetery and walked up a narrow footpath toward the old mill. Paul showed off his house, ten neat rooms with a screened porch and a detached greenhouse. The garage was the original carriage house with a black weathervane and four empty stalls. Paul especially enjoyed walking Herb through his garden, which in midsummer was a profusion of vibrant color. At day's end they sat around the weathered bench which encircled a massive oak, and Nora departed to make iced tea.

Herb closed his eyes and turned his pale face toward the sun. He liked this garden. After his cramped New York apartment, Paul's house seemed more like a castle. And this town! It was unbelievable. Norman Rockwell towns really did exist, and if you dressed the part and adopted the role, perhaps one could just manage to fit in. Managing to fit in was a goal Herb had abandoned long ago, and yet he was drawn to the possibility of how happiness might be attained if he were more like Paul and Nora.

Herb felt that meeting Paul had been a good omen. If he were religious, he might almost say it was a miracle capable of restoring a bit of faith and renewal into his jaded life. Herb breathed in the faint mixture of wild honeysuckle on a warm salt breeze as it drifted over the cemetery gate, and decided that he would no longer ridicule Paul's discreet suggestions for improvement. As soon as he got back to New York, he would ask Vince to color his hair back to its natural color.

Paul could not see what Herb knew. Right now and early on, the relationship was no more than an exotic diversion, a dangerous interlude, titillating, sensual, and brief. If he wanted Paul, and the mantle of Paul's life, to sooth his own demons, he must get started right away. The attraction Paul felt must become reliance; reliance was easily fitted to compulsion; and then to a kind of blind adherence. If layers of manipulation achieved the desired outcome, it would be Herb and Herb alone who would have the power to sustain or end the relationship. And then, in the delusional bravado of imagining himself solely in command, the internal cord constricting his heart might actually relax. Why did he think it could? Why did he hold on to such misplaced hope?

Having identified his prey, Herb was invigorated by the sense of power he would feel if utterly successful. He reminded himself that only a fool would fail to grasp this opportunity. At any time, a male version of Nora Dillihunt might come into Paul's life or reemerge from the past, and then he would be quickly forgotten.

In New York, Herb was fairly anonymous, but in the quaint town of Rockport he stood out like a pariah. To his eternal heartache, Herb had repeatedly grappled with the emptiness of his life, and he was tired of losing. Recently he had turned a few tricks in order to supplement his income and a return to old habits terrified him. Flirtation with 'the life' would soon necessitate a suicidal somersault into addiction. Herb had now been clean for eight months but had stopped attending his support meetings and no longer returned the calls of his AA sponsor. All too familiar with the self-loathing that accompanies relapse, Herb knew he did not have the will to wade through that miry clay again.

Herb surveyed Paul's garden. His eyes came to rest on the honeysuckle. In fragrant heaviness, laden branches fell over the fence toward a border of yellow and purple pansies. The knowledge came to him with unmistakable insistence: The time for change was now or never, life or death. His legs outstretched, he leaned against the gnarled oak and imagined Paul on the other side. Nora returned and passed out frosted glasses of tea with mint and lemon perched on the rims like miniature bouquets.

Paul and Nora lived within the borders of an ordered correctness which Herb had loudly derided but secretly admired and longed to emulate. He had always equated the seemingly effortless beauty of what he saw depicted in the glossy pages of decorator magazines as artificial hype, permanently beyond his grasp and, therefore, an unattainable fantasy. Now he looked about, weighing Paul's world against his own, and dared to hope. If he could own that same ordered existence, then maybe the gnawing hunger that seemed always to claw at his heels would be appeased.

As Nora took her place on the third portion of the circular bench, a picture flashed into Herb's mind of how they appeared from the top of the leafy canopy, and he had the distinct impression of being observed from above. They sipped their drinks but said not a word to one another for a long while. "Nora," Herb thought, "is thinking of how she can get rid of me and Paul . . ."

As though reading his mind Paul moved around the tree to sit beside him. Paul's hand gravitated toward his and held on tight. Herb studied the dappled patches of sunlight over the perfect lawn and felt a rare contentment. That devouring and perpetual uneasiness which haunted his waking hours was momentarily restrained. Almost involuntarily he prayed to that nameless God, the powers that be, the presence he sometimes felt at odd moments, hovering near.

This was an absolute, final chance for happiness. Could he manage himself and Paul well enough not to self-destruct? He needed Paul's stability and his neat, ordered life. He needed Paul with a desperation that would prove hard to conceal beneath the lackadaisical veneer of the one addiction he acknowledged, substituted for the one he could not name.

After a suitable period of apparent indecision, Herb moved into Paul's house and absorbed what he could quickly and deliberately. Among a thousand bits of useless trivia, he learned the appropriate way to spoon his soup away from him and which shape of decanter to fill with what. Nora and Paul were devoted to understatement with an unconscious passion that Herb found contradictory to his own concept of magazine living; and he went on a spending spree, bringing home odd bits of furniture and accessories that later made their way to the basement storage areas. He gave away his leather jacket, which Paul was clearly fond of, and with Paul's Gold Card in hand, he invited Nora to go shopping with him for a wardrobe his partner would approve. Repackaging the outside proved a simple enough endeavor, but refurbishing his shattered and depleted spirit was another matter entirely.

Nora could never entirely discard her distrust of Herb. When she saw that he had become a permanent fixture in Paul's life, she began the search for something to like, isolating those traits in her mind and concentrating on these, rather than the far more numerous others that irritated her.

Herb sensed Nora's ambivalence. He had not survived a childhood in foster homes and on the streets, with only his wits to sustain him, without acquiring certain skills. Even as he fielded her polite, deferential overtures of friendship, he gave the appearance of welcoming her inclusion into their lives. Herb knew that Nora would never abandon her friendship with Paul without a fight, and to his great frustration, his few attempts to drive a wedge between them had hopelessly backfired.

What, he wondered, *is this indestructible bond they share?* If it wasn't blood or love, then what was it? No stranger to shame, it seemed to Herb that Nora and Paul shared a secret that, for their mutual love of one another, they kept well hidden. He thought it might have something to do with the disappearance of Lydia Dillihunt, who he knew had been kidnapped while in their company. Paul and Nora never discussed Lydia within his hearing, and when he brought the subject up over dinner one evening, expressing his sympathy, the silence that followed was awkward.

"Thank you," Nora said. "But, this is not something we like to talk about."

"I was just curious, and I wanted to say that I know it must have been just terrible for both of you." He looked between Nora and Paul, who sat across the table from him over a late supper of cold chicken and salad. Paul glared at his plate; Nora reached for her wineglass; and Herb knew better than to broach the topic again.

The dynamics of Nora and Paul's relationship remained a mystery to Herb. He resented the memories and experiences they shared which excluded him, but he never felt secure enough to openly challenge that bond; and on the few occasions when jealousy had got the better of him, resulting in an argument over Nora, he had unfailingly emerged the loser. Like many other accommodations in life, Herb adjusted to what he considered Nora's intrusive presence, but always resented Paul's apparent need for her approval and company.

Paul remained oblivious to the many little sub dramas that orbited his new relationship. Herb was impetuous and endlessly entertaining, sometimes verbally abusive, but always willing to apologize and make amends. Then there was the passion fraught with the threat of danger which served to blind Paul to a multitude of deficiencies.

Out of counseling, facilitated by the much diminished pace of their social life, came periods of forced reflection. Paul naturally moved on to weigh the rocky, roller-coaster pattern inherent in all his past relationships. These had included components of physical and mental abuse which appeased the guilt and shame he could never shed. Risk and danger made Paul feel alive in some way that safety and ordinary existence failed. Being alive, no matter the cost, was preferable to feeling nothing at all. For, in the great mass of that dark void of numbness, breathed the threat of something far more terrible which stalked the rim of consciousness, and which the trappings of life with Herb, for the most part, had kept at bay.

At his most self-destructive, out of the chaotic melee of his internal life, Paul's thoughts took on an impersonal, scripted quality. And then a kind of programmed imperative to act or respond in certain ways that precluded choice, making solitude and reflection the enemy to avoid.

"I saw you once."

"When did you see me?" Paul asked and straightened a crimp in the IV tubing. He lifted the light blanket and checked the urinary catheter.

"Here in Rockport when we were teenagers."

Paul sighed. Herb was about to go off on another fanciful tangent and seemed even more confused than usual, but at least he was no longer reminding him to get tested for this new, deadly strain of the virus.

Herb had been on the verge of death before. In the past he had managed to snap back and resume daily life, although each setback required more recovery time, and he was progressively more susceptible to secondary infections.

"We first saw one another at that off-Broadway production of Rent. Liza introduced us. You do remember that, don't you? We all went to dinner and I contrived to sit next to you."

"Of course," Herb said, "but I'm speaking of a different time. I saw you once before that. I just never told you."

"Okay, I'll bite," Paul was now curious. "Where did you see me?"

"I was with Howard. He was my first real love, you know. I was crazy for that man."

"Howard? My Uncle Howard?"

"You were sailing and we passed by and nearly capsized you."

How well Paul remembered. This was the only time he had

seen Howard since the day he and his mother had left the mansion. Apprehension tore through his body.

"You and Howard were lovers? When?"

Paul's hands shook as he replaced the covers and tucked the blankets about Herb's wasted frame.

Time had suspended its progression, and his thoughts drew inward even as an overwhelming sense of apprehension tore through his body. The random encounter had been abrupt and unexpected. With difficulty he'd brought his much smaller skiff about, furious at the thoughtlessness of the larger craft, and then, through raised binoculars, he spied Howard on deck.

Herb's face was clouded by an expression that hurt Paul to see. He turned from the bed and walked to the window. Herb had never disguised the fact that he knew Howard. It was one of their first exchanges of information as they sat in that restaurant and savored their onion soup beneath a layer of thick cheese. "Who do you know that I know?" When Herb heard Paul's last name, he asked if he was related to Howard Marstead. But the news that they had ever been together, well that was different. Herb had never confided that, and Paul had never suspected. If he had ...

"I said to Howard, 'who is that boy?' Because it seemed to me he deliberately tried to cause trouble, speeding up to create those swells. He said, 'That's my nephew, Paul.' Howard rarely used profanity, but when he said your name it had that effect," Herb continued, oblivious to the change in Paul's demeanor.

"And that's when I knew there had been something between you, and it hadn't gone well. But Howard was hard to read. Of course, you would know that. He was always so polished and careful. My, he was careful, so I knew there was some kind of problem. Something about you had really disturbed him. I was curious, so I studied you through my binoculars just as you looked at him with yours. When you lowered them I saw the family resemblance, but you were even better looking than Howard was, and it was clear that you loathed him. I saw it on your face, and I knew."

Herb's voice trailed into silence.

"Go on," Paul pushed, the physical sensation of the room evaporating to a dull tintype.

"I wanted to be like you ... lucky. You looked so lucky and

blessed to be sailing that boat, and you had a rich family. I couldn't believe my luck when we actually met years later. Somehow I thought Howard's polish would rub off, and he would turn me into someone like you."

"But he didn't change you for the better, did he?"

"When we met I was already too old for him," Herb offered, his raspy voice wistful, yearning.

The words came at Paul like a whip. He pulled the curtain aside. He had moved Herb to this guestroom when round-the-clock nursing care was required. The furnishings had been his mother's, moved from across the hall after she died. Paul had replaced her antique, canopied bed with the hospital bed, but everything else remained the same.

Across the way was Nora's house. Paul could see the cemetery and a slice of the sea beyond. The room was wallpapered with orange winged cranes on a white background with small gold insects. A near thread-bare peach and orange oriental rug covered the hardwood floor. Bold floral chintz adorned the chairs, and Nora had painted him something for the wall.

Paul let his eyes drift over the painting and started. There clearly depicted was the boathouse in disrepair. He recognized the row of pine trees, which marked the entrance to the cove, and the knoll above where the Marstead mansion had once stood. Paul hadn't realized until this very moment what Nora had painted. It had been so long ago, and the family house was now gone. He wondered if the boathouse was still standing.

"Well, it has to be," he said aloud.

"What did you say?" Herb asked, but Paul had drawn inward and didn't hear.

He studied the boathouse, weathered and listing; captured just as it must have looked to Nora on that day that she painted it. Paul lifted the canvas from the wall. He opened the dark closet and none too gently tossed it in. Behind him Herb coughed. Herb hated the décor of this room, and suddenly Paul hated it too.

Unexpected tears pooled in Paul's eyes, but the anger he felt burned them quickly away. The sudden question flashed to mind. Who would take care of him when he became sick? Why must he think of himself now? Why now and not later, and how did Herb get sick in the first place? They were supposed to be monogamous. They had pledged fidelity. Paul had cast off the need for answers to all these questions until another time when once again his life would be his own. But how would he live without Herb? Herb was his life. Or, maybe not.

With effort Paul kept his voice neutral. "Why did you never tell me about you and Howard?"

The room was so still in the aftermath of the question that Paul could hear the drip of the IV. Then the furnace kicked in, and the sound of the bells from the white steeple over the cemetery wall rang out to mark the noon hour. On a normal day Nora might come home for lunch as an excuse to poke her head in to inquire how he was. It irritated Paul that she was more concerned about whether he was eating right and getting enough sleep than about Herb. Didn't Nora realize that Herb was dying?

Paul turned from the window. With forced step he walked to the bedside. "Why didn't you ever tell me about Howard?"

Herb was asleep. His head lolled to one side and drool slipped from the corner of his mouth. Paul dabbed at Herb's mouth, feeling impatience over the necessity. Dutifully he applied ointment and straightened the blankets. Every mundane, routine task of caring for Herb, expressions of love willingly offered, would henceforth not be performed in the same way ever again.

CHAPTER FIFTEEN

Paul stood in his garden, where under beds of leaves and strips of burlap his children slept. He felt paternal toward his garden. The night was cold, but the moon was bright and reflected through the low cloud cover. In the light from the kitchen and back porch, Paul paced the yard. He reached up to retrieve a twig half broken and suspended from a narrow limb of the Chinese Maple. He brushed snow from the back of the granite tortoise, which was a permanent fixture amid the Shasta daisies and the black-eyed Susan's. He imagined the crocus, the paper whites, and the many tulips that would emerge in spring, and he fingered a sprig of forsythia and then the lilac. No knobby protrusions yet.

"Not yet," he repeated aloud, his voice piercing the stillness of the night air.

All day, since Herb's disclosure, Paul had avoided the sick room. Twice he walked to the door but could not bring himself to step over the threshold. Connor came with his nurse, but for the first time, Paul was not on hand to support Herb. The cut-down was performed and the permanent catheter inserted into the vein without incident, and now, genuinely confused, Herb had not asked for him. Paul mixed himself a whiskey and ginger ale and offered Connor one when he came downstairs.

"You're kidding, right?" Connor said. "I have patients back at the office and a baby due, and you know I don't drink."

It struck Paul how much his friends accommodated Herb for his sake. He had taken them for granted and been oblivious to all their many kindnesses, refusing to see that most had never warmed to Herb.

"I don't think I've ever told you how much I appreciate you coming to the house for Herb," Paul said carefully. It made him feel disloyal to say the words, and he thought of the first years of their relationship, before they had burrowed into a busy, but settled predictability, which he had welcomed, but which Herb had strained against.

"Glad to be of help," Connor said. Connor had graduated from Rockport High School with him and Nora. His father ran a fishing trawler out of Gloucester and Paul had joined him one summer vacation; the hardest work he'd ever done. Connor had married his high school sweetheart while still in medical school, and now they had four children. Often he and Paul engaged in rousing debates, as if the high school debate team had never disbanded. Before Herb's illness they had played a regular game of golf in summer and handball in winter.

Herb never understood the friendship. Connor attended a conservative Bible church and stood for everything Herb hated. After witnessing a first caustic debate between the two, Herb had thought *good riddance,* certain the two would never speak again and so was astonished when a few days later, they greeted one another with a warm hug at St Joachim's annual bazaar.

"If that doctor tells me one more time about Jesus," Herb said to Paul one day, "I'm going to report him for medical harassment. He judges us; hates our relationship."

Paul laughed. "Well, yes … He tells me our life expectancy is lower because of the lifestyle, that I would be more prone to suicide and certain cancers. What can I say? He tells the truth."

"Why should you put up with that?"

"A lot of years under the bridge, I guess. Friendship is our habit, and we've always disagreed."

"Well, I hate it. I hate it for you especially. And Nora secretly agrees with him. She hates our lifestyle but doesn't say so to our faces." Herb spat out Nora's name with disdain.

"They're honest. I like that we can talk and say what we think and still really like each other because we have a lot else in common, and the sexual preferences are such a small part of who we are."

"You like a good argument, Paul. That's all this is. Let's find another doctor."

"You can if you want to, but bottom-line, he's the only show in town."

"What about the experts? He's just a GP."

"You see the experts. Connor consults with them, and they don't stop by after a busy day just to see for themselves what color your sputum is."

It was Connor who put the question of a living will to Herb.

And that one question that was most on Paul's mind. The one he could not bring himself to ask. Did Herb want to return to Boston and the hospital there, or did he want to die at home? Even if Paul refused to grasp the seriousness of his current state of health, patient and doctor did not.

Suddenly, Paul realized that Connor had asked him a question. Since Herb's disclosure regarding Howard, Paul had found himself replaying in his mind odd, seemingly unrelated, portions of his past life. Though he tried, he could not silence the voices or quell the unwanted images that sprang to mind.

"Are you feeling okay?" Connor repeated. "If you don't take care of yourself you'll be no use to Herb, and I'll have another patient to worry about."

"I'm fine."

Connor put a hand on Paul's shoulder. "And I'm a small animal vet. Call me if you want to talk. You know I'm praying for you both." Connor looked into Paul's eyes, seeming to invite conversation. But Paul looked away. "And get some sleep. Take care of yourself or I'll have a talk with Nora."

The storm door slammed. Paul followed and stood on the step, watching his friend trudge through the snow. His black SUV could be seen at the head of Mill Lane, which was too narrow for the snowplow to turn around. Once no more than a bridal path, the lane narrowed even more at the crest of the hill before descending to the old mill.

Walking was the preferred mode of transport for most that lived close to town. The physical perimeters were small, and many of Connor's patients drove in from Gloucester. People warned him that he might never have enough patients to support his growing family. But, like Paul, Connor did not desire to live anywhere else.

Paul considered Connor's assertion that he was praying. He imagined that Connor talked with God often, and if he was asking help for him and Herb, well ... that couldn't be a bad thing. Maybe at some point he would give it a try himself, but not now. Right now memories were gathering like storm clouds, momentarily held off, but threatening release; and he felt afraid to be alone.

When the night nurse came at six, Paul told her he was retiring early. She nodded her head approvingly, believing that he was finally taking her advice and getting more rest. She admired Paul's devotion to Herb, but his almost ritualistic attention to detail regarding each aspect of Herb's care seemed a futile attempt to bargain with the God he'd rejected. She too was praying for Paul and especially for Herb. She'd asked her mother to get her church circle praying, and her three prayer partners, all nurses working in home care with end stage, critically ill patients, met regularly for that purpose.

Paul made himself a tuna fish sandwich on cinnamon swirl bread with watercress and Major Grey's Chutney. He then retreated to his room but not before studying Herb's vast array of medications. He swallowed the sleeping pill with another shot of whiskey floating on top of his ginger ale. He then retired for a bath.

At three he awoke. He looked in on Herb and the nurse. Herb was awake, but Paul ducked out before he was spotted; and now he stood in his garden in the dead of night and shivered. He thought of taking another sleeping pill, but his head hurt and he didn't like the idea of that helpless, artificially induced oblivion. Though he tried, he could not recall leaving the bath or his head hitting the pillow.

Deciding abruptly, Paul ceased the aimless survey of his garden and, striding into the kitchen, he grabbed a set of keys. He let himself in through Nora's back door and, climbing what had once been the servants' staircase, he entered the upstairs foyer; turned left past the main staircase and entered her bedroom.

"Don't be scared," he whispered. "It's just me."

"I know. I saw you in the yard. I had that dream again. The one about Lydia."

Paul slipped into bed beside Nora. His feet felt like ice. They both shivered and lay quietly. Paul listened to Nora's even breathing and thought he might drift back to sleep. But first he would have to phone the nurse and tell her where he was. What if Herb needed him? What if the nurse needed him? If he called, the phone might disturb Herb just drifting off to sleep. He'd have to get up and cross the yard in the shrinking darkness, and then he would not be able to return to Nora. Something would keep him away.

Paul sighed as self talk pelted through his head like a

runaway train until he thought, *"Just once, just once I'd like silence in there."*

Paul wanted to move, but did not dare to move. He wanted to swallow, but his throat constricted, and his limbs felt weighted. Despite the warmth generated by Nora's nearness and the bed covers, he was cold, very cold and he would never be warm again. Never.

Nora spoke. "What are you doing here?"

In answer Paul could not suppress the sob. It came from the deepest place of his soul, emerging raw and primitive. Instinctively Nora turned her body into his and wrapped her arms about him.

"Is it Herb?" she asked. "Oh, Paul, I am so sorry for you. Don't you worry," she soothed. "We'll get through this together."

"You never liked him," Paul accused, tears staining the front of Nora's cotton gown.

"No, but we both made a valiant effort. Herb and I had an understanding. We had you in common, whom we both loved. We'll have the arrangements to make. I'll help you just as you helped me. Remember when my parents died? You were such a big help to me. I couldn't have gotten through that without you."

"He's not dead."

Nora sat up and turned on the light. She looked at Paul. He remained curled up under the covers, his face averted.

"Tell me," she said.

"I can't."

"Come here," she said sternly. Paul put his head in her lap and wrapped his arms about her hips. She stroked his hair and allowed him to cry. It was a long while before he stopped.

"I don't know why I should be so upset. Maybe it's just everything," Paul said. He released Nora and sat up. He punched a pillow behind him and leaned back against the headboard searching for the expected, right words that would close the fissure his lapse of control had opened.

"It's the pressure of Herb so sick and the thought that I'll soon be alone; and I'll never find anyone like him again. And who will take care of me when I get sick?"

"You're not sick. You've dodged a bullet with this virus thing. Can you get that through your head? Nada. Nothing."

"You can't know that."

"Oh, but I do. How many times does Connor have to explain this? You did notice that the paper is white and the ink is black? You gave me a copy. I have it around here somewhere. They must be tired of seeing your ID number at that lab."

"I don't know."

"Well, I do know, and so would you if you'd only listen to reason. But if you must hear it, I will indulge you and state the obvious. I will take care of you. If and when you get sick and, mind you, you won't because you are perfectly healthy if not mentally unhinged."

"I wouldn't expect that of you, Nora."

"Why not? Wouldn't you take care of me if I got sick?"

"Of course."

"Then stop obsessing and tell me what's really wrong."

Into the pause that followed, Nora reached for Paul's hand, but he removed it from her light touch. A palpable aura of anguish seeped from his pores. His skin felt clammy and so she pulled the down comforter up and tucked it around him.

"You remember me telling you about my Uncle Howard?" Paul ventured.

"The one who molested you?"

"He and Herb were together. They knew one another in New York long before we met. He should have told me! Why didn't he tell me?" Paul's tone was quietly outraged.

"Did you ask him? I hate to say it, but it seems to me that given his history that might have been wise."

"It never occurred to me. I can't help feeling betrayed. I realize how unreasonable I sound, but for years I've nearly succeeded in not thinking of that monster unless I absolutely must, because you know, Nora, I hate him. I still hate him."

"And with good reason," Nora stated with conviction. Paul often apologized for his feelings no matter how justified. It was a habit of his that drove Nora mad. "Did you ever confide in Herb? Did you ever tell him what Howard did to you?"

"I told him I'd been molested, but I didn't tell him who it was. He didn't react, and I was glad not to talk about it. But listen to what Herb said to me, Nora. This is what really disturbs me. Their relationship ended because he was already too old for Howard. Herb said: 'I was already too old for him when we met.' And that was somehow okay with Herb, so I guess it was the intimation of collusion -- the fact that he didn't sound all that outraged. You know what this means, Nora?"

"What does it mean?"

"Now I must think about it, decide what to do. Because Howard went on to molest other young boys and I've kept silent."

"Your mother made that decision. You were just a child."

"I never thought of myself as having a responsibility to expose him."

"Why am I only hearing about this now?"

Paul didn't respond. He went on speaking as though he hadn't heard the question. "Maybe I could have stopped Howard."

"It's not too late," Nora offered, her voice determined.

"He's dead. Remember a month ago when Hank asked me to be pallbearer at his father's funeral and I turned him down? The family was pissed because I didn't show. You and I should have gone to that funeral. When we talked, Hank especially asked for you. He wanted us there, but I was afraid I might look at Howard in that coffin and explode. You know... say something."

"What would you say?"

"I don't know. Something like, 'Your father was the monster who stole my childhood and altered my destiny forever.' "

"Do you feel that way, Paul? That your destiny was altered by that terrible crime?"

"Perhaps not entirely, but yes; maybe."

"Because I've always felt that you didn't have to live this way and be repeatedly hurt as though you were punishing yourself in a cycle of destructive relationships. Because I believe in choice and the liberty to decide that life can be better and even different."

Paul sighed. He reached for the crystal carafe of water and Nora noticed that his hands shook as he poured, lifting the tumbler with both hands in order to drink.

"Sometimes I think I wasn't born homosexual. That this one event that I do my very best to never, ever think of turned me onto another path. I've thought of it more in the last year than I ever did."

"Why do you think that is?"

"Counseling. I should never have started."

"Counseling has been good for you."

"I haven't had a really happy moment since we finished discussing Herb and our relationship. That bastard had to get into my childhood. And the really scary thing is that I've come to realize how much I pretended that everything was all right; like being normal was a job. It's like there is more. Something is waiting. Waiting to grab me, and I don't know what it is."

"This doesn't sound logical, Paul."

"I know. But if we're being completely honest, it was like there was an otherworldly component to that torture. Like Howard was knowingly trying to implant this darkness in me. He was getting sexual gratification, exercising sadistic power, but it was also a ritual. Gay or straight I'm saying that via this wounding there was an access point for something evil to set up residence. To pull the strings, constrain choice, script the hurtful behavior. Nora, I couldn't open that door. I couldn't tell Hank the truth. I might explode and do something crazy if I showed my face at that funeral. Especially if there was an open casket. So, I just made an excuse and said we couldn't come."

Nora was stunned. "Why would you even consider going? And besides, we sent flowers. That was far more than that man deserved. But ... " There was a pause and then Nora asked, "Howard. *That* uncle was Hank's father?"

"Yes."

She remembered well Hank's brief visits each summer. Paige Marstead remained close to Howard's former wife, but Hank was as different in temperament and outlook from Paul as two cousins could be, and yet their mothers persisted in the illusion that a close, enduring friendship existed.

The two boys spent their time sailing and playing golf during the two weeks of Hank's annual visit to Rockport that began sometime in July. Nora tagged along only at Paul's insistence. To keep him, he told her, from being bored by Hank's endless chatter, which revolved around sports, girls, and Hank's own inflated accomplishments.

"That uncle was Hank's father?" Nora asked again.

"Of course."

"No!"

"You knew that, Nora."

"No, I did not. And it just surprises me, that's all. The details

188

that you choose to tell me and then the ones you leave out. Don't you think that might be significant? That Howard was Hank's father? That Paige was Howard's sister. I guess I thought your mother had married into that family. Not that she was one of them."

"No, my mother kept her maiden name, and when my father bowed out of my life I took it myself. Doing so pleased her. And my grandfather too, I think."

Paul put his hands over his face and shook his head. "It's all in the past. Being molested as a child is not a subject I like to discuss. You only know so much about me because you are such a ruthless inquisitor."

"Well, that explains something about Hank, don't you think? Wasn't he here with his mother the weekend that Lydia disappeared?"

"He wasn't at the beach with us. He came down with strep, remember?"

"If I think about it … Yes, I do remember. But, I mean…." There was something more she wanted to say, but in a flood of confusion and uneasiness she changed her mind. She had to think. "With a father like that, I just think we could have been kinder to Hank while he was here."

"Hank didn't meet his father until he was a grown man and besides, that bore never knew we didn't like him. He still doesn't. He thought we'd like to come to his father's funeral! I can understand me. Hank doesn't know what Howard did to me, and we're family and all that rot, but not you! When was the last time you saw him, Nora?"

"It's been ages."

"It's been years, really," he answered his own question and continued as though a flood of talk could bury the open fissure of his disclosures with distracting debris.

"And he still expected you to be there. Can you imagine anything more ludicrous? And of course I'm an outcast because I wasn't there, not that I wasn't one already. Appearances are all they care about, Nora, and do you think any of them will stoop to attend Herb's funeral? Do you think if I asked Hank to be a pallbearer at the funeral of my same-sex partner, he'd jet right up to be here for me?"

"Stop, Paul. You need to rest."

189

"Not, hardly," he went on not hearing her. "But Connor; I've already asked Connor, and he'll do it. He believes homosexuality is a sin and I'm going to hell because I'm not a Christian, but he'll be there for me until the end and not just because he has hope he can convert me. Oh, no, Nora! He really loves me, and he loves you and even Herb. I don't understand it. How some families will just do what they can to destroy you and talk about love and leave outsiders to really love, because I hate to think of where I would be today if I hadn't known your grandmother and been so cared for by your parents! And without you, Nora? Where would I be if you'd gotten tired of telling me I was wrong and foolish and stopped laughing and crying with me? So you see... I just don't understand it!"

Paul had moved to the edge of the bed, his back to her. He gulped back a sob as his shoulders hunched, but no more sound emerged. Nora knew that if she could see his face, his expression would be distorted by fear. She'd never seen him like this before and realized that he wasn't actually talking to her. He was venting bottled up hurt and desperation, all brought about because Herb was dying. "*Well, no,*" she thought. "*There is more to it than that.*" And suddenly sympathy took on an aspect of curiosity. There was something more to know.

"Some memories are powerful. They don't get diluted by the present or amended by reason. I'll send Hank a sympathy card."

"Yes, by all means Nora, do send Hank a card. That'll solve everything!"

Nora slapped the back of his head. "Get back under the covers and don't take this out on me. We can make up the guest room pretty fast or you can go home."

"I'll stay here if you'll let me," he said, suddenly repentant. With that he lay back down and turned his back to her. Even as Nora drifted off to sleep, she knew that Paul was wide awake.

Before Paul had entered her bedroom Nora had awakened from a recurring dream. She had walked with Lydia down Main Street toward the harbor. Across the strand they moved and followed a path, soft with pine needles underfoot, to the high hill that overlooked it all. A ruined boathouse could be seen, and out in the inlet, the white sails from small boats snapping in the wind with the lobster buoys further out, rising on gentle swells.

Lydia's hand lay in hers like a baby bird tucked into a nest. She counted the row of pines, and the fingers curled into the shelter of her palm. She counted again, and then she realized Lydia's hand had slipped away and she hadn't even noticed. Nora woke in a rage of panic, each muscle in her body poised for flight.

Nora walked to her bedroom window. When they were children, she and Paul had strung tin cans between the two houses and signaled one another with flashlights. Now Herb lay dying in Paul's old room. After his mother died, he'd moved to her larger room, which overlooked the ocean on one side and down the lane toward the old mill on the other. The light was on, and although the nurse would be in attendance, Paul would be there as well. Nights were the hardest for Herb, who was not dying well.

Nora felt she was somewhat of an expert on the subject of death. Her father had died suddenly, but she knew he was not afraid to go. Her mother had died in the knowledge that she was going to Heaven and would be reunited with her husband and perhaps with Lydia. In Heaven there would be answers, while here on earth there were none regarding that one all-consuming desire to know the fate of her youngest child.

It was hardest of all for Nora to lose her grandmother. She had been a woman of strong, unquestioning faith; who loved life and people; and who had an intense curiosity in all that was around her. She didn't want to die. She knew that Nora still needed her and talked of all she wanted to do and places she had never seen, with genuine longing for a few more good years. Herb in contrast was angry and fearful, and Nora found it difficult to be around him. She did not have the faith of her parents, and it scared her that when her time came she would face it all more like Herb.

Nora's eyes dropped to Paul's garden. She thought she glimpsed a figure there walking, but not until he moved into the light did she recognize Paul. A few minutes later she heard his step on the back staircase. "Herb is dead," she whispered and felt exactly as she expected to feel; immense relief that for Paul's sake, the long ordeal was ended.

When Nora woke in the morning, she was alone. The place

beside her felt cold although the indentation of his head on the feather pillow remained. The smell of coffee led her downstairs, her bare feet cold over the intermittent spaces between the carpets and the hardwood floors. She found him in the kitchen, huddled in Grandmother Dillihunt's rocking chair. He wore thermal underwear and one of Nora's oversized sweatshirts, and his thick nut-brown hair was tousled just as she remembered it from childhood camping trips.

In the harsh light of morning, Paul looked to be drained of color, drained of emotion, and drained of will. He asked Nora to let the nurse know where he was, and after she was dressed and ready for work, Nora returned to the kitchen to find that he had barely stirred.

Taking charge, Nora called the nurse's registry and confirmed the day's schedule. Then she crossed between the yards and heard the report from the night nurse before letting her go. Nora sat with Herb until the day nurse arrived.

"I'm afraid that Paul is angry with me," Herb whispered, his voice barely audible. Nora bent her head close in order to hear.

"Paul's not feeling well. You know he can't be near you when he's sick."

"Sometimes I say what I shouldn't, Nora. I'm not at all discreet like the two of you. You really know how to keep secrets, don't you, Nora?"

Nora didn't answer. Instead she pretended to read the spiral notebook that held the nurse's notes.

"Is he okay? You can tell me the truth. Paul's mad at me, isn't that right?"

"He'll be by later, as soon as Connor has checked him out," Nora lied. "And if he's contagious, he can stay at my house and I'll sleep here if you want me to. An extra person in the house. Does that sound like a plan?"

Herb smiled weakly. "You don't have to do that. We both know I'll soon forget this conversation. Tell him I love…"

Herb drifted off to sleep. Nora noticed his breathing seemed different, not exactly labored as it had been in the past, but shallow. Those short, quick breaths worried Nora. She gave the nurse instructions for his tube feeding, then called Connor's office and described the change for his nurse.

Returning to Paul, ready to report on the sick room status

next door, Nora realized that for once he evidenced no anxiety at being away from Herb. He had unearthed a bottle of her grandmother's homemade dandelion cordial from the cellar. The amber jug stood open on the butcher block, cobwebs clinging to the fat base. Nora watched as he turned a generous shot into the dregs of his coffee.

"You realize you're taking your life in your hands drinking that," Nora said. She picked up the bottle and read the hand written label. "I didn't know any of this was left."

"There's quite a lot. You've got a small fortune in wine down there, Nora."

"Then couldn't you have selected something less likely to give you a fatal dose of Botulism."

"Your father collected wine, remember?"

"You loved my father."

"I did. And your grandmother too. Your whole family. Even Lydia, though she drove us nuts."

They'd made small talk long enough. Nora studied his face until, feeling her scrutiny, he looked away.

"Oh please, Nora, let's not have any profound conversations right now. I'll be all right," he stated, reading her correctly. "And in a few hours I'll be my old self again. It's just that right now I'm trying to shut off the voices in my head. I don't want to think or feel anything. Okay?"

"Of course, you'll be fine," Nora affirmed.

Paul finished the coffee and poured himself more cordial. Nora noticed that he failed to ask about Herb or express his usual guilt that he was not by the bedside. In the four years since Herb's struggle to maintain some semblance of health, Paul had been beside him every step of the way. He read everything he could get his hands on and drove the Boston specialists mad with his endless questioning. He monitored Herb's care, all the while encouraging and cajoling Herb to embrace any new treatment. Especially those homeopathic regimens that Herb called 'fads.'

I've taken care of Herb," Nora offered. "The registry sent someone who can stay until late afternoon. Why don't you go back to bed?"

"Who did they send?"

Nora told him, and he nodded his head, ignoring the fact that she was young and inexperienced, and in the past Paul had rejected her as unsuitable.

"What about you?" he asked his voice trailing. "What will you do today?"

Nora saw him swallow hard and thought he might cry again. He was clearly having some sort of breakdown. "I have to be at the studio. I'm expecting a shipment so I'm stuck there and can't leave. Will you do me a huge favor?"

"Of course," he said, calmed by the request.

"Bring us lunch at the gallery, but first go back upstairs and crawl into bed. Sleep is what you need, Paul."

Paul looked at Nora and felt as though the world had quietly shifted off its axis. Nothing was right. He felt a rush of terror invade his body, then cold and heat. Nora was stubborn and could be a relentless adversary in defense of a perceived wrong. Last night they had ventured into forbidden territory, but Nora hadn't seemed to notice, and the moment had passed with the potential ferment of secrets still dormant. Paul took another swallow, this time from the open neck of the bottle.

"Go on then," Nora said as she slipped into the old coast guard jacket. "Go to bed."

"Have you extended that invitation to any other man in this decade?" Paul asked, slurring his words.

"Don't think you can change the subject," Nora chided. "We are worried about you, not me. You've over-extended yourself, and if you don't get some rest you'll be no use to Herb because you'll be in the next hospital bed. And look at yourself. It's still morning and you're inebriated. This isn't like you, Paul." Nora picked up the bottle and poured the remainder of the amber liquid into the sink.

"I only hope I'm drunk enough," Paul said and felt the sort of immense relief one feels when catastrophe is narrowly avoided. He looked at Nora and felt that he loved her. Regret was a weight of immense and painful longing. "It is not right, Nora," he said, enunciating each word.

"What's not right?"

"That you should be alone, and all these years I've had Herb to love."

"You know why I'm alone."

"But why? I don't understand it."

"Yes, you do. I've made the choice to be alone. There is no dignity in living the way you do, Paul. I'd rather save myself the pain. Let's just not go there, okay?"

"You tried to move away once, but you stayed for me."

"You're wrong. I stayed for Lydia, on the off-chance that she might come looking for us. Or, more likely, we should hear something about her. I did what my family would have wanted."

The atmosphere between them was suddenly rapt with caution. Paul was clearly losing control. Did he really think she stayed entirely for him and what they once had and lost? Hadn't she given up her hopes for Paul long ago? Later when she talked with Connor, she would ask him to prescribe a sedative or even an antidepressant. Something more appropriate than half a bottle of dandelion cordial at eight in the morning, and who knows what else he had been drinking.

"When was the last time you had eight hours of uninterrupted sleep?" she asked.

"Last night, thanks to the wonders of modern medicine, and as you can see, it did me not a bit of good."

"Go to bed. Look, I'm taking the phone off the hook. I've instructed the nurse to phone the studio if Herb needs anything, and Connor might stop over lunch."

"If Connor calls by, you will come for me?"

"You know I will," was Nora's measured reply.

Paul stood and walked over to her, a bit unsteady. He was taller than she, although he was not a tall man. The top of her head came to his cheek. He pressed her against his chest and slipped his arms under her coat. She felt his limbs melt into hers and breathed in the mixture of herbal shampoo and cordial. She was startled at the intimacy of his embrace. How many times had they held one another with no hint of sexual tension between them?

"Remember the time we made love?" he whispered and gently bit her ear.

Nora remembered. How could she forget? She had once, in her naïveté, believed that the right woman could change Paul. He said he loved her, so why couldn't he just decide to really love her as other men loved women? It happened without preamble just after her mother had died. They were alone in the house and home from college. They sat on her bed loaded down with stuffed animals and dolls, despondent and sad, discussing the funeral and their parents and how life might change for them with only her grandmother left.

Paul had kissed her and she had responded. He later made light of the incident, referring to his sexual orientation like it was a sort of inevitable condition, not worth a backward glance. He wanted Nora to agree, but she lied when she pasted a brittle smile on her face and hid her pained heart; all the hopeful girlish wishes for something more behind the practiced charade of sibling-like affinity.

"I remember," Nora said. "You know I do."

"I wanted to be like other men. All my life I longed to be like your father. I wanted this ambivalence to just die away. What could I do? We are who we are, but I wanted you, Nora."

Nora disengaged herself from his embrace.

"I wish for that now," he drew her back and leaned in for what Nora knew would be a long fluid kiss. Once she would have welcomed that kiss. She felt his breath on her neck and his grip tightened, but Nora pushed a space between them and turned her head away. When she looked up there was a glint of resignation in his eyes.

"Like always you'll do anything to avoid facing the truth." Nora forced herself to sound stern. He mustn't know that she was tempted. She had come a long way since that day in her bedroom when she dreamed of marriage and a large wedding. She had learned to be alone for one thing.

"I'd apologize, if I weren't drunk," he said and smiled a charming smile.

"I'm not what you want, Paul. We came to grips with that a long time ago. This is really about loss, my friend. This is about grief and pain. Nothing can protect you from feeling it. Not even me."

Paul turned away, but feeling something akin to anger, Nora grasped his shoulders and made him look at her. "I'll be here for you. It will be hard, but you're not alone. Lots of people love you, really, really love you, Paul so don't do anything to hurt yourself. Herb wouldn't want that. My father, who loved you, wouldn't want that either."

Paul looked into her face and then broke away. She could not read his expression before he turned and carried his cup to the sink.

"And this is about Lydia," Paul thought grimly to himself. *"This is about Howard and me and Herb and you and all the mess of it."*

The door slammed and Nora was gone. Paul wandered through the rooms that in his childhood had so rarely been empty or silent or lacking warm cooking smells and bright greetings. Love lingered despite the family that was gone. He missed them terribly. Now it was just he and Nora that were left, living in parallel homes and with a tragic secret that was as much a bond as a wedge between them.

Why couldn't they have something together; a real family with a child, and that same kind of full and vibrant exchange of love? Maybe he couldn't change, but he didn't need to act out. Maybe he could heal enough to be a good father. Was this an impossible dream?

Paul felt he knew the answer. The script in his mind ran ... Nora was every bit as doomed by their failings as he was. There was no hope. There was no future. Herb was dying of a cruel illness, and love could not stave off the inevitable outcomes.

And yet, he had entertained the thought that it could. A wayward thought had flown past his defenses to hover above the breaking surf of his heart. As he held Nora in his arms he had felt a melting toward her, a brief peace that came to him and which eluded logic.

CHAPTER SIXTEEN

Nora made her way up Mill Lane keeping to the worn footpath the neighbors had defined in the snow. At the top of the lane was a granite block with a row of rings where people had once tethered their horses. From here the road descended toward Main Street. As always, she paused to admire the view over the rooftops, and although the trees were bare, she carried in her mind the look of the landscape in summer; the black weather vanes, white steeples, the sea gulls circling and the constant backdrop of shimmering blue ocean.

She kept to the sidewalk, the snow still pristine and piled along one edge. An occasional car went by and she returned the waves and smiles, but it was an absent wave and a smile preoccupied by worry.

As she walked, Nora thought of the Fourth of July weekend that Lydia disappeared. Hank Marstead and his mother had arrived on the heels of her own family, and Nora resented having to share Paul so soon with his cousin. She prayed that Hank would get sick, and when he came down with strep throat she could only be happy.

Key in hand, Nora opened the door to her studio. Soon she was busy mixing colors. Her brush moved confidently as she painted in, amid a sweeping branch of pine, a bird nest camouflaged as it would be in life. The stand of pines often figured in her work. Sometimes, as now, she painted all fifteen lined up in a row, and the little cove below, and then the boathouse. When the painting sold she would wait a while, sometimes as long as two years, before she found herself working on another interpretation of the same scene. The older locals immediately recognized the location. Is this what had triggered her dream? This painting she'd been working on to replace the one a tourist had purchased at the end of October, just as she closed her studio for the winter.

The door opened and a string of miniature mission bells clanked and jingled. Whittaker Wobus came in with her mail.

"Painting another one, I see," he said. "Why don't you just tell people it's not for sale and leave it in the window? Doesn't anyone complain that nothing you do is original?"

"Not yet," Nora laughed. She made an excellent living from her work and did an annual show in New York and another at a Gallery on Newbury Street in Boston. The rest of the time she worked from her studio in Rockport. Her own work sold too fast, so that in summer most of the gallery space was filled with the work of lesser known artists. This allowed her time to stockpile for those shows that provided the bulk of her income.

The year after college Nora worked for an advertising agency in New York. She became engaged to a stockbroker and, until Grandmother Dillihunt died, it looked as if her life would be entirely predictable. Nora came home to plan the funeral. As previously arranged, her grandmother was buried alongside her husband and Nora's parents.

Nora recalled standing by the newly dug grave with the other headstones close by and realizing that there would be no room for her. During her last meeting at the mortuary, Nora made arrangements to purchase another plot for herself and was nearly out the door when she turned to write a second check. No one was more surprised than she to find herself scribbling the name of Lydia Diane Dillihunt in the space marked recipient. Although logic said otherwise, perhaps something would be found out about Lydia. Someday. Maybe.

After the funeral, Nora stayed an extra week to close the house. The pink and fuchsia impatiens had faded, but the white geraniums languished in the window boxes and the ivy retained a waxy sheen. Most of the summer cottages had been closed, though the tourists continued to descend at weekend intervals.

Paul was brisk and short with her as he helped fasten and latch the outside shutters. He found it incomprehensible that she would choose to live any other place. His reproach was evident, even in his reminder that, except in anticipation of a storm, the shutters had never been closed for any length of time. Nora was not due to return to Rockport until her two-week vacation the following July. That seemed a paltry, meager span and she knew that inevitably, even to her closest neighbors and friends, she would be demoted to the rank of summer folk.

As she sorted and packed, Nora felt a traitor for abandoning the neat rooms with the high ceilings. She spread the dust covers, great billowing tents that obliterated the blue and white of her grandmother's chintz and the green and red stripe of the dining room chairs. Gathering another armload and feeling like an executioner, she mounted the back stairs and could almost hear a moan from the pinks and butter yellow, the reds and harbor blue of the bedrooms as she snuffed from sight her grandmother's love of color. When finished she surveyed the sterile result which spoke to her more clearly of death than the gleaming casket, or the long line of mourners who wrung her hand and kissed her cheek until her face was numb.

Nora began to pack a box to take back to her apartment in New York. She gathered her grandmother's collection of atomizers from the top of her vanity and carefully enclosed the fragile glass in bubble-wrap. Each space no longer occupied rang out to her with a gathering sense of its own absence. Nora moved into the living room to the Limoges boxes, some that she and Lydia had given as gifts, and then the collection of silver snuff boxes and thimbles that had once belonged to her father's great Aunt Nellie, the first Dillihunt to live at Mill Lane.

If inanimate objects could speak, they spoke to her now with a certain hollow clarity whose message she fought to ignore until she picked up her grandmother's Bible, open at Psalm 139. Nora leafed through the pages. Many passages were highlighted and notes filled the borders. Tucked between the pages were cards and scraps of paper; many notes that she and Lydia had written as children. Outside, a hovering dusk burned brighter than the room as early twilight slanted bars across the floor. She fought to see, forgetting entirely the light beside the bed.

Gathering strength Nora stood and wrapped the Bible in tissue paper. On the way out she dropped it on the top of an open crate, ready for the dim hibernation of storage. At the threshold she paused. Her hands felt strangely light. The pull to wrap her hands over the binding and keep it close was nearly physical. Feeling on some level very foolish, Nora retraced her steps and placed the book back where it had been, on the bedside table in her grandmother's room. It will be there, she told herself, when I return. Must she go? The entire house seemed hushed and pensive; at odds with the very fate that had propelled her far from home. She couldn't stay. She would not stay.

Paul drove her to Boston in his restored 1954 MG Midget, a passive aggressive exclamation mark of disapproval if there ever was one. The MG was uncomfortable, and with little room for her luggage, most would have to be shipped separately. She took the inconvenience personally when he informed her that his mother's Cadillac convertible, which he had inherited, was in the garage. On the way into Boston they fought over Nora's fiancé.

"He's a jock, Nora. The sort of perpetual frat boy who thinks it entertaining to cruise gay bars and pick fights. It galls me to know you would end up with someone like him."

"Don't be ridiculous," Nora said. "You hardly know him."

"I know his type well enough and I'm frankly disappointed in you."

"Oh yeah, this from a man whose last boyfriend beat him up and stole his credit cards."

They struggled over grilled swordfish at the No Name Restaurant, for once finding little to speak of, before heading for South Station in the noon traffic. She felt angry; angry with him and irritated with herself. Even before the train pulled away he had left the platform. For the first time ever, they had not parted friends.

Nora measured distance outside the fleeing landscape of the train window. She counted thin slices of life and narrow vignettes of canvas through countless small towns, by factories, over rivers and bridges. She had relied on these lengthening miles to mount a barricade between herself and home, finally lifting the mantle of her disquiet.

She slept and dreamt of the gasps and death-groaning of inanimate objects under lengths of white sheeting and all the while the relentless ring of the phone. Persistent and pulsing, the sound raced through the abandoned interior of the house until, in a last death knell echo, it fell to silence.

Nora woke in a rush of panic. What if that long awaited phone call came? What if the doorbell rang and the house was closed and still? Nora heard the two syllable sound of her name distinctly called. She was not dreaming. No one on that train knew her. But her name came clear and resolute as though to punctuate the substance of the dream. *"Nora."*

Before the train pulled into Grand Central she made up her mind. She would catch the next train back to Boston. Nora was only irritated that Paul was not surprised to see her as, without comment, he happily went for the ladder and hooked back the shutters.

In her heart Nora knew that Lydia was dead, and yet it was impossible to extinguish hope that answers could be found. The all-consuming questions which had haunted her family were revisited on her. What really happened on that Fourth of July weekend? This was the impetus that powered her life and orchestrated her decisions and inspired her work with far more clarity and precision than ambition or acclaim or even a significant relationship with a man.

Nora left most of her grandmother and parents' possessions packed and made the house on Mill Lane her own. Without planning, she turned her love of painting into full time work. When it was necessary to be away from home, she was never able to enjoy herself and preferred her friends come to her, which they did in summer. In winter the town was an entirely different place, settled and genuine with a certain untainted flavor of timelessness. During the off-season, with the tourists and summer residents gone, Nora could more easily imagine a horse and carriage rolling over the narrow streets than a car.

"You know who planted those pines, don't you?"

Nora was startled. She had almost forgotten Whittaker's presence. He looked over her shoulder and studied the painting. "Who?" Nora asked, as he dropped his mailbag with a thud and helped himself to coffee. In winter his route took half the time, but no one thought to adjust his schedule. He often passed along bits of news and sometimes a book from one neighbor to another, all the while freely dispensing his Yankee brand of pragmatism.

"It was old Mr. Marstead. Paul's grandfather. He restored the old mansion, and it was he that planted those pines so he could recognize his cove from a few miles out. He wasn't much of a sailor, and he kept missing the cove," Whittaker chuckled. "He bought a fine boat though. The same one that Herb ran up on that sand bar a few summers past."

Nora wiped her hands on a rag and poured herself a cup of

coffee. She was in for a longer than normal visit and might as well get caught up on local news. She and Whittaker enjoyed the same books and liked to talk about the latest mutual read. He would give her a report on the shut-ins along his route and would pass the word that she was at work in her studio. If so inclined a neighbor or two might poke their heads in to say hello and inquire after Paul and Herb.

"That boat was too much for Herb and it was too much for Paul's grandfather. Old man Marstead had no sense of direction and would lose his bearings right off." Whittaker chuckled again.

"So what happened?"

"Eventually pride won out and that beauty sat in dry dock until Paul restored it." Whittaker bestowed his highest compliment. "A fine sailor, Paul. How many boats he have now?"

Paul bought and sold schooners and occasionally a car that caught his fancy. He spent hours restoring, working at his own speed. Only after he'd bid on a new salvage project, making room in the old carriage shop transformed into a workshop, did he let any go.

Nora shrugged in answer. She thought she knew everything there was to know about Paul. "What happened to Paul's grandfather?"

"Samuel was his name. The elder and not to be confused with his namesake and younger son who now runs the family law firm. He'd be long dead."

"Did you know Howard Marstead, Paul's uncle?"

"He was older than me, but I knew him all right and I don't like to say, but I didn't much like the man. That's all. Someone like him didn't talk to someone like me, if you get my drift, Nora. He was a movie star, you know?"

"No, he wasn't," Nora said, amused.

"He was," Whittaker asserted. "Made two Hollywood movies, but then just sort of retired. I heard down at the courthouse that Paul inherited that land from him a few months back. And choice property it is, too."

"A movie star, right?" Nora was dubious.

"You can ask Paul if you don't believe me."

"I will," Nora said.

Whittaker walked over to the huge tarp that covered Nora's most recently completed project. "Finished it, aye?"

"Yes. I generally keep it covered," Nora added, unable to stop Whit from lifting the tarp. The wood was unfinished ash when Herb had it delivered to her studio asking that she paint it for him. "Follow your instincts," was his only instruction. It was just like Herb to want something unorthodox, even at his own funeral. Now it awaited the upholsterer and Herb's choice of satin, but after seeing Herb this morning Nora doubted he would ever be up to the challenge of selecting fabric and color. She would have to decide for him and made a mental note to get that started.

Whittaker replaced the covering.

"I feel sorry about Paul. Sorry he turned out the way he did. I know it's a cliché Nora, but I wouldn't have wanted Paige Marstead for a mother. Most people, who didn't know her really well, liked her. She was enmeshed with Paul in a way that felt assaultive."

Paul had told Nora that the dubious distinction of being the town's most prominent homosexual was preferable to the anonymity of living in a place like New York or San Francisco. He was far more involved with community life than her, having served on the city council, the tourist board, and followed his mother as president of the garden club.

"Well, I must be on my way. Thanks for coffee Nora, best in town." Whittaker hoisted his satchel over one shoulder. "By the way, how's Herb doing? I haven't seen him about for a while."

Nora decided to indulge Whittaker with news he could pass along his route. A little sympathy was sure to bring Paul enough frozen casseroles and quick bread to last the month. She had just finished returning the freezer containers from Herb's last crisis and knew that Paul hardly ever cooked for himself anymore.

"Not well, Whit. He is on tube feedings and needs oxygen round the clock."

"Is Paul still convinced he'll pull out of it?"

"Yes," Nora said simply. "Paul is hopelessly hopeful. He won't even look at that," Nora said and gestured toward the coffin, which sat suspended between two sawhorses.

"Poor boy. This will be hard on him." He sounded genuinely

sad, and Nora forgave him his earlier comments. The door slammed, the bells jingled, and she returned to her work.

Nora wondered why people persisted in referring to Paul as a boy. No one had called her a girl for a very long time. She guessed it was the absence of guile in his personality. A certain quality he projected of being open and uncomplicated. Behind the façade, a need to be liked and accepted by everyone.

Nora switched on a Van Morrison CD. She sang along with the lyrics of "Ball and Chain," and thought about Paul. When Herb was not well enough to leave the house, neighbors visited. The ladies from the church benevolent society took turns ferrying books from the library and doing the grocery shopping for Paul, who was reluctant to leave Herb's side.

"Why don't they bring me a book I can read," Herb would complain to Nora and Paul.

"You've read many of those books," Nora reminded him.

"You need to write those ladies a thank you note," Paul said, adding, "Something suitable to be published in a church bulletin, where, I might add, it will certainly end up."

"What am I, a debutante?"

"Use that nice note paper I bought you for Christmas. The ivory with your monogram in sepia," Paul said as Nora suppressed a giggle.

The ladies often stayed to visit with Herb. They treated him, Nora noted, with the same respectful consideration as Bitsy Faron when she was dying of cancer, and they hadn't liked Bitsy any better. It was her husband Hal, just as it was now Paul, they truly extended themselves for. Each summer Bitsy had chosen a tourist to have an affair with and then was selectively blind enough to convince herself that no one noticed. The town had a way of ostracizing those they disapproved of with a certain benign, but distant politeness. Nora noticed, but didn't care. Paul, if they hadn't done such a good job of protecting him, would have been mortified.

But Herb couldn't help himself. The habit of baiting and being provocative, always challenging the pitfalls of distrust without giving trust a chance was a life strategy. He was too often sarcastic and talked freely of wishing he could live some other place. He had a way of insulting them and then deluding himself into believing they were too obtuse to understand the double entendres and half implied slights. Openly they speculated as to whether Herb was truly in the relationship for Paul or was it Paul's money that he liked, or the trips they took, or a hundred other comforts? They especially did not like the manner in which Herb spoke to Paul in public, sometimes belittling him, or his fondness of alluding to money and possessions, or his habit of eyeing their husbands and sons. Paul was one of their own. Herb was not.

Nora had her own past to contend with. For several months, and then with decreasing frequency, the disappearance of Lydia Dillihunt was rehashed on the daily news. Lydia had vanished with such sudden and mysterious swiftness that, for a time, it affected the tourist business whose frantic flurry in summer supported many through the solitude of winter.

The story that Paul and Nora told was entirely plausible, which made Lydia's disappearance all the more disturbing. Every parent could easily relate to the events of that flawless summer day and suddenly began to keep track of their children with hawk-like vigilance.

One minute little Lydia was with Paul and Nora and the next she was gone. They had walked up the ramp from Front Beach to buy butter brickle ice cream cones from the pharmacy soda fountain. They passed over their money, bathing suits still damp and bare feet covered with sand. Outside the weekend tourist traffic was thick; the cars on Main Street moving bumper to bumper, and the pedestrians on the sidewalk heel to toe.

The following day was the Fourth of July parade followed by a bonfire and fireworks launched over the water. Nora and Lydia had already staked out their seats on the cemetery wall across from Front Beach, while Paul had the distinct honor of being one of the children who would ride on the yacht club float.

The children darted between the bodies on the sidewalk and Nora reached back for Lydia's hand. They walked a few feet, but Lydia was lagging and Nora let go. When she turned back at the edge of the ramp that descended to the beach her sister was gone. Simply and utterly vanished.

When the mission bells rang out Nora did not bother to turn around. Whit would have forgotten to tell her something or discovered another piece of her mail. She was absorbed in the stroke of her brush. Sometimes it seemed to move of its own accord, but even she could see that this painting was finished. She thought about what size canvas she would like to use next. Often that was how a new work was begun. The size that appealed to her and the snowy blankness that begged for form and color.

Nora did not consider herself a great artist. Not like Burns Padgett Shiel whom her mother had so admired. Nora had to have a feeling and then be surprised by the result. She didn't want to be a good illustrator. She wanted to be an artist, and if that emotional connection did not exist and somehow get conveyed, then she couldn't work. Minutes passed and the door was forgotten until she sensed movement.

"Forget something?" she said to the shadow, just at the edge of her peripheral vision.

"Yes," replied a stranger's voice. "I'd forgotten how cute you are."

Nora turned. "You should know that 'cute' is not a word real woman aspire to."

"I'll try to remember that," he said and smiled.

He looked familiar, but she could not place him. Then she recalled he had been in her studio late October. She had seen him in passing as he left with her painting, 'A Stand of Pines', under one arm.

Nora remembered their eyes meeting and he glancing away, but most of all she recalled feeling disappointed. Checking the day's receipts she noted that he had paid in cash and the artist who was watching the studio that day explained that he did not want his name included on her mailing list. Nora recalled counting the money, which was too much to have on hand, so she immediately left for the bank.

"I'm Jared Shiel," he said and offered his hand. His grasp was firm and swallowed hers.

"I know who you are, Mr. Shiel. The painting you bought last fall is a little out of reach of a policeman's salary, isn't it?"

"Uh, but you forget. I was Burns' only heir."

"I'm sorry. I am being rude. You've been on vacation?"

"Medical leave actually, but sitting around is not my style. It seems I've felt compelled to unearth the particulars of an unsolved case. So when you called, I was glad. After our last conversation, I didn't expect to hear from you."

"I'm sorry," Nora said. "It's just that there have been so many disappointments, and I didn't want to set myself up for another. But if you think you can discover some new information then I want to be of help. My family would have wanted me to cooperate with any valid investigation," Nora added, with special emphasis on the word 'valid'.

Once more Nora wiped her hands on a rag and cleaned her brush, replacing it tip-up in a red S.S. Pierce coffee can jammed with others. She led Jared to the two down filled sofas that faced one another in front of the large slanted window, but almost immediately, and without explanation, he excused himself and returned from his car moments later balancing in his arms three large filing crates.

"These of course comprise only a portion of the original investigation into Lydia's disappearance." He let them fall with a thud on the old trunk Nora used as a coffee table.

"Getting right into this, are we?"

"Yes."

"I suppose you expect me to read all that. A bit presumptuous don't you think?"

"She was your sister, not mine," Jared challenged. "You should know I don't need your permission to study this case."

His expression seemed to add, *so why do I have the feeling that I care more than you?* He looked to be a man devoted to a regular workout. His dark hair waved slightly over his brow, and she thought that if she ever painted him, she would have the hair longer. It would create a softer, more vulnerable impression, but would in no way diminish the strength of his features. Nora swallowed the bitter reply that sprang to mind. Even when no more than a voice over the phone, she had found Jared abrasive and meeting him now did not mitigate that first impression.

"Sit down, won't you?" she invited, but he was already seated and this too irritated her.

"Unfortunately your sister disappeared during the Fourth of July weekend." Stating the obvious, he removed the top from one of the boxes.

"You'll have to do better than that," Nora said and noticed the inside jammed with folders.

"The town was thick with tourists and no one could be found

who saw anything suspicious," he continued, ignoring her comment. "My guess is … Lydia may have recognized the person who took her. Either that or he knew enough about her to establish a connection that she might trust him or want to help him."

"Like looking for a lost puppy."

"Yes or maybe something even more personal. Like your father is sick and your mother sent me to get you. All that has worked before to lure children into grasp."

Nora regarded Jared with new interest. She agreed, but had been told that every available piece of information that could have linked an acquaintance or family friend with the events of that day had been thoroughly investigated. Still, Nora knew that Lydia was a strong personality who rather enjoyed too much the drama of protest. If a stranger had grabbed her sister and forced her into one of the slow moving cars, locked in a one-way crawl up Main Street, that car would have passed her and Paul.

One thing Nora was sure of. If Lydia had believed herself to be in any danger, she would not have gone to her fate passively. But, if she were with someone that she knew, well this was different. She might have been tempted to spite them over not being included, yet again, in their activities. And maybe there was no car. Just a person who grabbed her or convinced her to walk off in the opposite direction.

"But the authorities told us it was a stranger abduction."

"What else can they say when they have nothing?"

Nora did not reply, but Jared saw that she agreed with him. "You and … who was the boy who was with you?" he asked.

"Paul Marstead. We grew up together."

"Right. And Paul Marstead is your neighbor and friend."

"If you already knew that, why did you ask?"

"Habit, I guess. I need to hear certain affirmations in your own words. So . . . Marstead; what did he claim to see?"

"Nothing more than I." Nora's reply was dismissive. She didn't like his tactics, and he had said the name Marstead as though it left a bad taste in his mouth.

"You and Paul returned to the beach. You realized you'd be in trouble, not having Lydia with you," Jared prompted.

Nora decided to make an effort. After all, Jared had come in response to her message though she had clearly overreacted to that girl who had waited all night outside the house. Though she regretted calling him, there could be no purpose to her rudeness. Nora sank back against the soft cushion and studied the ceiling as she gathered her thoughts. Then she leaned slightly forward, her arms resting on her knees. It was an inelegant pose, and she felt his scrutiny.

"Lydia put up with a lot trailing after Paul and me. We were best friends, and we resented her. Two sisters could not have been more different. Lydia liked to play with dolls and didn't like to get dirty. We sailed without permission, but she would tell our mother, and then I would be grounded. After Paul's mother realized the punishment I had been given, she would sometimes follow suit. I liked to play ball and climb trees. Paul and I were the same age, our birthdays only days apart. We preferred our own company. Lydia was so much younger. A typical sibling dilemma, you see."

"And you feel guilty?"

"Of course, every day. I didn't want to go back for her, my own sister! But Paul insisted so we retraced our steps. I wasn't worried because even if she tried she couldn't possibly get lost. But... the very last thing my grandmother said to us was a reminder to stay together." Nora's voice trailed off. "She always thought that if we children stayed in a group there wouldn't be any trouble. I should have listened."

"How much time elapsed while you and Paul debated going back?"

"A couple of minutes. No more. Lydia let go of my hand less than a block from the beach."

"Did she let go of your hand, or was she pulled away?"

"I've never thought about it like that. I still dream about her hand in mine. Like a baby bird in a nest ... I didn't let go first. She did. I'm certain of that."

"Show me."

The route had been gone over countless times, but no one had ever invited Nora to be a guide. She was strangely moved by the request. She closed the studio door without locking up, and they walked in silence until Nora stopped before the clothing boutique that had once been a soda fountain and pharmacy.

"What do you remember about being here?" Jared asked.

"Nothing helpful."

211

"Try me."

Between the buildings an invisible blast of cold swept off the ocean. Nora looked down the narrow alley and let herself be drawn in to how the ocean beyond the breakwater blended into the horizon. She pulled her collar up and stepped from between the buildings, shoving her hands deeper into her pockets. The cold didn't seem to affect Jared. He wore jeans and a bright blue ski jacket with navy trim. A faded lift-pass dangled from the zipper. He didn't appear at all sick to her. Was it an accident; in the line of duty? She'd find out.

Nora reminded herself not to encourage him by appearing grateful. There was just too much going on right now. It looked as though Paul was at last coming to grips with the seriousness of Herb's health and was additionally having a nervous breakdown. Not the best time to subject Paul to these painful memories via a bulldog like Jared Shiel.

"I remember incidentals. That we all ordered the same flavor of ice cream, which never happened. Lydia had been swimming and we planned to get away without her, but she was too quick. I remember that she had a red and blue cartoon towel over her shoulders, and her hair was wet. We argued over that towel earlier in the morning. I wanted it only because it was her favorite. I was not always nice to my sister."

Nora paused and Jared thought that she was right. Not cute at all, but a classic, tom-boyish beauty. In this moment Nora was vulnerable in a way she rarely allowed herself to be. Push too hard or in the wrong direction and Jared realized, with any excuse, those defensive walls would be back in place higher and stronger than ever.

"Lydia knew you loved her."

"And you know that because..." The look she gave him was abrasive, disbelieving. Nora shook herself and continued.

"The sidewalk was hot. We ran to get inside. I remember that Lydia wanted us to take her sailing later. Paul was not allowed to be out by himself, but we went anyway, and she threatened to tell if we didn't include her."

"You were young to be sailing by yourselves."

"We mostly stayed in sight of the harbor, and Paul's mother could be pretty dense. She tended to assume Paul did precisely what she asked, while my parents were smarter about such things. My mother was nearly forty when I was born, and my father was ten years older. They didn't deserve to lose Lydia."

"No one deserves to lose a child."

"No."

"Go on," he encouraged.

He had lowered his tone to match hers. Now he inclined his head and moved a step forward, ostensibly to hear better. Nora felt he had invaded her space. She turned abruptly and walked back up the block. They came to the ramp, which led down to Front Beach. Across the street was the cemetery and at the crest of the hill her own house and Paul's.

"We're an easy day trip from Boston. You can't imagine how crowded it gets here on weekends. We have more commonwealth visitors than actual tourists. They hunt the galleries and the antique shops, eat fried clams, stroll down Bear Skin Neck and feel they've escaped the city. After Lydia disappeared, my mother and I moved here permanently and my father stayed in Belmont. They always thought Lydia would come home." Nora's voice trailed. Now she sounded truly sad. "You know, they thought they'd open the door, and there she would be on the front step, little changed no matter the years. They died with that expectation still fixed in their minds."

"And you?"

Gusts of wind whipped Nora's short hair to a frenzy. They had strolled to the edge of the ramp that descended to the beach. Pools of steam rose from the shallows where the rocks formed a barrier between one stretch of sand and another. She watched the white vapor dissipate as it hit the cold air, and considered Jared's question.

"I firmly believe my sister to be dead, and yet I cannot live my life as though she is. God knows I've tried to move from here, but when I go away on business I'm restless and consumed with anxiety to be back. I think the call will finally come. Lydia will be at the door knocking. And because I'm not at home, or because she can't find me, she'll disappear for good. It's not logical. It makes no sense, but that's the shape of how this legacy plays out."

"For both of you? You and Paul Marstead?"

"Yes, for both of us."

"Was it always like that?"

"Not for me. In the beginning my family kept that vigil quite well. Both Paul and I went away to college, we took trips, did things. But after my grandmother died I realized that I was all that was left, and this futile waiting was a kind of bequeathal. A sort of mandate I could not escape."

Jared looked reflective, even sympathetic. Nora felt an unreasonable urge to lay her head on his shoulder. She hadn't talked like this to anyone in a very long time. A knife was turning in her heart. *Snap out of it! Get a grip; shut up!*

"I understand you were hypnotized in order to recall additional detail? Did anything come of that?"

"I never saw the report. In those days they didn't share information with children. There was a different attitude."

"I'd like a copy of that report. For some reason it never made its way into the police file."

"I saw a doctor at the Massachusetts Mental Health Center, but I can't recall his name. I'll sign a waiver if you need one."

"Was Paul hypnotized?"

Nora nodded. "It wouldn't work. Paul wanted to help and was devastated when the doctor couldn't get anywhere with him. I remember he cried inconsolably and my father had to go over and tell him it wasn't his fault."

"I want you to go over all the police reports. Have you ever done that?"

"No. My parents did. My father kept up with all that, but not me. They wanted me to have a normal life. Like normal was possible after something like this."

"They had few leads. As you read the contents of what I brought take notes. When you finish we'll talk and I'll bring more."

"What are you hoping for?"

Jared had the look of someone to be reckoned with, but now a veil lifted from his eyes, and he appeared unsure of himself. Still, Nora had the distinct impression that he had anticipated her question and had already selected his words with care.

"It surprised me how little you and Paul were involved in the initial investigation. Reading between the lines, it especially appeared that Paige Marstead was anxious to protect Paul. I understand she tried to put him out of reach of the police altogether?"

Nora nodded. "Until Paul was older, he visited his father and sometimes over a long weekend, so that wasn't unusual."

"Yes, but never during July when you and Lydia were here. Without notifying the authorities, she had his plane ticket and his bags packed until the police were alerted by your father. Paige Marstead was none too happy when they suggested she keep Paul available for further questioning."

"That was a difficult era," Nora said and saw immediately that he was disappointed in her reply. He wanted her to say more, but Nora was numb to such expectations.

"You were interviewed, both in the presence of your parents and out, while Paul was never left alone for a minute. A family attorney was involved, Samuel Marstead."

Jared paused, waiting, but Nora missed her cue.

Did you know Samuel Marstead?"

"No."

"I looked up one of the old-timers on the original case. He said that no one liked Paige, and if she hadn't been a woman and had an ironclad alibi, her behavior would have identified her as a suspect. Then her family closed ranks around Paul. No one could get near him. To this day he is convinced that Paige Marstead was holding back; had something to hide."

"I can see why he might think that," Nora said, feeling strangely disloyal to Paul.

"Was she normally overprotective of her son?"

"She was, and often she was not smart. What you describe was completely in character for Paige. She was short on common sense. There was little discipline or routine in Paul's life, but she gave him plenty of attention. Sometimes she relied on him too much and treated him like he was older. I envied Paul his freedom, some of his possessions, and the unlimited allowance. I never envied him his mother."

"He has a trust fund?"

She looked at him askance. "If inherited wealth were a crime, I guess you'd be just as guilty."

Jared shifted gears. "I'm hoping, as you go through the files, you'll remember something important. Some detail in this material may strike a chord, seem odd, or worth commenting on. Read once as the adult you are now and then ... stop and consider how you felt at the time."

"Like what?"

"Anything at all that feels authentic and brings a question or memory to mind. I'd like Paul to do the same. Will he cooperate?"

"Paul loved Lydia as much as I did. He was like a brother to us. You may find him more willing to cooperate than I." Nora was defensive.

Back at her studio, just inside the door, Paul was signing for Nora's delivery of art supplies and rolled canvas.

"Did you forget about lunch?" he asked Nora.

"Actually, yes," Nora said as Jared walked in behind her. She introduced the two men.

"You're welcome to join us," Paul offered. "I've brought enough to share."

"He can't," Nora said. "We're finished here."

"I'd like that," Jared replied, ignoring Nora's comment.

He put on a different face for Paul, amiable and charming, as they chatted over pastrami and dill sandwiches, with Verner's ginger ale and homemade chips. Although Paul was slightly more animated than usual, Nora saw no evidence of his drinking. He seemed more like his former self, before Herb's long illness had begun to take its toll. With ease, he repeated much of what she had already related, but painting a more vivid picture. He spoke of lunching on the beach with Nora's mother and grandmother, and his and Nora's plans to sneak away for a sail soon after. He described the mix of tourists and summer residents and their childish anticipation of the Fourth of July parade until Nora too was transported back to that hot, July afternoon.

Nora noted Jared's habit of asking a question and then observing each gesture and nuance associated with the response. She watched as Paul warmed to Jared despite the grim topic and grew increasingly uneasy as Paul described that last walk, Lydia trailing behind. Abruptly, she decided enough was enough. Paul's words had evoked vivid images of the days that followed as Main Street was closed off, and the town fanned out to search for Lydia. Then the coast guard was called in and precious time was wasted as the authorities explored the possibility of her drowning, a theory that some still held to.

Nora left her place by the large window and sat beside Paul.

"Have you seen Herb?" she changed the subject.

"Not yet."

She could feel Jared watching her and resented the feeling of being on display, but he had been pulling their strings long enough. She felt like a wooden puppet suspended above a child's painted stage. She didn't want to come alive and feel the pain and anguish of that loss all over again. And the guilt. She looked at Paul and tried to catch his eye, but he was looking at Jared with fresh interest. She imagined that Paul could be easily drawn into another futile investigation and especially now when he so needed a distraction from the larger issue of Herb's pending death.

Nora placed her hand over Paul's. "Why don't you go along? I'll say goodbye to Jared, and we can get started on these files later tonight if you're up to it."

Paul shook Jared's hand. "I hope that I can help. I know it's natural, but I've always felt I could have done more," he added wistfully, looking at Nora as he spoke.

"Well, actually there is something you can do. You can allow yourself to be hypnotized. I understand your current psychiatrist is an expert at uncovering lost memory."

Paul was startled. "You seem to know quite a lot about me."

"It could be that the opposition, which revolved around this lack of access to you as a witness, stalled the first investigation."

Jared's tone was now impersonal, without the warmth that made Paul want to like him. It occurred to Nora that Jared wielded charm like a weapon, putting on whatever persona was called for in order to gain the desired information.

"Well, actually," Nora interrupted acidly. "This is not your job. You are investigating a case without actual authority, out of your jurisdiction and on your own time. A case, I might add, that everyone else thinks is hopeless."

"That's all right, Nora. I don't mind," Paul said. "I'm just surprised that Jared took the time to learn that I was seeing a psychiatrist. Of course I'll try again," Paul said earnestly to Jared. "I don't expect we'll find Lydia alive, but I wouldn't want to impede any real investigation. I'll do whatever I can." Paul was almost at the door.

"One other thing?"

This time Paul turned to face Jared with a show of reluctance.

"Were you ever sexually molested?"

Nora felt, rather than saw, Paul recoil from the question.

"I hope I haven't offended you," Jared said. "It's one of the first questions an investigator would ask today, but back then, if they inquired at all, it would have been of your mother. With no other evidence, they would have accepted whatever she told them."

Paul looked at the floor and then at Nora. "Actually, yes. A relative did molest me. It was before we moved to Mill Lane; before I knew Lydia or Nora."

Jared turned to Nora. "What about you?"

Nora shook her head. "No, never."

"Who was it?" Jared fired the question at Paul without raising his voice, but distinctly changing the cadence. The question came so fast that Paul responded without thinking.

"It was my uncle. My mother's eldest brother. Howard Marstead."

"Related to Samuel Marstead?"

"Yes."

"I may know the family from another case actually. Ever hear the names Andrea and Dr. Dudley Wodsende? Stephanie Wodsende?"

Nora and Paul shook their heads.

"He was a movie star," Nora offered, feeling strangely obligated to change the subject.

Paul looked at Nora, surprised. "Well, no," he corrected. "Howard was hardly a movie star. He had two or three supporting roles in unremarkable films. Between the time he molested me and now, I only saw him once, and that was when our boats passed out there." Paul gestured vaguely to the view of the harbor outside Nora's window. "I didn't even go to his funeral," he added.

"He's dead?" Jared inquired.

"He died recently. He was old, but I understand it was unexpected."

"Do you have a photo of him?"

"No, but his son would have one. Media outlets also I imagine. He had a certain public presence. I wouldn't want Hank to know about his father; what happened to me. That I disclosed this to you."

Paul and Jared shook hands and Nora saw how glad Paul was to escape. After the door closed she accused, "You ambushed him."

"Had to. Pedophilia is a motivation for child abduction, especially where no ransom demand exists. We look at the family, then the acquaintances and the neighborhood. And sad to say at this point, with the number of tourists, we can't rule out an opportunistic stranger abduction."

"But you said it wasn't likely a stranger. That the abduction was planned."

"That's my gut instinct. Yours too, I think."

"What about the theory that she went back to the beach and was swept out to sea."

"That seems the most farfetched. Your father and the Coast Guard report agreed. No rip tides, beautiful weather, a still sea. For now we'll table that theory until we exhaust the others, but I will track down and re-interview all those that were on the beach that day and gave witness statements."

Nora questioned why Lydia's disappearance should be so important to Jared. She disliked his arrogance and Machiavellian penchant for manipulation. He believed he was clever. Perhaps that came with the police work and the jaded view of life one must be daily confronted with. Nora had one goal. To get Jared out the door so she could be alone with those boxes filled with details of the case she'd never been privy to.

He handed her two cards. "I'm usually at the farm in Wood's End, but at least for the near future I'll be in the city. I wrote my address on the back; call me any time day or night."

He was almost at the door, before he turned back. "I understand Paul's companion is very ill. If there's anything I can do?"

"Why do I doubt the sincerity of that offer?"

In answer Jared smiled at her. His eyes were a dark ash blue. Again she noticed no evidence of an injury significant enough to release him from the Boston Police Force. He had a certain presence about him that she couldn't put her finger on. Nora was annoyed for noticing, but there was no denying. She was both attracted and repelled by him at the same time.

PART FOUR

CHAPTER SEVENTEEN

NORA

"You've been avoiding me."

Paul ignored Herb's accusation and maneuvered himself between the IV tubing and the catheter. It was March, but hinted spring as the wind came up and hit the swelling fullness of the tide and the white-tipped swells that rolled over the breakwater.

There seemed to be no place to touch Herb, and yet Paul felt an overwhelming desire to be embraced. Soon he would be alone. Only the ingrained habit of a lifetime allowed Paul to maintain the precarious masquerade that all was normal.

"Why did you never tell me about Howard?" Paul asked and sat cross-legged at the end of Herb's bed. The nurse had been sent to the kitchen for a break. Dusk settled over the room, and a dim light brightened on the small chest beside them.

The specter of death had not diminished the essence of who Herb was. He had always tossed himself into the melee of whatever captivated him with greedy enthusiasm. Even now an indomitable energy flowed from the ruin of his body, but all too soon the last vestiges of life as Paul knew it would pass with the body of his partner into the grave, and he would be alone.

Amidst the false cheer and disingenuous trappings of an atypical Christmas, Herb had rallied, relapsed, and rallied again. Through it all Paul had not found the courage to ask that question that, of late, kept his thinking, hostage.

"Why didn't you ever tell me about Howard?" Paul repeated and looked into Herb's shrunken face.

"I couldn't. I thought it might end things between us. If I hadn't been confused, I would never have told you about Howard and myself. I am so sorry."

"You should have told me. But a long time ago." *In the very beginning, before we ever began as a couple.* Paul added this last silently to himself. He had begun to think that he'd thrown his life away on someone who had never been faithful.

"Would it have made a difference?" Herb asked.

Paul was careful with his reply. The time when discussions like this could be at all productive had long past.

"Never," he lied, careful to keep contained the mounting rage that had begun to steal past his defenses. Herb seemed to believe him. He reached out his hand, which Paul took and gently folded into his.

"Because of you I'm a better man," Herb said. Economy of speech had become a necessity, but now Herb pushed himself. "I've lived longer than I would have because you loved me, and I'm not talking of this illness. Appetites are more important to some people than right or wrong. Consumed with satisfying themselves, they're always pushing empty. Howard was like that, you know. You saved me from being like him."

"Like it was my job, part of the bargain we made. I don't think so." He let go of Herbs hand. The thought that Herb could be at all like Howard was abhorrent, and he was shaken by the comparison that he himself had made only minutes before.

"Tears sprang to Herb's eyes. He gasped for breath. Not often prone to introspection, Paul could see the fullness of all, Herb, longed to say burst over his face, but he did not want to hear. Ever so gently Paul wrapped his arms about Herb's frail body, careful not to let his own weight rest. Herb was a sandcastle being washed away in tiny chunks by an onrushing tide and Paul wished that despite the certainty of nature's laws, he alone had power to prevent it.

With his ear close to Herb's chest, he heard how full the lungs sounded and reached for a stethoscope. He felt a stab of guilt that the worsening of this symptom had escaped his attention. There were tinges of blue beneath the fair, paper thin skin, and it registered how cold Herb's hand felt in his. Connor had wanted his patient in the hospital, but Herb had protested; and then one of the consulting physicians at Mass General suggested they start a new spectrum of drugs and wait another forty eight hours.

Paul elevated the back of the bed and turned on the suction machine. Herb shook his head in protest, but Paul ignored him. Putting on gloves he carefully inserted the tubing. Finally he wiped Herb's mouth with a lemon bliss stick and applied more ointment to his lips. Herb started to speak, but Paul silenced him.

"It's all right. We'll talk later."

"But there is something more. Something I must tell you."

"We'll talk later," Paul repeated, harsher than he intended.

Herb reached out, only managing to pluck at Paul's sleeve. In the grip of an immense reluctance, Paul turned back. Whatever Herb had to say at this late date wouldn't matter to the man who wasn't all there.

Paul leaned over the bed. "What do you want to say?"

Herb's face constricted in pain. Tears returned to his eyes. "It's gone. I don't remember. Just know that I love you," he whispered.

"I know."

Herb had never seemed more vulnerable, and yet Paul could not stand another millisecond under that needy gaze. His beloved house felt oppressive and the gathering gloom of impending death and his future unbearable to contemplate. If he had his way he would pack a bag and be gone. He would do it now. He could do it now, but at the same time, fleeing his responsibility to Herb went against the grain of who he was.

Paul wondered how his entire perspective could shift so abruptly with the simple news of what he should have guessed at long ago. Herb and Howard had once been lovers, if one could apply that term to a monster like Howard. Herb was his life partner, his cherished friend, but against his will cosseted layers of denial were being stripped and shredded amid emotionally charged hurricane strength winds. Paul felt betrayed by that part of his brain, which job it was to maintain the equilibrium; the delusional façade. Beginning with counseling some internal filter had short circuited.

Paul wanted a drink. Later, after Herb was gone, if he could just keep it together ...

Paul's house was the oldest on Mill Lane and actually predated the gristmill. The rooms were smaller and the ceilings lower than Nora's with five working fireplaces and narrow, steep stairs leading to the second floor and third floor attic. Paul's mother had extended the back of the house, adding on a large sunny kitchen and porch. Later Paul had added the green house. Paul descended slowly and paused momentarily at the landing. He looked across the hall and into the low-beamed living room at Nora.

They had gone to Essex for an early dinner, and now she was slouched in a chair before the fire. She wore an outfit he had bought her for her birthday the year before. Her short boots were off and her slender legs, encased in navy tights, stretched out over the ottoman.

His glance lingered. How, Paul wondered, could he admire Nora, even be attracted to her, but not allow a different relationship? Suddenly he was submerged in regret. How much different his life would be today, if only they had married. Although they never discussed it, he understood perfectly that at one time she had desired him and even dreamed of marriage. And yet he had slammed the door on that possibility believing that there were no real choices to be made. Was he really re-thinking his options, his bruised heart suddenly longing for a different lifestyle? They might have had children and now he would never be a father. Why, as Herb lay dying, must he dredge up and question what he had wholeheartedly embraced with no such conflicted longing?

They sat across from one another, and shared the same ottoman, passing occasional folders and sheets of paper back and forth, all so carefully copied and organized by Jared. Nora had always been protected from knowing the details of her sister's disappearance, but was now engrossed, feeling an urgency to make up for lost time. This was in sharp contrast to Paul's lack of enthusiasm. The two had executed a role reversal much like passing the puck off for the hoped for strike.

The fire cracked as pinecones sputtered, and the occasional start of the suction machine drifted down the narrow stair case. Nora lay her papers aside and studied Paul. He appeared to be absorbed, but she knew that none of the words were registering. During the time that she had sipped half a glass of Piesporter, he had consumed the remainder of the bottle and had just opened another. Nora was surprised when, in the late afternoon, Paul suggested dinner. It was rare that she could wrest him away from Herb's bedside, but lately Paul was grateful for any excuse to be away.

Paul lifted the crystal hock to his lips and glared at Nora over the rim of the glass. "What, already! You've been shooting me looks all night. Spit it out. What's on your mind, Nora?"

Nora did not hesitate to answer. It was as though she had waited for the breach afforded by his question. Thoughts had been incubating; pictures spilling into consciousness.

"Why haven't you told Jared that Hank was here the weekend that Lydia disappeared?"

"Jared already knows. It's recorded here someplace," Paul said and waved at the files scattered between them.

"I haven't seen it. Your mother didn't tell them. And . . . if Hank was here, maybe Howard came too. It would have been an opportunity for him to see his son, even if only from a distance."

Paul gave Nora a searching look. "Then you suspect Howard?"

"Don't you?"

"When did you first think of Howard?" Paul asked.

"That night you climbed into my bed and let me think that Herb was dead. Then you told me that the relative who had molested you was Hank's father. I wish I'd known that earlier."

"What difference would it have made?"

"You have the nerve to ask. Because we know Howard had an excuse to be in Rockport that weekend, and we certainly know he was capable of harming a child."

"But he didn't know Lydia. Why would he take her?"

Nora had thought a lot about this very question. "Maybe he wanted you. Because of you his life was never the same. He wouldn't blame himself for being caught out. Evil people never do. He might have been disinherited. The Marstead money would be a significant loss."

"He got his share."

"Okay, so perhaps his intention was to catch a glimpse of Hank; the son he'd lost custody of. Hell, I don't know. It might have been a crime of opportunity. Don't you remember? Lydia was the one who fell behind, while you and I walked together. Maybe Howard was frustrated because he couldn't get his hands on you, or because Hank wasn't with us. If it was Howard, I actually think that you or Hank would have been his logical targets."

"So now it's my fault that Lydia disappeared?"

"I didn't say that," Nora replied evenly, never shifting her gaze from his face.

"This is ludicrous! Will you listen to yourself, Nora? You have no grounds for such a theory. None at all! You could destroy lives with such groundless allegations!" There was an outraged, pleading quality to Paul's voice.

"This is all I have," Nora erupted, extending her hands palm up in supplication. "Look at these blasted files," she shouted. "They didn't even have a possible sex offender to interrogate, and they took their own sweet time about labeling it abduction. There was no ransom note, and as far as I can conclude, the FBI wasn't consulted until it was too late."

"I disagree. They did a very thorough job with this investigation. I can't imagine what more they could have done."

"Are you crazy? Are we reading the same material? For the first time, I realize how much time they wasted trying to convince my parents that Lydia was with a friend or relative or had drowned or gone back to Belmont, as if someone on the train wouldn't have noticed a child in a bathing suit. And all the while, your mother sat in this house and said not a word about Howard!"

"Why should she? This is wild speculation, Nora, pure fantasy!" Paul's tone matched Nora's.

"It's a hell of a lot better than what the authorities had. This is at least a theory that makes sense, and it feels right. Don't you think it feels right, Paul?"

Abruptly Nora stood, oblivious to the papers that fell from her lap. "Remember what Jared said. He said look for something that feels authentic. Well, this could be it!"

Paul remained silent, his face furrowed in exasperation.

"Look," Nora said, lifting a file into the air. "I see nothing in here about Howard. Your mother never told them you'd been molested! I was the only one you confided in. That was years later and I never betrayed that confidence. As a little girl, I didn't really understand it anyway. My parents didn't know, so it wouldn't occur to them that your family might have such a connection to a child predator. Maybe the police asked your mother some of those questions, and maybe they didn't; but she certainly did not volunteer the information."

"Why should she?" Paul was horrified.

"The appropriate question is why wouldn't she tell them? Why wouldn't she make a connection, in view of Howard's history?"

"You know the answer to that, Nora. She was protecting me."

"Or more likely herself and her family name. Need I remind you that your Uncle Howard was a pervert? A sexual predator! We have just learned from Herb that you weren't his first victim or his last. Paul, listen to me! If it turns out he took Lydia, no one would blame you. You couldn't possibly predict such a thing. You were only a child."

"But," Paul stumbled over the words, "it can't be. For one thing, he wasn't interested in girls. He seemed to think he was gay."

"Oh please. Even you know better. He wasn't a homosexual. He was a pedophile and like many pedophiles he got married. I only know that we have to look at the facts. We have to learn more about Howard. I want you to call your cousin, Hank. I want you to ask Herb for information."

"I can't!"

"You must, Paul. Herb will trust you, and we need to know before we lose another chance and someone else dies."

Paul winced as though she'd physically struck him.

"As you so aptly point out, Herb is dying," he said. "It's wrong to burden him with this, and what do you imagine I would say to Hank? 'Your father molested me when I was a boy, and now we suspect him of kidnapping Lydia Dillihunt.' Hank came to love his father. He'd sue me for slander."

Nora was dumbfounded. She could not understand Paul's reticent refusal to see the possibilities. If Paige Marstead had shared this information, years before, Howard would most certainly have been investigated and even cleared. Or perhaps not, and her sister would be alive today. Nora had no idea if she was right or wrong. She only knew that she felt an urgent and powerful need to explore the possibilities, and that Paul was not right beside her, helping and encouraging as he always had, was hurtful and even perplexing.

"You were always pushing me to pursue every avenue. Now that we have legitimate information that deserves close scrutiny you won't help," Nora said softly. "Why is that, Paul?"

"Because you have no proof; because Herb is dying so why upset him over a theory that has no basis in fact?"

Paul bounded from the chair and walked to the fireplace. Picking up a poker, he furiously stabbed at the flames and then tossed on another log. Sparks went flying but he ignored them. His neck stiffened, and he seemed to feel the intensity of Nora's gaze on his back.

Nora was baffled. In all the years she had known Paul, he had never been so defensive. "You mean you won't help me? You won't help because you gave Herb the best years of your life, and now you know that he was unfaithful. You only have to wonder how often and with how many other men, and when you add Howard to that equation, the possibilities are truly frightening."

"I won't believe that of Herb," Paul asserted lamely.

"Then you're a fool."

Nora began to pace. She strode across the long narrow room, stabbing at the air to emphasis her point. Paul began to speak again, but she cut him off with her own tirade.

"Oh, please. Then what about this illness? What about the fact that he has it and you don't? Every fight you ever had was an excuse for him to disappear for a few days. He wasn't capable of a monogamous relationship and you knew that right from the start. What planet are you living on? Wake up, Paul, before it's too late."

"Stop it!" Paul screamed, his face flush with anger.

Nora was suddenly still. She looked at Paul intently. "No, I won't stop it, Paul. He was never kind to you. He was barely nice to you most of the time, and I had to stand by and watch you be insulted because if I'd told you the truth I would have lost your friendship. Isn't it true that in a heartbeat you would have chosen Herb over me?"

"You never asked me to make a choice."

"No, but I should have."

Common sense warned Nora to tread softly, but a torrent of suppressed suspicion had been unleashed, and she could no longer hold back.

"Herb was rude and self-centered and nothing you did was ever right. He tore you down, and he often did it publicly because he and everyone else knew he didn't deserve you. For Lydia's sake you have to consider the possibilities, Paul. You have to be honest and demand honesty from Herb before it's too late, because at the very least ... " Nora's voice broke, but she quickly regained control. "At the very least, he may know something about what happened."

"Too late for what? What could Herb tell you that we don't already know? Don't you see Nora, how deranged you sound?"

"If you won't ask him about Howard and exactly what that monster was capable of, then I must!"

Nora strode toward the stairs, but Paul intercepted her. With a firm grip about her arm he turned her to face him.

"You will *not* ask him anything! I won't have you disturbing what little time he has left!"

"I intend to ask if Howard continued to molest children, because you know what the experts say. These people don't stop! They continue committing these horrid crimes, despite any threat or consequence. And then I'll ask Herb if he thinks Howard could have murdered Lydia. And guess what, Paul? You can't stop me!"

Nora broke free and once more started for the stairs. Paul followed at her heels and was again reaching for her arm, when she stopped abruptly. They both looked up. The nurse stood on the third stair, her face pinched in disapproval, her arms crossed defensively across her chest. It struck Paul that Herb had probably overheard their argument, and in a flood of unguarded feeling, he was mortified, happy and glad all at once. What followed a moment later was a flood of guilt so painful it came as a sinking, physical sensation.

How could he be glad to see Herb suffer? How had he allowed this conversation with Nora to get so out of hand, and especially now, at a time like this?

"I'm afraid there's just too much fluid in Herb's lungs for ordinary suctioning. I've called an ambulance, so if you'll just phone Dr. Connor and have him meet us at the emergency room."

Alexandra Clair

CHAPTER EIGHTEEN

Paul remained at Herb's bed side, and Nora went to open the garden gate as the ambulance backed down the narrow alley behind the house. She knew that Herb would fight, holding on for as long as possible. No one, it seemed could help Herb face death with anything but bitterness and dread. That he would not give up more easily and sign the papers that would release Paul sooner had made Nora resentful, but now she was grateful. There was time, God had given a reprieve. Nora lifted her gaze, faced the wind, and concentrated.

The drop of the hill and the white grave stones were a milky tilt against the sea behind her. She closed her eyes and paced words in rhythm with the waves. It was awkward to pray. She was out of practice, and yet had fond memories of praying with her family at meal times. Some of the prayers had been formal and others were conversations. She wondered if God would hear her after all this time of silence. Was He angry at her neglect and the doubt she indulged? She no longer considered questions of eternity, heaven, and hell. Faith had seemed too simple a solution to the complications that surrounded Lydia's disappearance, and she wondered how God could allow such a thing to happen. She hadn't stopped believing, she told herself now. But she had willfully turned her back on God, who seemed distant from their suffering.

The cold wind snatched tears from her face before they could fall as she pleaded with God for one, just one, last lucid conversation with Herb. For Lydia's sake, a final exchange that would either put the worst of her suspicions to rest forever, or send her off in an entirely new direction.

Paul sat huddled into a corner of the waiting room sofa. His whispered tone was curt although the intensive care unit that had swallowed Herb in a rush of activity only moments before had placed Herb safely out of hearing distance. They had never quarreled so bitterly.

"You don't need to stay, Nora. In fact, I'd like you to leave."

"Will you give us a minute, Connor?" Nora asked, not taking her eyes from Paul's face.

"No, stay," Paul countered.

Connor looked between them, mystified by the animosity. "Look, you two, this is not the time to fight. Whatever is wrong, forget it," he advised with his usual directness.

Silence settled between them as they watched after Connor long after he had disappeared into the hallway. They heard the almost imperceptible swoosh of the wide double doors that opened into ICU, knowing they would be sensitive to that sound until they knew the outcome of Herb's fate.

"Well?" Paul finally challenged her.

"I have no intention of leaving."

"I don't want you here!" Paul hissed.

"Why? Because I verbalized all your fears? Because I stated the obvious? You can't even say why you're angry at me, Paul."

"I won't have you talking to Herb about Howard!"

"Afraid your house of cards is going to burn or stand on what he might tell me?"

Immediately Nora regretted her choice of words. "Look, Paul, I'm sorry that I overreacted. Don't let my suspicions drive a wedge between us. Not at a time like this. If you don't want me to talk with Herb about anything serious, then I'll respect your wishes and I'll understand."

Paul looked at Nora, seeming to hesitate over a difficult decision; but Nora couldn't risk the wrong response. "Just let me be here for you. I'm not angry with you. I love you."

Paul stood abruptly and rested his forehead against the wall. There were several air bubbles trapped under the paint. He counted them. Nora had said 'I love you,' but Paul could not express the degree to which he suddenly despised the ring of those words. The distinct sound of a fist connecting with flesh echoed. He pushed the flashback from his mind and pressed his forehead harder into the wall for balance.

The strain of shielding himself from Nora's scrutiny was more than he could tolerate. She could always sense what no one else could, and even now might perceive disjointed shreds of memory rising from deep pits of loathing. All logic to the contrary, Paul felt naked and exposed.

Could Nora be right? Could Howard have taken Lydia? Paul just did not want to think about that. Not now. As the longing for a drink washed over him, Paul consoled himself with the conviction that soon he would stop consuming so much alcohol. Both Connor and Nora had remarked on his drinking, and on some level it had embarrassed him, but on another he couldn't care.

Paul spoke to himself sternly. He would promise anything to stem, postpone, or stifle what was coming. As soon as Herb was well enough to leave the hospital, Paul vowed that he would call his doctor and resume therapy, but for now he must simply get a grip on his emotions and stomp these memories back to where, like a breathing thing with an independent mind, they'd once been content to reside.

Nora walked up to Paul. She turned him to face her, his body no longer rigid, but in a sudden wash of exhaustion, he was slack and passive. A wave of guilt assailed her. She was being far too hard on Paul, even brutal, and yet there was no denying the urgency which propelled her actions and roused her to speak. A slim window of opportunity had opened which afforded no alternative. She must shove that window wider or risk a lifetime of regret.

Not disguising their curiosity, the other family watched them, but Paul seemed unaware. Nora led him to the sofa. They sat, their thighs touching, and studied the far wall until Paul had lost a bit of that absent, haunted expression. Whatever there was to do would have to be accomplished without Paul's help. Nora glanced at his profile, now stoic and remote.

After a bit, they had moved to opposite ends of the sofa. It happened by degrees, with trips to the restroom, for water and on the pretense of reading an outdated magazine. Their faces averted, as though by design, they did not speak, the silence between them alive, their bodies tense and waiting.

Finally Connor joined them. "Herb's awake and resting. I took him off the ventilator and he's breathing on his own. He wants to see you."

"Thank God," Paul said and headed for the door.

"I'm sorry, Paul, but Herb is asking for Nora."

"I won't have it. You can't let her in there!" Paul exploded with sudden passion.

Connor looked at Paul, astonished. "You can't prevent her. Herb is clearly upset about something that somehow involves Nora. He needs to get it off his chest so he can rest."

"But why Nora? Why not me?"

"You can see him as soon as she has her ten minutes." Connor turned to Nora. "No longer than that, Nora, and don't upset him. He's too weak."

Paul dropped to his corner of the sofa, fighting an urge to draw his knees up and hug his body tightly. There was a time when he had sat like that for long periods and perhaps hours. As quickly as the thought came, he cast off the image and looked instead at Nora.

"If you bring up Howard, if you upset him in any way, I'll never speak to you again. Never. Are we clear about this, Nora?"

Nora nodded. She tried and failed to hold his gaze. He turned away as though she was of no more importance than a gnat.

"There is something else I must tell you both," Connor added. "Herb has asked not to be hooked up to a ventilator if he has another episode like the last. He wants us to let him go, so you both need to say your goodbyes. It's only a question of time."

"He's in no state to make that decision. His lungs will fill up with fluid and he'll drown," Paul asserted.

Connor spoke gently. His attitude caught their mutual attention more than any words. "Herb is perfectly lucid. He and I have prayed together, and he understands the decision he has made."

There followed a few seconds of stunned silence.

"Oh, that's just bloody wonderful! What does that mean?" Paul erupted as though Connor had betrayed him also. "Now Herb's a Christian so it's okay for him to die! We can stop fighting to save his life. Is that what you're saying, you simpering hypocrite?"

"It's hopeless, Paul. He can pass away tonight or next week, but barring a miracle he cannot survive this illness. He has finally made his peace with Jesus Christ. Only a personal relationship with a living God can give one peace at a time like this. When you talk with him ... you'll see that he is changed."

"You've been after him with that religious voodoo since the first day you diagnosed his illness."

Paul had sunk to the sofa where Connor joined him, placing

an arm about his shoulders, but Paul pulled away. His eyes were on Nora as, grim-faced, he watched her walk from the room.

Herb's head was elevated. He had two IV bags running, and instead of a nasal oxygen tube, a mask covered his mouth and nose. Away from the softer lighting of home he truly looked like a dying man, and yet what Connor said was true. He was strangely peaceful, aware of some special comfort. Was it God? Was it because he had prayed with Connor?

Nora walked to the bedside and took his hand. It felt limp and cold until she felt his fingers curl into her palm and his head turned in her direction, though he failed to open his eyes. He gestured to the mask, which Nora removed and replaced with the nasal catheter. It struck her how she and Paul had grown comfortable with all this medical apparatus which had once greatly intimidated them.

Herb tried to speak but no sound emerged. His throat was raw from all the suctioning. His bed had been rolled up to waist level. Nora ducked under the tubing, lowered the bed rail, and leaned her waist against the mattress.

"What is it, Herb?"

"I heard you fighting, Nora. I'm sorry."

"Sorry for what?" Nora asked and held her breath.

"I'm dying. Must tell you," he whispered. "Must tell someone, but not Paul."

"I'm listening, Herb. Take your time. I'm listening."

"No time."

"Just say what you can."

"There are videos, pictures."

Nora was certain she had not heard correctly, but then Herb repeated the phrase more clearly.

"Pictures of what? What about Lydia?"

"In the wall," he said.

"I'm sorry, I don't understand," she said.

Once again Nora was convinced that Herb was confused. He shook his head as though in disagreement. She must ask her question. It was now or never.

"Herb, you must tell me. Was Howard in Rockport that weekend that Lydia disappeared? Was he capable of taking my sister? Maybe revenge because he couldn't see Hank or was exposed by Paul."

Herb opened his huge, cavernous eyes. "That family. Nora, I'm telling you. Don't think you can grasp who they are; some are not entirely human. Lots of genetic mistakes, lots of them. When you get to Howard's apartment. To recover," he gasped, picked up his oxygen mask and breathed deeply. She thought he was done, but he rallied, forcing himself to speak. "Be careful, be very careful."

A spasm of coughing wracked Herb's frail body. He closed his eyes and seemed to drift off as she held the oxygen mask in place. Nora squeezed his arm. 'Not entirely human,' well, Nora was convinced. Herb was delusional. But there were also pearls of truth. She was convinced of this.

"Please Herb. Tell me something, anything that will let me know about Lydia."

Herb appeared to be looking for something. There was a photograph in a silver frame beside the bed, which Paul insisted accompany Herb whenever he went to the hospital. He wanted to remind the nurses of how Herb had looked when he was well and healthy. Herb was particularly fond of the photograph, which Nora had snapped of the two men on the bridge of the Chris Craft, their arms draped about one another's shoulders and the open sea beyond. Nora was glad that on that day none of them knew the future.

Nora held it up for Herb to see, but he shook his head. The bleep of the monitor raced faster, and he was becoming agitated. He grabbed a line of IV tubing, but Nora pried his fingers loose. She tried to place the oxygen mask back over his face, but he waved it away with surprising strength. He leaned forward, his body stiff, and Nora thought he might collapse forward.

"Nora," he whispered, but with an intensity that caught her off guard.

"It's all right, Herb," Nora nearly sobbed. "We can talk later. You must rest," she pleaded, convinced that she had gone too far. Paul was right. It was wrong for her to question Herb at a time like this. Paul would certainly have confided the details of Lydia's disappearance to Herb, but apart from that one instance at dinner, Herb had never again alluded to the tragic events of that summer. At the time, Nora had valued such decorum.

"Pictures of Howard and Paul. You must destroy them, Nora.

Paul doesn't remember. I don't want him to remember."

Nora felt the deceptive calmness of all her suspicions jell into one moment.

"Where are they?"

Nora saw a blaze in Herb's eyes. He was making one final effort to communicate, and now she believed him. He wasn't confused. He was trying to tell her something important, and she was not listening.

"In the walls," he whispered, the brief restoration of his voice lost again.

"On which wall? At Mill Lane?"

Herb fell back against the pillow. "No," he rasped out in frustration. "At Howard's."

The red dot of the monitor chased across the screen until the bleep sounded faster before lapsing into one continuous drift of jarring current.

A nurse raced into the room and elbowed Nora away from the bed. Another came and then another. Nora stood helplessly back and watched, stunned by Herb's words.

"You'll have to leave, Miss," the nurse said to Nora. But Nora was soon forgotten. She backed as far as she was able against the wall and watched as the bed was flattened and another nurse placed a black ambu-bag over Herb's face. From just outside the door a red crash cart was hurled to the side of the bed as Connor raced into the room, white coat flying. He waved away the crash cart and removed the bag from the nurse's grip.

When they pronounced Herb dead a short five minutes later, Nora felt stunned by the swiftness of it all. Compared to the long, drawn out drama of a prolonged illness, death itself was an anticlimax. Nora was still there when Paul was ushered in. He bent over Herb's body. Gently he pulled back the sheets and placed his palm lightly over the still chest, as though to confirm that there was indeed no heartbeat. Nora noticed that Herb's facial expression was transfixed in death by what could only be great emotional release and even joy. How was that possible? Had he seen or known something just as consciousness lifted away and his heart stopped beating? It wasn't what she expected of Herb, and she felt momentarily confused.

"You must have an angel to guard your grave. I want Connor to say a prayer, and we'll ask him to play the pipes. Oh, Herb,"

Paul said, his voice breaking. "I wish it was summer so the flowers could come from our garden."

Paul's voice trailed into silence, more sorrowful than words. He clearly believed himself to be alone. He crossed his arms and hugged his own body for futile comfort, and leaning forward he stared into Herb's face as though he could will his partner to wake.

"I'll help you make the arrangements," Nora said gently and stepped out of the shadows. "I want to help you, Paul, if you'll let me."

Paul turned in Nora's direction. His expression was tortured, and she felt a stab of remorse that they had ever quarreled.

"You won't help me, Nora. I don't want you anywhere near Herb or me."

"But, Paul," Nora started to speak.

"Did you find out what you wanted? Was it worth it, Nora? I begged you not to upset him." Nora could see the nurses behind their crescent shaped desk turn in Paul's direction. Connor put down Herb's chart and walked toward the room. This was not the place to argue. All the other glassed rooms were occupied, and it was only because of Connor that they had been allowed to linger.

"Paul, I'm so sorry and I–" Nora spoke.

"Don't apologize to me. You, who never loved him. Don't deny that you ruined his last moments by asking a lot of hateful questions. Leave this room, Nora, or I'll have you thrown out. It's my turn to be alone with Herb."

Herb's body lay outstretched, the clutter of an aborted rescue scattered about. Paul looked for some evidence of Herb's eleventh-hour conversion to faith in that same expression that had startled Nora. But he saw only emptiness and an eloquent stillness, which Paul found reminiscent of gossamer cocoons, suddenly obsolete as they clung to the wet, black branches of spring. He thought of snakeskin lifted from the garden with the prong of a rake, and the empty shells of horseshoe crabs scattered on the shore. Herb was gone. He was simply and undeniably no longer at home in the shell of this once vital body. It was a death disconcerting to ponder, but to ponder later; much later.

Nora hesitated to leave. She desired nothing more than to wrap her arms about Paul's stricken frame. She wanted to plead her case and change his mind, but Connor laid a firm hand on her arm and escorted her into the hallway.

"Don't worry," Connor said. "I'll take him home with me tonight, and the two of you can work things out tomorrow."

"Try to understand this, Connor. I know him better than you do. Paul may never forgive me. Not this time."

A sob caught and strangled in the back of her throat, and Connor reached his arms around her.

"That's the thing about Paul," he reassured. "He's generous to a fault and quick to forgive. I go to church with a few people who could learn a thing or two from him. And, Nora ... ?"

She lifted her face to look at him, and he held her gaze as though with a child to whom he had something important to impart.

"Paul didn't mean a thing he said back there to either of us. He's drunk and in shock and everything will look different after he's had a little rest. You can see him tomorrow."

"If he'll allow it," Nora whispered, unsure.

Connor walked her to the ICU entrance, still holding her hand, and there they separated. Her footsteps sounded hollow as she approached the elevator. She watched the reflection of her feet across the floor's antiseptic finish and felt a heightened mixture of triumph and sadness. Nora thought of the coffin she had painted and was glad she had taken the time to get it to the upholsterer. Herb would be amused. He would like the bright, discordant colors and the Celtic scroll design. In a normal world she would be upstairs grieving with Paul, but suddenly her world had shifted, and something more compelling demanded her attention.

Herb had given credence to her theory, and this theory now had a layer of flesh whose shape jumped near complete into her mind. Suspicion had moved to plausibility. It was more than anyone else involved in the earlier investigation ever had. And there was only one person she could think of who knew the next steps and would help her.

For the first time Nora had hope. Not that Lydia could be alive, but that answers were close at hand. The heightened emotion of that possibility was felt as much for her grandmother and parents as for herself. The reality struck her in a wave of emotion so powerful it drove her to her knees. Nora leaned her head against the door of her car and looked up at the sky, lit by stars so bright she had only seen them so on the ocean miles from shore. "Oh God," was all she could say before sobs strangled in her throat.

Getting to her feet, Nora considered. Herb was gone. Whatever change had taken place that God had truly healed his heart, somehow prompted this con artist of little conscience to be honest. She couldn't feel close to Herb, she had never liked him, but she was grateful ... to God.

Nora slid onto the car seat. Turning on the dome light she found the card Jared Shiel had given her, punching his number into her cell.

"What's up? You okay?"

Nora couldn't help herself. Jared sounded groggy and human, and Nora felt raw and vulnerable. Tears came as Jared waited.

"Paul's mad at me," was all she could manage.

Ah, well, I know this wasn't a lovers tiff, but I imagine Paul will forgive you. You'll make up."

"You don't understand."

"Sorry, I don't," Jared acknowledged sensing that she was on the edge ... of something. "Why don't you just tell me, Nora."

"Herb is dead."

"Did you kill him?"

Nora's crying turned to brief laughter. "No. It's true that I wanted to plenty of times; seriously considered it you understand, but I managed to weigh prison against momentary satisfaction."

"Wise decision. So what's really going on?"

"I need to see you," her voice broke.

"Where are you? Five minutes, I'm on my way."

Nora stifled a sob. "No, no. I'll come to you. Are you in Wood's End or Boston?"

"I'm in the city. Do you have the address?"

"You wrote it on the back of your card, remember? As they say, leave the light on."

Nora ended the call and punched up the genius of her favorite musician-poet for the drive ahead. She didn't want to think. No need. As firmly as any zealot, thanks to Herb, she was convinced she had the bare bones of what transpired on that long ago summer day. She wanted justice and she didn't much care how she got it.

The irascible, determined, maddeningly obnoxious Jared Shiel was just crazy enough to take the risks necessary to make that happen ... sooner rather than later.

*"Ere the bonnie boat was won as we sailed into the mystic..."**

* "Into the Mystic", written by Van Morrison, ©
Warner/Chappell Music, Inc.

Alexandra Clair

CHAPTER NINETEEN

Outside Gloucester, Nora picked up Route 128. Although it was an unnecessary detour, she took the Winchester exit and followed Route 3 through Arlington and into Belmont. She passed down the tree-lined street that had once been residential, looking for the place where her home had been.

At the corner she slowed and locked eyes with an elderly woman walking a cat on a leash. There was something familiar about the woman who lifted a gloved hand. Eventually she came to Storrow Drive and the Harvard lights burning over the Charles River and the Mass Avenue Bridge. Left at Marlboro Street and she was skirting the common into Beacon Hill.

Jared Shiel lived only blocks from the gallery that hosted one of her largest annual shows. Life was knit together with threads of coincidence, she reflected as Jared let her in wearing faded jeans torn at the knee and a white t-shirt. Despite the informality, he was showered, shaved and ready for the day still some hours off. In silence Nora followed him into the kitchen where the smell of coffee was pungent.

On the way through she glanced into adjoining rooms, surprised by the formal décor of period pieces that Nora guessed would be genuine and inherited. A Child Hassam adorned one wall, and she recognized a work by Willard Metcalf, as well as the painting of her own that Jared had purchased at the end of her last season. Nora felt proud to be in such good company, but was disappointed to see no sign of Burns' work and guessed the bulk of it would be on extended loan to museums.

The kitchen was unremarkable though cluttered with file boxes and two computers. On one wall was a large poster with photographs and names connected one to another. At the top was a photo of Lydia at age six; the year she disappeared.

Nora walked over and read the names. She felt Jared's eyes on her back. Dillihunt, Marstead and her own photo and that of her family. Paul, Paige, the three Marstead siblings as well as Hank and his mother, Pearl. Off to one side, the name

Wodsende and another group of photos. A line was drawn across the board to Samuel Marstead.

"I don't understand all this," she said and turned back to face Jared.

"It would be a lot to explain right now and I think you came here for my help. You have something to tell me and I want to help you, Nora. I care about you and all you've been through. Just know I'm here in Boston right now to be closer to these two cases. What the one says about the other and how that will inform what happened to Lydia."

Two cases? Nora let it pass. Her eyes drifted to a stack of photographs on the farm-style serving table.

"What's this?" she asked and then caught her breath.

Over the grainy black and white surface was an image of a young woman. Nora knew instantly that she was looking at the computer-aged enhancement of her sister's face. The family resemblance was obvious as Lydia peered back at her, entirely and completely herself.

The effect on Nora was electric. She was looking into the eyes of a woman who lived and breathed and performed ordinary, routine tasks of life just as she did. This was the sister who, in Nora's mind, had never grown up; and yet here she was, presumably alive and well. But, Nora knew what she had always known. Lydia could not possibly be alive.

"She would have been beautiful," she whispered, hardly aware of the tears that pooled in her eyes. "May I have this?"

"Of course," Jared said.

"It's odd," Nora continued, speaking slowly; and Jared knew that she was not at that moment addressing him.

"It's odd how the truth emerges. Not as instant revelation, but ever so slowly, through bits and pieces of random happenstance that may suddenly slip the bonds of obscurity into a particular pattern."

Nora looked into Jared's eyes, her penetrating stare catching him off guard. "Have you ever felt that way?"

Energy flowed out to Jared from that look, and for the first time he thought that he loved Nora. He had been attracted to her even before all this started, from the time that he saw her at a neighborhood showing of her work at the gallery on Newbury Street. When he sought her out to remind her of their former brief acquaintance as children, she was nowhere to be found. He knew she had a reputation for being aloof and distant, but when he finally met her, he was unprepared for that tough exterior; the direct, almost defensive way she pushed aside any and every offer of help.

Jared knew that if he'd met her in the midst of an investigation, he would have focused on her as a suspect. He sensed the absence of boundaries between Nora and Paul that only existed among lovers or people who shared dreadful secrets that left them in a kind of bondage to one another.

Nora and Paul were a handsome couple, and he knew that Paul was often her escort when she attended various social functions to promote her work. Paul was sociable and friendly, playing off Nora's penchant for distance, and yet they had a way of completing one another's sentences like an old married couple who'd long ago lost the mystery.

On that day at her Rockport Gallery, when Jared had seen Nora painting at her easel, and she had been unaware of his watching, he could not escape a vision of her as fresh and uncomplicated, an impression that quickly evaporated the moment she spoke. The contrast was compelling and he studied her now, her short hair gathered behind her ears to reveal the porcelain symmetry of a delicate profile.

Nora was not the kind of woman he was normally attracted to. Even now as he looked at her, once more appearing vulnerable and yielding, he had to fight an urge to take her in his arms and comfort her. Deliberately, he turned away, busying himself with mugs and spoons.

"Have you ever felt that way?" Nora repeated her question.

Jared turned to her with a slight, almost imperceptible intake of breath. "Yes," he said. "Each time I approach an investigation I hope eventually to feel just that way. It's the moment that transforms the ugly chaos of crime into craft."

Jared handed her a blue mug with the crest of the Boston Police Department on the outside. Their hands touched and almost unwittingly his lingered seconds longer than necessary, but she seemed not to notice.

"I have a story to tell you. It may, or may not be true, but I'm certain that at least parts of it are. This is the place to reopen the investigation into Lydia's disappearance."

Jared took Nora's hand in his. That she did not pull away prompted a surge of desire that he wished he could ignore. He thought of Andrea Wodsende and the similar attraction he had felt for her. Seeing Andrea helpless as she lay in restraints in that hospital room, he had wanted to shield and protect her and he didn't think he was wrong to see her as the likely victim and not the perpetrator. In the same way he could not imagine Nora as someone who would take a life. Soon he would get back to the Wodsende case, but for now Jared pushed the thought of Andrea from his mind and prepared to hear whatever it was Nora would share. He had entertained the theory that Nora and Paul may have, at the very least, concealed an accident they felt responsible for. Certain crimes delivered consequences far beyond the immediate sphere of impact, eroding the freshness of life for those left in the wake of violence. Jared knew this from bitter personal experience.

Still holding Nora's hand he led her to one of two comfortable chairs by the window, and with the other hand he brushed off yesterday's *Times* and *Globe*, letting them fall to the floor. As her hand fell away he felt the absence of her touch and realized that he couldn't protect her.

"Okay, I'm listening."

"I wish I could begin this story as though it were a fairy tale," Nora started. "You know, 'once upon a time' or 'in a far off place.' But I can't. The place was home and the time was real. It might have been yesterday, because it's so very hard to forget how our lives changed. My grandmother buried a young husband and then her son and daughter-in-law. I can't imagine how she bore that and still kept her faith in God. But she did. I really believe that if she hadn't had her faith and believed she would see them again, grief would have claimed her also. But she held onto that Bible verse, and you know I don't read the Bible all that much. But she quoted it so often that I remember. *I know who I have believed and am persuaded that He is able to keep that which I have committed to Him until that day.* Don't ask me where that verse is because I couldn't tell you, and I'm not sure I have the words exactly right."

Nora paused. Jared thought she might break down again.

"I'm not proud of that. She wanted me to have the same relationship with her Jesus that she did. She trusted her family to God, and she believed that we would all be reunited after death, and that justice would somehow prevail. Sometimes I imagine her up there nagging God. Saying something like, 'Okay, Jesus, you promised when I was living down there on earth that you would resolve this for our family, and Nora is the only one left.'"

Nora took a sip of coffee.

"My father had to sell our home in Belmont to pay for all the business of chasing down those rabbit trails that always came to nothing. It killed them. Can you possibly understand what a loss this was to my family? I think more often of them than of my sister. I think if only I still had my father and my mother, how much richer my life would be today. Because you know I miss them every day. They were remarkable. And with them alive, we were a remarkable family just living a normal life, and yet extraordinary for that. And then there is the burden of wishing and thinking that if only Paul and I had done this or that differently."

Nora stood and walked to the sink, pouring out her coffee.

"Would you rather have a drink? Something to steady your nerves?" Jared asked.

"No. I need my wits about me. As I mentioned on the phone, Herb died."

"I'm sorry."

"He told me something curious. He asked specifically for me, to talk with me and not Paul. Something he wanted me to do."

"And this upset Paul?" Jared wanted to confirm.

"That would be an understatement."

"What did Herb want you to do?"

"I think he wanted me to break into Howard's old apartment and look for certain evidence ... to destroy it. He didn't say so exactly. But he confirmed to Paul that Howard Marstead was a pedophile who'd harmed other children."

"After Paul told me who had molested him," Jared offered. "I looked to see if Howard had any kind of criminal record and particularly any assaults against children."

"And did he?" Nora asked.

"My old partner is checking to see if he frequented travel to certain countries where the exploitation of children is part of the tourist trade. I thought maybe I'd get the report today or tomorrow, but so far it seems that Howard Marstead managed to operate off the grid. And of course, if he did get caught, he had a very powerful family law firm that would have put the machine into operation to get him off; keep his record clean."

"He kidnapped Lydia, I'm sure of it."

Nora's expression was one of barely concealed rage, and Jared knew that if the object of that rage were anywhere near, she wouldn't hesitate to act.

CHAPTER TWENTY

No more than the rooftops of houses could be seen from the street and sometimes not even that. The beginning of one property was determined from another strictly by the shade of brick in the neighboring wall. They drove slowly, hunting for numbers until they finally settled on an unmarked drive. Jared rang the bell and the gate swung open. They were expected.

Hank was clearly surprised by Nora's early morning phone call. He had not seen her in years and was curious at her insistence that they meet immediately. As Nora introduced Jared, identifying him as an investigator from Boston, Hank eyed him with open curiosity. They sat in an office off the library, a tray of coffee, on a Chinese butler's cart, within arm's reach. Without asking, Hank poured them each a cup of the fragrant streaming brew. Cynthia's own blend.

"It was certainly a surprise to hear from you, Nora. Is this a social call?" Hank asked, ever aware of his schedule and impatient to be off. He looked pointedly at Jared. "If you need my legal services we might just as well have met at my office."

"You may want to sit down, Mr. Marstead. We have some startling news for you."

But Hank remained standing, impatient to get this interview behind him.

"I understand that despite your father's age, his death was not expected. Was there an autopsy?" This was not the question Nora expected Jared to ask, but she realized that just as his line of inquiry had yielded results with Paul and herself, it might do the same with Hank.

"I can't imagine why this should concern you, but I will say that I did insist upon one. I am sorry to say that my father's death was preventable. He died of suffocation."

"Did that seem odd to you?" Jared asked, catching the hesitancy in Hank's tone.

"Actually, yes, it did. My father was partially paralyzed and could not turn on his own, so the thought that he could have suffocated seemed ludicrous to me. My wife and I discussed the final report and decided an investigation was not warranted. My father could not speak as a result of his stroke. He suffered permanent brain damage, but there was evidence of a seizure, which explained the manner in which a carelessly left plastic bag draped over the bed rail, could have covered his face. His death was ruled accidental. We are considering a lawsuit against the healthcare agency, but they of course claim the attendant is completely innocent and cannot say where that bag came from."

"Did you have any other thoughts concerning the death?"

Hank sat at his desk and placed his palms on the leather-trimmed blotter. He wondered where the conversation was leading. In the first throes of grief, he had confided to Cynthia his suspicion that Daria was somehow responsible. Cynthia had no qualms about telling him he was deranged for suggesting such an absurdity.

The emotional side of Hank had thought immediately of Daria, but logically he knew he sounded somehow paranoid; and yet even now as she came to mind he felt a deep chill of foreboding and was tempted to share his thoughts. It would be a relief to tell someone who might listen and even take him seriously. As he wrestled with the idea of bringing up Daria's name, an innate cautiousness prevented him from doing so. Thanks to Cynthia he had come to appreciate just how bizarre that theory would sound to sane ears.

Hank found his gaze seeking Nora. Several times she appeared about to speak as she sat at the edge of a jacquard wing chair. He thought her surprisingly unchanged from the young girl he had summered with in Rockport. She had always been a bit of an enigma to Hank, confident beyond her years with a clean sort of prettiness.

Hank recalled with some discomfort his attempts to attract Nora's attention. Other girls liked him and thought him handsome and even entertaining, so why didn't Nora? No matter what he did, he could never breach that impenetrable space she affected between herself and others, and perhaps taking her cue from Paul, she had seemed to regard him behind a veil of ironic humor, completely immune to his adolescent attempts at flirtation.

That was long ago, but even today Hank could recall with

some bitterness how he had longed to be included in that exclusive world which his cousin and Nora seemed to inhabit. After the tragedy involving Nora's sister, that hedge of protection had only grown thornier. She and Paul closed ranks, growing ever more distant and secretive. It galled him that they hadn't seemed to need anyone but each other, and now he wondered how that relationship had changed. He felt an almost perverse satisfaction about her sitting here in his home and finally needing something from him.

After Lydia's disappearance there were no more summer visits on Mill Lane for Hank and his mother. The last time Paul and he had been at a social function together was at his wedding to Cynthia, where Paul had agreed to be one of the groomsmen and Nora had accompanied him. They were content to let others assume they were a couple.

Hank regarded Nora with interest. Could he still be a little in love with her, even after all this time? He had expected Nora to accompany Paul to his father's funeral and was particularly hurt when neither came. Perhaps they had never realized how important they were to him and that ignorance of his feelings was far more insulting than their absence.

Hank decided to change the subject. He was angry with Paul and Nora and felt a sudden wash of self-pity. He would dispense with Nora and her investigator friend as quickly as possible. Whatever problem had brought them to his door could not possibly be as important as the two appointments he had cancelled just to satisfy a childish curiosity.

"Is Paul in some sort of trouble?" Hank ventured. "Because I am hardly the person to help. Perhaps you are unaware that my cousin and I are not on speaking terms at the moment."

"You were disappointed when he failed to attend your father's funeral," Jared stated dispassionately. "You asked him to be a pallbearer and all you got in answer was a sympathy card some weeks later."

"That's right."

"Are you aware of the reason?"

"I can't imagine any good reason, and I no longer care," Hank replied, feigning indifference. "I asked him to take part in the funeral when others were courting me for that honor, and he never even had the courtesy to respond."

"Paul was sexually abused by your father, Howard Marstead."

There was the barest flicker of emotion at Jared's assertion. Then Hank's lawyer persona shifted into gear. Nora could almost see him draw into himself. His body straightened in a formal way and his eyes narrowed.

"And you have proof of this?"

"Yes," Jared said simply.

"I mean more proof than my cousin's word, because you do know that he tends toward the fantastical."

Nora bit her lip rather than give voice to the retort that sprang to mind. Jared had insisted on conducting the interview, and now she understood why.

"To your knowledge, has your father ever been charged with any sort of crime?"

"My father was a paragon of respectability. He and my mother were divorced, but he had an illustrious career as a philanthropist. Over eight hundred people attended his memorial service and the condolences are still flooding in from three continents."

"In regard to child pornography and pedophilia there are no economic or educational barriers," Jared replied evenly. "You might make a list of those who sent cards and notes for the authorities. They will certainly be asking." Nora realized that Jared was deliberately provoking Hank, just as he had tried to provoke her and Paul on that first day in her studio.

"I must ask you to leave my home," Hank said, pointing a finger at Nora. "These are serious allegations. You damage the reputation of my family in any way and you'll find yourself in court."

"This is your right, of course," Jared said.

Nora stood, ready to leave, but Jared remained. He leaned back in his chair, looking to all appearances like a man ready to settle down with the Sunday paper and his first cup of morning coffee.

"A dead man cannot be prosecuted. There would be nothing to be gained by dragging your family name through the mud, and I'm sure Paul wouldn't want that either. But crimes have been committed and others are involved."

"Let me escort you to the door! Nora, I am disappointed that you would come to my home under the pretext of needing help, only to attack my family name. I thought we meant more to one another than that."

"But I do need your help, Hank," Nora said, entering the conversation for the first time. "You must remember my sister. My sister Lydia?"

Hank leveled a cold stare at Nora. "I can see where this is going," he said. "Many people, my mother and Aunt Paige included, have always believed that Lydia wandered back to the beach and drowned. The undertow is unpredictable, even with the breakwater off Front Beach. So you see how ludicrous it is to think that a man of my father's caliber would stoop to kidnapping a child. Get out of my house. If I hear from you again, I'll not hesitate to obtain a restraining order. I'll see you in court, and all you think you own will disappear as you defend yourself against slander and defamation of character and a few other choice charges."

The phone rang. Hank walked back to his desk and shouted a demanding, "Yes?" into the receiver. Once again Jared failed to follow Nora to the door. She turned back to see him calmly sipping coffee as he studied Hank over the rim of his cup.

Irritated by Jared's scrutiny, Hank tried to calm himself as he listened to the voice on the other end of the phone.

"I am sorry," he said. "Would you repeat that?"

"Mr. Marstead, this is Rowan Greer, with the construction crew working on the apartment."

Even in his shock over Jared's allegations, Hank was struck by Rowan's stern tone. Rowan and his hired crew had done extensive work for them over the years on various pieces of property. Cynthia was very fond of him. With the title to the New York apartment now firmly in their possession, Hank had given Cynthia the go-ahead to begin a total refurbishing, and they had hired Rowan to begin the first stage. Cynthia had persuaded Hank to purchase the newly vacated apartment on the floor above and Rowan, following the architect's plans, was now combining the two into one. It would make an impressive second home, and Cynthia fully expected the premier architectural design magazine to feature the finished result in a future issue.

"I know who you are, Rowan," Hank said impatiently and turned his back against Jared's scrutiny.

"We've knocked out the east bedroom wall and have found something here that needs your immediate attention."

"What are you talking about?" Hank demanded. Nora and Paul looked at one another. "You're there to renovate, not explore in places you are not supposed to be."

"This is the wall your architect asked us to remove. Now, if you don't get down here within the hour, we'll be phoning the police. I know you never lived in this apartment, and I appreciate what you did for my grandson; so I'm giving you an opportunity to get here first. Am I making myself clear?"

Hank thought back. It was Cynthia's idea to arrange for several private interviews which would assure the boy was seriously considered by several Ivy League colleges, including their own Alma Mater. Rowan's grandson was accepted at MIT on his own merit, but Cynthia often contrived useless deeds for people which resulted in big rewards.

Hank's voice dropped to a whisper, and Jared and Nora could no longer hear. Finally, he replaced the receiver with strained deliberation. He rang for his butler.

"Show these two out," Hank said to Lawrence. "Remember their faces. They are not welcome back, and keep your eye on them until they are actually off the premises."

"No need. We're ready to go." Jared took Nora's hand, nearly sprinting to the car.

"What are we doing?" Nora asked.

"Intriguing conversational exchange, don't you think? And that body language. I think we owe it to ourselves to find out where he's off to in such a hurry."

"Hank was uncomfortable and understandably anxious to see us go, but ... "

Jared interrupted. "My guess that car of his will be coming from the direction of the garage in just a moment. So we'll just meander slowly up the drive and catch his tail as he leaves."

"We're following him?"

"Of course."

Nora agreed that Hank's whole demeanor had changed with that one phone call. It had not escaped her how he had stared at her, allowing his gaze to linger longer than seemed appropriate. She wondered what he remembered from that July weekend. Had he stayed in bed all day as was claimed? She was sure that

Hank being in Rockport had brought Howard as well.

Herb had told her she did not know who the Marstead family were. *"Be careful,"* Herb had said. "Some are not quite human." Was it wise to put this assertion down to lack of oxygen; the delusional ranting of a man in the last minutes of life?

Paige Marstead had gone to extreme lengths to keep Paul from the police. Until Nora read the reports she had no idea how this cat and mouse game had frustrated, not only her father, but also the investigators at the time. It seemed that Pearl and Paige Marstead had been more concerned with closing ranks around Paul and Hank than helping to find Lydia. Pearl had packed up her sick son and promptly left the country. Neither was concerned for future victims, distancing themselves from the investigation as though from the plague. That Paige had withheld the crucial information of this pedophile connection was criminal. As Alexandra Clair wrote in her book, Discerning Spirits, they were passive facilitators, a role all perpetrators select and groom weaker persons to play. In Nora's mind, this made Paige equally culpable. Somewhere in Paige's back ground there was an accommodation, a cowardly pay-off of some kind. Nora had never liked Paige, but now she thought she might actually hate her.

Alexandra Clair

PART FIVE

CHAPTER TWENTY-ONE

RYAN

"Do you have it?" Mat asked as he and Ryan exited the baggage area.

"Yes, but if I may be so bold as to ask, what's the mystery? Why do you need Elliott's schedule for the day? Why not just phone like a normal person and invite him for a drink?"

"I'm in a bit of a hurry."

"I can see that. You chartered a plane."

Mat didn't respond.

"I have a funeral to attend day after tomorrow," Ryan continued, assuming Mat planned to stay with him. "I'll be gone overnight, but I'll leave you my keys."

"Who died?"

"No one you know. AIDS, I think. A new incombinent strain of the virus, or so I was told."

"Sorry."

"Yeah," Ryan said off-handedly. "I just heard this morning. Haven't seen him since he got so sick, but I need to be there. Now tell me, what's going on with you?" Ryan insisted, changing the subject.

As he talked he handed Mat the network visitor's pass and schedule he'd asked his assistant to surreptitiously obtain from Elliott's secretary. Mat pocketed the pass and studied the schedule.

"Looks like Elliott has a planning meeting with the northeastern affiliates," he read out loud.

"That would be in the eighty-second-floor meeting room. Not a gathering to interrupt. Only a medical emergency could free Elliott. If you plan on a confrontation, it's far too public."

"Perfect. I just have time to waltz in uninvited and appropriately late." Mat tossed his suitcase into a waiting cab.

"I have a car. Let me drive you."

"This is all I need," Mat said and held up Elliott's schedule. Suddenly he turned serious. "Actually, Ryan, you might want to distance yourself from me for a while."

Ryan eyed Mateo with ironic interest. "I guess you're telling me gently that you won't be staying at my place while you're in town. And to think I made up a bed and everything."

"That would mean you've cleared a corner of that closet you call an apartment and set up an army cot with a sleeping bag," Mat replied.

For over ten years Ryan had occupied a three-room walk-up on a dead-end mews-type courtyard. The seedy decor did not fit what was expected of a young man on the rise, which a consumer culture associates with media success. The lapse of image irritated those who thought they knew him well enough to offer advice. When pressed, Ryan would reply, "I just had the place fumigated, sprinkled and blessed, so why should I fix the place up? I'm good for another year."

After sharing hotel rooms with Ryan, Mat knew the truth. No matter how much money Ryan made, he would never acquire much by way of material possessions. A victim of chronic insomnia, Mat had heard stories of Ryan's bizarre sleeping habits, but not until they roomed together while on the world team did Mat take the rumors seriously. While Ryan began the night in bed, he never ended there. Mat would wake to find him propped in a chair or most often in the bottom of a closet completely ignorant of how he got there and yet sadly resigned to this odd, seemingly unconscious ritual. It seemed that any enclosed or barricaded corner would do, but Mat also noticed that his friend slept most soundly in busy airports, ice rinks, or any public place where he could catch a few winks.

"If you need someone at your back, I'm not afraid of a little trouble," Ryan offered, and Mat knew he was serious.

"Besides," he continued, "I don't recall you distancing yourself from me, and I imagine there was a time when you got plenty of that advice."

"True," Mat smiled grimly. "But unfortunately this is not the same. There might actually be some legal implications that the network won't want you associated with. But I appreciate the offer, my friend."

"Oh, but what if I insist?"

"Thank you. It's just that you attract more attention than I want at the moment, but I'll let you know if that changes."

"At least tell me what's wrong! We've been friends since the day you dropped that gold medal in my bag. I owe you," Ryan pressed.

"There was something more I should have done for you that day. No matter what you said, I should have gotten you some real help. I should have told someone what I saw." The two men held one another's gaze. Ryan shrugged and Mat smiled grimly.

"Where did that come from?" Ryan asked with some discomfort. "Hey, I don't think about that anymore."

"Even if I believed you I couldn't confide in you just yet. Later," Mat said and closed the door of the cab as it pulled away from the curb.

Mat left his luggage at the front desk of the hotel and took a cab directly to the network building. One of the photographs held back from the flames left little doubt as to the identity of two of the three men on camera. Instinct warned that catching Elliott off guard, before he had time to marshal his defenses, might yield the best outcome. There were so many questions. Among them, did Daria have a family, and if so, why hadn't they protected her?

With the yellow pass pinned to his lapel, Mat signed the visitors' log and followed Ryan's directions to the meeting room. A receptionist looked inquisitively his way and then recognized him. Mat could always tell that moment when people realized they had seen him before. A blank expression suspended their features as they questioned their judgment. Sometimes a little notoriety came in handy.

A long table filled the length of the room, as people milled about taking an afternoon break. Mat saw Elliott, the center of a group of laughing admirers. Elliott could always command an audience. To these people he was a media personality as well as a successful businessman.

"Mateo, what a surprise. What are you doing here? Allow me to introduce you," Elliott said cordially, as in a rush he made brief introductions to the group standing about. Mat smiled and handed Elliott the envelope as he shook a few hands.

"What is this? Something that can't wait?" Elliott asked, emitting an indulgent, self important chuckle as if happy to do a favor for a friend.

Elliott lifted out the photograph, carelessly laying it atop the envelope. Immediately his smile was replaced by a horrified grimace as he resisted that first stab of comprehension. In one frantic motion he jammed the photo back into its sheath, and to hide his hands shaking, shoved them to his side like a marionette stiff with fear.

There was something about observing the disintegration of Elliott's famous composure that was immensely satisfying. Conversation receded as those closest to him could not ignore the sight of his trademark tan as his skin color sank to green pallor. For the first time Mat wished he had confided in Daria and brought her along to witness this moment. It was her moment, not his, and he stored away the details in his memory for the time when he could tell her.

Elliott's reaction confirmed what Mat already knew. "We can talk here, or we can take what I have to say some place more private."

Elliott walked from the room with Mat following. "What is this? Some sort of blackmail scheme!" he hissed, his tone accusatory, jumping to a first offensive. "I would have thought this sort of behavior beneath you, Mat."

"Would you have preferred I go directly to the police?"

They stood in the privacy of Elliott's retro corner office. Breaking the impression were three original Miro's. The door opened and Elliott's assistant poked her head in. "They need you back in conference," she said and looked with annoyance at Mat.

"Tell them to go on without me," he said and nearly slammed the door in her astonished face. As he slid the bolt into place the phone rang. Elliott strode back across the room and picked up the receiver.

"I don't care what you tell them," he said, his tone seething. "What do we pay you for, anyway? Manufacture something believable, but under no circumstances are you to put through another call until I say otherwise."

Elliott replaced the receiver and leveled a stare at Mat. It was a look Mat had seen often through the years of watching Elliott cut people with smug caustic barbs considered pithy only by sadists and his employers.

"What do you want?" he asked. "Money? A spot with the network? Name it!"

"I want the identity of the other men in this photograph. I want an explanation of how Daria found herself in these circumstances. I want answers."

"I have nothing to say." Elliott reached for the phone. He punched in a single number letting Mat know that whoever it was he thought of calling was someone he had on speed dial.

"Not a wise move to call for reinforcements just now, Elliott. You want to get this settled here and now between the two of us. No one wants to ruin your reputation or cause my wife any more pain," Mat lied.

Elliott replaced the receiver. For a brief moment he looked hopeful.

"But if you don't cooperate and tell me what I want to know, I'll phone the police. You and I both know that this one photograph is merely the tip of the rubbish heap."

"What about Daria?"

"Daria wants the truth to come out. She wants to see you all prosecuted," Mat lied. "All that is standing between you and a prison sentence, not to mention complete financial and personal ruin, is my good will. So start talking."

Mat could see the hesitation. Elliott stared at the phone as though struggling to make a decision. Twice he reached out his hand before letting it drop back to his side. Mat wondered who he thought of calling; security, a friend, another pedophile reprobate?

"Allow me to make this easy for you!" Lifting the photograph out of the envelope Mat slammed it face up before a shaken Elliott. "This is you!" he said pointing. "This is Sasha Eymrnov! Now who is this?"

Elliott looked like a beaten man. His voice had lost the bravado that so characterized his usual manner.

"After a manner, Sasha Eymrnov was executed. You didn't know that, did you? It's not public knowledge. I think his government is still giving out progress reports on the cancer that will soon claim his life. They found out a few things about Sasha. Soon they'll have a mock funeral and I imagine the mourners will be few. They can get away with that sort of maneuver in some countries."

Elliott sounded envious.

"You may have wondered why Daria had such trouble getting permission to stay in this country and why you had to marry her to smooth it all out," he continued. "Our government knew, of course and hoped Daria could give them more details."

"More details of what?" Mat demanded.

"It seems your Daria helped herself to large sums of money, which she wisely invested out of the country. Ownership of that money is in serious dispute. Some say the government. Others... don't snicker; illuminati Satanists and various networked cult-fronts loyal to no country or government. Out of certain rituals come power, and these rituals require children."

"And what do you say happened to the money?" Mat asked, feeling that Elliott was attempting to draw him in to this conspiracy trap. If drawn in to making sense of what Elliott was saying he would go away no wiser and be no closer obtaining justice for Daria.

"When Sasha returned home without Daria, he had no idea she'd betrayed him. If he had, he would have followed her example and taken off for one of the many safe houses his justified paranoia motivated him to prepare over the decades. Daria left detailed information in certain hands, which effectively sealed Sasha's fate, and if you hadn't rescued her, we would have killed her ourselves. So you see, Daria gambled heavily on your Sir Lancelot mentality and was planning to escape with that stash with or without your help."

This explained Daria's need to marry in order to stay on in the country and her long interrogation at the FBI office in Los Angeles. But he saw nothing to indicate that Daria had access to large sums of money. In fact money did not seem to be at all important to her. And he could not believe these conspiracy theories about global control, cults operating within governments, illuminati demon worshippers.

"An interesting story, Elliott, but not what I want to know." Mat pointed to the man who had been poised over Daria in each of the photographs. "Who is this?"

"You will be surprised. Perhaps even astonished, but then hero worship would never have been your proclivity."

"Get on with it Elliott. I might have places to go, people to see; formal complaints to file. You get my drift."

Elliott's tone shifted to a certain fawning eagerness. "You are opening a Pandora's box, my boy. Do you promise to embrace the truth when you hear it? You realize you are sealing my fate just as Daria did Sasha's. I am a dead man even as I utter the words."

Mat rushed over to Elliott and brought a fist within inches of his face. "Stop playing with me, Elliott. As far as I'm concerned you don't deserve to live, and I would be perfectly justified in killing you now."

Elliott's voice came wistful, self-pitying. "I imagine the world would agree with you. Your stay in prison would be minimal, but then there is so much more to know. Just the tip of the rubbish heap, as you so eloquently pointed out."

Elliott emitted an elitist chuckle. "People like you can't see the forest for the trees. Fact is we're mowing down the trees and you're not even feeling the shock," Elliott reached for the phone. He punched in a number and put the phone to his ear.

Mat spun around with dance like grace and leveled his foot into a blow at Elliott's arm. Elliott recoiled as Mat grabbed him in a choke hold, the white leather desk chair bending back with the weight. Elliott sputtered and gagged, his arms flailing helplessly.

The feel of Mat's fingers as they felt fragile resistance against Elliott's fleshy throat was immensely satisfying, a culmination of primal imaginings interrupted only as the chair toppled over and the two men fell in a heap on the floor. Mat let go. Elliott was right. If he died now the truth would die with him.

As Elliott staggered to his feet, Mat walked to the bar and poured a shot of whiskey. Amber liquid sloshed over the rim of the glass as he slammed it down before Elliott.

"Start talking and this time leave your opinion out of it," he said, fixing Elliott with a menacing stare.

"Howard Marstead," he rasped.

"Howard?" Mat repeated.

"You do recall the party you attended in January at his son Hank's home? You didn't realize that Ryan was there as well, did you? In fact, we came together, because you see, Ryan and I have a long history and Ryan is more connected than you can ever know. Ryan is bloodline."

"I don't want to know about any bloodline crap, whatever that is?"

"Oh, I can see the question on your face. Why didn't you see Ryan and me? Where were we while you and Daria were holed up in that closet; otherwise occupied?"

"I can't imagine Ryan agreeing to go anywhere with you."

"Indeed. It's not easy to persuade a cab to drive that far out on a Saturday night. I had a network limo at my disposal, and, although it's been the bane of my existence, Ryan and I do share the same employer, as you well know. Actually, Mat, you might want to consider that Ryan Kollyn is not the person you think he is."

Elliott walked to the mirrored bar. Retrieving an ice cube he rubbed it gingerly across his throat where ugly red marks were forming.

"You, my boy, were the talk of the party." Elliott stabbed at the air with his glass, leaving a spray of amber droplets over the white carpet. In haste, he gulped what was left of his drink and poured another shot.

"Yes," he said, as always enjoying center stage. "It was on everyone's lips. How you and Daria locked yourselves in that closet. Very Hollywood, but not in the least original. Howard died that same night."

Mat thought back to that dark conclave in Canada, or so he had come to think of that sinister meeting. Sasha, Glen, Elliott, the two Marstead brothers gathered unobtrusively, cloaked by an innocent party atmosphere, on the night he helped Daria escape. Howard kept a low profile while continuing to wield tremendous influence behind the scenes. Elliott had said that children were required. What Mat inferred from that, that some pedophiles, not fully in the loop helped to supply these children. It was hard, almost too much to contemplate. A level of courage was needed and he wasn't sure he was up to the challenge.

Mat had anticipated the time when he could confront the man who had raped Daria. Each still of that event had been burned indelibly into his brain. For a split second Mat longed for doubt, but as he looked into Elliott's avid face, he saw that this was just what was hoped for and even expected. A shunning of reality that prompts vacillation and then a grateful excuse not to follow the bread crumbs. The very doubt upon which evil counts and predators feed.

Death had placed Howard permanently beyond his grasp. Mat felt deflated. He thought of Daria and their reunion on the night that Howard died. He saw her in that green dress with red hair shining and the smell of her perfume and the feel of her arms about his neck. He remembered the snow falling and the delay as he waited for her in the car.

"Was Howard's death an accident?" Mat asked with all the calmness he could muster and hating himself for that dawning suspicion that limped its way into words.

"He'd had a very bad stroke. Much worse than anyone let on. Cynthia Marstead allowed only a handful of his very best friends to visit and of course I was one," Elliott stated proudly.

Mat felt immense relief. How could he think Daria capable of murder?

"But he was a great man," Elliott lamented. "A gentleman, a true intellectual."

"Howard Marstead was a monster who preyed on defenseless children, and he did not deserve the privilege of expiring comfortably in his own bed."

"I did not molest Daria," Elliott countered.

"I don't know what else you'd call it. You stood back and watched, didn't you? Even if I believed you, I'd have to say that constitutes the same thing. Maybe worse because you could have helped Daria but didn't."

"I couldn't possibly have helped Daria. I'd be dead myself if I tried, and it was all a horrible mistake. Howard had never been so reckless. He intended to take someone else. Both boys were bloodline and very important to..."

Mat erupted, "what is this craziness? What bloodline are you talking about?"

"He was after someone he would have returned. He panicked; took her instead, then didn't know what to do and the publicity was brutal. Your Daria was going to be a throwaway. I can tell you we all had some sleepless nights."

"People were looking for her?"

"She wasn't supposed to live, but then we thought of Sasha. He happened to be in town and the minute he laid eyes on her he wanted her and promised to keep her for no more than a few hours. But Sasha liked to save things, and you wouldn't know it now, but Daria was like a Dresden doll, and Sasha had this most remarkable collection of memorabilia."

Elliott spoke in a rush, caught up in the web of his own evil mind. Mat felt sick. He bit his lip, willing himself to keep silent as Elliott stood and walked to the window. He pressed his cheek against the triple pane and then turned his head and stared out at the row of empty flower boxes that lined the walled ledge.

"Howard's mistake was trusting Sasha, but we'd done business with him before without a problem. Only a man with Sasha's monumental ego would risk taking a trophy like that out of the country, and the next thing we knew she had this whole other identity. She was an orphan, and there were plenty of those in his country, so I guess no one took notice of one more. Suddenly she was Sasha's Pygmalion, and he was teaching her to skate. He was rubbing our faces in it. He'd always been an outsider, and now he was forcing his way in and we were helpless to stop him."

"And that worried you?"

"Yes, you idiot, that worried us! When Howard confronted Sasha, he told us that, with programming Daria had lost all memory. Howard threatened him, but Sasha was holding all the cards and used every one of them. As long as Daria remained alive, Howard was firmly under Sasha's control. Before that no one wanted much to do with him. He was too crass and too opinionated. An undisputable liability, but suddenly he started attending certain events. The council in Milan found him useful and the word came down that he was untouchable. They got him to modify his behavior, but that Bolshevik was always a loose cannon."

Elliott turned and leveled a stare at Mat. "Didn't you ever wonder why a skater of Daria's talent rarely competed internationally? Sasha had to keep her away from Howard. She was his insurance policy, so if she turned out to be temperamental and a little crazy, well that only served his purpose. Howard would have killed her in a heartbeat, if only one of us could have gotten close enough."

Elliott's eyes burned into Mat's. "There is only one reason why Daria is alive today, because if Howard had his way, the two of you would never have crossed the Canadian border."

Mat was stunned. Elliott was telling him that Daria was an

American. 'I know Boston,' she had said. 'I want to go home.'

He pointed to a place off center. "Someone took these photographs. I want the name of that person!"

An evil grin tore across Elliott's features. Mat had never understood the phrase 'chilled to the bone', but now he understood it perfectly. He felt that he was standing on the precipice of evil and looking its substance and design firmly in the face. Elliott seemed to have no idea of the impact of his words, but Mat was now beyond anger. He was looking into the face of a rabid dog, and he appreciated how one could rationalize murder. He felt he would be doing the world a favor if he killed Elliott rather than allow the legal system to deal with him. This was no longer just about Daria. There had to be other children whose treatment demanded retribution, and it didn't matter that he didn't know their names.

What rankled most about Elliott's delivery was his apparent lack of awareness of how his words sounded to civilized ears. If Elliott had begun life with a conscience, it was now totally obliterated. Mat thought of Howard, Sasha, and now Elliott. It seemed that depravity ran in packs, just like dogs, but who was the fourth dog? He had to know.

Despite his apparent poise Mat noticed that Elliott's eyes were shadowed by anxiety, and his hands had never lost the tremor that had arrived with a first glance of that photograph. His fading blonde hair was streaked with gray, and his Nordic blue eyes regarded Mat warily. There was no evidence of remorse. Elliott was only sorry to be found out.

"There's nothing more dangerous than an honorable man and you have always been so predictably ethical. It's boring, Mat. You *are* boring. Wouldn't you rather give people a little mystery. Well, I can help you with that. I can make you bigger and richer than you've ever dreamed of."

"Don't waste your breath, Elliott. You'll need it when you confess to the authorities."

"With great sadness I must say. I'm glad people like you don't dominate the human race, because if you did no one would have any rights at all. Our time is coming. You're probably a Christian, but I wouldn't have quite labeled you a born again, witch hating, book burner. People like you are dangerous."

Mat could hardly speak. If the evil he saw in Elliott was real, there had to be a God to overcome it. Otherwise there would be no goodness, nothing to live for, and no purpose or dignity to his existence. He hadn't intended to pray, but words flashed to his mind, rising from some deep place of need within himself. *God, please help me. Please rescue children like Daria from men like Elliott.*

"As we've been chatting I've been racking my brain, wondering. What can I offer Mat in exchange for silence? The answer seems painfully obvious? I can offer you nothing. Is this not correct?"

Mat nodded his head.

"Well, then. Where do we go from here? Are you going to destroy Daria? Or will you allow her to go on and enjoy the success and acclaim she's won, because you know the press will have a field day with this when it gets out."

"You make it sound like Daria has something to be ashamed of. Make no mistake, I'll not keep silent to accommodate you. Somewhere out there Daria has a family and a past. You've already told me people missed her and were looking for her. That means she was no throw-away as you put it. I'll help her blow the whistle so loud your ears will explode."

Mat stepped threateningly into Elliott's orbit. "I won't ask again! You are, were, a ring of pedophiles. Who took this photograph?"

"You do us no justice, Mat. You have not been listening."

"I'm all ears."

"Some of us, of course. But others, no. We use pedophiles, we manufacture assassins' and world politicians, bankers, military chieftains. All on the take before they realize what they're involved in. Oh I dread to tell you and I've already said too much. But wherever I'm off to I'll enjoy hearing from the watchers just how you struggle to put these pieces together. Especially because it seems I shall gain nothing for my cooperation," he tested and studied Mat's face.

"Right," Eliot said. "Therefore I have nothing more to say."

Elliott was playing with him, but that was okay. Mat felt overwhelmed with all there was to think about.

"Time is running out, Elliott."

"Pour me another scotch, will you; straight up and neat. Then I'll do what I must."

The Year Between the Wood

Mat walked to the bar. He lifted the crystal decanter and heard the sound of glass sliding against metal. A March wind, an incongruous whiff of thawing ground that promised budding trees and grass easing into green, even in mid-town Manhattan raced like a freight train through the room. Why had he not registered the empty pots enclosing a wide ledge into a patio?

Before the crystal had shattered against the marble rim of the bar Mat had sprinted halfway across the room, but all he managed to grab hold of was the fabric of Elliott's sleeve as it slid like a paper burn across his palm.

Alexandra Clair

CHAPTER TWENTY-TWO

Jared had difficulty keeping up with Hank's gray BMW. He drove wildly, dodging traffic and twice occupying the right shoulder. Just before the bridge Hank was stopped for speeding. Jared pulled ahead waiting for him to pass.

Once in the city Hank's car disappeared into an underground garage.

"I'll pull over and go inside. After you've parked you can join us," Jared told Nora.

"How will you get in without being announced?" Nora asked, noting the elite address.

Jared flashed his badge. "I'll let them know my assistant is following."

Nora grabbed the badge as Jared double-parked. "No," she said, "I'll let them know my assistant will be following." Impulsively she leaned over and kissed his cheek. She felt suddenly buoyant and hopeful. It seemed an odd little burst of emotion that could not last.

"Don't even think of trying to talk me out of this," she said when she saw his face cloud over.

He would have but it was too late. She was already gone.

All eyes were on Hank as he walked into the apartment. Half a dozen men stood about in work coveralls and a film of dry wall particles floated in the air. Although it was early, most were in the process of packing up their equipment for a quick departure. None of the men would hold Hank's gaze.

"What's going on, Rowan?" Hank asked.

"This way, Mr. Marstead."

Hank followed the large-boned, middle-aged grandfather into what had once been two bedrooms. The area was now gutted with partial walls removed and only a supporting beam left in place. Rowan pointed to a four-foot depression in the floor. Hank allowed his gaze to follow the depression toward the remaining wall, where stacks of what looked like canisters of old reel to reel movies and the later variety of video tapes were wedged into shelving from floor to ceiling. Color-coded files and rows of folders clearly labeled with a series of numbers ran along the depression in the floor and were meticulously arranged to fit precisely the depth. Rowan picked up a folder and handed it to Hank.

"These numbers correspond to others on some of these old reels and tapes," he said. "This operation has been going on for many years. It was your father who used to live here, wasn't it? That's what your Missus told me."

"Oh my God," Hank cried out audibly, his words an anguished plea of shock. As he leafed through the photographs, he felt contaminated and defiled by the little that he looked at. It was horrifying to think that there was more, and yet there was. Even he felt overwhelmed as he considered the impossibility of imposing much damage control. He took a deep breath. He had to try.

"Have the police been called?" Hank asked.

"Not yet," Rowan responded. "Looks like invoices over there," he pointed. "Had a profitable little business going on. Something to see him through retirement," Rowan's tone was contemptuous.

Hank took a deep breath and steeled himself to speak. "Stop those men from leaving. We can destroy all this within the hour. I'll do anything. Give them money." Hank's legendary composure was disintegrating. He removed his jacket and rolled up his shirtsleeves as though to begin the work of destroying evidence immediately.

"Your troubles are just beginning," Rowan replied sympathetically. "After we found all this," Rowan waved his arm to encompass the room, "some of the men went looking for more. I told them to wait for the authorities, but I'm afraid it was already too late. Come this way."

The cold chill of disaster pricked at the hairs of Hank's neck, and his palms felt hot with a sudden blood surge of apprehension. With great reluctance he followed Rowan deeper into the apartment. Rowan pointed to a wall and spoke with the professional tone of any contractor explaining why some whim of thoughtless design could not be carried out.

"Looks like nothing, doesn't it?" Rowan pounded his fist

against a concealed panel and a hollow sound reverberated. "This is not on the architect's plans and doesn't lay flush on the other side. Here," he said, leading Hank by the arm. He pushed and the panel swung open. The room was small and lifeless. A cot lay on the floor and old children's fantasy posters lined the wall.

For a long moment Hank refused to see anything unusual. *So what*, his mind soothed. *So what*, until his gaze took in the miniature leather restraints lined with lamb's wool. As though in a dream Hank bent to pick one up. It was small and slender with openings, as though for belt loops, and at the center a large ugly buckle. With false composure Hank noted the inventory of characteristics until suddenly, as though burned, he threw the restraint from him. The inside cuff was stained brown, the color seen in police evidence rooms, the distinct shade of old blood.

"It seems to me you've got no choice, Son. You've got to phone the authorities. It will look better for your family if you do it yourself."

Hank turned to see Rowan's crew standing in the hallway opening. He realized that even though they had prepared to depart they were drawn to this macabre drama like moths to a flame. They observed his reactions with cautious wariness, clearly wondering if he were somehow involved. Hank knew that this kind of crime had a way of clinging to and contaminating anyone associated, no matter how innocent.

When he spoke, Hank was stunned at the calm, concise quality of his voice. He was back in law school, role-playing one of the criminal cases he'd decided was not his sort of law. Gearing up for arguments, confident that he would prevail, he was, for the moment, only interested in the quickest course to resolution.

"None of you are rich men. How does half a million dollars sound, divided equally between the seven of you?"

"Most of us have children. You think we could sleep nights knowing a place like this exists and we haven't told anyone?" One man spoke for the others who nodded and murmured in agreement.

"My father is dead. He can't hurt anyone else. As you can see, I had no idea."

"How do we know that?" "Maybe not," came duel responses

and then a concurring murmur.

"Do you think I'd turn this place over to seven strangers to tear apart if I even suspected the truth? Not to mention the architect and my wife's decorator and her team of assistants."

"I don't know," someone wavered, and for a second Hank let himself think he was winning the room.

"How does seven hundred thousand sound? That's a cool hundred grand for each of you, and all you have to do is walk away. Don't any of you have mortgages or children you'd like to put through college?"

"What about all the people he corresponded with? All the people he sold this wickedness to?" one man asked.

"From what Rowan claims, your father had no time to cover his tracks. Somewhere around here there must be a mailing list that ought to provide the authorities with some long overdue answers."

"On the day my father had his stroke, all this died with him," Hank tried to reason.

"I know you're scared, Mr. Marstead," Rowan said. "But taking a bribe is not my style. Now I tried to do you a favor, but I can see this has all been too much of a shock. One of us will be calling the police in the next couple of seconds. Who will it be? You or me?"

"No, wait," Hank said, grabbing Rowan's arm, now desperate. "We can work something out. I am a rich man. I'll just come up with more money, and all you have to do is walk away."

"I'm afraid there will be no more of that." They all turned at the sound of a woman's voice. "You can't protect your father's reputation, Hank. Or anyone else involved for that matter. Jared will be here in a moment and he'll call the police."

Those blocking the door moved aside as Nora stepped up to the threshold. Hank was struck by how small she was, and yet there was a certain noble polish to her demeanor that commanded attention. He couldn't help thinking that she would make a good witness. A jury would believe her. It was a good thing for his family that his father was dead.

Tears glistened in Nora's eyes as she spoke. "My sister may have been imprisoned in this room. That could be her blood on those restraints," she said and stooped to pick up the cuff that Hank had earlier thrown down in horror and disgust. She turned it over, almost lovingly in her palm. Unlike Hank she seemed loath to relinquish this thread to what could possibly be Lydia's fate.

Taking in the scene at a glance, Jared came up behind Nora and gently took the cuff from her. Ever the professional, she noticed that he had put on gloves and wondered where they came from.

"This is a crime scene," he pronounced. "I'll have to ask you all to move into the next room and wait there without touching anything until NYPD arrive. You," he pointed sternly to one of the workers getting ready to depart, "will be going nowhere."

Hank slumped to a nearby chair.

"Don't you think I have a right to know what happened to my sister, Hank?"

At the steadiness of Nora's gaze, Hank flinched. Abruptly the reality of his father had rudely shattered all those carefully constructed fantasies which he had fabricated to form the illusion of the complete family that had never been his. He had been a fool for indulging such sentiment and wondered what Cynthia would say. He would call her. Her instincts were intently focused on furthering their causes. She always knew the correct posture and position, the right spin to diffuse a difficult situation.

Hank looked into Nora's face and attempted to conjure up an image of Lydia Dillihunt, but it was difficult, for she was now just a vague memory of a child with red hair, who continuously complained and whined as, much like him, she chased after Nora and Paul.

Hank recalled that he had been sick in bed the weekend that Lydia disappeared. His last glimpse of the trio had occurred as he looked out the guest bedroom window. Lydia complained of carrying the beach ball instead of the picnic basket and Nora's calm reasoning voice explained that she, as the eldest, would carry that basket. Paul had finally settled the dispute and appeased Lydia by taking it himself. Hank watched enviously as they stepped onto the rock slab at the side of the gate, too old to open without difficulty, and jumped into the cemetery for the usual short cut to Front Beach. Had anyone else been in the lane that day? As he thought about it, Hank conjured up an image of a man walking to the gate; looking after the children.

Was that imagination or fact?

Arms laden with bright beach paraphernalia, Paul, Nora, and Lydia disappeared down the hillside, amidst the granite headstones and burnt grass of summer. Despite his illness Hank lingered at the window until the last of their voices, suspended on the hot sea-air, could no longer be heard.

There was no escaping the truth in Jared's allegations. It remained to be proven if his father had anything at all to do with Lydia's disappearance, but that Howard was guilty of unspeakable and shocking acts was not in doubt. Hank felt a profound sadness displace his initial panic. In a desperate attempt to recapture and rewrite the past, he had loved a helpless stranger and called him father. He had invested him with all sorts of attributes and sentiment that had been nothing more substantial than a mirage.

Hank thought of church and the minister he hardly knew. He and Cynthia went to church to be seen and to establish useful contacts. That he was a member of a church could help rehabilitate the hit to his persona that was about to be severely damaged, but for now all Hank wanted was to withdraw someplace safe and be comforted by Cynthia. As always she would arrive at a course of action. For now Hank felt helpless and so profoundly disappointed. He wanted to cry. Hank staggered and Rowan caught his arm.

"Forgive me, Rowan, for so foolishly trying to compromise your ethics. Now if you will excuse me I have some phone calls to make. The first to the police."

Hank watched as the men left him alone, but loitered in the next room waiting. Hank turned his back and dialed Cynthia.

Upon entering his hotel room Mat filled the massive marble tub with steaming water. He felt drained and exhausted. Fragments of Elliott's conversation, the scope and horror of his disclosures, replayed in his mind as he shed his clothes and settled himself into the bath. Mat felt somehow contaminated by Elliott. He had looked over the white blocks of the terrace and seen Elliott spread-eagled on the pavement below, and he had not been sorry. From far up Elliott could be sunbathing with no hint of the twisted body splayed on the pavement below as bystanders gathered about.

When the first officers arrived Mat acknowledged the locked door, the exchange with the secretary, and Elliott's obvious discomfort as they left the meeting room. Any temptation to explain the truth was only fleeting. He had to think of Daria. Claiming to have no idea why Elliott would suddenly decide to kill himself, Mat remained vague but acutely aware of how conspicuous his omissions sounded to reasonable ears. There was no note, no reason any of Elliott's co-workers could give to explain his shocking plummet from the balcony ledge of the network building. Judging by the shock and grief on the faces of Elliott's co-workers as they suspiciously looked in his direction, Mat surmised that even though the police had not named him a suspect, they certainly considered him one.

Two detectives arrived and the polite inquiries took a more assertive bent. After interviewing those in the boardroom and Elliott's secretary, Mat was asked if he would voluntarily supply his fingerprints.

"We'd like you to take a lie detector test. Maybe this evening," the younger of the two detectives told him and then wrote down the name of the hotel where Mat was staying.

But Mat was evasive. He certainly had wanted to kill Elliott and now could not be sorry that he was dead. He wondered what it would be like to answer a barrage of questions about Elliott's last hour, as an impersonal machine interpreted data on his pulse and respirations. He could not risk a lie detector test. There was too much to hide.

"I'll let you know after I've consulted my attorney," he said, trying not to sound as nervous as he felt.

Although he could not hear the conversation, he knew there was a debate over whether they should bring him back to the station for a more formal interview. Mentioning his attorney had temporarily forestalled this. Mat tried to remember how much of the ledge he had actually touched as he attempted to stop Elliott from jumping. His grip on Elliott's throat would have produced obvious bruising. How would he explain that? He could postpone the inevitable, but eventually would have to tell the truth.

Getting up from his place in the outside hallway Mat walked to the reception area off Elliott's office. Through the open door he watched as a lab worker finished dusting and lifting fingerprints from the contents of the desk, over the window ledge and balcony door. As he moved to the bar area Mat had the impression of events careening out of control while he struggled to keep pace. He decided to leave, noting that everyone else interviewed by the police, including Elliott's secretary, had been told they could go. It was time to test the waters. Either those two detectives would stop him and haul him down to the police station or they would not. He walked toward the elevator.

"We wouldn't want you to leave the city without letting us know," one of the detectives reminded Mat. Mat hesitated, locking gaze with the detective. Then with purpose he walked back into Elliott's office. Before the detective could stop him he put Elliott's desk phone on speaker and pushed redial.

"Marstead Firm, may I help you?"

"You want to know where to start this investigation? Start there," Jared said to the stunned detective. He then walked to the elevator, surprised anew that they let him go.

As Mat sank deeper into the warm water and felt his muscles ease, he switched channels, catching bits and pieces of the evening news. The local networks reported Elliott's death as an apparent accident. No mention was made of the police investigation and no other explanation was given, but Mat knew that could not last. He was only thankful that for now he could postpone calling Daria. He did a mental calculation of where she was right now. She would now be in Kansas City, joining up with Glen Winston's tour. He expected her to call soon after checking into her hotel.

Mat closed his eyes and leaned his head against the padded neck-rest of the ivory bath and allowed his concentration to drift. He was nearly asleep when the cell phone erupted. Sandalwood bath oil dripped from his arm as he put the phone to his ear.

"What room are you in?" Ryan demanded, his shrill tone jarring Mat back to the present. "I'm coming up."

Mat wrapped a towel around his waist, and went to unbolt the door, leaving it ajar. He was just belting the hotel robe when Ryan burst into the room.

"I just drove by Howard Marstead's old place and at least six police cars are out front, and then I get a text that Elliott has jumped to his death with you in the same room and the door locked. Did you push him?" Ryan demanded.

"Is that what people are saying?"

"Yes. And if you did, I can't actually say that I feel anything but jubilation. We'll just have to hire the best defense attorney money can buy."

Mat regarded Ryan with interest. His pupils were dilated while his body exuded an intense energy. Could he have relapsed and be back on drugs? Mat hoped not, but knew it was entirely possible.

"Do you want dinner? I'm actually starving," Mat picked up the phone and dialed room service. "Lamb okay? It's excellent here." Ryan's impatience was evident as Mat calmly ordered lamb with new potatoes, green beans, and sorbet.

"Just tell me if you killed him, because, there is only one scenario I can imagine where Elliott would take his own life."

"It seems to me, your dislike of Elliott goes beyond network rivalry. This is all somehow connected, and for Daria's sake I need you to tell me the full story."

In answer Ryan gave him a wooden stare.

"Don't you trust me, Ryan?" Mat pulled a pair of wrinkled cargo pants from his suitcase. He ran his hands through damp hair, and donned a flannel shirt.

"I think you know. I think if you've spoken with Elliott and as a result he killed himself, well then. You had the big guns out; you could enlighten me about a few things."

"Humor me."

Ryan sat at the foot of the bed. He turned his hands over and studied the lines in his palms as though deliberating and then coming to a decision.

"Family doesn't mean the same thing to me as it does to you."

"I could have guessed that."

"My father spends a lot of time in Europe. I'm nothing to him but a valuable piece of DNA. Mother... well, I think by anyone's standards one would say she is an alcoholic. When I go home, maybe she is there and maybe not. There are servants, hired by my father to keep an eye on her and some are a little creepy."

"I'm sorry."

"As far as I know, my parents never went against anything

that Howard, and later Glen wanted to do. They were responsible for my programming."

"Programming? Are we talking about mind control?"

"That's what they call it. All about controlling human beings like robots; micro targeting for the macro agenda of controlling planet earth. The research on this jelled under Hitler, but has been going on for a long time. The battle ground is in the mind, and if you control what people think and disable critical thinking skills through fear based programming; trauma and ignorance you control a population. When I was too young to fight back or even understand how it started, I was spending a lot of time with Elliott and then it was Howard. As I'm sure you know they molested me."

"What about Glen?"

"Glen wasn't a pedophile. He seemed to know my breaking point. Sometimes he found excuses to keep Howard away. Especially as competition season geared up; my primary motivation for doing well."

Ryan spoke in a flat, mechanical manner, almost as if reciting.

"Their manipulation in order to break me grew more sophisticated as I became older. Howard had pictures that chronicled my life. Not the sort you'd put in silver frames on the grand piano, you understand. Just the thought that those photos would surface if I told, was pretty effective blackmail until I decided I'd rather die than go on. That's when I realized I held power denied them. They actually had far more to lose than I."

"Why didn't you tell anyone?"

Ryan's expression came alive to one of withering contempt, and Mat wished he could retrieve the question.

"There is always some fool who must ask! Why did you marry that person? Why were you walking by yourself at night? Why did you dress the way you did, why not run or scream? Why not leave Ireland when food became scarce or escape Germany when friends began to disappear? As if every outcome can be foretold, and that one minor mistake of judgment that sets you on the road to destruction justifies the consequences. If it's my fault, then you can delude yourself into thinking that evil could never touch you or someone you love. Well, Mat, it has touched you. I suspect it has rammed into you like a runaway train. And you did nothing to invite it, did you, Mat? But you sure as hell spent some time denying and doubting your instincts. Everyone does."

"I'm not asking about everyone. I'm asking about you."

"I don't think of myself as a victim. I hate that word."

"Ryan," Mat pleaded in desperation. "Elliott talked about some kind of illuminati conspiracy. So I already believe these people are a cult and crazy and somehow you and Daria are involved with them. Please Ryan, just tell me."

"Once I told a visiting coach who didn't want to get involved. Somewhere a police report exists, but I figured that if no one would hold the great Glen Winston accountable for his behavior, how much more they would disbelieve anything I had to say about Howard."

"What about Howard?

"It's more than you think, Mat. Just the thought of trying to explain to someone like you who hasn't a clue is exhausting. It's like literally... Like, I want to crawl into bed and sleep until you give up asking questions."

"Try me."

"And there is risk. You won't see it, but I will."

"Please, Ryan. Trust me."

"It's a whole system expert as dissemination and discrediting anyone who speaks out. And since the public doesn't want to think along these lines they cooperate. I was dedicated to demons before I was born. They believe some things that Christians do about the end of planet earth and judgment only they fully believe they can win this battle and ascribe a very different outcome; trying to change God's prophetic time table. These people like to say they don't believe in the devil because fact is they believe in thousands of devils; many groups worshipping different powerful demons. They expect the last very powerful antichrist to come from one of the bloodline families. Any male bloodline child could be that candidate and they compete for the honor and the power it will bring. This last antichrist is the principle of reversal coming to fruition. This Satan will be the antithesis of Jesus Christ coming at the end."

"So, let me get this straight. As far as these lunatics are concerned, being bloodline, you could be that antichrist figure?"

"I'm sure my father would like to think so. It would mean

more power for our family. After they tear you down through abuse they program you to be whatever is needed."

"Enough? You're giving me a headache! What does this have to do with Daria? I'm not interested in some crazy conspiracy-religious theory, right now. I only care about saving my wife from these people!"

"You asked and I'm trying to let you know what you're up against. And if you want to help Daria you'll listen, because she won't respect anyone who doesn't understand what she's been exposed to. Your refusal to face facts serves Daria, but it also makes for a dangerous situation. And that's why she turned to me, Mat, and not to you."

"They were blackmailing me. That's how I learned about Elliott and Sasha. They sent these photographs."

"No, they did not!"

"Yes, they did."

"Stop playing the fool and think, Mat. Did Elliott look shocked when he viewed those photographs? That's why you went to see him right? No one from that cult, as you like to call it, sent those photographs. Ask yourself! Elliott had no conscience. He was so sure of himself he believed he would never be found out. Exposure would represent a minor adjustment to Elliott. He'd ride it out and survive. So why did he kill himself?"

"Okay, I'll bite. Why?"

"He was programmed to do so. Rather than threaten higher ups it became his job to die per suicide programming. Ideally any subsequent investigation would end with Elliott."

"You're asking me to believe some pretty crazy stuff. Okay. So who did send these photographs?"

"We do have enemies."

"And these enemies sent...?"

"They were playing you. They wanted you to put a dent in this segment of this particular American bloodline group and I can guess the dissenter behind it."

"Who?"

"He's a Catholic priest; part of a Christian activist group that includes several denominations. Originally he belonged to a powerful American bloodline group. His mother managed to escape with he and his brother while they were still quite young;

before the major damage could be done. They had help because they stayed under the radar; dropped off the grid. The target, through Daria, is the Wodsende family and run today, by Samuel Marstead, Howard's younger brother. You might explore that connection."

"And you belong to this family."

"No, I'm part of the German family, based for now in Milan, Italy."

"Why don't you leave."

"There is no leaving. There is death like Sasha and Elliott. There is dropping off the face of the earth like this priest I mentioned. There is total immersement in the families, or like me, there is survival. Survival until they decide they need me for something. Then the shit hits the fan."

It was almost more than Mat could take in. The thought came to him, "that funeral you're going to. Is that another of Howard's victims?"

Ryan stopped talking. Silence stretched into minutes as almost hypnotically Ryan stared at a fixed point across the room.

"What's wrong?" Mat asked, breaking through the impasse, putting his hand on Ryan's shoulder.

Ryan looked up. "If the police are clearing out Howard Marstead's old apartment, if they connect what they find there to Elliiott's suicide, everything will change."

This brought Mat up sharply. He would have to tell Daria, all that he knew and suspected. It would be a relief to have it all out in the open. He wondered if Ryan would agree to go with him to speak with Daria. Whatever there was to say he wanted it said face to face.

Ryan leveled an ironic look at Mat. "Do you wonder why I live alone? Why I've never had a significant relationship with a woman? It's because I can't get close to anyone. On some level I just don't feel. I'm a shell. They did that to me. It's part of the insurance they count on."

Mat was disturbed.

"You and I are close," he asserted, wanting more than anything to deny the significance of Ryan's words. Daria could just as easily have parroted that same sentiment. She could be just as damaged, a hollow shell of a person, but Mat refused to believe that aside from Joey, the two people he felt closest to in all the world, could not heal and change.

"Maybe we are close," Ryan was noncommittal. "I can't explain that, except to remind you that we safely live on opposite coasts and see one another in small controlled doses. If you hadn't met and married Daria, you would not have stumbled on the truth, and I sure as hell wouldn't have volunteered."

"I hope you know that you can trust me, Ryan … and what do you call this conversation; idle chit-chat?"

"Sorry, Mat, but I call this damage control. Fact is the little that I did tell you is enough for you to decide I'm delusional. You can go back to your safe, head in the sand, white-bread life and forget all this conspiracy crap."

"I am your friend. You've been my friend. It's a relationship we've sustained over time. That should count for something," Mat insisted.

"They count on a slow annihilation of all the traits that make us human. At a young age you are introduced to blatant evil, wearing a human face and walking about in a human shell. It threatens to kill you or suck you in and you believe that these are the only choices. That lawyer I told you about. The one that helped me file for emancipation getting out from under Glen's control. He told me I could be washed clean in the blood of Jesus. If I would just confess my sins, God would forgive me. More than once I've just about made up my mind to give that a try. I just feel dirty. I can't imagine a righteous God wanting anything to do with me, and then there is the question of authority. I'm not sure I can give authority over to anyone else, ever again; not even God."

"Speaking of authority, I guess we'll have to call the police eventually and tell them everything we know."

"I can't do that."

"They'll understand. You couldn't help yourself. You were a child."

Ryan shook his head vehemently. "You still don't get it! I'd rather follow Elliott out that window than open my past."

"We need to help the authorities. Silence isn't a luxury we can afford, Ryan. There's been enough of that already."

"If you thought the police could help Daria, you'd be there

right now, spilling your guts. You had a perfect opportunity this afternoon and you let them run with that bogus theory that you might have actually murdered Elliott. So don't hypocritically talk about the authorities and lay the responsibility on me."

"I need your help, Ryan."

"I've made a life for myself. I talk the language and make the right moves and it's all just a carefully choreographed parody and I, an imposter miming my way through life. But I make a pretty good salary for all the pretending, and it's my life. The only way I know how to live. I won't give it up for you, and certainly not for Daria."

"There were photographs of Daria. There are photos of you. We can't predict where or how they'll turn up. But after the day I've had, I can guarantee the police will be looking very carefully at Elliott."

"If it comes to that, I'll deny they are of me, and I'll keep on denying until no one cares. Everything grows old, and besides, Daria has already seen to Sasha and Howard, and you, thank God, have taken care of Elliott."

The dispassionate revelation slammed into Mat's consciousness. He could accept that Daria had arranged for Sasha's downfall. He wouldn't have hesitated to expose him. But... that she had actually killed Howard? That was murder!

Mat thought of the evening that Howard had died. For a moment he was back in that car outside Hank Marstead's house. He saw the snow as it fell, obliterating the lacy pattern of frost on the window, and he heard the drone of the engine as it paced the rhythm of his impatience. All he could think of was the tender reunion that lay ahead of him and Daria. Soon after they would marry, and all that was lost, all that was so abruptly interrupted, would be restored. Just thinking of that second chance for a life with her had made him happy. He could feel Ryan scrutinizing his expression.

"There were three men in the photographs that I saw," Mat stated, forcing his concentration back to the present. "Someone was setting me up to be blackmailed. So now I have to wonder who took those photographs."

"Wake up, will you? I'm not repeating this again. Blackmail had nothing to do with it. There was never going to be a demand for money in exchange for silence. Silence is the last thing these people want. Organized dissenters, Christian's planted that information to bring down a pedophile ring, tired of seeing one investigation after another shut down. They know exactly who Daria is, somehow found out, and knowing what a boy scout you are they predicted what you would do."

"I'd like to know who took those photographs."

"Not to worry. Daria will get around to him soon enough."

There was a knock at the door and the tray of food was wheeled in. Mat was no longer hungry, but Ryan was. He poured himself a drink and cut into the lamb with relish. Mat watched as he spooned out a generous helping of the mint and ginger chutney.

As he studied Ryan, Mat felt a cold sweat break over his brow. Time seemed to pause at the threshold of realization, like horses at the gate before a race. He gathered the courage to ask.

"Are you saying that Daria killed Howard?"

Ryan laid aside his fork. His chair toppled over as he made a mad dash for the lavatory. Mat listened to the sound of Ryan's retching and felt a numb quiet steal through his body. When Ryan emerged he was pale, his face drawn."

"Are you deaf? To what extremes are you going to take this denial thing?" he erupted, his voice dripping ridicule. "Of course that's what I'm saying. Daria killed Sasha, she killed Howard, and you saved her the trouble of taking Elliott out. The Daria that I know might not thank you for that."

Turning his back on Mat, Ryan walked to the window seat. He drew up his legs and sat looking out at the city lights and the street below. Not since those brief tears of rage in the aftermath of that altercation with Glen Winston at nationals, had Mat seen Ryan cry.

Far below traffic melded in a blurred river of brilliance as miniature stick figures moved about. From here the world looked manageable, and one could almost imagine a God-like invincibility that would never be the province of man.

Overcoming great odds, Ryan had survived a childhood, the ramifications of which Mat could only guess at. A picture of Elliott's face flashed to mind. Ryan was not like Elliott, and yet the hint of a new wariness rose in Mat and he was loath to make a comparison that reason mocked was absurd. At the end, unable to hide the truth, Elliott had defended himself by speaking a foreign language in which an entire range of emotions like empathy and culpability had been replaced by qualities one could not humanly relate to. Elliott's only true lament had been that Sasha had not murdered Howard's throwaway child as he had promised, and now Daria had resurfaced to become a monumental inconvenience and threat to him; to Ellliott. There was no comprehension of the pain and havoc that had been reaped in Daria's life.

Mat looked at Ryan and it seemed to him that his friend had never appeared so isolated. Always there had been this tough, no-nonsense shell and the sarcastic barbs and humor to ward off any real conversation and too often he had let Ryan get away with that. A real friend would have demanded more.

Mat sat behind him on the narrow window seat and joined his arms about Ryan's chest. Ryan pulled away, but Mat drew him firmly back. As he felt Ryan's body stiffen, he was drawn into a tangible oppression, like the blending of watercolors on a wet page. Resisting what he felt Mat held on tight, refusing to let go. Ryan's heart was pounding dangerously fast against his palm as unsung sobs strained against the boundary of flesh. Time passed and by degrees Ryan's muscles eased and his breathing returned to normal. In a rare abdication of all those dearly-won defenses, Ryan let his head drop back against Mat's shoulder. Minutes passed and Mat knew he held a child and not a man. He would not be the first to let go.

"Will you go to that funeral with me?" Ryan asked, rising suddenly as though stung; putting distance between them.

"Why?" Mat was surprised.

"Trust me. You need to be at that funeral."

"Where is it?"

"Up the coast; near Boston."

"The detectives told me not to leave the city."

"Call your lawyer in the morning and let him deal with it. Anyway it was a suggestion. They haven't charged you so they can't keep you here."

Mat started to speak. He wanted to ask more about Howard and that fourth man. The one behind the camera whose identity he felt he needed in order to protect Daria. Ellliott was right. A Pandora's box had been opened, but Mat would follow the trail of truth wherever it led.

"This is about all the male bonding I can tolerate. Anymore and you'll be admitting me to Bellevue. Now you need to think about what you're going to tell Daria before she catches some exaggerated gossip."

Mat looked at his watch. "I'll call her later, tonight. I need to think about what to say."

"I wouldn't wait. You don't want Daria to hear that you were with Ellliott when he jumped from anyone else. Nor, that you are suspect material."

Ryan picked up Mat's cell phone and tossed it on the bed.

"Just call her. Also... I'd change hotels. In fact I'll call the Drake and make a reservation under my name. While you pack I'll go pick up the key and bring it back to you."

"You think that's necessary?"

"I'm done explaining things to you. I told you what I think so start packing. Once you change hotels, until I come for you in the morning, don't open your door to anyone. No one, got that?"

"You think I'm in danger?"

"You've got a disease that we could label the proverbial selective hearing. Wake up! Ellliott was important. The space he occupied, able to influence media, represents a significant loss. You and I will assume a bot could already have been dispatched to silence you."

"They'll shoot me?"

"Nothing in such bad taste. No, they have murder down to a science. More like a brain aneurism, anaphylactic shock or a tragic accident of some kind. Be careful about anything you ingest."

With those parting words the heavy door closed behind Ryan. Mat stood in the center of the room, undecided. Then he felt a quiet assurance. A supernatural kind of affirmation that Ryan was right. Mat began to pack. Afterwards he would phone Daria.

Part of Mat believed it all. The practiced, socially trained denial part of him questioned. Could clinical paranoia construct such a sophisticated stronghold of fantasy that others would buy in and the system of belief, like a self fulfilling prophesy evolve and move into the realm of fact? And where did that leave him? Leave Daria?

CHAPTER TWENTY-THREE

When Daria arrived at practice the other skaters had already assembled with the choreographer. She had been sent a video to familiarize herself with the group routines, but a mental run through in her mind and actually skating were not the same. Feeling awkward and out of place, she skated through the number with few errors.

If there was any ill feeling about her last minute addition to the show, none was evident. The other skaters were curious about her life and seemed to welcome the opportunity to get to know her better. Although the film was still in post, some of the ladies congratulated her on the opportunity. Daria maneuvered her path about their friendliness like footfalls in a minefield.

For the remainder of the afternoon she practiced two other group numbers and then performed her solo for the choreographer, who suggested only minor changes. She was just finishing and was due for an appointment with wardrobe when she caught a glimpse of Glen Winston. He had been a brooding presence in and out of the rink area during much of the practice but had yet to greet her. It was a surprise to all when the music was suspended and Glen's voice boomed out over the ice.

"For those of you who have not yet heard, I have some tragic news. I regret to inform you that the rumor is correct. Ellliott Smythe is dead as a result of an apparent accidental fall from a balcony. The show will go on as planned. We will dedicate tomorrow night's performance to his memory. Those of you who imagine that we will cancel any engagements so that you can attend his funeral should think again."

There was a prolonged moment of stunned silence and then a drone of whispering began. As Daria skated toward the boards she caught snatches of conversation.

"Fell from his balcony?"

"There has to be more to this story."

"Mateo Araujo was with Ellliott when he fell," one of the principal male skaters offered and glanced at Daria as she skated by, his voice dropping to a whisper too late. Daria could not help but hear the speculation as she slipped her guards into place and headed for the closest exit.

"Leaving?" Daria looked into the face of Glen Winston and blinked. "I understand that you have a fitting in wardrobe."

Daria had forgotten. All she could think of was the comment that Ellliott had been with Mat when he fell. Could that be true?

"Thank you for reminding me," Daria said. "I am sorry to hear about Ellliott, Mr. Winston. I understand you were good friends."

When he failed to answer, Daria moved to retrace her steps, but Glen remained in her path. She had rehearsed this moment countless times but could not escape the dreaded nervousness which enveloped her in a cloud of uncertainty.

"After the fitting I thought I'd return to the hotel for a rest before tonight's performance," Daria said, reaching for the futile blanket of words to cover her discomfort.

"Good idea. Shall we leave passes with the gate for your husband?"

"I don't think so. He and Ryan might be," Daria put a hand to her forehead, "doing something. But I know Mat will call tonight and plans to catch up with the tour."

"What a treat!"

Glen's sarcasm was clearly directed at Mat and not at her. Didn't he recognize the far larger threat that she presented? Even Howard Marstead, that shriveled-up excuse for humanity, had opened his eyes and been horrified to see her leaning over him. For the mere heartbeat of seconds, as she looked into his face, Daria wondered if she had been right about Glen Winston.

All that she knew of him had been bolstered by Ryan's recollections. In spite of that she now doubted that Glen was among those monsters that had exercised full reign over her childhood nightmares and the thought was disconcerting. Daria already knew that memory could be manipulated. Was she wrong about this? More significant, was there reason to doubt Ryan?

Daria heard the distinctive ring of her cell phone. It had to be Mat? But Glen continued to bar her path.

Daria looked carefully into Glen's face, thinking that he was an anomaly. She had yet to meet anyone who did not like and admire her husband. She opened her mouth to speak but found that she could not. Instead, alien words projected over that mysterious flash of splitting in which the multiple, if only briefly, occupied the same spot of constraint, poised at the threshold of emergence to become separate and whole.

Daria came to herself keys in hand; fumbling to open a door her arms laden with packages.

Her cell was ringing and then stopped. Bursting into the room she got tangled in the strap of a purse she didn't recognize. Irritated she tossed all on the bed and reached for the hotel phone, just erupting in jarring sound.

"Where have you been?"

Daria looked at her watch feeling like a woman fighting her way up from a deep dive of sombulant numbness.

Lost time. Where was she? Hotel room?

He had been speaking for some time, and perhaps she had responded, but she only just now caught, "Daria I need to tell you something. And I don't want you to be upset."

"I know, Ellliott committed suicide," Daria took up her cue.

"I have to tell you that I was in the room with him when he jumped. It was too quick and I couldn't stop him."

"I'm not surprised."

"You may hear a rumor that I'm responsible for his death. I'm not; nothing like that." Mat asserted.

"He wasn't a nice person."

"There is more. I'm going to a funeral tomorrow with Ryan and then catching the next flight home. I want you to leave the tour and meet me there."

"You said I couldn't get out of the tour. There is a contract."

"We'll let the lawyers sort it out. You and I have a lot to talk about. There may be some details regarding Ellliott that I will have to deal with. But first we'll be together so we can get everything out on the table. I love you. Completely honest..."

"I so agree; completely honest."

"I'm so glad to hear you say that, Daria." Mat sounded relieved. "I've pressured you onto a career path you didn't want, haven't listened to you enough. But that's all going to change. I'm so sorry."

Lifting what she'd recently heard from a radio talk show word for word. "Perhaps I could learn to say 'no' and mean it. I love you too. Love covers a multitude of sins."

Mat ended the call and thought that had gone better than expected. Daria would finally confide in him. He took his bags to the front desk and checked out. Then he settled down with a newspaper to wait for Ryan. He wondered if he could get out of the funeral tomorrow. Mat felt an urgency to be with Daria, but he thought not. For some reason his going had been important to Ryan. Something he couldn't say, but what Mat needed to know. He'd play along for another twenty-four hours. Then he would concentrate on Daria.

CHAPTER TWENTY-FOUR

Nora stood beside Paul. The house was congested. Like water seeking its own level, spilling into the first floor rooms as mourners jockeyed for space. The evening was milder than normal though an Atlantic bite lingered off the coast and sent a moist chill over the granite gray of the headstones, across the fieldstone wall that bordered Mill Lane.

Herb's last minute, deathbed conversion to Christianity, was viewed by some with a jaundiced eye. Friends from the garden club graciously organized and served the eclectic stream of dishes which steadily arrived on the dining room table now pushed into the library to make room for the casket Nora had painted.

Nora glanced at Paul. It felt good to be standing beside him, shoulder to shoulder. She and Jared had driven back the night before arriving late. Settling Jared in Lydia's old room, Nora undressed and slid between the flannel sheets of her own bed. She dozed intermittently, but real sleep eluded her. First light, just easing the March sky, drew her to the window, and she looked out over Paul's backyard. The greenhouse door was open. Her heart beating fast, Nora slipped into faded jeans and, tucking her nightgown into the waistband, moved quietly down the stairs. In the darkness her feet found the back door Wellingtons, and grabbing the pea coat she went to investigate.

Washed in the gray blue of a breaking dawn, the greenhouse felt decidedly empty and Nora was disappointed. Prepared to endure Paul's wrath in whatever form it would take, she had steeled herself for this first meeting since the debacle at Herb's hospital bed.

As she walked deeper into the glassed enclosure, tears burned in her eyes. Dropping her head Nora wrapped her arms about her own slim body as though for comfort. Defeated, she turned to study the house beyond, where no light burned, until her startled gaze picked Paul's form out of the dimness. Wrapped in Herb's crocheted Afghan, he sat on the top of an empty bedding table, wedged into a corner.

"Hello," Nora said into the silence.

She noticed the clay pots and the hoses neatly coiled and the late winter onions sprouting next to the spinach, carefully divided by wood barriers. The brick floor, sloping toward a drain, was dry. Overhead bunches of dried flowers, which under normal circumstances would have been recycled into flower arrangements and wreaths to give away, still dangled from a low-slung rafter to brush the top of her head. In all seasons the greenhouse overflowed with the activity of new life sprouting and old recycled, but with Herb's last relapse there was little time, and it was now eerily empty of its usual thriving abundance.

"Hi," Nora said again, thinking that Paul had not seen her. He seemed stiff, almost catatonic, and when he finally turned in her direction she had the distinct impression that she had called him back from a very far place.

"Are you all right?" Nora asked.

"I'm hanging in there. An apt phrase really." Paul's tone sounded tentative and his voice cracked in the way it does from prolonged disuse.

Nora nodded, letting a little silence gather in acknowledgment, and then she took a deep breath and spoke. "I need to tell you something but I don't know if you want to hear; or if now is the time."

"Now is the time," Paul stated flatly, and so Nora told him.

Paul hardly responded as she related Hank's reaction to their charge that Howard had molested him. Sliding up on the opposite table and propping her feet across the narrow aisle, she described the unfolding police investigation, which was for now centered on the massive amounts of evidence uncovered in Howard's apartment.

"The detective told me that if they find any connection between Howard and Lydia's disappearance, it'd be fairly certain she'd be dead."

The pause was long as Nora awaited Paul's reaction.

"If Howard hadn't had that stroke, do you think he would have destroyed everything?" he asked.

"Maybe not destroyed it, but certainly moved it or turned it over to someone else. Jared thought Howard's role would have been upper management; distribution coming from another location since most of what Howard had, in tech terms, could be considered antiquated; stuff he held on to as a serial pedophile."

"Time to open all those locked drawers and I guess that can't be helped."

"I'm sorry Paul. I know you're worried."

"I just hope that Howard had the mental capacity to agonize over the possibility of discovery each and every day that he sat immobile and speechless in that wheelchair."

"I thought the same."

"Did the police take everything?"

"When I left they were just beginning to process the crime scene. The next day they interviewed Jared and me. I learned that the building housed that singer-songwriter, William Chase and his family. For that reason there was added security paid for by him. There were several attempted break-ins which they assumed were fans, but now they will revisit that and will review the security tapes. I personally think someone may have tried to get at and destroy evidence."

Paul turned his attention back to the sky above the geometric configuration of the greenhouse windows. The air was warmer, somehow heavier, and Nora knew that by mid morning the sun would burn through a milky haze and the snow would melt into wet pools, which would freeze again by nightfall, turning the lane into a treacherous pond. Spring thaw, just a hopeless pipedream the week before, now seemed a certainty, and even the trees and gulls and night sounds appeared to express faith in its arrival, and yet March could be a cruel month. No true New Englander ever counted on March or April.

"Paul, do you forgive me?" Nora asked. "I said some harsh words to you."

"We've always told one another the truth, haven't we? We've lied to everyone else, but not to each other."

"There's more I need to tell you, but it can wait until after the funeral."

With renovations begun on that apartment this was all going to unravel, and the photographs of Paul, that Herb begged her to retrieve, would certainly surface. Did Herb also guess that his request on Paul's behalf might lead her to the truth about her sister? Did he know of the existence of that secret chamber, and was he aware of the international scope of Howard's child pornography business? Jared had reminded her that if Paul did not already remember, she had a responsibility to tell him before the authorities arrived with all their harsh, intrusive questions.

"You seem to be doing okay. Better than I expected," Nora offered.

"I tried to find out something about Herb's family. I thought there might be a sibling or distant relative I could reach out to. It seems he had a made up birth certificate. Wasn't even his real name, but that of a child that died in the first year of life. My lawyer's office found an arrest record for prostitution and that's pretty much it. If Herb ever worked it wasn't with a valid social security card."

"We were his family," Nora said.

"I named us both in his obituary. There is nothing more I can do for Herb, is there? When he was alive he needed me. Now he's gone."

"There is something more we can do. Herb never wanted a somber event for a funeral. I imagine half the town will show. Will you let me help?"

Paul was silent for long seconds. "Herb looks nice," he finally said. "I have him in that gray suit he liked with my college tie and the emerald earring I gave him our first Christmas together. You want to see him?"

Nora nodded her head as Paul moved stiffly off the bedding table. Draping their arms around one another they walked back to the house. The sky was lighter now and Nora could see Paul's face more clearly. The night sounds had faded and the first birds could be heard singing in the bare branches of the trees.

"Are you hungry?" Paul asked. "I'll boil us a couple of eight minute eggs. There are scones and cream Whit brought over. Then we can catch a few hours of sleep before people start arriving. You haven't slept, have you?" he looked at her sternly. Nora felt a thrill of joy at his reproach. She hugged him and would not let go until he hugged her back.

Nora and Paul slept until noon and then she slipped back across the yard to shower and dress. Jared spent the morning on the phone, networking with the New York detectives.

"I'm glad you made yourself at home," Nora said. "Sorry I abandoned you."

"No problem. Happy that you and Paul are talking."

"Any news?" Nora asked.

"They'll be testing your blood sample against that found at the scene. The FBI is coming on board. They said they would do their best to keep Lydia's name out of it for as long as possible."

There was little for Nora to do. Paul had seen to most everything. He had arranged to have their first Christmas card reissued by the local serigraph artist who had done the original. A printer friend had inscribed the inside with the twenty-third Psalm and placed Herb's photograph on the last page as a memento. Then Connor had suggested adding the following words, which Paul agreed to, only because it seemed dishonest not to validate in some way Herb's last hours.

"Before he breathed his last, Herb made a profession of faith in Jesus Christ and is, at this very moment, glorifying his Savior in Heaven. *Come to me, all you who are weary and burdened, and I will give you rest. Take my yoke upon you and learn from me, for I am gentle and humble in heart and you will find rest for your souls. For my yoke is easy and my burden is light (Matthew 11: 28, 29).*

All afternoon Nora and Paul stood by the fireplace and followed the bright holiday flash of those cards as they greeted guests.

"Do you think Herb would have approved of all this lack of piety? I mean, since he discovered religion and all that?" Nora asked.

"Not to mention drunkenness." Paul added. "It's very possible that you and I, some of the locals, and maybe those two late arrivals over there," Paul gestured, "are the only sober people present."

Nora glanced toward the dining room, where Herb lay, with his head on a satin pillow in the colorful coffin she had painted. From the hospital Herb's body was transported to the funeral home in Gloucester for embalming before returning to Mill Lane. Tomorrow morning a hearse would back down the alley for the short ride to Connor's church. After the services he would be interred in the Marstead family plot.

"Herb liked nothing better than a good party, but I think even this would have stunned him a little," Paul said, allowing his gaze to scan the room. It was an intriguing group of people who had assembled with little advance notice. Friends arrived from New York, Boston, and as far away as Wichita, New Orleans, San Francisco and Taos.

"Are you surprised?" Nora asked.

"I'm surprised that so many people came with such little notice and that I can't claim to have met many of them. You were right, you know. Herb had a whole other life."

Nora wore a slim black dress and jacket trimmed with matching satin and Paul wore black trousers and a gray wool shirt with silver buttons. Though his face was pale and his eyes rimmed red, Nora thought he looked very handsome.

"Then you forgive me?" she asked.

"I'll consider it, only after you explain what your boyfriend thinks he's doing."

"Not my boyfriend," Nora deflected. "Not yet, anyway."

Paul noted that Jared seemed to be making a concerted effort to personally speak to as many of Herb's friends as possible. "I would never have thought Jared could be such a good host. And this isn't even his party," was Paul's wry observation.

"He definitely has an agenda, but you might want to wait a few days for an explanation."

"You know, Nora," Paul said, turning serious. "I am sorry that Herb is gone, but I feel somehow lighter, and I have this notion that he is happy. As I was sitting in the greenhouse last night, I felt that he was looking down at me from a better place. I know this sounds strange, but I felt that distinctly and it was comforting."

"Then you're not sorry Connor prayed with him?"

"Herb was always so defensive of the lifestyle. It just seemed a betrayal of everything he stood for, and it seemed to me that Connor took advantage of that moment and robbed Herb of the dignity of staying true to what he believed."

"But Herb was scared. He was afraid to die. Could it be, that in the end, that radical social stance he was so vocal about just wasn't going to replace his need for God? His death was a long slow process and he had plenty of time to reflect."

"Maybe, and I sure didn't have any answers for him. In the

end it was Connor whose belief system never wavered. Maybe you and I should look at that, Nora. I've been thinking that Herb and I were never honest with each other. How can there be love without honesty?"

"Maybe in the end you'll only remember that you loved one another very much."

"That's a nice thought, Nora, but if I find that Herb had any involvement in Howard's activities, I shall have to hate him."

"I suspect that Herb, too, was exploited by Howard."

"Perhaps, but that's not the point, is it? There are lots of victims in the world and most do not grow up to become perpetrators. If I had known the truth, I would never have committed myself to loving Herb. In fact, I could not have loved him because there are some abhorrent lines one should never cross and abuse of children is right up there."

"But you loved one another. I saw that love. It was real, Paul. Up to the very end it was real."

"Was it? Let's not shade the truth just because we have a funeral. And are you forgetting everything you said the day we took him to the hospital? You said he never loved me. And how does that stack up against all the emotion that I invested in our relationship over the years?"

"I don't know," Nora acknowledged. "We don't have to think about all that right now, Paul."

"Ever since January, ever since Herb first acknowledged knowing Howard, and not in the superficial acquaintance first implied, I have been thinking about little else. He lied to me. When you give someone your youth and later you find that love was never reciprocated, you can't take it back. What does that say about me? That I was stupid to trust him? That I was foolish not to have guessed? Or that he was despicable for not telling me the truth about Howard because, even if he wasn't involved in Howard's activities, he did tolerate his behavior? I think that Herb made the decision to deceive me because he knew the truth would have ended things before they began."

"Paul," Nora began, but he cut her off.

"He robbed me of choice, Nora. And yes, you were right. He was unfaithful and with more than one person in this room with the abominable lack of taste to share their own grief, implying and telling more than I want to know. They didn't live with him and meld their finances with him and operate like a couple, trusting that the relationship was exclusive, did they?"

This tortuous questioning was just beginning for Paul. Nora wanted to stop the process and save him the pain, but knew that she could not. Nothing could hurt and then heal like the truth. Paul went to the kitchen and returned with two glasses of ginger ale. He had stopped drinking as suddenly as he had begun. He handed Nora a tall glass.

"I may be in love, you know," Nora said, changing the subject. She squeezed Paul's arm, simply grateful to be back on speaking terms. What would she have done, Nora asked herself, if Paul had really cut himself out of her life? That wouldn't have happened. She wouldn't have allowed it to happen! They watched as Jared introduced himself to the two late arrivals. Both looked familiar to Nora, but she couldn't place them.

"In love!" Paul said, amused. "How do you know?"

"I'm quite familiar with the symptoms from watching you, thank you very much. He hasn't said that he cares for me. Still, I think that everything he does is absolutely marvelous and endlessly entertaining. Yet I can't help arguing with him at every turn and indulging a certain thrill of heightened reality when he looks at me. That's what you had with Herb."

"That's what we had in the beginning, always in the beginning," Paul acknowledged wistfully. "Only you could come up with such an analytical definition of love. Well, Nora, I'll be happy for you if I must. A little jealous. Yes, definitely jealous," Paul said as though weighing his emotions. "But decidedly happy for you, and if he hurts you in any way I'll pound him into oblivion. Well, no, I couldn't actually," Paul said, eyeing Jared, who stood across the room speaking to a very handsome stranger who did not seem to be keeping up his end of the conversation. "But I'll hire someone."

Nora laughed. "Jealous. How could you be jealous?" she cajoled.

Paul was reflective. "I've had you to myself all these years. I guess you could say I also had the cake. Now I'll be alone for the first time in my life and to me loneliness felt like death. Don't you think there's a certain fateful symmetry in the reversal of our lives?"

Paul's hand found Nora's and he held on tight.

"Let me ask you something."

"What?" she prompted.

"Did we ever have a chance, you and I? If I had just tried could we have had a life together and maybe children? Because it seems to me that you would have tried and that you might have been waiting. And I wasn't listening or seeing. Is it too late for us, Nora?"

Jared was intrigued from the moment they entered the room. The man more formally dressed, in dark suit and tie with a black raincoat over one arm, held back as the other approached Herb's casket.

Neither followed the protocol displayed in near identical manner by the other mourners. They did not greet Nora or Paul, nor did they kneel and say a short prayer. Despite the offered pen, they declined to sign the guest book that stood on a podium at the entrance to the dining room, where Herb's last bed sat festooned with baskets of flowers, wreaths, and plants.

Only the second man, dressed informally in jeans and cashmere blazer, actually approached the casket. Placing one hand on the rim of the raised hood he leaned forward and gazed for long moments into Herb's face. Some close by noticed, but glanced quickly away, for the length of that prolonged scrutiny seemed irreverent.

What is he thinking? Jared asked himself, but the coffin stand had been wheeled and locked against the far wall, and it was impossible to see his expression. Jared turned his attention back to the first guest, who remained at the threshold. He made no attempt to speak to anyone and yet was not awkward in the way of people with nothing to say and no one to visit with in a group. Others noticed him as well, but there was something unapproachable in his manner. Jared thought he looked familiar.

Jared intercepted Ryan as he turned from his odd vigil at the casket. "Jared Shiel, I don't think we've met."

Ryan didn't respond.

Gesturing toward the casket, "did you check his pulse? Is he really dead?" Jared hoped to provoke a reaction; any reaction. He had circulated all night and found only what was expected. Too many former lovers, rapt with fear as they considered the nature of Herb's illness at the mercy of a strain of virus the medical community had little defense against. Whatever Ryan had been thinking as he peered into Herb's death mask was now safely hidden behind what Jared instantly felt was a carefully constructed façade.

"I'm Mat Araujo," his companion intervened. "This is Ryan Kollyn."

"Right? You work in television."

There was no fleeting look of irritation, and yet Jared felt it just the same. Ryan had taken an instant dislike to him and why wouldn't he? Jared planned to exploit that momentum as he always did. But there was something about Ryan. An undercurrent of world-weary exhaustion jaded and drained of some human element. This was a dangerous numbness to goodness; an absence of life, he'd sensed only a few times among cunning predators. When was the last time? *Dudley Wodsende at the bedside of Andrea.* A mere hour before he'd been shot and nearly died; that violent attack propelling him on the arduous road to recovery.

"And you," Jared turned his attention to Mat.

"A friend of mine actually," Ryan interjected, speaking for the first time. "Are you a friend of the deceased, because I don't recall Herb mentioning your name?"

"A Friend of Nora's," Jared admitted and nodded toward where Connor had just joined Paul and Nora. Connor stood between them, a hand on each of their shoulders. Ryan and Mat glanced into the next room, but Mat seemed unable to tear his eyes away. Finally he looked back at Jared.

"And Nora is Paul's wife?" Mat asked.

"Sometimes I wonder," Jared chuckled wryly. "But, no. I'm sure Ryan can tell you that Paul was Herb's companion and Nora is a close friend." He looked at both men. "Did you know Howard Marstead?" he asked and then noticed that Mat was gone. Without preamble he had turned and walked toward Nora. Jared started to follow, but Ryan recaptured his attention.

"Yes, I knew Howard." He let his eyes roam about the room and even coolly nodded towards a few people.

This was at least a straight answer to a question Jared had been asking all night. When he pressed the few who admitted to knowing Howard, he confronted a common unwillingness to shed light on Herb's association with Howard. As news leaked of Howard's crimes, however remote the connection, all would close ranks.

"How were you and Howard acquainted," Jared asked.

"I'd say at least a dozen men in this room knew Howard, but I imagine most have had the good sense to peg you a cop and have denied it."

"Busted," Jared acknowledged. "I'm not here officially investigating, you understand. More doing a favor for a friend."

"That's far worse. You're a man unrestrained by politics and protocol; a man on a mission. So, tell me. What is it that you think you know?"

"Enough to know there's reams more."

"And you'd like to compare notes."

Giving Ryan a measured look, Jared nodded his head.

"That would be a job for someone with a death wish. I'm not quite there yet," Ryan said glancing at the casket behind him. But then, still keeping Jared occupied and away from Mat, "I'm not opposed to answering the right questions carefully phrased."

"So as to be generally denied at a later time," Jared offered.

"Exactly."

Later Mat would be unable to explain how he knew that Nora was related to Daria. He just knew. It was the way she lifted her glass, the familiar heaviness of those sleek red strands that bobbed about her chin. It was the tilt of her head and the line and posture of her body, which made her appear taller than she actually was. Put together, it was a thousand details of persona and spirit which drew his eye and jelled to inward certainty.

Mat shook Paul's hand and, for the moment, avoided looking at Nora. His heart pounded as the caustic chill of discovery threatened to paralyze his limbs. "I'm sorry for your loss," he offered awkwardly.

"Thank you. Were you a friend of Herb's?" Paul asked, as he had already inquired of the steady stream of out-of-town mourners who entered his home and spoke words of condolence to him and Nora. Paul felt at an awkward disadvantage as he shook those hands, surprised at the number of people Herb had kept in touch with through the years, and then how full his life had been away from Rockport and their life together.

"I'm a friend of Ryan's," Mat said and looked over his shoulder at where Ryan and Jared continued in conversation.

"I hope you don't mind my being here?"

"Not at all. There are actually quite a lot of people here that I've never met. One more doesn't matter. It's turned out to be a lively bunch," Paul offered when he realized that Mat was not going to move off as the others had. "We didn't intend a party, but it seems we have one anyway."

Mat looked about the room as though for the first time. "I'd like something like this for myself when I die. Old friends meeting after a long absence, a bittersweet tribute that's not false or over-burdened with ceremony. I don't imagine something like this can actually be planned. It just happens."

Paul seemed pleased by Mat's observation. He smiled warmly. "How did Herb and, Ryan, is it? Come to know one another?"

"Through Ellliott Smythe and Howard Marstead, I think. Did you know Howard?"

"He was my uncle," Paul replied, all trace of friendliness suddenly vanished. Nora stepped closer and took Paul's arm. Mat caught the protective gesture and glanced briefly in her direction. Nora fascinated him, yet just looking at her raised the hackles on the back of his neck, and he was reminded of his mother's phrase to explain such a feeling. "Someone just walked over my grave," she would say.

"I'm sorry if I upset you," Mat offered, tearing his eyes from Nora's face with difficulty.

"How could you possibly know enough to be sorry," Paul replied, a razor sharp note slicing the last trace of warmth from his tone.

Unbidden, those horrid photographs of Daria sprang to Mat's mind. He spoke carefully, already knowing that he must risk the words. He looked searchingly into Paul's eyes. "Because Howard was an evil man and I do not use that word lightly. I am sorry he was related to someone as nice as you seem to be."

Paul's face clouded over. He opened his mouth to speak, but Nora interrupted. "He was an evil man," she asserted. "Did you know something about that?"

For the first time Mat turned fully in Nora's direction and let his gaze linger over familiar features. This woman was somehow related to Daria. Mat could not conceal his scrutiny. He couldn't afford to be gentle with her and ease into the many questions that flooded his mind. There was no time for such luxury. "I'm sorry. I don't mean to stare, but it's uncanny how you remind me of my wife," he began tentatively.

"Did you know Howard well," Nora asked again, clearly impatient for the answer and ignoring Mat's question.

"I was not a friend of Howard's. We never met socially and I'd only seen him in passing."

"But you knew him. I mean," Nora hesitated and seemed to struggle over the words. "I mean, you knew ABOUT him."

"Forgive me," Mat heard himself ask Nora. "Do you have a sister? Because I want, need to ask you--" His voice trailed.

A certain feeling descended, like the calm heaviness that precedes a storm. Nora thought of the silver-backed leaves in a summer wood turned up against the impending rain. She thought of mackerel gulls gathering inland for protection before the wind rises and the surf pounds. She registered the closeness of the room and the voices. Connor had left them, and now the sound of a tin whistle, a fiddle, and Eilleann pipes erupted from back toward the kitchen in sudden impromptu harmony. Connor was playing the pipes he'd inherited from his Irish grandfather. Nora recognized the tune. 'Be Thou My Vision'.

Nora studied Mat. He had asked her a question and she somehow knew that this was not an aimless inquiry prompted by banal intent.

"I have a sister. She disappeared when she was six. We think she was abducted," Nora replied, breaking her own best rule against volunteering information to strangers. But she'd answered his question as though he deserved an explanation and now she watched for his reaction, rather than turn away in defense as she would normally have done. And at what point, she reprimanded herself, had she stopped speaking of her sister in the past tense? Did she really think that Lydia could possibly be alive?

Mat spied a stack of magazines. He found the recent publication near the top. Turning pages he handed it to Nora who glanced with impatience at where his finger directed.

Paul looked over Nora's shoulder. "This is you. I didn't know we had a celebrity in our midst," Paul said.

As it turned out they had not made the cover, but he and Daria had been satisfied with the article, a point far from Mat's mind as he watched for Nora's reaction.

Her face drained of color. If she registered Mat's image on that glossy page at all it was doubtful. Instead the full weight of her gaze was riveted on the face of Daria. How did he know? Nora looked beyond Mat and tried to catch Jared's attention, but he seemed to be concentrating on a wary Ryan.

With shaking hands Nora reached into the inside pocket of her jacket. With one swift movement of her arm she sent the Wedgewood box, silver-rimmed photos, and two abandoned glasses tumbling to the floor. Exhibiting far more care she unfolded a piece of paper and spread it lovingly over the cluttered end table.

One of Paul's friends from the garden club scooped up the fallen items and cast Nora a puzzled look. Not noticing and with trembling hands, Nora placed the folded photo taken from Jared's kitchen only a few days before beside that of the magazine article. Mat and Paul looked over her shoulder.

"What is this?" Paul asked, baffled by the unexpected twist of events. They were looking at the age progressed photo of Lydia and then at the magazine image of a smiling Mat with Daria leaning slightly against him as they sat on the veranda of Mat's home in California.

"Lydia Dillihunt," Mat read the print beneath the age-enhanced photograph. *Disappeared at age six – date – place.*

"And who is this?" Nora asked, her voice trembling as she pointed to the magazine page of Daria's smiling face.

"My wife," Mat replied, his voice hushed as though in church. "I imagine she remembers little about her true identity."

Thinking of the same event, Nora and Paul looked at one another.

"No," Paul said. "I think she knows exactly who she is. Lydia... or Daria, was here and stood out there, watching Nora's house most of the night, though we didn't know until morning." Paul pointed out the window toward the lane. "It was just before Christmas and it had snowed in the early morning hours."

His voice trailed. Almost involuntarily Paul's eyes drifted to the hallway. Herb had asserted that a threatening figure had stood over his bed that morning. Clearly he was frightened and now Paul wondered if he had recognized Daria. It made sense to Paul who could no longer believe that Herb was merely confused. He recalled the snowy footprints on the rug when he returned with the newspaper after talking to Nora and telling her about that girl who had remained the entire night outside.

Which house had the stranger been drawn to? It was not Nora's home she chose to enter. Had she known Herb? Known that he was there? Was there some connection with Howard and had she truly intended harm, as Herb believed?"

Irritated, Paul had retrieved a rag from the kitchen and blotted the rugs, assuming those melting footprints belonged to the nurse assigned to take care of Herb that day. She was on her break in the kitchen, and if she had walked out the front for any reason he would have seen her. How blind he had been! Was such stupidity and refusal to assess the obvious a defense against having to face the truth? Paul shuddered. It was all unraveling and both terrified and elated he could sense the phantom breath of discovery teasing all the missing pieces together.

Alexandra Clair

CHAPTER TWENTY-FIVE

Daria called room service and ordered cranberry juice, pasta, and a small salad. That task completed, she lay on the bed and ran through her breathing exercises, but it proved impossible to relax. She had lost time, but the good news was that she was still in the hotel room and nothing looked amiss, though she desperately regretted not asking Mat more questions. Whose funeral and why with Ryan?

Rosa had called, wanting to confirm when her plane was due to arrive so that they could send a car for her. It was Rosa who pointed out the potential weather problem developing along the upper eastern seaboard. Mat would have difficulty getting out as planned; all the more reason for her to stay put, shift attention, and accomplish the task ahead.

"In that case I may stay with the show a few more days."

"Elliott's death is all over the news. The phone has been ringing off the hook. Mat instructed us to beef up security, to close the vineyard until after you'd both arrived home and could decide how to handle this."

"I have some things to do."

"What things? If the press hasn't already found you and pressed for some kind of comment, they soon will."

Daria felt pressure at her temple; not an unpleasant feeling. Her lungs expanded and compressed as her brain seemed to float. Seconds elapsed as the Lie announced her unique presence by blowing out a noxious stream of carbon dioxide so powerful it could wilt plants and melt plastic. Daria had no memory of how the conversation ended with Rosa.

Lie walked to the mirror and brushed at Daria's long hair. She looked at her nails. It was a good thing she'd arrived, for this body needed a major overhaul, and yet there was not time. The most that could be managed was a hot oil treatment for the hair and spa appointments for the following day. That completed, she walked to the mini bar with key in hand. It occurred to her that in such extreme circumstances a drink was warranted, but first she would order room service.

"Room service, room service is what we need," she sang into the receiver. "I *need* chocolate cake. Do you have chocolate cake? You do? Prekrasno! I want a big piece. As opposed to a small piece. You know ... large with a generous scoop of French vanilla ice cream and two shrimp cocktails. Oh, and goulash. Do you make that? What is the word? You know ... beef stroganoff only Russian style. No ... well, you should. Okay then. This is it. Please, and be quick. Good day."

She then recalled the drugs. Where were they?

Lie rose from the bed and rummaged in suitcases. She riffled through the makeup bag, pockets, and crevices leaving chaos in her wake. Assassin had hidden those drugs well, and she wasn't even certain what they were for, except perhaps to kill Glen Winston who, no matter what anyone said or did, would certainly die.

Heaving a helpless little-girl sigh, she let her gaze survey the room, shifting from ceiling to floor until her eyes locked on an oddly bunched place in the beige carpet just beside a corner wardrobe. Walking directly over she peeled back the rug and pad to find what she was looking for. The drug was wrapped in a plastic bag and covered with tin foil, which she removed to reveal a white powdery substance that she immediately recognized as coming from Howard Marstead's home on the night Assassin had snuffed out his life.

Lie sniffed at the powdery substance. Her nostrils flared and began to burn. Eyes watered and instinctively she rushed to the sink to make herself sick. Choking and gagging over the bowl she splashed cold water onto flushed skin. Then, as though rounding on living prey, she scooped up what she could of the tiny packet, careful not to let any of that powder come in contact with her skin, flushing what remained down the drain. In doing so she felt a thrill of satisfaction for she was rarely, if ever, decisive.

Taking a deep breath the Lie stretched her arms wide and lifting her head, she waited in the hollow shelter of the shower stall for her punishment. Minutes passed, until it finally dawned on her that Assassin and few of those others had not been aware of her actions. Fire was not going to rein down from heaven just yet. The world was not going to tilt on its already tilted axis, and the very least that she expected; a torrent of wrath, the rage of banishment, never surfaced to usurp that precious space Lie now occupied in the forefront of Daria's body. Sometimes she worked in concert with Mocking and Flirt, the good ole days, not necessarily better days since Sasha was alive at that time; but potentially fun, fun, fun.

Lie could hardly believe her luck. The hotel room was as silent and empty of competing cries of outrage as the small church at the vineyard where she sometimes woke to find herself standing in the dreaded stillness of night. Perhaps that Assassin was not so all knowing and omnipresent as they had imagined.

"Maybe," she whispered aloud. "The emperor really does have clothes."

Or, the thought came to her. *Daria was usurping a bit more control. Change was afoot eroding the delicate construct of a multiple existence.*

For something to do, Lie propelled the limbs back and forth across the limited space of the hotel room. She did some stretching exercises until a knock came, and she looked with bewilderment at the salad and pasta. She opened her mouth to protest just as another tray was delivered.

As she ate she wished Daria hadn't been so quick to turn down an invitation to do some browsing at the Plaza shopping area with some of the other women from the show. And this thought prompted another. She would change her clothes. She walked to the suitcase, although almost everything had already been dumped out on the floor while searching for those drugs. She examined the few items hanging in the closet. It was clear that someone with no sense of adventure and limited imagination had packed. There was nothing, absolutely nothing that she could possibly be seen in.

Shopping was the needed diversion; a bit of fun. And this hotel? My goodness, it wasn't first rate, now was it? They needed the suburb service and opulence of a five star experience. The Lie gathered their belongings, none too neatly, and exited the room with a bellhop trailing.

Where were the credit cards? She had forgotten to check Daria's wallet. Did she have Daria's wallet? Oh well. Everything would work out. It always did, although Lie never stayed around long enough to find out exactly how.

Thoughts hit like a pelting rain; like an avalanche of rocks. Why must one ever be scared? It was not their job to experience fear. And Ryan! Why couldn't Ryan imagine what she was going through at this particular instant and call to let her know that nothing had changed? Lie and Mocking searched what memory they shared. What friend did Daria and Ryan have in common that had been so sick that death came knocking? Herb! They could think of no one else.

Tears came. Little-girl sobs and whimpers.

The cab driver turned to look over his shoulder. "Are you all right, Miss?" But she had already switched. Abruptly the crying stopped. The skin tightened over the face which literally snarled at the cab driver, who recoiled in astonishment. The alien alter stepped from the cab and surveyed the gray stone facade of the Ritz Carlton Hotel with haughty contempt.

Another mess to unravel, another immature personality to rescue, and then *it* would have to get back into the former hotel room in order to retrieve the murder weapon.

CHAPTER TWENTY-SIX

Secrets, Mat thought, casting Ryan a disgusted look. He was choking on secrets and he was sick and tired of weighing the damage. It was now after midnight. Connor and his wife had remained in the role of host while Paul, Nora, and Jared along with Ryan and Mat, had retreated to the quiet of Nora's kitchen.

Nora made coffee and for something to do defrosted a pound cake, but no one was hungry. It sat on a round plate in the center of the table, and for long minutes they all looked at it rather than at each other. Across the yard, Paul's house had finally fallen silent. Connor saw his wife to the car and joined them in the kitchen.

Jared's notepad sat open on the table. Pen in hand he had succeeded in jumpstarting the needed dialogue with a few questions. Over the last two hours, all but Ryan had been intensely caught up with discussing and piecing together the past. Ryan, in sharp contrast, had been quiet, almost sullen and contributing very little, even to those events which Mat knew he was painfully familiar.

"You brought me here to learn the truth. You could have saved us all a lot of trouble and simply told me." Mat spoke in a low, furious whisper. He had pulled Ryan aside so as not to be overheard by the others. "What were you thinking?"

"Can't you see these people are not our friends," Ryan said and pointed to where Jared, Paul, and Nora remained at the kitchen table going over Jared's notes. Only Connor stood aloof from the process of discovery, observing in quiet intentness. At times he turned his head away to close his eyes, and Ryan wondered if he were praying. Connor, had hardly spoken to him, and yet there was something about the doctor that drew Ryan. Perhaps later he could explore that feeling, but not now. Right now he was in protective overdrive, and he couldn't fully understand Mat's anger. Why couldn't his friend see the danger? Why not just shut up until they could be alone?

"You are NOT going to suck me into this. No one can quote

what I refuse to say. I'm not the one with a self-destructive mandate to understand everything," Ryan shot back in answer to Mat's question. "I'd rather die than see the past dissected in the tabloids, or worse still in a court of law."

"Ryan, you must realize that it's already too late. The police are processing Howard's old apartment as a crime scene." Mat gestured to Jared. "Tell him what you told me."

"I'm not interested in what Jared has to say. Assuming Glen Winston was the fourth man in those photographs, which I know you suspect," Ryan looked for confirmation into Mat's eyes. "If that's true Glen can't be long for this world? Don't you know that Daria is crazy? Ask her the right questions and push the right buttons, and she'd be certifiable."

Ryan glanced at his watch and continued. "No, my guess is that Glen Winston will be dead by now. I vote for cocaine laced with strychnine."

"What are you talking about? I spoke with Daria before we left New York. She was completely rational."

"Strychnine laced with cocaine. Daria, sorry to say, was privy to all of Sasha's dirty tricks. Following Sasha's example, Howard adopted the habit of keeping a particularly deadly synthesized supply on hand. Last time I checked, Howard's little stash was missing."

Almost against his will Mat remembered the glimpse he had of Daria as she slipped something colorful into her pocket before turning to him in the limousine outside of Hank Marstead's house.

"Where did Daria get strychnine?" Jared asked. The two men looked at him as though they'd forgotten his nearness.

"Howard kept it in a miniature Chinese apothecary jar. I'd seen it at Hank Marstead's in the past. As far as Hank was concerned it was just part of his father's extensive porcelain collection. I tried to solve the problem by offering to buy the entire collection months earlier, but Hank refused. When I arrived at the party, Howard was already dead and you and Daria had just made your memorable exit. Striking coincidence, wouldn't you say?"

"How did you know, at that point that Howard was dead?" Jared asked. "Hank told Nora and me that Howard wasn't discovered until after Cynthia Marstead went up to say goodnight. That was some time after the last guest departed."

Ryan looked at Jared with withering disdain. "Maybe I was going to take Howard out myself, and save Daria the trouble. Or more likely I was after a key to the apartment. But, alas. No key to be found and the man in question already dead."

"And you didn't call the alarm?" Jared asked.

"Why should I? There was a party going on downstairs."

"He doesn't mean that the way it sounds," Mat covered.

"So you knew about the vast collection and distribution of pornography and you, like Ellliott, realized Howard probably hadn't had time to destroy incriminating evidence before his paralyzing stroke. You were... how old the year Lydia disappeared?"

Ryan looked at Jared, nonplused.

Conner answered the question. "Ryan would have been too young to be anything, but a victim himself. Let's remember that."

Ryan turned abruptly from Jared. He was halfway down the hall with jacket in hand when Mat caught up with him. Turning him about and slamming him against the wall, he raised his fist and hit the wall with a resounding thud barely an inch from Ryan's face.

"You will answer his questions, Ryan. You will tell him what he needs to know, because if you don't you can forget that we were ever friends. So if you really don't care, if you're really as dead inside as you claim, then you're useless. You might as well keep walking when you cross that lane, right through that cemetery and into that ocean beyond." Mat stabbed in the direction of the door. The two men stared at one another, their faces nearly touching.

"Do you really want Howard and Ellliott to win?" Mat continued. "Then don't help us! Don't change! Keep hiding from yourself and everyone else that cares about you."

Ryan pushed Mat back, and breathing hard, perspiration running down his neck as though the decision he had to make was physically as well as mentally wrenching, he finally spoke. Ignoring Mat, he turned to Jared.

"Everything you suspect and more is probably true. Where you're wrong is that Sasha was always a much bigger player than Howard, who at the time of the kidnapping, and unlike his father and brother, was pretty low level due to his very risky, out of control behavior."

"The Marstead family knew he was a pedophile?"

"Yes, they sent him for retraining, but chemical or medical castration was never the goal. The goal was that Howard operate smarter and stay out of trouble. Andrea Wodsende and Daria are proof positive that programming can backfire."

Andrea Wodsende? Programming? Jared came acidly alert. He looked at Ryan who coolly looked back a half smile playing at his lips. Inserting Andrea's name as he did; out of context and unnecessary... Jared knew. Ryan had just tossed him a bone and for that he could only be grateful.

The others had gathered at the halls entrance. "Programmers," Paul asked, decidedly uncomfortable at the thought.

"They are universally despised by group members. They train and sometimes retrain people to keep them in line. Especially those who find God, enter counseling, or decide they can escape their responsibilities within the various cults."

"Let's all sit down," Paul offered. "Let's try and keep the strong feelings under control." Paul took Ryan's arm and guided him back to the kitchen, but Ryan remained standing.

"It was Sasha who turned Howard's proclivities into a thriving international enterprise. Howard became chairman of the board and vice-president of American operations, and he never even applied for the position. Of course, no one was ever going to read a quarterly report or see stock issued."

"I want you to understand that my background is law enforcement," Jared felt strangely obligated to make clear. "And, though I'm out of it at the moment."

"Once a cop, always a copy," Ryan finished.

"If you incriminate yourself I can't stay silent. Not if I discover you had anything at all to do with Lydia's disappearance or profited in any way from Howard and Sasha's operation."

"Yes, well this is the time to make myself perfectly clear." Ryan looked about the room making eye contact with each person. "Any of you quote me later in print or otherwise and I'll make sure you never do so again." Ryan took a deep breath. "And that goes double for you," he said and raised his chin in

Jared's direction.

Ryan removed his coat and threw it over the butcher block. He settled into a chair at the kitchen table. Suddenly he turned in Nora's direction, and his stare was a silent invitation for her to sit across from him.

"You want to know about your sister?" he asked.

"Please," Nora said simply. She sat pensively on the edge of the chair, wishing she could instantly assimilate everything Ryan knew.

"I only saw her once, but I couldn't help her. I was just a kid myself and I wasn't free to leave that place."

Nora reached across the table and touched the back of Ryan's hand. "I'm sorry for what you must have suffered," she said gently, surprising everyone with her words of sincere condolence.

Ryan looked uncomfortable and stared down for a long moment at the back of Nora's small white hand as it covered his. She wore no nail polish, and he noticed a tiny bit of cobalt blue paint embedded around one cuticle. Her hands looked older than they should have, from all the years of cleaning them with turpentine. He focused his attention on the blue speck and resisted the urge to peel it away. Then slowly, as though extricating himself from the open jaws of a tiger, he withdrew his hand.

"I knew she was in that room," he continued and looked Nora full in the face, though she could tell he didn't want to. "They gave her to Sasha, but I didn't know that either. Not until much later. I assumed they'd killed her, because that's what they said they planned to do."

"You know what happened to her," Nora stated. It was almost a question, but not quite.

"You don't want to know the details."

Nora opened her mouth to protest, but Ryan cut her off. "Because really that's up to your sister to tell you or not tell you. She's an adult today and nothing like what she would have been if this hadn't happened. She has the right to privacy and dignity and not to have everything known."

"But I need to know so I can help her," Nora said, stifling a sob.

"You only think that because you imagine that by knowing

317

you'll understand. If you can only understand, you can repair the damage. The best you can do for Daria, or Lydia, or whatever you end up calling her, is to realize right now that you can't change a thing. No amount of therapy or love or money or guilt is going to give back to you the person she would have been if she'd never been taken. And if you lay a lot of unreasonable expectations on her she'll either never be honest or she'll disappear and you won't ever have the chance to know her."

Nora wanted to rebel against everything he said.

"I can shut up or tell you the truth. Your call," Ryan said.

"Okay, go on. Please."

"She's screwed up. Big time. And, what's wrong with her very few professionals have any luck at fixing, and most who claim they can do the job are not dealing with the real thing."

There was a long pause as Ryan and Nora regarded one another. "You believe in God?" Ryan asked, surprising them all and unable to resist a quick glance at Connor, who caught his eye and nodded.

Nora also looked at Connor. Suddenly she realized that she did believe in God, and she wanted to say so. She especially wanted to tell Connor. It was true that she hadn't entirely lost that early faith. Her grandmother's Bible was the place to start, and she was suddenly glad that she had not packed it away on that long ago day when she had tried to flee the legacy of that tragic event.

"I've heard of miracles. That's what she'll need, because you'll learn that there is an unseen, supernatural fight going on. I know that I was somehow rescued over and over again. I think the Bible says that angels watch over us and I really think that God sent them to watch over me."

The verse is Psalm 91: 11, 12. Would you like me to tell you what it says?"

Ryan looked at Connor, surprised. He nodded his head.

For he will command his angels concerning you to guard you in all your ways; they will lift you up in their hands, so that you will not strike your foot against a stone.

Ryan appeared to consider the words. "I had a lot of close calls. There were times when circumstances conspired to protect me and I suspect it was the same for Daria and even Herb. I really did want to die, but some spark kept me going, kept me fighting for survival. I was also filled with hate. I wanted to get even. I wanted them to suffer all that they had inflicted on me." Ryan had been speaking to Nora, but now and then he glanced at Connor. Nora nodded her head as though she really did understand, encouraging him to go on, but Ryan realized that the anguish of discovery was just beginning for her.

"Like Mat, I saw her sometimes at foreign competitions and we even managed to speak a few times. True to form we pretended not to know each other, no flashbacks, no emotion."

Here Ryan looked over Nora's shoulder at Mat. "Remember when you asked me to say hello to Daria for you in Canada? I hadn't seen her in a couple of years. I walked up to her, and I could see right away that she thought I might hurt her; might even be an assassin."

"Assassin?" Jared asked.

"Yes, they have those too and they've done such a good job at framing public opinion that if you say illuminati financiers and bloodline families wanting one world government in order to extend the reign of the coming antichrist beyond the seven years described in the Bible you are immediately labeled a paranoid-crazy, religious zealot. Now do you really want to get off track with that apparent craziness?" Ryan confronted Jared.

"But, you believe this?" Jared had to ask.

Ryan nodded his head. "They operate in a paradigm of evil and tap into power sources that the world won't acknowledge. Daria is a survivor. She started as Sasha's little insurance policy and ended up destroying him. Anyway, it was crowded and she had a bodyguard, but Sasha was watching the last skater on the ice and everyone was distracted. She knew that Howard and Elliott wanted her dead. So I told her right off that I was just like her, that anything she said to me wouldn't be repeated."

"And just like that she trusted you," Jared probed.

"Trust? Hardly. But we didn't have to pretend with each other. You wouldn't understand how rare and precious those moments are. We looked into each other's eyes, and we understood something. I told her I had a message from Mat, and she handed me that patch so quickly I almost didn't know I had it until I'd walked away. After that our relationship sort of evolved."

"What do you mean, 'relationship'?" Mat asked.

"Well, no offense, Mat, but she couldn't play me the way she did you. She didn't always like that and she could be absolutely scary. Me, I was actually afraid of her sometimes and if you had any sense you would have been too."

Ryan looked carefully at Mat as though weighing how much to say. "That time you called me in New York to ask if I'd keep an eye out for her. Well, she was actually staying with me. Came and went during that time and especially when she traveled down from Boston to meet with Hank."

"And you didn't tell me. You knew how worried I..."

"She was in no shape to deal with you just then."

"Why not?" Mat asked, clearly hurt.

"Because she was someone else entirely and that person didn't care a snit about you or your neat little life and especially not for all those expectations she would never live up to. Besides, she had other things on her mind."

"Like what?"

"Like she was hot on the trail of Howard; had just figured out that Hank Marstead was his son and she was out to learn as much as she could from him."

"And you know all this because?" Jared asked.

"Because, stupid, she told me. She was having some bogus legal work done, thinking she could get to Howard through Hank. She was furious with me for not telling her, but I did not feel I'd been given an edict to facilitate murder."

Jared interjected. "Was that because you didn't want to be on her hit list?"

"I knew she planned to go down that list and coolly check off each name like groceries going into a shopping cart instead of a grave. And yes, who knows how confused her memory was. When we catch up with her you can ask her if my name was on that list."

"You told me," Mat said, "that Ellliott was programmed to kill himself. Tell Jared about that."

"Yes, under certain circumstances."

Jared was stunned. He let that sink in and thought this was something to get Thor's take on.

Mat was feeling something very different. He thought back to those desperate days after Daria had left him without explanation. He had turned to his friend for advice and sympathy, but Ryan had kept silent as he poured out his love for Daria and went through the long litany of everything he had done to drive her away. Was Daria sitting right there listening to him go on and on about how worried he was as he agonized over her loss and wondered where she was at that very moment?

Suddenly Mat felt jealous. It was the way and use of Ryan's word 'relationship.'

"Did you sleep with her?" he had to ask.

Ryan gave him a hard look. "You don't want to know this."

Mat stepped forward, but Jared put a restraining arm on his shoulder.

"Did you sleep with my wife?" he asked threateningly.

"You weren't married to her at the time. But no, I didn't sleep with her. I slept with someone else."

"What are you talking about?"

"I didn't sleep with Daria and I wouldn't even say it was consensual the first time, because I didn't want her that way. I am spoiled for sex. It's rare that I ever want anyone in that way."

Despite himself, Mat remembered how aggressive Daria had been with him on that first night at the cabin and with a physical strength she only rarely exhibited after.

"If you don't start making sense," Mat shrugged off Jared's restraining arm.

Ryan smiled. "It's not like you to be so combative, Mat. But okay. I'll say this as clearly as I can. The woman you know is probably the closest to the original Lydia Dillihunt that you will ever find. She's almost sweet and she wouldn't hurt a fly. She would never have deliberately plotted the murder of her enemies and then taken enormous pleasure in seeing her intricate scheme for Sasha's death come to fruition. But Daria is not alone. She's alive today for only one reason. The same reason that makes her an assassin; Daria, or Lydia is a multiple."

Daria sat straight up in bed. Some jolt of alarm had propelled her out of a deep sleep. She threw a robe over her shoulders. As though for safety's sake, she nearly ran to the window and pressed her palms against the cool glass. She took a deep breath. She didn't recognize the room. Where was she? She had to think.

Something had changed Mat. If Ryan had told him about Herb and taken him to that funeral, what else did Ryan reveal? She would have killed Herb, but he was already dying. She recaptured the memory of standing over his bed, looking into his pale ashen face. It was fully in her power at that time to take his life, but clearly Herb looked to be in the grip of more suffering than she had time or inclination to inflict.

Still Daria had wanted him to open his eyes and see her face. She wanted him to recognize the danger he was in and to experience the torment of hell just a little sooner than God had planned. "Herb," she had whispered and reached out to shake his shoulder. His sticky eyelids fluttered and his gaze focused just as the muffled sound of thick-soled nurses' shoes came from the back stair.

Silence itself, Daria slipped out of the room. Like a ghostly apparition she settled her straight frame into the shadows of the dark hall. There was no fear of discovery as she glimpsed Paul walking through the foyer below. It pained her to see him and she was filled with a bitter-sweet longing. He was a man now, but she would have recognized him anywhere. How keenly she had admired him. Paul clutched his newspaper and looked down at footprints of melting snow on the rug, and she resisted the nearly overpowering urge to call out.

"It's me, Paul. It's me! Do you remember?"

Such a reckless inclination sent a warning knell of anxiety into the far reaches of the inmost caverns. Daria felt an imbalance in herself; a dizzying sensation. It took a great effort of will not to give over the field completely.

Paul never looked up, and the moment passed. There was work to do. A task to accomplish that was far from finished. A great deluge of fear descended. The feeling of imbalance grew stronger as she fell into herself, retreat an irresistible and well-practiced lure.

A moment later she had fully switched. But, going against the practiced protocol Daria fought to watch, her presence muffled by distance, her emotions entwined in a cloaking numbness.

Paul wiped the floor just as Herb's nurse turned the corner into the sick room. In that moment Daria's body was in full sight of both. *It was true*, the chorus proclaimed. They were invisible and completely and utterly protected. Nothing at all, not death, or discovery could touch them. But Daria felt at odds with that inner chorus. She had wanted Paul to see her and then the thought came to her. How did she know the voices in her head could lie? How did one strengthen the muscle that questioned? With that a brick was removed from a very high wall; the slight hand that removed it that of a child. And through the gap, a slender beam of light.

CHAPTER TWENTY-SEVEN

No one disputed Ryan's assertion that Daria suffered from multiple personality disorder, but the others looked to Mat as though for a conflicting opinion. She was, after all, his wife and he would know. Mat felt the weight of that inspection, and as much as he longed to deny that it was true, a dreadful chill of certainty clutched at his heart.

The two friends regarded one another. Ryan could almost see Mat's mind working back to all those shifts of personality and absence of memory for what had preceded a recent event or circumstance. The signs had been there all along and yet Mat had never thought to connect Daria's behavior with anything other than the abuse she had suffered under Sasha's coaching. What did they call it now; Dissociative Identity Disorder? The phrase seemed woefully inadequate. A phase packaged to distract from the variance and vagaries of what an industry wouldn't see. Turning abruptly, he grabbed his coat.

"Where are you going?" Ryan asked in alarm, taking a few steps after him.

Mat cinched the belt of his black trench coat and pulled on leather gloves. He took a few steps towards the door before looking back at Ryan.

"I guess we have less in common than I thought, because no matter how despicable the target, murder is not a solution I can live with."

"Where are you going?" Ryan repeated, desperation creeping into his voice.

"I'm going to charter a plane and get to Kansas City as fast as possible. Maybe what you say is true and no one will ever connect Daria to Howard's murder, but I hope to prevent another that could possibly send my wife to jail and make it impossible for her to have a reunion with the little that's left of her family. And you, more than everyone else in this room Ryan, should understand that."

"Wait, I'm going with you," Nora asserted.

"I'm afraid no one is going anywhere tonight," Paul interrupted. He walked over and took Nora's hand. In spite of himself, Jared felt a stab of jealousy and wondered if he and Nora would ever be as close.

"The rain turned to snow a few hours ago," Paul offered. "Snow on a layer of ice makes for lethal driving conditions. The highway patrol has blocked all travel along 128 until late tomorrow morning, and that lane out there is a river of ice. The roads will be just as treacherous up and down the coast from Portsmouth to Boston. I doubt we'll even get Herb to the gravesite tomorrow morning."

As though to confirm what he was saying the electricity went off and they were plunged into darkness. By the time Nora had lit two kerosene lamps it came back on.

"I'll get the generator ready," Paul said, and left with Connor following.

Nora came back downstairs to shut off the lights and put the dishes in the dishwasher, but the table was already clear and all else put away. Paul had left with Ryan, Connor, and Mat to spend the night at his house, and Jared would stay with her as he had the night before. She saw him in the small sitting room off the kitchen and walked in just as he replaced the receiver.

"Thanks for straightening up."

"Happy to help. I was just talking with Hank Marstead," Jared offered.

"I'm surprised he took your call."

"He's scared. I really think all this has ambushed him."

"Did he say anything worth hearing?" Nora asked.

"I wanted to know if Ryan was a frequent visitor at his house before Howard's death, and it seems he was. Ryan and Ellliott were among the few of former friends that Cynthia allowed to interact with Howard. They often arrived together."

"And Hank said that. 'Friends?'"

"Yes, he did."

Nora was reflective. "The hype is that Ellliott and Ryan hated one another. Not only was their feud public and ongoing, but Ellliott had good reason to be afraid of Ryan. He knew the truth."

"Fear of disclosure makes for strange bedfellows'," Jared

replied. "It seems there was a high degree of collusion between those two. Hank told me that Ellliott was after them to buy Howard's apartment, but Cynthia Marstead wanted it for herself. There was no way she was selling."

"I agree that something seems amiss between those two, but I can't waste energy right now. I have to think about Lydia and I'm grateful to Ryan, however murky his motivation."

"Ryan and Ellliott had high-profile careers that would be jeopardized by all that information falling into the wrong hands. Those two were perfect blackmail targets, and Hank did say that Howard's New York apartment was broken into several times. Someone was trying to recover that material."

"And you've concluded it was Ryan." Suddenly Nora sounded irritated and Jared was instantly alert. He didn't understand why Nora felt the need to defend Ryan. He was the last person to have seen Lydia as her family remembered her, and maybe that was the reason.

"You must realize that at some point Ryan knew, that Lydia was alive? Not only that, but he knew with whom she was living and at any time during those years could have gone to the authorities. Could have made an anonymous report, but you think I'm being too hard on Ryan?"

"I think that Howard, Sasha, and Ellliott are all dead, and Ryan is all you have. I also think he was a victim. So maybe we should reserve judgment until we know more."

"You seem to forget that reserving judgment is not my forte. If detectives took that bleeding-heart view of potential suspects, no one would ever get arrested."

"What do you make of this illuminati stuff, Nora asked, changing the subject. A secret, global organization that has networked other secret groups, infiltrated governments, and wants to rule the world."

"Well, I can't dismiss that. Burns believed we had a group operating at the next farm; that the location was somehow a portal that demons came through. He told me there were various family groups situated over the globe, and these groups were competing to have the last antichrist born out of their bloodline. Sounds eerily familiar to Ryan's story; a story that has been alive in the collective imagination for at least two centuries."

"And you believe that can be true."

"I try to leave conjecture out of any investigation. As Ryan said, 'they believe it.' For that reason I'll follow the evidence."

Okay... Step out on a limb and tell me. Sound as paranoid and crazy as you like," Nora encouraged. "Give it a go."

Jared laughed. "You'd have to start from two ends of a very broad spectrum and see the United States as a microcosm. First you'd have to get certain groups identified as dangerous, subversive cults and at the same time preserve religious liberty and the first amendment. Germany understands this. They banned scientology from operating in their country. You'd have to look for proof that some are working within different paradigms toward a common goal to have global control. They would break down borders, create real and fabricated crisis. You can't oppose what you don't see. If we can allow for criminal prosecution of those that use psychological torture and programming to achieve societal and political aims. Layers up you'd have to look at covert operations; shadow government systems with funds derailed to meet hidden budgets. Like why any president would want to lift banking regulations, would operate to destroy constitutional restraints and why elected officials from both parties would collude facilitating that. The reason some don't want an armed populace. Why wouldn't you pull these threads and many others together and see a larger conspiracy?"

"What about an antichrist?"

"I wouldn't know. My friend, *Thorson Dillihunt*, believes this last antichrist figure is predicted in scripture."

"Dillihunt?"

"Your cousin I believe."

"Yes, I've never met him, but I'd agree. We've had evil prototypes wrecking havoc throughout human history. So, okay, now my head hurts," Nora said. "I can't let Lydia get lost in all this. These people took her. I want her back. For now; end of story."

Nora felt exhausted and yet nervously elated. Tomorrow she would see her sister, and she could not imagine how they would greet one another. Would Lydia know her? Did she harbor anger and feel she was abandoned on that long ago summer day?

"Let's not disagree about anything more tonight," she said,

and Jared perceived a frailty in her that she rarely showed. He stood and walked toward her and would have put his arms about her if she had not turned away and seemed so preoccupied. He felt a momentary stab of disappointment.

Nora and Jared shut off the lights, he automatically helping as her own father had often helped her mother. Together they walked up the stairs. At the entrance to Lydia's old room they paused, and Jared kissed her cheek before closing the door behind him.

Still feeling the fresh impression of that feather kiss on her cheek, Nora took a few steps into her bedroom and wondered if Jared would be warm enough. The temperatures had dipped below zero, and under the light from the windows, frantic snowflakes swirled and pummeled the windowpanes.

Nora was almost grateful for the delay of weather. She wanted time to sort out her thoughts and prepare, and yet she knew there could be no true preparation for what was coming. She perched on the edge of her bed and thought about tomorrow's promised reunion. Daria. She would have to call her sister by this other name, at least until they got used to one another and she found out which was preferred.

A blast of wind through the trees and the sudden rhythmic pounding of Paul's garden gate jolted Nora alert. She went to the hall linen closet and removed two wool blankets. Without thinking she opened the door to Jared's room. He had just removed his shirt and hesitated before turning in her direction. The scar was clearly visible and caught her eye immediately. It was long and curved like a sickle and came from below his shoulder to his waist. The red was fading, but fresh scar tissue molded the line of angry flesh. Nora reached out and traced the healing suture line.

"Does this still hurt?" she whispered.

He shivered slightly and turned his body, his face inches from hers. He smelled of mint toothpaste and the fresh milled guest soap in the hall bath, and she noticed the evening stubble on his face and that his lips were just a little dry.

"Not at all. Fortunately one can live without a spleen, and I had two kidneys, both in good working order."

"I'm sorry," Nora said. "When you said you were on medical leave I had no idea. What happened?"

"I was surprised by, I guess you could say ... and to use Ryan's term, an assassin. I thought I knew who it was, but after listening to Ryan tonight I'm thinking it may have been a contract hit. It was this other case and I was getting too close. I wasn't buying the story that Dr. Dudley Wodsende was innocent and Andrea guilty. The investigation was heading in a direction someone couldn't control."

Nora visualized the intricate display on Jared's kitchen wall; all those family relationships connected by threads and photographs with note cards and reference numbers.

"It was a murder investigation," Jared continued. Supposedly this Andrea Wodsende murdered her husband's new wife in a fit of jealous rage. After I was attacked she was sectioned to a locked psychiatric ward; never stood trial for the actual murder."

"Considered not competent?" Nora clarified.

"That's right."

"But you didn't believe that, did you?" Nora leaned against the door frame and looked up at Jared.

"Not at the time and especially not now. I think this cult framework that Ryan has talked about impacted this other case. Too many people, this cast of characters around your sister's disappearance, cross over."

"Like who?"

"The Marstead family, for one. I have a lot of digging to do before I can draw any firm conclusions."

"Will you go back to work?"

"No. I'll be retired, just awaiting the formalities to play out. They might offer me a kind of desk job, but I'll decline."

"Then you'll get back to this Andrea Wodsende case, I imagine. If you find there is a connection to Paul; something he should be aware of no matter how dark. You will tell me first and let me be with you when you talk with Paul. Promise me that, Jared."

"I admire your loyalty, Nora."

They looked into one another's eyes. Nora was suddenly flooded by insecurity. What if she had only imagined a mutual attraction between she and Jared? It had been years since anyone had held her. Years since she had been passionately kissed. He saw the hesitation. She drew back, almost involuntarily, but Jared put his arms about her and held her fast.

"I really like you Nora and I think you feel the same about me. I'm going to kiss you," he whispered against her ear. "If you plan on objecting now is the time." He paused a moment, but Nora said nothing.

His kiss was at first light and a bit tentative. It was as though he had been waiting for her to stop him, and guessed the scope of her ambivalence. Then his lips softened and her body awoke to an eruption of senses, and yet, another feeling came over her as well. This was not right. She knew what she had always known. All the years of self-imposed isolation now had a purpose and timing beyond the incidental happenstance of chance. This was not her man. She'd really only loved and wanted one man almost her entire life, and what they had survived was far more enduring than mere chemistry. Nora pulled away.

Alexandra Clair

CHAPTER TWENTY-EIGHT

On the flight out to Kansas City Nora sat beside Jared. She did not know what to think about the night before. He was comforting her now as a friend and had graciously accepted her rejection. She could no longer think of him as a potential partner and hoped he felt the same. A door had closed and she was glad to have her own feelings clarified. Eventually they would talk about it, just not now.

Alternately nervous and frightened she was also elated, a jumble of emotions seesawing in anticipation. She wished that Paul had been able to come, but he had stayed behind in order to see Herb buried, and Connor had agreed to come in his place, should a doctor be needed.

Nora felt lonely. Only Paul could know the depth of her uncertainty. A reunion with Lydia should be as important to him as it was to her. Once more that old familiar resentment surfaced that he had chosen this last obligation to Herb over her own needs and wants.

What would be different in the future? She would have to take a long hard look at this question. As soon as she got back she would tell Paul everything she felt and thought about their relationship and its marvelous potential to begin the healing process, not only for them, but for Lydia as well. If he rejected her again, if he hesitated even for five minutes, she would do the unthinkable. She would sell the house on Mill Lane and concentrate on Lydia. Perhaps she would move to California and live with her sister and Mat, if they would have her.

Nora felt frightened at the prospect of losing Paul. She guessed the unhealthy description would be enmeshed and codependent. Dysfunction and shared tragedy made for strong cords and so the ultimatum she had always hesitated to issue would have to be clearly stated. She could, she would have a life apart from Paul.

Jared noticed that Ryan seemed to avoid him. He sat beside

Mat on the chartered Cessna, his body turned toward the window, avoiding eye contact. Ryan's trademark humor, so often a buffer and frequent vehicle for communication, was absent in a way that made him seem intrinsically empty. Ryan had to be frightened. The unexpected resurrection of all his childhood traumas could all too easily be sensationalized by the press. The threat of that exposure, which would certainly re-victimize him, had to be exerting strong influence.

Mat had told him that behind the numb exterior, Ryan was in pain and hurting. The explanation seemed a little too simplistic. Mat was too willing to explain away Ryan's obsessive need to control the flow of information at everyone else's expense. Despite the strong words of the night before, Jared noted that Mat had reverted to a kind of passive approval of Ryan's outrageous behavior. Ryan had clearly betrayed the friendship when he slept with Daria. In addition, Ryan had lied to all of them each time he withheld crucial information that would have saved them all a lot of time, not to mention heartache, and this too was overlooked by Mat.

None of this seemed healthy, but Jared felt no obligation to help Mat see things differently. After all, he was not a counselor. What he had noticed was that people who successfully managed to maintain secrets over long periods of time attracted personalities who opted for blindness at any cost. For now he would give up the probing and questioning, but he would keep his eye on Ryan in the same way he would a hissing cobra.

A late wash of daylight reflected off metallic puddles that dotted the wet streets. Spring had arrived in this part of the country weeks earlier than the Northeast. Here the snow had melted, and the air was rife with the promised riches of color and new things growing. A low sun burned on the horizon as a pale moon brightened with the streetlights. If they were lucky, they would be on time for the first evening performance.

Mat wanted Nora to see Daria skate. Although it made no sense to anyone else, he thought it would somehow ease her nervousness and help her recognize the kind of person he knew Daria to be. Not crazy as Ryan described, or to be pitied as he could see they all pitied her, but as a survivor with an inner strength and beauty which superseded the entire trauma and tragedy of her life.

If it was true that Daria intended to kill Glen, then Mat had to stop her because Ryan was right. The deaths of Ellliott and Sasha could be explained, while the facts surrounding Howard's demise seemed dubious and might not continue to appear accidental under close examination. New light would be cast in their direction as the police continued to investigate the contents of Howard's New York apartment. A final death among the key players might prove impossible to explain and Daria would emerge the prime suspect.

The arena was in a low well of a place in sight of two connecting overpasses. In the fading twilight, Mat could see the river below the levies, and overhead the bridge they'd recently crossed into the city. Old warehouses lined the narrow streets, but the wide berth of parking was filled to overflowing.

Ignoring the signs and barriers, Ryan pulled the car to the front of the building and parked illegally below the many steps that led up to the arena. Jared placed his business card on the dash and another under the window wiper and hoped security wouldn't tow the vehicle.

They crossed the wide corridor that encircled the interior, rimmed by souvenir and refreshment stands. The show had already begun, and as they pushed open the wide doors, they looked down on a large oval surface of gleaming ice. As though on cue, Daria's name and skating credits were announced and a single spotlight picked her out of the darkness, center ice.

She wore a white dress, which sparkled silver under the light. As the first notes of music pierced the air, she began to glide. Nora's first thought was that her sister looked like a swan, floating weightlessly over a frozen pond. With stunning competence she landed a triple-flip, double-toe combination to an eruption of applause from the audience. Jared came up on one side of Nora and took her hand, but the intrusion perturbed her. She didn't need protection and was ready for whatever lay ahead.

"I'd know her anywhere," Connor whispered in her ear, and Nora felt closer to him in that moment than she ever had, for he had spoken aloud the very words that rang in her heart and momentarily replaced her anxiety with a surge of pride.

"Let's go," Mat urged and led Nora, Connor, and Jared across the stands and down to ice level.

So glamorous from above, here the spell of fantasy was quickly replaced by the cold block walls and slab flooring. They were stopped twice by security guards until Mat was recognized, and now Nora noticed that Ryan was not with them. She wondered why, but it was only a passing thought. She was about to meet her sister, and yet in the grip of so many conflicting emotions, there was a lingering anxiety that this long awaited reunion would never take place.

As a change in music bellowed out over the unseen arena, Nora imagined her sister abandoning the spotlight. As they made their way down a tunnel like corridor, another group of skaters filed from the dressing area in bright costumes, as others went through a routine of stretching in order to keep their muscles warm and limber. Several smiled or waved in Mat's direction, but he barely acknowledged the greetings. More than anything else, Mat's single-minded air of urgency struck new fear into Nora.

"Wait here," he said and walked ahead to where the other skaters were disappearing into the spotlight, but Nora would not be put off.

"Did you notice where Ryan went?" Jared whispered in her ear, but Nora shook her head impatiently. Jared's treatment of Ryan had disappointed her. She felt that like Paul, he had suffered more than anyone could know, and she was willing to wait for answers before she formed a judgment, but she could not think of that now. Over the music she struggled to hear what Mat was saying.

"Have you seen my wife?" Nora heard Mat ask a man with a clipboard, but she could not hear the answer. She had learned to live with the guilt of that moment when Lydia's hand had slipped out of hers seemingly forever. She had accepted the sad fact that forgiveness could never be asked for and then given. Although her feelings were not logical, now only minutes from seeing her sister with limited physical space between them, she could not escape the sneering doubt that this was all a cruel joke.

"Have you seen my wife?" Mat asked the ice monitor.

"She's supposed to be out there." He pointed to the arena, lit bright under roving spotlights of pink, green, and red. The animated flow of performers alternately skated and jumped to a fifties' rock and roll medley, their dance like footwork impressive to watch.

"You may not notice, but there is a gaping hole out there. When Glen hears about this he'll be livid. He didn't want her joining the show so late. He said she was unreliable and something like this would happen."

"Where's Glen?" Mat demanded, nearly choked by impatience.

"Well," the man hesitated and looked about as though suddenly baffled. "He's usually close by, but I don't know. You might check back there," he waved vaguely in the general direction from where they'd just come. "We lost some of the set in transport and Glen might be checking it out."

"When was the last time you saw Daria?"

"Look, I have a job to do." The man started to walk away, but Mat deliberately stood in his path.

"Hold on," he said menacingly. "I asked you a question and I expect an answer."

"I saw her right here," he stabbed a finger at the ground. "And she was supposed to do a quick change and be out there," he pointed at the ice in disgust.

It did not escape Mat that this hire was typical of the sort of person Glen surrounded himself with. Inadequate types who blindly reflected Glen's opinions while they successfully deflected criticism away from him. He would not be popular with the other skaters and yet would make Glen look like a saint in comparison.

"Which way did Daria go?"

"When she stepped off the ice Ryan Kollyn was here. I guess Kollyn thinks he's grown so important that he can divert an ice show with an interview. How should I know where they went? I have better things to do; I have a show to run."

"If you worked for me I'd fire you," Mat tossed behind him as he turned away.

"Yeah, well, I guess there was no reason to think the ice princess wasn't professional enough to do the quick change required of her and get back out there for that group number. Yeah, like Glen and I didn't call that one," he shot after Mat, who was already jogging down the corridor.

Mat was frantically trying to remember the layout of the arena. It had been years since he had skated in Kansas City.

Nora, Jared, and Connor followed. "What do you think is wrong?" Nora could not help asking. "Where is my sister? Why isn't she here?" But Mat did not answer her questions, and his expression of single-minded anxiety alarmed Nora.

"Don't worry," Jared said. "We'll find her. Why don't we split up?" he suggested. "Connor can check the dressing area, and I'll talk to some of the other skaters as they get off the ice. Nora, you can–"

"I'm going with Mat," she said, already turning away and then running to catch up with Mat, who had just disappeared up a staircase.

"Aren't you going to shoot him?" Ryan spoke to Daria with a flatness that struck fear into Glen. She pointed the gun in his direction and he had backed as far as he was able into the corner of an abandoned receipt office.

"Shoot him," Ryan demanded. "Shoot him NOW," but Daria stood as still as a deer transfixed by headlights.

"Ryan, I don't understand," Glen pleaded. He somehow knew it was useless to address Daria. She had a dead, glazed look on her face, which frightened him almost more than the gun itself. If she wanted to shoot him, she would do so and nothing could stop her. Nothing except Ryan, who seemed to be telling her what to do, as though she had been programmed to do his bidding. As he contemplated her expression in a haze of panic, it occurred to Glen that she might even relish that bloodthirsty prospect.

"Ryan," Glen tried again, his voice breaking. His legs felt as though they'd been stripped of muscle, and he wasn't sure they would continue to hold him upright.

"Please, Ryan, whatever I've done let's talk about it. You've always been my favorite. I loved you as though you were the son I never had. Didn't I protect you and take care of you? Oh, maybe I was too hard on you, but I only wanted the best... Ryan! Please! Listen to me!"

"S-H-U-T U-P, shut-up," Ryan erupted, his tone seething hatred, as his handsome face contorted in a kind of tortured rage. At the sound of his voice, Glen heard the unmistakable sound of the gun cocked, and imagined that impersonal steel bullet gliding into the greased chamber. In anticipation of death he squeezed his eyes shut.

The sound when it came was deafening. It echoed off the walls in hollow agony, and he waited for the searing pain and felt he would die in the torment of anticipation. It took him a moment to realize that the cry he heard was not his own. Laboriously he forced his eyes open, as chilling sweat dripped off his brow, and a warm trickle of urine slid down his leg.

He could hardly believe his luck. Daria had swung the gun away from him in a deliberate arch. Glen pressed his back harder into the wall and inched a few steps toward the door. He felt certain that at any second she would turn in his direction, re-aim and shoot again, but for now she had the gun leveled at Ryan. She shot off another blast and Glen saw Ryan's body spin around and drop to the floor. He wasn't dead. Incredibly he wrapped his arms about his middle and glared up at Daria in an odd grimace of astonishment and pain.

"It was you," she said. "It wasn't Glen. It was YOU!" Shock at having uttered this was clear in her voice, all her senses straining towards that one conflict of realization as her fingers tightened on the trigger. She stood in stocking feet, dressed in her shimmering white costume, with a gold ribbon braided into her long hair.

"No," Ryan struggled to speak, his hands attempting to stem the blood flow from his wound. "We've been over this a thousand times, and now you're confused again. Daria, you know it was Glen. He held the camera, set up the lights, and tightened your restraints."

"I can see it now," Daria said. "You all counted on me losing my memory. But I remember how you argued with the other men. You could have helped me escape. There were opportunities."

"And what did we argue about, Daria? Think. We argued about you. I begged them to let you go."

"But they didn't, did they? They forced you to go along with them, knowing it would make you as despicable as them. You could have helped me. You could have!"

Once again the click of the chamber. Glen knew that if he chanced to live, he would hear that unforgiving sound in nightmares for the rest of his life, but this time it freed him to move. He ran blindly, careening around the corner and directly into Mat. Others hurried behind, summoned by the sound of the gun and Ryan's scream of pain. Mat took in the scene at a glance and put up his hand for the others to stop.

Connor was grateful he'd brought along his equivalent of the old doctor's black bag; a nylon satchel much lighter and easier to carry. He clicked off in his mind the contents, hoping he had everything needed until the paramedics arrived. And yet it was clear to him as he observed the scene that they were all in danger. They might never reach Ryan before Daria shot off another round.

Jared reached under his jacket and removed his gun. Nora gave a gasp of disapproval, but he ignored her reaction. She looked at him stubbornly, a fierce gleam in her eyes, and shook her head. Nothing was going to stand in the way of Nora being there, not even the threat of her own death.

Mat stepped further into the room, ahead of Nora and Jared, while Connor pressed his back against the wall and inched closer to Ryan. They all noticed that Daria seemed oblivious to the commotion. She was bent on one task and one task alone as she stared down at Ryan's suddenly still form. Ryan was pale. In agony he drew into a fetal position and Mat realized Ryan would die if he could not get through to Daria. As he studied the set of her features, he realized he had never seen this woman before, and he wondered if she knew him.

"Daria."

She heard his voice and hesitated.

"Wait, Daria."

"Mat?"

He stepped into the room and walked a few steps forward.

"You heard, did you hear? You think you know everything, but you can't possibly," Daria stated, her voice tempered by confusion. There was a wild look in her eyes, which Mat had never seen before, but at least she knew him and had spoken his name.

"I know enough, Daria. We can beat this thing and I don't care," he emphasized. "I only care about you. I'll help you. Give me the gun." He stepped closer. She had lowered her weapon, but now she raised it back in the direction of Ryan's skull.

"Stop right there," she said to Mat, in that odd tang of an accent that came and went for no good reason.

It occurred to Mat that he had heard that accent only when they argued or the few times that she had been aggressive in a combative way that unsettled him. He thought about Ryan's claim that Daria had multiple personality disorder. What did that really mean? He would think about that later. For now he refused to be afraid of his wife.

"Stop right there," she repeated. "I can kill you too."

"You won't kill me, Daria. You can't kill me, we have a life together."

Daria stood unwavering and it was then that Mat saw that Ryan was far worse off than first thought. A flood of bright, slick blood pooled from beneath the place that Ryan lay on the hard concrete. Mat caught Connor's eye as though to say, *watch for your chance.* The fear had left Ryan's face, and Mat realized that shock was setting in. Ryan moaned again and attempted to shift his position. That sudden movement captured the full intensity of Daria's stare. Once more she swung the gun in Ryan's direction.

"Daria, I want you to think about something. Imagine Ryan's face at that time. It was the face of a boy, and that's why you didn't recognize him when you met him years later. He wasn't much older than you were, and Howard was trying to blackmail him by involving him in their crimes. They had to ensure his silence because they did the same to him."

"He protected Sasha. I don't care what you say. He could have gone to the police. He could have joined the dissenters and killed them himself."

Her tone was savage as she spit out the words. It was again that cold and alien voice that he didn't recognize. Mat wondered. How could he call forth the Daria that he loved? The one he had laughed with and discovered a sweet intimacy with that had made them both so very happy. There had to be something he could do. *Think,* he told himself silently and uttered a swift prayer of desperation. Mat concentrated on her face. It was still the face he remembered; the face he loved, and he held on to that knowledge like a drowning man to a life-raft.

Over her shoulder, Mat saw Jared approach, but Daria caught the shift of attention and swung about. At that very moment, as she turned away, Connor slid to the ground beside Ryan. With expert swiftness he pressed a compress to the bleeding shoulder and another to the growing stain of his middle.

Jared admired the risk Connor had taken. He didn't seem to be afraid of Daria, but was now intent on his patient. The gun fired and ricocheted off the wall, and if he'd counted right Jared estimated that Daria must be almost out of bullets.

Daria lifted her arms to the ceiling and pointed the gun above her head. She swirled around and began to lower the weapon back at Ryan. Noticing Connor for the first time she hesitated. The expression on her face went momentarily blank, and then a look of surprise followed one of recognition.

"I know you. Do I know you?"

"I haven't seen you for many years, but yes. You do know me," Connor said, still working over Ryan. "We were friends long ago. But now you need to let me help Ryan. Will you put the gun down? Just lay it down here on the floor."

Connor spoke gently and Mat took a few hurried steps in Daria's direction. There was no time to bridge the distance, for she stepped back and once more lifted the weapon, seeming to ignore Nora, who had remained in the hallway, a look of grief clouding her expression.

"Daria, think of us. We have a life together and your sister is here."

"Nora?" Her response was a question followed by an animal-like whimper.

"Nora wants to see you and get to know you. You both deserve that opportunity. Don't let what Ryan did so many years ago rob us of a future. You don't have to do this..."

Slowly Mat had begun to bridge the gap between them. He was inches from her when he reached for the gun, surprised that she released that sleek heaviness with such ease. Almost in a heap Daria collapsed against him, and he wrapped his arms about her as they sank in unison to the floor.

Mat kissed her and held her against his chest. He brushed wet strands of hair away from her face. She was a tortured soul, struggling against the cruel assault of contradictory infringements, her fragile defenses quaking inward against a deluge of treacherous muttering, that he could never know.

Mat's eyes searched for Nora. She took a few steps forward

and stopped, unsure of herself. He smiled at her. It was comforting to know that he would have some help.

"The paramedics will be here soon," Jared said to Connor who was still bent over Ryan, loosening clothing and then covering him with his own jacket.

"I'm cold and I'm going to die. I don't want to die." Ryan whispered.

"You said you believed in God," Connor said, removing a compress soaked in blood and pressing another to the wound. "Would you like me to pray with you?"

Ryan whispered 'yes' and Jared was stunned. Why, he wondered, was Connor taking the time to pray when he had a patient who might die? Jared had seen lots of gunshot victims, and as he studied Ryan he doubted recovery was possible. The second bullet had clearly lodged somewhere they couldn't see, and there had to be internal bleeding.

But as he prayed Connor continued to minister his emergency medical expertise. In the distance they heard sirens and knew that help was on the way.

"*Dear Jesus. You love this man. He has acknowledged to us that you have rescued him many times from disaster and an early death. And yet perhaps he has never actually prayed and asked you into his heart. Perhaps he doesn't really know God's Son and His Holy Spirit. And so, Jesus, we issue that invitation to you now.*

Ryan, don't try to speak. Just say these words in your mind, and no matter what happens to your body, you will live. *I believe, Jesus, that you are God.*" Connor paused for Ryan to pray, repeating the words. *You are the promised Messiah, who died on the cross to save me from my sins. Come into my life now. Forgive me for all that I have done that has grieved you and been wrong. I am sinful, and only you, God, are good. Be for me the comforter and teacher, who will never leave me or forsake me. We claim your words Jesus as true: **for God so loved the world that He gave His only begotten son, that whoever believes in Him shall not perish, but will have eternal life (John 3:16).***

Mat felt the weight of Ryan's gaze turn in his direction. He wanted to go to Ryan, but he held on to Daria, who seemed to melt into his protective embrace as though to hide. Now, perhaps close to death, that air of being separate and unaffected was gone. Ryan was as pale and gray as the concrete slab he lay against. His lips moved soundlessly, and despite tears that glistened in his eyes, Ryan attempted an unruffled smile of perfect ease that seemed to echo down the long corridor of their past. But this smile was different. It wasn't a barrier meant to put off any that would penetrate a hard exterior. No, Mat thought. This was a smile of relief and even peace.

Connor bent to whisper in Ryan's ear something they could not hear. For a long moment Ryan and Connor looked deeply into one another's eyes. Connor grasped his hand until Ryan's grip fell loose. His eyelids fluttered, closing forever on this world.

THE END

www.ingramcontent.com/pod-product-compliance
Lightning Source LLC
Chambersburg PA
CBHW071522260626
47170CB00002B/464